P9-CCC-738

SILENT SEDUCTION

She kissed him again, and it was all he could do to pull away.

"We'd better go easy here—" His whisper was rough yet gentle.

She didn't answer. Instead, her arms wound more firmly around his chest and she pulled him even closer.

"Damn it Zelda, you're playing with fire, a man can only take so much—"

He drew back, scowling at her, and like a thunderbolt, the truth struck him. It was clear by the expression in her eyes, the look on her face, the slight trembling of her arms around him, that she wanted him to go on. Wordlessly, she was asking him to make love to her.

A DISTANT ECHO

BOBBY HUTCHINSON

LOVE SPELL  NEW YORK CITY

LOVE SPELL®

May 1996

Published by

Dorchester Publishing Co., Inc.
276 Fifth Avenue
New York, NY 10001

Printed in the United States of America.

Dedicated to my father, Robert Rothel, my grandfather, Charles William Rothel, and my brother, Ole Rothel, each of whom went into that awesome underground darkness day after day to mine the coal that earned their daily bread.

"There is a patience in the Earth to allow us to go into her, and dig, and hurt with tunnels and shafts, and if we put back the flesh we have torn from her and so make good what we have weakened, she is content to let us bleed her. But when we take, and leave her weak where we have taken, she has a soreness, and an anger that we should be so cruel to her and so thoughtless of her comfort. So she waits for us, and finding us, bears down, and bearing down, makes us part of her, flesh of her flesh, with our clay in place of the clay we have thoughtlessly shovelled away."

—*How Green Was My Valley* by Richard Llewellyn

Chapter One

"You come in there with me, Jackson, you slippery son of a gun. It's not right to make me do this alone." Tom scowled across at his partner. They'd been arguing for the better part of ten minutes, standing beside Tom's mud-stained red Bronco in the parking lot of the senior citizens' residence.

It was still early afternoon, but the April sun was already dropping behind the snow-capped peaks of the craggy Rocky Mountains that surrounded both the village and the Crowsnest Valley in this remote part of Alberta, Canada.

Tom had a gut feeling he was about to lose the argument.

Jackson was digging in his pocket for a coin to flip, his favorite method of ending an altercation—mainly because he was always luckier at gambling than Tom.

"Heads, you go in and talk to her alone. Tails, I come along," Jackson proposed, expertly flipping the U.S. quarter he finally dug from the pocket of his well-tailored pants. "And it's—ahhhaaa, hallelujah. It's good old Ben himself. You get to do the honors, Tommy, old son. And a good thing, too, because like I've been saying all along, my talents with the fair sex don't extend to cantankerous old women."

Jackson Zalco's white pirate's smile split his handsome, tanned face, turning his features from dangerous to devilish. "Give the venerable Ms. Lawrence my regards, Tom. I'll wait for you at the tavern. I've got the spare keys for the truck. You can walk back. No telling how long you'll be. It's only a couple blocks. The fresh air'll do you good."

His traitorous partner roared off in Tom's truck, leaving him stranded and cursing in the wet slush of the parking lot.

Tom hadn't ever had occasion to be inside a senior citizens' residence before, and it made him nervous. The building smelled of pine-scented disinfectant with an overtone of hot roast beef, cooked cabbage, and a generous dash of urine. He did his best to breathe through his mouth.

It was just past four, but it seemed the evening meal was already over. Elderly men and women wandered along the halls as cheerful staff members collected the orange plastic supper trays and chatted with the old folks.

The chubby pink-smocked attendant, who'd taken charge of Tom the moment he stepped through the door, bustled down the hallway beside him. He was a foot taller than her five four, and he was conscious of towering over her. He was also aware that his Western boots made an ungodly racket on the mirror-bright polished floor, and that even though he was nearing forty, the men and women who stared at him as he passed their wheelchairs and walkers made him feel like a rawboned kid again.

"Folks in here like to eat early. We serve dinner at four. Then there's time for a snack before bedtime," the attendant explained. "Meals are a big deal here, that and television. This is Miss Lawrence's room," she added.

The door was open, and she bustled in ahead of Tom. The room was sparsely furnished, holding only two straight-backed chairs, a wardrobe, a bedside table, a pink brocaded armchair, a television, and the hospital bed where the old woman lay. The most striking element was the wide picture window, framing a spectacular view of blue sky, snow-topped mountain peaks, and evergreens.

"Evenin', Evelyn." The attendant's voice was determinedly cheerful. "Seems this gorgeous cowboy's come all the way from the States to visit you, you lucky thing." She gave Tom a wink and a coquettish simper before she hurried out again.

The bulbous old woman in the hospital bed by the window turned to stare at him and let out what could only be described as a snort. She had sparse, frizzy white hair and an enormous pair of horn-rimmed glasses perched on a tiny nose that seemed to have sunken down into the folds of flesh surrounding it. A thick, hardbound book she'd been reading lay on the patchwork quilt mounded over her bulk.

Tom tried for a grin and held out his hand. "Evenin', Ms. Lawrence. I'm Tom Chapman. Pleased to meet you at last."

"Have you no manners, young man?" The voice was precise and schoolmarmish. "Here in Canada a gentleman removes his hat when he's in the presence of a lady. You Yankees have a great deal of nerve and no training in etiquette, seems to me."

The old woman's numerous chins jiggled with outrage, and Tom snatched off his Stetson before he once again held out a hand.

She left it hanging until he withdrew it. It was obvious she wasn't pleased at all to meet him, even though she'd agreed, with great reluctance, that he could come. She scowled over her glasses and tapped her fingers on the cover of her book.

Tom set his hat on a chair and met her displeasure with a show of bravery, studying her with as much intensity as she did him.

This unpleasant woman might hold the key to a fortune in gold ingots, and he had to do this right. He tried to figure out from looking at her whether she had all her marbles, and if she did, what might be the best way to charm her. He, like Jackson, had precious little experience with old women.

They'd discussed bringing her flowers and decided against it. This was a business meeting, after all. They didn't want her to think they were trying to con her in any way, did they?

Though chocolates might have been a good idea. She sure as hell looked and sounded as if she could use some sweetening up—and it was obvious she liked to eat.

Evelyn Lawrence was exceedingly fat, and if her

clothes were any indication, she must also be color-blind. She wore a voluminous purple flannel night-dress with a thick red sweater over it, despite the fact that it was hot and stuffy in the room. There were several gravy stains down the front of the sweater.

Tom had done whatever sketchy research he could on her. He knew she was eighty-two, the spinster daughter of a local doctor, now long dead. She'd been a schoolteacher. She'd broken her hip in a fall three months ago.

That was about all he'd been able to find out, besides the annoying fact that she was something of a recluse. She hadn't responded to a single one of his three letters and had refused four separate times to speak with him on the phone. He still didn't quite understand what had prompted her to answer his fifth call or to agree that he could visit her.

"So you're that pesky Yankee who kept writing and phoning me before Christmas. From some godforsaken little place in New Mexico, aren't you?"

Her voice was wheezy, as if she was recovering from a chest cold, but it certainly sounded to Tom as though her mind was functioning.

Tom nodded. "Yes, ma'am. I wrote and called you several times from Albuquerque." He smothered a grin at her labeling the city of Albuquerque either little or godforsaken. In his opinion, Blairmore, Alberta, more than fit that label.

"You described yourself as an adventurer." Her gray eyes, almost buried in folds of flesh, were assessing him coldly. "A modern-day treasure hunter,

I believe you put it." There was more than a trace of sarcasm in her tone.

So she'd read his letters after all. He hadn't been sure, because she sure as hell hadn't answered them. "Yes, ma'am." He gave her the smile that always endeared him to females, but there wasn't so much as a twitch of response from Evelyn.

You sure put paid to the idea that fat people are jolly, old lady. "See, ma'am, my partner and I research old stories and myths about treasure of one sort or another, and if there's enough basis for it, we go looking for whatever's lost," he explained. "Sometimes we work for ourselves. Other times we hire out. This time, we're on our own."

"And you're here because of that worn-out old tale of gold buried under our Slide here at Frank." The words dripped with scorn. "Well, you've come on a fool's errand, young man, because there's not a word of truth to it. If there had been any gold buried under that Slide, it would have been recovered years ago. The Slide occurred in 1903, you know." She sounded exasperated.

"I realize that, and you could very well be right, Ms. Lawrence," he lied. He didn't think for a moment she was, but he sure as hell wasn't about to contradict her. "Nine out of ten of the stories I research turn out to be nothing more than tall tales." And if he hadn't been more than reasonably certain this one fit the remaining small category, he and Jackson wouldn't have driven across half of North America to get here.

She was studying him. "How old are you, young man?"

"Thirty-nine."

She let out a snort. "Aren't we all. And this treasure hunting is all you do for a living?" There was outright disdain in her voice now.

"Yes, ma'am, it is." In his mind's eye he saw the upscale apartment building he'd just purchased in Albuquerque, the latest in a number of lucrative real estate investments he'd made in various locations throughout the United States. Unlikely as it might sound, hunting for treasure and then putting the profits into careful investments had made him a wealthy man, and he was quietly proud of it.

"And where is your home, Tom Chapman? Where do you live when you aren't gallivanting after fool's gold?"

That was a tough one. "I'm sort of a wanderer, ma'am. I keep a mailing address in Albuquerque, but I don't really have a home base to speak of." Truth was, he and Jackson kept most of what they needed in the back of whatever vehicle they were driving. Tom leased space in a warehouse where he stored his growing collection of vintage motorcycles, but he didn't own much else in the way of possessions.

Investments, now, that was different. But things—he and Jackson preferred to travel light.

"Humph." Her eyes swept over his weathered buckskin jacket lined in fleece, his checkered shirt, faded, well-worn jeans, and the comfortable boots he'd polished for this visit. From the expression on her face, it was obvious that Evelyn thought it probable he was on social welfare. She studied his features one by one, and he tried not to look as self-conscious as he felt.

"You're certainly a big, good-looking man," she

pronounced, making it sound like an indictment. "I imagine most foolish women lose whatever wits they have around you, what with that curly hair and those ridiculous eyelashes. Wasted on a man. Are you married?"

"No, I'm not," he answered. "Never have been."

Same as you, old woman.

She humphed again. "Darned good thing, too, if you spend your precious time running around after buried treasure like a half-wit dog chasing his tail. At your age, you ought to have grown out of such nonsense."

Whew. Jackson, you rotten sod, you were born lucky to have won that coin toss. This old gal has a mouth on her. Must have scared the living daylights out of the poor kids she taught.

Still, something about her amused him. She might look pitiful, but it was plain there was a razor-sharp mind inside all that flesh. Tom decided the best thing to do was to come straight out with what he wanted from her and take it from there. If he didn't get down to business, he'd be here all night fending off her insults, and he had a feeling she probably wasn't going to cooperate anyway. Better get it over with, get himself tossed out on his ear, and at least have time for a few beers with Jackson.

"I believe your father was a treasure hunter, wasn't he?" It was her father and his memoirs that had brought Tom and Jackson to this remote region as well as their desire to see the Canadian Rockies. They'd spent an inordinate amount of time in various deserts lately, and Jackson insisted he'd always wanted to visit Banff. The National

Park wasn't far from here—a few hours' drive west. It had seemed a perfect opportunity to combine relaxation and pleasure.

"You were interviewed several years ago by a local paper, and you mentioned a diary your father kept."

She made a rude noise. "I ran off at the mouth to that beguiling young reporter, and I've regretted it ever since. No fool like an old fool!" she snapped. "I wish I'd shut up about the darned diary. You aren't the first young whippersnapper to come sniffing around, thinking a good look at it would lead to gold. I've put the run on quite a few fortune hunters by now."

"I realize that, ma'am." Tom gave her a level look. "Only difference between me and them is that I'm totally professional about this. It's my business. Also, I'd like to be the first to prove your father was right about that lost Klondike gold. He must have been disappointed not to locate it himself." It was a blatant shot at sentimentality, and he should have known it was the wrong approach.

She scowled at him. Her face grew red, and she leaned forward and spat out, "My father spent half his misguided life clambering over that pile of rocks down the road and never found a plugged nickel. Nothing to find, I say. More fool him. He'd have been better off tending to his patients and paying some attention to his family. He was obsessed with that slide and whatever he believed was underneath it, and my mother and I suffered as a result."

Her voice dripped with venom. "Professional treasure hunter, you call yourself? Hah. You'd be better off getting yourself decent training of some kind and settling down to earn an honest living."

"What we do isn't dishonest in any way, I assure you," Tom said in a mild tone, even though her vitriol was wearing on him.

"There are strict rules about recovered treasure, and we follow them to the letter. We always apply for permission from the government of the area we're interested in exploring, and a percentage of whatever we find goes to descendants or survivors, if there are any. And, of course, a portion is allocated to the state by law—I believe you call them provinces here."

He shifted his weight from one leg to the other. He was getting tired of standing, but she hadn't invited him to sit, and he'd be damned if he'd give her another chance to jab at his manners.

Sweat was pouring down his back, though, and he peeled off his heavy coat, flipping it across the back of the chair that held his Stetson, as he detailed his request.

"In this particular case, we'd be searching for a shipment of gold bullion, one of the last large shipments sent out of the Klondike, in early 1903. The gold arrived in Vancouver by boat where it was fired into gold bars and, with much secrecy, dispatched via Canadian Pacific Railway across the country to be deposited into banks in eastern Canada." As always, even his preliminary research had been detailed and extensive. "For some reason, the theft of that shipment was never given the publicity it deserved."

"I've heard dozens of different fairy tales about gold being buried under the Slide, and not one of them was ever proven true. You might as well amuse me with your version." She settled herself on her pillows and waited a scant moment before she jerked her chin at him. "Well, get on with it."

Tom cleared his throat. She was testing him, and although it was absurd, he felt like a schoolboy called on to recite a lesson.

He was determined to do well at it, too. "In the heart of these Rocky Mountains, in late April of 1903," he began, "a spectacular and well-planned train robbery occurred."

Without being conscious of it, he lapsed into the terminology of the moldy books he'd read and re-read until he had them memorized. His voice conveyed the sense of excitement the story still created in him. "Three bandits rode off with that fortune in gold bullion. The guards on the train recognized one of the men. He was a well-known train robber named Bill Miner. The second man was never identified. The third was a sometime partner of Miner's called Lewis Schraeger. The bandits loaded the heavy boxes into a wagon, and with the North West Mounted hot on their trail, they brought the gold to a location near here, the little coal mining town called Frank, where Bill Miner had been living incognito for some time.

"In a bizarre coincidence, the very night of the robbery was also the night the top of the limestone mountain near Frank gave way, sliding down and covering half the town and most of the surrounding valley. In the chaos after the Slide, it was assumed that the gold and the robbers had been buried as well. But then Lewis Schraeger was arrested months later in Montana for cattle rustling and charged with the murder of a rancher. He was sentenced to twenty years in San Quentin, and questioned over and over about the train robbery, the fate of the other two men, and the whereabouts of the lost gold. He staunchly denied any knowledge of where his former partners might be, and he insisted, at least to the authorities, that there wasn't any gold."

"And I suppose you feel he told my father a different story."

Tom nodded. He couldn't tell whether or not he'd captured her interest. She sounded bored, and she just lay there like a beached whale, her glasses reflecting light from the overhead neon fixture, her hands folded where her lap should be.

Tom took a deep breath of the thick, overheated air. "As you know, your father, Dr. Lawrence, was one of the prison doctors at San Quentin at that time. Lewis Schraeger had tuberculosis, and before too long, he got pneumonia and died. But I'm certain he told your father something more about the lost gold, probably in return for special privileges"—Tom's voice held irony—"like decent food and warm blankets. Conditions at San Quentin were atrocious."

There was no further response from her. Behind her glasses, Evelyn's eyes had closed. At least she wasn't snoring. Tom could only surmise she was listening and not sound asleep.

He cleared his throat and went on. "The reason I believe Schraeger talked was that Dr. Lawrence quit the prison service immediately after Schraeger's death, telling no one where he was going, although I've learned that one of the guards insisted it had to do with the missing gold."

He paused. No response.

"Lawrence came out here, which seems to substantiate the guard's story, and you said yourself he spent a lot of time climbing over the Frank Slide. I think that, although he didn't find it, the gold from that robbery is still here all right, and my partner and I likely can locate it. We use our own system of computer imaging and low-frequency radar waves to detect buried objects and identify them. Of course, to do that we need at least an approximate location, which I believe you said your father's memoirs contained. If you could let me read them, and if they prove helpful in locating the gold, I'd of course have a legal document drawn up which would entitle you to a generous share of it, or a sum of money you feel is adequate to recompense you for the information."

To Tom's amazement, she tipped her head back on the flowered pillowcase and burst into laughter, hearty, rich belly laughs that shocked him.

The rolls of fat on her neck quivered, the bed trembled, and her face turned an alarming shade of mottled red. She chortled and coughed and finally choked. He grabbed a glass of water from a small table at the bedside and handed it to her.

"You okay, Ms. Lawrence? You want me to go get a nurse?"

Maybe she was crazy as a loon after all.

She shook her head and gradually regained her breath.

"You're good for me, Tom Chapman," she wheezed after a moment. "I swear I haven't laughed like that in weeks. A *generous share of the recovered gold."* She shook her head. "That tickles my funny bone. You see, I'm already one of the wealthiest women in this area, thanks to wise investments and careful saving. I'm a spinster, eighty-two years old. I've got a shattered hip that won't heal. I don't have a relative left in the world, and my friends are all too old and senile even to remember who I am for longer than five minutes." In spite of her show of bravado, her voice trembled.

"You're my first male visitor in months, besides that confounded young idiot of a doctor. Just my government pension more than pays for this luxury hotel, and there's nothing else for me to spend my money on. What in heaven do you think I'd do with a generous share of recovered gold anyway? Go on a cruise, buy myself jewelry and furs, have a face-lift?" She slapped the bedcovers with the flat of her hand. "I can't even get out of here without four strong orderlies and a crane."

She reached behind her and punched her pillow into submission, and then looked straight into Tom's eyes. "I finally bullied that idiot doctor into admitting I have bone cancer. No one comes out and says it, but truth of the matter is, I'm dying, Mr. Chapman. It's slow, but it's happening. I've no earthly use for gold. Can't take it where I'm going. You ever see them towing a U-Haul behind a hearse?" She laughed again, but this time there was no real humor in it.

For a long moment, Tom felt mortified. He should have assessed the situation much better, handled her with more tact.

Then embarrassment slowly turned to anger, at her and at himself. He felt as if she'd deliberately let him make a fool of himself, standing here and spouting off what he knew like some slow pupil.

"Well, I guess there's nothing more to say except sorry to have bothered you, ma'am." He reached for his jacket, thrusting his arms into the sleeves. He recovered his Stetson and rebelliously plunked it on his head, tugging the brim low over his eyes. He was almost out the door when her voice stopped him.

"Mr. Chapman, come back in here." The words were bossy, but the tone had a weary sadness in it. "No need to get on your high horse. Maybe we can make a deal, after all."

He hesitated, then shrugged deeper into his jacket. More than anything, he wanted out of this overheated room, away from this nasty caricature of a woman. To hell with the diary and the gold. There were other places to explore, other riches to uncover. This had been a long shot anyway.

"My father's so-called diary was more a collection of scribbling," she wheezed in a petulant voice. "There was reference to a wagon buried under the Slide."

Knowing there was a good possibility she was playing him like a fat brook trout on a line, Tom still turned and retraced his steps to her bedside.

"Now take that fool hat off again and sit down this time. Makes me nervous, having you loom over me like that."

Tom was through letting her call the shots. He left his Stetson in place and stood beside the bed, giving her a narrow-eyed look.

"Contrary as all get out, are you? Well, I always did favor folks with a touch of spirit." She shoved her huge glasses up her nose with one fat finger and turned to stare out the window for a long moment, making a show of ignoring him.

"Maybe we can strike a deal here after all, Tom Chapman," she said in a different voice when she turned to look at him. "I don't need money, but I might like to hear more about some of these treasure hunts of yours."

He frowned, trying to understand what she meant.

She turned over the fat book she'd been reading and tapped her finger on its cover. Tom tipped his head to read the title.

"*A History of the Crowsnest and Its People?*" He still didn't understand what she was getting at.

"It's a collection of local people's memoirs. I had a hand in getting it published. It's history, Tom Chapman, the history of this area. History's the only true treasure worth uncovering."

That made sense to him, even though he didn't fully agree that history was a treasure in itself.

Tom, too, had a passion for books and for history. It was what made him such a meticulous researcher; it was how he unearthed the stories and legends behind the very real antiquities and treasures he and Jackson had located over the years.

"I've spent a great deal of my life studying the history of this area and getting it preserved, including the true facts about that Slide down the road. The Frank Slide may not be important to you folks from Albuquerque, except for the gold you figure is under it. But having a mountain break off and cover half a town affected plenty of lives around here, believe me. And even now, we all live in the shadow of the mountains. They're like family to us. For years, the coal we mined out of them was our major industry. I'm very fond of our mountains."

She turned her head and looked out at the view of the snowcapped Rockies her window provided. "But I'm also fond of hearing about other people's history," she declared, turning back to him. "I never traveled much, and now I wish I had. Seems to me you must have picked up at least a smattering of interesting stories, poking your nose into other people's business and backgrounds the way you do." Her words were still acerbic, but her tone this time was almost pleading.

Tom didn't trust her. "Let me get this straight. You're telling me you'll let me see your father's memoirs in return for . . ." He left the sentence hanging. He still wasn't at all sure what the bargain was, and he was damn certain he wasn't going to like it once he got it straight.

"Don't be obtuse, young man, it doesn't suit you!" she snapped. "I'm offering you a look at my father's precious notebooks in return for a few paltry hours of your time and some of your recollections of places you've been. You seem to have a good memory and you tell a story well enough. You must have taken pictures and I'd like to see them, too, if you've got any handy. Give me something new to think about, lying here flat on my back."

Tom's heart sank. Flowers, chocolates, a reasonable fee, even a share of the gold if they found it—he'd give her any or all of them gladly. But to have to spin stories in return for a look at the damned journals. . . . Wasn't there some story about a woman who had to beguile a king with a series of stories to keep herself alive? And didn't it take a thousand and one nights to spin enough to satisfy the old codger?

Even if this only took him a few days, it wasn't worth it. He looked at Evelyn Lawrence and opened his mouth to tell her politely to go to hell, and all of a sudden, he realized what this was really about.

Tom had no family and, apart from Jackson, no close friends. He'd been lonely at different times in his life. He understood loneliness, and he knew he was looking straight at it. Evelyn was bargaining the only thing she had of value for a few hours of human contact.

Tom had grown up rough. He'd been on his own since he was fifteen years old, and he had few illusions about altruism or the goodness of the human spirit. He was honest, because he'd found in the long run it was easiest to tell the truth. He was friendly and affable, because it wasn't in his nature to be mean, but he was basically a loner. He didn't know how to get close to other people.

He and Jackson had worked out a relationship that allowed both of them plenty of privacy. The rules were simple: They never put the move on each other's women; they didn't delve into each other's psyches; and they covered one another's back when the going got rough.

Spending an extended period of time talking to anyone, male or female, wasn't something Tom had ever done. His relationships with women had been basic, superficial, and physical. Talking hadn't been a priority, and he didn't fancy spending hours doing it now, particularly in a room this small with a gal like Evelyn Lawrence.

Still, to his own amazement, he heard himself agreeing to her proposal. Maybe it was her mantle of lonely pride, or maybe it was just her cussedness.

"I don't have photos, but I've got a video camera and film I can hook up to your television set. When should I come?"

"Tomorrow morning will be fine. Breakfast is at seven. Come around eight."

He thought there was anticipation and even excitement in the watery pale eyes behind the glasses.

"And you've got the journals? You'll let me read them?"

"I've got them, although why I've kept them is beyond me. I've glanced through them now and again."

Strange, for a woman obsessed by history, not to study her own father's records, Tom mused. "I understand," he agreed, even though he didn't. "I'll see you tomorrow morning then."

Chapter Two

The moment he was out of her room, Tom cursed himself for being ten kinds of an idiot. By the time he'd walked the few short blocks to the Greenhill Hotel, his temper was frayed tissue-thin.

"Hell, maybe you could work up a regular patter," Jackson jibed when Tom told him about the bargain he'd made with Lawrence.

"We could probably get you gigs in rest homes all over the country. We could call it Chapman's Bedside Chats."

"Put a sock in it, Zalco." Tom gave him a narrow-eyed, warning look, but he still had to endure more of Jackson's good-natured teasing during dinner.

Afterwards, when Jackson suggested they spend the rest of the evening in the saloon, Tom rebelled. "I'm going for a drive. I want to have a look at this Frank Slide. You stay here if you want to."

"Why the hell leave a nice warm pub to go look at a pile of rocks?" Jackson grumbled. "It'll be dark soon. We can see the damned thing a whole lot better tomorrow when it's daylight, can't we?"

Tom shrugged. "There's still enough light to have a look. The guy at the hotel desk told me about an old road that goes through the middle of the Slide, near where the town of Frank used to be. I want to drive down there. He says there's nothing there now except a meadow and one old fire hydrant, but it'll give us an idea of the magnitude of the thing."

Jackson grumbled, but in the end he came along.

Around them, the Rocky Mountains rose, lowering sentinels protecting the small mining towns that lay strung like grimy beads along the valley floor. The twilight was rapidly fading, but the Slide was only a mile down the road.

Tom turned off the highway near a sawmill, crossed a set of railway tracks, and found himself on a narrow, bumpy dirt track. He drove past a grassy field intersected by a stream swollen to overflowing by the spring runoff and through a stand of poplars and evergreens. Then, between one breath and the next, he and Jackson found themselves in a landscape that might have been lunar in its rocky barrenness.

Immense boulders dwarfed the truck, and jagged shoals of limestone rock extended right across the entire valley floor. Tom slowed and stopped, and after a silent moment, he and Jackson got out of the truck slowly.

Jackson limped a few paces down the road and looked around at the millions of tons of rock. He squinted up at the scarred, forbidding face of the mountain looming over the valley.

"How many people died when this sucker came down?" His voice was awed.

"About seventy." For some peculiar reason, Tom's chest ached with emotion, and he had to swallow hard against the thickness in his throat before he could continue. "There wasn't any exact number. The majority of the bodies were never recovered."

"I can sure as hell see why." Jackson shook his head, and his long blond pony tail switched on his shoulders. "Moving this mess would be next to impossible." He gestured at the mountain, which seemed close enough to touch in the twilight. "They figure it was mining that caused this, right?"

Tom nodded. "It was a contributing factor, all right. The limestone was unstable, and apparently they mined huge chambers which they figure weakened the mountain at its base."

Jackson nodded. "I remember reading in one of those pamphlets you had about the miners trapped inside that night and thinking how it must have felt, entombed in the guts of a damn mountain. Where's the old mine entrance supposed to be?"

"It's gone now. There's nothing left of the town of Frank or the mine."

"Just this gigantic tombstone." Jackson gestured at the piles of rock, and a chill shivered its way up Tom's spine.

He felt the hairs on his nape and his forearms stand on end, and he was suddenly icy cold.

Someone walking on my grave? Or me, standing on the bones of all those still buried under here?

For several minutes neither spoke, and then Jackson broke the silence. "If that shipment of Klondike gold is under here, Tommy, we'd better hope this old doc had some idea where it was located, and that he wrote it down in that journal of his. A man could spend a lifetime and a good supply of shoe leather clambering around this mess."

"Ms. Lawrence said her father did exactly that," Tom said. "According to her, the doctor spent most of his spare time tramping around out here. Seems to me if old Schraeger told Lawrence exactly where to look, he'd have dug up the gold and given up hiking. So he probably didn't know just where it was. We've likely come all this way on a wild-goose chase."

Jackson shrugged, unperturbed. "So what? Won't be the first or last. In our line of business, chasing wild geese is the rule rather than the exception. Besides, like I said, I always wanted to visit this part of Canada. I saw a travelogue on it one time."

"Yeah, and I'll bet they suggested you stay at the Greenhill Hotel in downtown Blairmore," Tom jibed. "This area's not exactly on Fodor's list of spectacular places to visit." He stared out over the rocks and added softly, "Although maybe it oughta be."

The peculiar, sick foreboding rose in him again, and in spite of the evening chill, sweat dotted his forehead. "Maybe we should hit the road first thing in the morning, Jackson, and forget about this damned Klondike gold idea," he suggested. "We've got other irons in the fire. There's that story of buried artifacts at the Alamo."

Jackson shook his head. "We came all this way, might as well stick around and see what happens.

Hell, you're just tryin' to avoid this old lady Lawrence, my friend. Sound of her, can't say I blame you." Jackson knuckled Tom's shoulder with a friendly fist. "C'mon, partner, let's head back to the nice warm saloon and you can fortify yourself against the morning." He hunched his shoulders deeper into his jacket. "This rock pile gives me the creeps."

They climbed back in the truck, and Tom turned the vehicle in the direction they'd come. It was growing dark rapidly, and he turned the lights on. He also pushed the button on the heater to banish the chill that had snaked up his back and was still making him shiver. Immense relief filled him when they were out of the rocks and back on the highway. He kept his hands tight on the steering wheel, embarrassed because they were trembling.

What the hell was wrong with him? He'd been in places where tragedy had struck in much vaster proportions than it had there. Although he'd often felt sad and sorry for the victims, he'd never experienced the soul-wrenching reactions he'd felt in the past few minutes, looking out over the Slide.

Why in hell should a long-ago tragedy in an obscure Canadian valley affect him this way?

"Well, at least you're prompt," Evelyn Lawrence greeted Tom the next morning, setting aside the inky pages of a newspaper she was reading.

It was three minutes before eight, and she was wearing a fluorescent pink bed jacket over a canary-yellow gown. Her sparse white hair resembled a messy bird's nest, and her glasses were perched firmly on her minute nose.

"Are you a drinker, young man? Because your eyes are bloodshot and you look hung over. Drink can be the utter downfall of a man. I hope you realize that."

Tom decided not to honor that crack with an answer. The truth was, he was simply weary. He'd slept badly, which was unlike him.

He'd had unsettling dreams about that damned Slide, and each time he woke, he remembered that he was going to have to come here and entertain Evelyn Lawrence.

"Put all that stuff down, and stop hovering." He was carrying the video camera and a box of tapes. He set them on the floor.

"Morning to you, Ms. Lawrence." He removed his hat and hung his coat over the back of a chair and sat down, determined not to let her get under his skin. "Nice morning." It was still windy, but the sky was washed denim blue, and the sun had already tipped the snowy mountain peaks with a pinkish glow. Their beauty had actually brought a lump to his throat.

She nodded, turning to look out the window. "I've always liked mornings. Years ago I used to get up at five or six and go for a walk, all by myself." She turned from the window and caught him eyeing her bulk. "I wasn't always this heavy, you know. As a child I even did my share of climbing over the Slide, imitating my father, I suppose." She shook her head and her chins jiggled. "I never liked being there, though. I always felt I was disturbing ghosts, but then a girl will do almost anything to gain her father's approval."

"Did it work?" Maybe if he could get her talking, he wouldn't have to.

The humor faded from her expression, and her jowls jiggled as she shook her head. "Not for a minute. My father barely knew I was alive, or my mother, either. She was a convenience to him, hot meals, clean clothing, tidy house. He didn't even remember her birthday, not once that I ever recall. Or mine, either, for that matter." There was enormous bitterness in her tone.

"Oh, he was an adequate doctor. In those days doctoring was a matter of setting bones, delivering babies, and handing out remedies for rheumatism. I pity the poor person who ever went to him for anything else, because he hadn't a clue what made people tick." She shook her head, her mouth pulled into a little knot. "All he cared about was getting away by himself to wander over the Slide."

Tom felt distinctly uncomfortable. He really didn't want to know about her childhood; he didn't want to imagine her being a young girl and unhappy. It was enough that he'd been forced to recognize that she was lonely and old.

"We drove up there last night to have a look at your Frank Slide," he said, hoping to divert her.

Her gray eyes lost their unfocused look and sharpened behind her glasses. "And what did you see?"

He shrugged, uncertain how to answer. "A monstrous pile of limestone rocks and the mountain, of course. Turtle Mountain, that's its name, right?"

She nodded, waiting for him to go on.

He felt like a schoolboy, unprepared to answer a question. He struggled to put something of what he'd felt in words. "It was twilight, pretty gloomy, but then I guess it's not a very cheerful sight at any time. It was cold and sort of spooky."

It wasn't very descriptive, but his answer seemed to satisfy her. "You're right, it is. I always felt that myself. It's historic, though. If you're going to spend time here, you should understand that Slide and the effect it had on this area."

She waved her hand at the window. "There's an Interpretive Center up on the mountain, overlooking the Slide. Go on up there and walk through the museum. Watch the movie they've made about the night the mountain fell. It'll give you the history of the area. And speaking of history, young man, you're here to enlighten me about the world outside these Rockies, so let's get on with it."

Tom's heart sank. This was the part he'd dreaded. He loved what he did while he was doing it, but it made him feel self-conscious and foolish having to talk about it afterward.

And he was also fed up with her calling him "young man," he decided irritably. "Why not just call me Tom?"

"Well, Thomas, then you might as well use Evelyn. 'Ms. Lawrence' and all that Yankee 'ma'aming' of yours makes me feel too much like a spinster schoolteacher, God forbid." There was something almost roguish in the grin that split her fat cheeks and bared impossibly white dentures.

"Evelyn it is," he agreed, answering her smile with a weak one of his own. There was a long, uncomfortable pause, and then he blurted, "See, I don't know exactly how to start, or what it is you want to know."

"This isn't an exam!" she snapped. "Just tell me about one of these so-called treasure hunts you've been on. Or better still, tell me what ever started you on this preposterous business in the first place."

He thought back to that period in his life. It had been a long time since that first expedition. As he tried to sort out how much to tell her and what to leave out, he must have taken too long because she smacked her hand down on the mattress, and said, "You may have all the time in the world, Thomas, but I thought I made it clear mine is limited. Talk, for heaven's sakes."

Startled, he began in the middle of a thought. "I guess it was seven years ago now we went on our first expedition, just after Jackson got his leg hurt. Both of us had been in the hospital, but all I had was a shattered collarbone. He was the one with the serious injury."

She frowned at him. "What on earth from? Were you in a wreck of some sort?"

He grinned. "You could say that. We worked for the U.S. Army Intelligence, Special Squad, and the last assignment we had was in the Middle East. It wasn't what you'd call a success, and we both figured maybe it was time to get into some other profession."

He didn't want to get into details about how they'd been injured. Even now, he didn't want to remember the horror of that botched assignment, so he hurried on before she could start asking questions.

"Anyhow, we'd had a job offer some months before that, while we were in Singapore, and after the—ummm, the accident, we decided to take it. We'd met this crazy little man, Harold Woo, one night at a club, and he talked for hours about mounting an expedition to recover the treasure from a pirate ship sunk during the seventeenth century off the coast of Portugal. For some reason, he took a fancy to Jackson and me and decided he wanted us to mastermind the whole operation. We found out a little more about him, to be sure he wasn't just a loonie shooting off his mouth. When we found out he was on the level, we got in touch with him and said we'd do it."

"I take it you found out he was wealthy," she interjected dryly.

Tom nodded. "He wasn't just wealthy. Harold was filthy rich. But he wasn't too good at the practical shit—sorry, Evelyn."

She waved a hand at him impatiently. "Four-letter words are allowed, as long as you use them in the proper context. They add color. Go on, go on."

"Well, Jackson and I also figured that he had more money than brains, and that this was just a Disneyland dream of his, this pirate-ship caper. So when he offered us either a share in the profits or generous wages, we didn't even blink. We chose wages."

She grunted her approval. "That's the first sign I've seen that you've got a practical nature, Thomas," she said.

"Yeah?" It felt so good to puncture her smug, little balloon. "Well, it was probably the single biggest mistake either of us ever made. See, that pirate ship was right where Harold figured, and it had gold and silver artifacts worth a fortune. If we'd taken even a small percentage, we'd be even wealthier men today."

"So you decided to go into the salvage business on your own," she prompted. She'd folded her hands on the sheet that covered her legs, and she was obviously paying attention to every word.

This wasn't quite as bad as he'd feared it would be. "Yeah," he went on. "We did. We figured if there was one sunken ship out there, there had to be more. So I started doing research."

"And where did you attend university, Thomas?"

"I didn't," he said shortly.

"And why was that? You obviously have a good mind."

Damn, he hated this probing. He didn't mind talking about pirate ships and treasure so much, but when it came to his personal business, it riled him to have her question him.

"I didn't finish high school until I joined the Army." Grade school, either, if the truth was told. He was seventeen before he even discovered how much he liked to read. "They let me take college courses."

"So you're self-taught."

"Yes, ma'am, uhh, Evelyn. I guess you could say that."

The now-familiar scowl contorted her features. "Where did you grow up, for goodness' sake? What kind of parents did you have, not to recognize you were bright and encourage you to get an education? There must be scholarships and bursaries, even in the United States." Her schoolteacher persona was activated, and her parochial attitude toward Canada would have amused him if he hadn't been uncomfortable with her questions.

She went on, "There's a line on television. 'A mind is a terrible thing to waste.' They repeat it so much it's tiresome, but it's also true."

"My folks were poor," he said briefly. It was all he intended to say, and she must have properly interpreted the tautness of his jaw and the warning in his eyes, because she let it drop.

"Well. So you learned to do research."

Immense relief flooded him. They were off dangerous ground, at least for the moment.

"Yeah. I started looking for stories of lost treasure and found they were endless, but lots of them aren't based on much factual information. I try to sort out which ones seem to be the most promising, and then Jackson and I go after them. Not all the time," he corrected. "Not even most of the time. About seventy percent of our work is funded by somebody else, wealthy individuals or organizations. It makes the business viable."

"And how often are you successful?"

His grin was both wide and rueful. "About once in every twenty attempts," he admitted. "That's why we usually work for wages, for somebody else. But once in a while, we can't resist chasing something down on our own."

"Like the mythical gold under the Frank Slide." She looked straight at him. "My mother was quite insane for years before she died, you know."

He couldn't figure out for the life of him what the hell she was talking about. Her mother, the Slide. What the hell had one thing to do with the other?

"You could say it was this same wild-goose chase that did it. You see, she loved my father. She never stopped loving him, even after all the years he neglected and ignored her, and all he loved was—a dream, a fable." There was weary resignation in her tone. "He traded his marriage and his daughter for a treasure hunt, Thomas. Don't let that happen to you." She turned again to the window, and the sounds from the corridor filtered in through the closed door, a television tuned to a game show, a petulant voice asking over and over for orange juice.

"Money's cold comfort when you're old and alone," she went on at last. "I wish now I'd married, had half a dozen children. I'd be a grandmother. A great-grandmother, probably. Most girls marry young around here. It's the fresh mountain air." A trace of her mischievous grin came and went again. "There was a man once, a decent man. But loving has to be learned, just like any other skill. I never learned, and I drove him away. I got to thinking money was the important thing."

Tom was distinctly uncomfortable with all this talk of love. He shifted in his chair, wondering how much longer before he could escape, with or without the diary he was trading his life's blood for.

She noticed and abruptly changed the subject. "Enough of all that. Show me slides, tell me stories."

For the next two hours, he did his best to entertain her.

There were pictures of the South China Sea in the Philippines, and the artifacts from a forgotten civilization that he and Jackson had unearthed. There was the ill-fated expedition to the Arctic, and their futile search for the remains of a Viking ship supposedly frozen in the ice. They'd come close to death on that one. And there was the eerie exploration of a series of caves in Mexico, funded by a wealthy archaeologist, which had resulted in the discovery of human skeletons, skeletons so large they could only have come from a race of long-dead giants.

She asked dozens of eager questions, and he did his best to answer. Time passed much more quickly than Tom had dared hope, but it was still an enormous relief when a tap came at the door and a pink-smocked aide appeared with a trolley.

"Lunchtime, Miss Evelyn. Fish and chips and chocolate sundaes for dessert."

Tom sprang to his feet. "Think I'll go have some lunch myself." The sun shone outside the window like a beacon signaling freedom.

"I sleep in the afternoon, Thomas, and then they use some confounded machine on my hip in the misguided belief that they're doing some good. So you're off the hook until this evening. I'll expect you at five. You might as well leave all that video equipment here until then."

Tom understood it was a way of guaranteeing his return.

"Oh, and remind me to give you the first of those ledgers tonight before you leave," she added with a roguish grin.

So, just as he'd feared, she was going to ration them out, one by one, like lollipops for good behavior. He thought of asking how many there were, and decided against it. By the mischievous look on her face, he knew she was anticipating the question.

He was beginning to understand her better, and he had some idea now of just how lonely she really was—lonely enough to coerce a total stranger into spending time with her. It made Tom feel sad, as well as trapped and resentful.

Like a wild animal scenting freedom, he shoved his arms into his jacket and picked up his hat.

"See you later then, Evelyn." Along with utter relief at making his escape, compassion for her curled inside of him. It must be a bitch to have to lie there and watch him put on his coat and hat and walk out into the blue-canopied day.

"I'd strongly suggest that you and this Jackson person go up to the Interpretive Center this afternoon, Thomas. You probably don't realize it, but tomorrow is April 29, the anniversary of the Slide. It happened at 4:10 in the morning, April 29, 1903. This is the day before the Slide."

Annoyance and amusement mingled in him. She was a petty tyrant. He'd known her all of a day and already she couldn't resist trying to arrange his life for him.

"The Interpretive Center might be called my only progeny, Thomas," she added with fierce pride in her voice. "Not to brag, but I was the one who lobbied the government, both local and provincial, and finally shamed them into building it."

The aide was arranging the luncheon tray on the adjustable arm of the bedside table. "Our Miss Evelyn's famous around here," she said archly. "She was on Calgary TV a couple of times, and she got written up in the paper and everything."

"Large stones, small pools," Evelyn snorted, but it was evident she was pleased.

Tom opened the door and turned to give her a jaunty salute. "We might just drive on up there later this afternoon," he lied. "See you later, Evelyn."

When he thought it over afterwards, Tom was never sure what prompted him and Jackson to visit the Interpretive Center that afternoon.

They ate burgers for lunch at a fast-food outlet, then washed the truck at a garage car wash. They found a cash machine and replenished their supply of Canadian money and paid a visit to the tourist booth on the highway to find out about fishing guides and to get some local maps that would show them the best route to Banff.

As the afternoon waned, Tom drove aimlessly down the highway, enjoying the brightness of the day and the magnificent, snow-topped mountains that cupped the valley. The truck's stereo was turned high, playing cowboy ballads, and Jackson sang along in his clear, true tenor.

The sign for the Interpretive Center turnoff was well placed and clearly visible, and impulsively Tom turned up the paved, winding road, intending only to have a quick look and drive back down again.

The road led in a series of switchbacks up the side of a steep hillside, ending finally in a paved parking lot. Steps led still higher, to a pinnacle where a modern glass and concrete building commanded a view across the narrow valley of the fractured face of Turtle Mountain. It loomed like a gray, scarred, topless sentinel over the miles of boulders and limestone debris which buried the valley floor.

The building was constructed on the very edge of

the Slide, so close that a visitor could reach out and touch the neat line of rocks where the Slide had ended.

There were only two other cars in the lot. Tom parked and turned off the ignition.

"Want to go inside and have a look?"

"Why not? It'll earn you brownie points with your old lady," Jackson teased. "And we don't exactly have any other pressing engagements until your date with her at five."

They climbed the steps, stopping at the top to gaze out over the panoramic view before them.

Again, shivers ran down Tom's back and his breath caught in his throat as he stared out at the tumbled limestone boulders. From this vantage point, the extent of the Slide was made plain.

Tom could see at a glance the entire mass of giant rocks and the highway snaking its way through them like a toy road in a giant's sandbox.

The scar on the face of Turtle Mountain was somehow ominous. Even now, the outline of the Slide rock stood out in light contrast with the adjacent dark greens and browns of the surrounding landscape.

"Must have been one hell of a bang when that sucker decided to come down," Jackson muttered, standing shoulder to shoulder with Tom and staring out over the scarred valley.

They stood for another long moment, silently studying the Slide. Then they turned and went inside the building. Tom paid the nominal admission charge.

"The lower level consists of a small museum that provides a history of the Crowsnest Pass area, and particularly the coal mining that has always been our major industry," the smiling young female guide informed them as they bought their tickets. "Upstairs is our theater where a movie graphically portraying the Slide is presented, but I'm afraid we won't be able to show you that this afternoon. We're closing early today. Tomorrow is the anniversary of the Slide, you see, and we're having a special presentation with the mayor and other dignitaries. Maybe you'd like to come back then?"

Tom was certain that until that moment, Jackson hadn't given a single thought to sitting through any movie. But telling Jackson Zalco he couldn't do a thing because of rules was like waving a red flag in front of a bull.

"No movie? Ahhh, now, honey, that's a real shame." Jackson suddenly acquired a Southern drawl, and he directed every ounce of his considerable charm at the girl. "Ain't that a shame, Tom? See, ma'am, we drove all the way up here from New Mexico, and we heard about this place and that there movie. We can't come by again. We're headin' on down the highway. We're downright fascinated by this whole Slide thing, and we'd be mighty glad to pay you extra for your trouble."

The young woman colored and gave Jackson a look from under her eyelashes. "Well, maybe we could bend the rules just this once. No extra charge. Look around down here, and I'll let you know when the projectionist is ready."

They wandered around, examining the exhibits. A great many of them depicted underground coal mining techniques used in the early part of the century.

Jackson fingered an antique kerosene lamp, used by miners a century before. "Didn't you tell me once your pa was a coal miner, Tom?"

"He was, yeah." A sense of acute discomfort had been growing in Tom as they walked past one mining artifact after another.

They moved on, and Tom was relieved when the young guide appeared. She directed them upstairs to a small, circular theater with steeply tiered seats that looked down on a tiny stage backed by a wide movie screen.

Except for the two of them, the room was empty. It was dimly lit. They closed the doors and slumped into seats, taking off their coats and trying to find a comfortable position for their long legs in the cramped space. The meager lighting suddenly dimmed to blackness.

"Wish I'd saved my breath to cool my porridge," Jackson muttered as minutes went by and nothing further happened. "This is a sinful waste of valuable drinking time."

Suddenly the sound system came alive, although the screen still remained dark, and a woman's haunting soprano filled the room, singing a coal miner's ballad.

The screen flickered to life. *In the Shadow of the Mountain,* the title proclaimed, and the movie began, depicting the booming coal town of Frank as it was before the Slide.

Not expecting professionalism, Tom was impressed by the quality of the film. The visual effects and particularly the sound, coming from wraparound speakers, were both expert and subtle.

The camera took the viewer inside the mine with

the unsuspecting night shift of miners on the night of the Slide.

Conversation and men's laughter echoed as the tunnel narrowed in the simulated flicker of a miner's lamp, and Tom's skin crawled with recognition. He felt again the claustrophobic sensation of being in the bowels of a mountain with untold tons of earth pressing down on wooden beams—all that kept the narrow passageway from collapsing. He heard the endless, infernal dripping of water all around him in the suffocating darkness. Cold sweat broke out on his forehead and soaked his shirt.

To his relief, the camera moved outside again to view the slumbering village as it must have been seconds before the Slide, sleeping in the long-ago cold April night.

The voice-over faded away, the flickering lights on the screen dimmed and gradually went out. For a long, tense moment, the theater was again blanketed in darkness.

Tension built in Tom, and he was grateful for Jackson's bulk, motionless beside him. And then a single rock tumbled in eerie isolation down the mountain slope, bouncing ominously against the limestone walls, its passage echoing throughout the silence of the valley.

For another long moment, there was peace, then the theater seemed to reverberate as the visual and audio depiction of the Slide began. The sound simulated ninety million tons of rock breaking away from Turtle Mountain and plummeting down, sweeping over the mine entrance, obliterating a portion of the town in a scant hundred seconds of wind, falling rock, and dust.

Tom jumped half out of his skin at the noise, and every muscle in his body tensed. His breath came in short, shallow gasps.

The damn film was entirely too realistic.

Tom had researched every aspect of the Slide, and he knew that seconds before the deadly rock fall, a solid blast of icy air raced across the valley ahead of the churning mass of rock.

He knew it had to be his imagination, but he shuddered all the same. It felt as if that same freezing air was whipping over him right now, blowing his hair back and making his eyes sting with cold. He couldn't seem to get his breath, and his lungs ached.

He wanted to get the hell out of there. He grabbed his coat and turned to tell Jackson they were leaving, but something was now wrong with the projector.

The room was once again plunged into inky blackness, although the audio effects of the avalanche went on and on, filling his ears with noise too overwhelming to bear. The audio grew louder and still louder. It felt as if his eardrums were breaking. He shouted in pain and put his hands up to cover his ears, staggering to his feet, trying to holler over the infernal dim. "Jackson—Jackson—"

But the icy air knocked him backwards, into an endless void. He tumbled as he fell. He screamed and threw out his arms to break the impact, but there was nothing there, no bottom, no sides, no ceiling. . . .

Terror filled him and he went on falling and falling. He knew that he was dying, drowning, choking, in a void of empty space that endlessly and forever reverberated with the awful cacophony of the avalanche.

Chapter Three

Cold. Icy cold.

Tom opened his eyes, shuddering. He moved his head from one side to the other.

He was outside, he concluded. Lying on his back on hard, rocky earth, under a dark night sky that stretched like a pewter canopy above him. No moon or stars, but even as he watched, the color in the heavens changed, growing infinitesimally lighter.

Dawn? Dawn where?

He sat up gingerly, trying each limb to see if anything was broken. He was bruised and half frozen, but he seemed to be in one piece. He was on a hillside, in a small clearing surrounded by shadowy pine trees. He looked at the digital watch on his wrist.

4:10 A.M. A.M.? Where had the intervening hours gone?

His Stetson had disappeared but his jacket lay nearby. He snatched it up gratefully, shook dust out of it, and forced his arms into the sleeves.

"Jackson." It came out in a hoarse whisper, and Tom cleared dust from his throat and struggled to his feet.

"Jackson?" This time his voice was louder, frantic and fearful. "Hey, Zalco, are you there?" Where was there? Where was here, for that matter?

He turned in a circle, searching for a landmark, something that would indicate where he was, but there was nothing he recognized.

Trees, a clearing, a valley below—no lights, no sign of the Interpretive Center, or of his truck, or even a road. Where in God's name was he? And where was his partner? His heart was thundering against his ribs, and foreboding churned in his gut.

"Jackson, where the hell are you? Answer me," Tom roared, and at last a response came from out of the gray darkness.

"Over here. I'm over here."

Tremendous relief flooded through Tom, and he ran, stumbling over stones and fallen logs in the half-light.

"Hey, buddy, you okay?"

Jackson didn't answer right away. He was sitting a few hundred feet away, bent forward so that his head rested on his knees. He sat up straighter as Tom approached, revealing a jagged cut on his forehead from which blood was oozing slowly. "What the hell happened? There was that godforsaken noise, and then . . . Where are we?"

Tom knelt beside his partner, groping in his pocket for a tissue to wipe the blood away. "I don't know where we are, and God only knows how we got here. We were in that theater, and then—"

To his relief, the wound on Jackson's head was no more than a deep scratch.

"Must have hit my head on a rock when I landed," Jackson said in a dazed voice. He looked around again, confusion in his gray eyes. "Last thing I remember is that awful noise. And it was freezin' cold in there. Lucky thing I grabbed my coat before all hell broke loose. It seemed like there was an explosion of some kind. We must have been blown clear, huh? Where *is* the damned Interpretive Center, anyhow?" He peered around, frowning, swiping blood from his eyes with the back of his hand.

Tom shook his head. "Got me. It's gone. Disappeared." He searched for a logical explanation and came up blank. "I haven't the foggiest notion what happened to us, but I'm damned glad we're in this together, whatever it is." He got to his feet and helped Jackson up. "Your leg okay?"

Jackson took an experimental step on his bad leg, and then another. "No worse than it ever was." He squinted up at the sky. "Looks like it's comin' daylight, anyhow."

They made their way through the thick trees, heading up the rise of the hill. The ground began to level, and they came out on a flat plateau that overlooked a shallow, familiar valley. It was the Crowsnest. Tom recognized the distinctive shape of one of the mountains, but he couldn't pinpoint exactly where they'd landed. There was a subtle difference in the landscape.

"There's lights down there," Jackson said, pointing. "But it doesn't look like Blairmore to me."

Tom shook his head. "Nope. That town's set right smack up against the mountain. Blairmore was more spread out than that. And there sure as blazes wasn't any mountain that close to the town. And there isn't any highway down there, either, although that looks like railroad tracks." He pointed his finger.

There was something else missing, something that sent a chill up Tom's backbone. "There's no Slide either, Jackson." His voice didn't reveal the growing apprehension he felt.

Jackson whistled, long and low, staring out over the valley, shaking his head. "That doesn't seem possible. We must have got blown a fair distance away, that's what it is. Well, let's have a good look around up here and see if we can locate anything at all. If there was an explosion, you'd think there'd be emergency vehicles around. Someone must have heard something. We couldn't be the only ones who survived."

For the next half-hour, as the indigo sky became deep gray, then began to turn a faded gray-blue, they stumbled through pine woods searching for something—anything—that was familiar. But there was nothing anywhere to indicate buildings had ever existed on the hillside.

At last, back on the plateau where they'd begun, they had to admit defeat.

"This is the damndest thing I've ever seen." Jackson clapped his cold hands together and shoved them deep in the pockets of his jacket. "This hillside feels like the same place that Center was on, but there's nothing here. No roads, no buildings, no parking lot. Sure as hell no people."

"No truck, either." Tom was looking out over the valley toward the flickering lights of the town. "Let's go down there and find out what's going on. Someone must have heard something. We're going to have to hike straight down the side of this mountain to get there, though. Wherever the road was, it's disappeared."

Jackson sighed and nodded. "Let's get started then. It's gonna be one hell of a long walk, and walkin's not my strong suit with this game leg."

Tom estimated that it took them the better part of an hour to make it to the outskirts of the little town.

Jackson's injured leg gave out several times, and they had to sit and rest until he could again put weight on it. The sun came up, spilling rose and gold over a snowy mountain peak, and slowly the icy chill in the high mountain air began to dissipate.

They crossed the railroad tracks and reached a roadway of sorts, a rough dirt track that led toward the village, and they slowly made their way along it.

"Something's mighty screwy here," Jackson muttered as they walked past the first buildings on the town's outskirts. "This place looks like it's straight out of the Old West, like some of those ghost towns in New Mexico. But this one's inhabited. There's all that smoke coming out of chimneys, which is another weird thing. It's like nobody here ever heard of natural gas or oil or pollution."

Tom, too, had the strangest feeling about the place. The buildings were mostly of wood, antiquated two-story affairs on either side of a wide, unpaved street. There was no concrete roadway, no streetlights, no neon signs. The sidewalks were wooden, many of the buildings had false fronts, and there were hitching rails all along the street instead of parking meters. There were no fast-food outlets, no filling stations.

"Damn, is that a horse and buggy that guy's drivin'?" Jackson pointed further down the street. "Y'know, there're no cars anywhere, Tom. I haven't seen one single vehicle."

Tom had noticed, and it didn't make him feel any better about the place.

They walked on, apprehension growing, reading the crudely painted signs on the front and sides of buildings they passed.

Dominion Avenue, an ornately carved wooden street sign indicated. Alberta Mercantile Company, another read, painted in white letters on the side of a store. They stopped and gaped at the array of goods in the small window. A woman's dress, black, floor-length . . . Even Tom, who had little idea of what was fashionable in women's clothing, could tell it was a style from a century ago. There was a bowler hat, shiny high-topped boots, and several mine lanterns of the same antique sort they'd seen—yesterday?—at the Interpretive Center.

"The whole place is a bloody museum," Jackson concluded, immense relief in his tone. "That's what this is. It's some ghost town they've fixed up like a museum, same as the ones we saw down in Tennessee. It's probably another part of that Interpretive Center that your Miss Lawrence never got round to telling you about."

But Tom knew for certain Evelyn would have mentioned something like this. Apprehension built in him as they passed other businesses, all of them antiquated by any sort of modern standards.

A shudder ran down his spine. "Jackson, look there. This town's named Frank. That sign over there says Frank Drug Store, and over there, Frank Barber Shop."

The smell of frying bacon and the enticing odor of coffee came wafting from a building whose sign said Palm Restaurant, Meals At All Hours.

"The hell with it, Tom, I can't figure it out and I'm fed up tryin'. Besides, I'm damned nearly frozen and hungry as a bear. Let's go get something to eat." Jackson headed, limping heavily, for the restaurant door.

Blessed warmth enveloped them as they stepped inside. About a dozen men were seated at round tables covered with red-checkered cloths, drinking coffee from thick white mugs and eating from plates stacked with eggs, bacon, pancakes, and toast. The only woman in the room was the waitress, a buxom, ruddy-faced woman of about forty.

There were antique light fixtures on the ceiling from which emanated pale electric light. But there was no music playing from any radio, no morning news, no television set stuck up in a corner.

There was only the buzz of men's voices, and even the sound of their conversation faded as Tom and Jackson stood dumbfounded, staring at the scene and being stared at in turn.

The room smelled of hot bacon frying, of tobacco smoke, coffee, stale sweat. The peculiar oily odor of burning coal fire came from a fat-bellied stove in a corner, a heaping bucket and a small shovel beside it.

There were framed pictures on the walls that would have brought a fine sum at an antique auction, and ornate lace curtains covered the small windows.

Tom could only think that it was like walking onto a movie set, a movie set in much earlier times.

Even the gaping men looked different from Tom and Jackson, roughly dressed in overalls and sturdy work clothes, their caps dangling from chair backs. Many were puffing on pipes. Some had handlebar moustaches, and two wore suits of a cut and style that Tom had never seen off a movie screen. It was plain to him that their clothing and their haircuts were both from a much earlier era, and again apprehension roiled in his gut.

The woman's skirt came to her ankles, which were encased in sturdy high-topped black boots, and her white shirt was high-necked and long-sleeved. She wore a voluminous red apron. Her brown hair was gathered into a puff on top of her head from which strands were escaping, and her shiny face bore not the slightest trace of makeup.

She broke the tension their entrance had created. Blowing a wisp of hair out of her eyes and waving a hand at Tom and Jackson, she said in a cheerful tone, "You gentlemen looking for some breakfast? Sit yourselves down over there, why don't you?"

She indicated an empty table near the stove and

they walked to it, removing their coats and hanging them on the wooden chair backs. They were uncomfortably aware that the men were still staring at them, taking in their close-fitting denim jeans, the bright red sweatshirt Jackson wore that proclaimed "Life is a Beach." His clump of long blond hair particularly drew their eyes, tied as usual at his nape with a leather thong.

The waitress arrived with two steaming mugs of coffee. She, too, looked at them curiously, but she also smiled in a friendly fashion. "You're new around here. Welcome to Frank. You want the breakfast special? Bacon, eggs, hash browns, sausage, toast," she reeled off.

"Sounds good," Tom agreed.

Jackson, who habitually flirted with any waitress, fourteen to eighty, simply stared at this one, a deep, puzzled frown creasing his bruised forehead.

"Me, too," he finally said in a subdued tone.

She moved away, and he leaned close to Tom, his elbows propped on the table, his eyes flitting around the room. "Would you tell me what is going on here? I swear we're in some sort of time warp. No television, no radio, no jukebox. And get a load of this crowd. I've never seen so many men smoking. You'd think they'd never heard the health warnings. They're givin' us the once-over, and *they're* the ones who look like they're wearin' costumes for a play or something. And yet I'd bet my ass they're not actors."

Tom knew they weren't. He shuddered and took a long, welcome gulp of the strong coffee. The heat from the stove washed over him in waves, and combined with the strangeness of the scene and the stress of the past few hours, he began to feel groggy and totally disoriented. He took another swallow of his coffee.

Maybe the caffeine would jolt his brain into action, so that something would begin to make sense.

"Here you go. Now get yourselves around that. You look half frozen." The waitress set two loaded platters in front of them, frowning at the clotted blood on Jackson's forehead.

"What'd you do, fall off your horse?"

"Fell off somethin' or other," Jackson muttered, not meeting her eyes.

"Nippy out there this morning, ain't it?"

"Freezing," Tom agreed, searching for a way to make sense out of all this. "Is it always cold here at this time of year?"

"Couldn't say for sure," she remarked, her hands on her hips, her head cocked to one side. "We just came West last September, me and Willy, just before the official opening of this here town, so I don't know much about springtime in these parts. Back East, though, April's likely to be unsettled, so it's prob'ly the same out here. Although it sure seems as if the snow's gone early, so that's a blessing."

She shifted from one ample hip to the other, took a deep breath, and settled in for a chat. "Now you take two years ago back home, that was a proper mess if ever I seen one. Snowed right on into June, started again in September, hardly had no summer at all. Folks blamed it on the turn of the century, said it affected the weather, but I don't hold none with that."

"Turn of the century?" Jackson's voice held none of its usual bravado, and his hawk-like features had lost most of their perpetual tan. "Turn of *what* century?"

She looked puzzled for a moment, but then she laughed loudly and whisked a dismissing hand in Jackson's direction. "You're a right caution, ain't you, Mister? Pretending not to know we're in the 1900s now."

1900s?

"Please, miss, what's the exact date?" Tom's throat felt constricted, and his voice sounded strange to his own ears.

She turned her attention from Jackson to Tom, frowning. "Why, it's April twenty-ninth, of course. Where you fellows been?"

Tom cleared his throat before he could speak. "And the year?"

"The year?" She gave him an incredulous look. "Land sakes, it's nineteen hundred two." She edged away until she was several feet from them, eyeing them both suspiciously. "Have you gentlemen been drinking spirits and pickled your brains that you don't even know what year it is?"

1902. Jackson had turned so pale Tom actually thought he might pass out. His own lips felt numb, and there was a buzzing in his ears. "Thank you, ma'am," he managed to say, and was grateful when she moved away, turning back to give them a long, considering look before she hurried into the kitchen.

1902. They were in the town of Frank, in April of 1902—April twenty-ninth, exactly a year before the Slide. Tom felt as if he'd been gut-punched, and from the stunned look on Jackson's face, it was obvious he felt the same. Their eyes met across the plates of food, and Tom saw his own incredulous disbelief mirrored in Jackson's gray gaze.

He swallowed hard. "Well, partner, you were right about that time warp," he finally managed to croak. He lifted his coffee and took a long draught, feeling as if his throat were going to close up on him. "Somehow we got fired back in time. Like in the movies, only for real."

"That's not possible, is it?" Jackson slumped back in his chair, dazed and shocked. "How can that be possible?"

Tom shook his head. "I don't know. I only know it seems to have happened."

The waitress appeared at their table again with a huge enamel coffeepot. "You want more coffee, gentlemen?" She eyed their untouched plates of food. "Somethin' wrong with the breakfast?"

"No, it's fine. We just haven't gotten around to eating yet." Tom lifted his fork and made a stab at an egg, but his appetite was gone.

"Where you gents from, may I ask?"

Tom caught Jackson's eye. Together, he and his partner had faced gunfire, foreign wars, drug dealers, storms at sea, and once even found themselves in an old Cessna running out of fuel 20,000 feet over the French Alps. In every one of those desperate situations, Jackson's cool was legendary. Not once, not even in a crisis, had Tom seen his partner totally lose control, but at this moment, Jackson looked as if he might be on the verge of hysteria. A muscle twitched beside his mouth, and his eyes were wild.

Insane laughter began to build inside of Tom. *Where were they from?* He struggled to answer the waitress's question with something approximating the truth.

"We're—from out of town," he said in a strangled tone. "Travelers, we're travelers." Time travelers, the hysterical voice in his brain proclaimed.

"You plannin' on staying here in Frank? Mines are workin' full time. There's usually jobs to be had underground."

"No." The word exploded from his lips, and he saw surprise and shock on the woman's face at his vehemence.

"No, actually, we're planning to move on as soon as we can," he amended in a more reasonable tone. "We're . . . just looking around."

God Almighty, was there a way to get back? There must be. They'd have to find it. He and Jackson had been in tight spots before, plenty of them, and they'd always managed to escape, Tom assured himself. They'd do that this time, too. Damn straight, they would.

Jackson seemed to be recovering from his initial shock. He swallowed hard and held his coffee cup out to the waitress. "I've let this get stone cold, ma'am," he said with a poor facsimile of his usual flirtatious grin. "Any chance of a hot refill?"

"Sure thing." She took the cup and bustled away.

"Well. Guess we might as well eat," Jackson said, sprinkling pepper on his food and then taking a huge mouthful of potato. "Way we're goin' today, no telling how many years it'll be till our next meal."

Tom grinned and lifted his own fork, grateful to have his partner's humor restored at least. For several moments they chewed and swallowed in silence.

They were almost finished with their food when the door to the restaurant opened and a man came in. He wore a Stetson, a snug-fitting distinctive red coat, breeches, and highly polished knee-high boots.

"Holy hell, it's a Canadian Mountie, in full dress uniform," Jackson murmured in awe. "First one I've ever seen duded up like that off a postcard."

"His jacket's a little short," Tom remarked. "And get a load of that side arm."

The policeman's eyes swept over the room; then his attention zeroed in on their table. He walked over slowly, his leather heels clicking on the wooden floor, his dark mustached face somber under the down-tilted brim of his Stetson.

"Morning, Officer." Tom looked up into steely blue eyes and a stern face.

"I'm Constable Liard, North West Mounted," the policeman announced in a formal tone. "I must ask you men to identify yourselves."

Tom's heart sank. A look at their wallets was going to confuse this officer no end. He'd be willing to bet there weren't any bank cards, photo drivers' licenses, or Social Security numbers in this era. He reached around to get his wallet from the back pocket of his jeans, and in one swift movement the Mountie drew his gun, a vintage Colt 44. He pointed it first at Tom's head and then at Jackson's.

"Put your hands where I can see them, and get to your feet."

"What the . . . What's this all about, Officer?" Jackson, his eyes narrowed on the gun, got up slowly. Tom saw the Mountie's eyes drop to Jackson's belt, checking for weapons.

"You, too, on your feet." The command came in a clipped, officious tone and the gun moved momentarily toward Tom. "Now. Nice and slow and easy."

Tom did as he said, very careful not to make any sudden moves.

"Now, keep those hands where I can see them and move over to the door, real slow." The cumbersome-looking gun was still pointing at first one of them and then the other.

"Our coats . . ." Tom jerked his chin at their jackets, tossed over the chair.

"Andy, you bring those coats along. I want a look in the pockets before they put them on."

A short man at a table nearby jumped to his feet, toppling his chair in his eagerness to do the policeman's bidding. He gathered up Tom and Jackson's jackets and followed them to the door.

If their entrance had commanded almost everyone's attention, this exit topped it. Several more of the customers were now standing, excitement plain on their faces, obviously willing and able to help Constable Liard should the need arise.

Voices rose and questions flew.

"What'd they do, Constable?"

"Who are they?"

"You want us to come along until you get to the barracks, 'case they try and make a break for it?"

The Mountie shook his head, centering his attention on Jackson and Tom as they sidled between tables and moved toward the door.

"They was talkin' pretty crazy, and they didn't pay for their breakfasts yet, Robert," the waitress sang out, poised halfway into the kitchen with an armload of dirty dishes. "They owe me fifty cents each."

"I'll see they pay, Gertie," Liard promised, herding them out the door.

Tom shivered as the door swung shut behind them, and the cold air sent icy blasts through his sweatshirt and jeans.

"Where are your horses?" Liard glanced up and down the street, then led them to a sleek brown mare tethered to a hitching post a few yards away.

"Horses?" Tom shook his head in bewildered frustration. "We don't have horses, for God's sake. Look, this is all a big mistake, Officer. What are you arresting us for, anyhow? Don't we at least have the right to know why you're arresting us?"

"Two men answering your description robbed the bank in Pincher Creek in the early hours of the morning," Liard pronounced.

"Damnation." Jackson rolled his eyes and shook his head. "Well, it wasn't us. I promise you, we aren't bank robbers, and we weren't anywhere near this Pincher Creek place, not this morning, not ever."

"What are your names?"

"I'm Jackson Zalco and this is Thomas Chapman."

"Give me an account of your whereabouts last night," Liard demanded.

Tom and Jackson looked at one another, knowing that if they told the truth, there was no way on earth this young constable was going to believe it.

Tom tried to think of how they could prove who they were and where they had been last night, but it seemed impossible.

"Look, we're not even Canadian citizens," he tried

to explain. "We're Americans. We're just visiting in this country."

The Mountie was singularly unimpressed. "Bank robbery's illegal on both sides of the border, gentlemen. If you can't give an account of yourselves, I have no choice except to arrest you."

A horrible thought struck Tom. Was lynching a common thing in Canada in this early part of the century?

He wondered how much cash Jackson had on him. Tom had a couple of hundred. Would they have enough between them to hire a good lawyer?

Was there such a thing as a good lawyer at this end of the century? Was there any lawyer at all in Frank in 1902? If by some miracle there was, and they didn't have enough cash, would he accept a charge card?

"We'll talk at the barracks," Liard said. "Andy, let me see those coats." He went through all the pockets, pulling out Tom's ring of keys and frowning at them. With equal puzzlement, he studied an unopened package of tissues from Jackson's pocket, as well as a stick of gum and a dispenser of breath mints.

At last he handed their jackets over, and Tom and Jackson gratefully put them on.

"It's a bit of a walk to the barracks." Liard unclipped handcuffs from his belt and cuffed Tom's right hand to Jackson's left. From a saddlebag, he withdrew a length of lariat and swiftly tied one end to the handcuffs and the other to his saddle.

"We'll go at a good brisk pace so you don't get too cold," Liard promised with a grin. "It's only about a quarter of a mile."

He mounted and clicked his tongue to the horse. In another moment, Tom found himself herded down the main street of Frank like any common criminal in an outdated Western video, his wrist hooked tightly to Jackson's.

Jackson was cursing steadily under his breath and limping badly.

Two small boys bundled against the cold were playing with a ball in the middle of the street. They stopped and stared wide-eyed as the procession neared.

"Hey, look, Willy, that copper's caught some bad guys!" one hollered.

"You takin' them to jail, sir?" the other queried. "You gonna shoot 'em or just string 'em up? Kin we come and watch?"

"Get lost, kid," Jackson growled. "You been watchin' too much TV."

"No TV, not for years yet," Tom muttered under his breath.

Jackson heard, shook his head, then turned a baleful look on Tom. "I want you to know I blame this whole sad, sorry mess on that old woman of yours," he gritted out between his teeth. "We hadn't gone to that cursed Center, this never woulda happened."

Tom, shivering in the cold, slogging through mud up to his ankles in expensive boots, which he'd carefully polished back in his own time, thought of Evelyn Lawrence and had to grin.

With her passion for the historical events of this confounded valley, the old girl would probably trade her dentures for the chance to hear this story.

I'll tell you all about it, Evelyn, he promised desperately. When we get out of this, when we get back there, I promise you'll hear every detail.

If we get out of this, some cold and rational portion of his brain corrected as mud from the horses' hooves splashed liberally over what had been clean jeans only hours before.

Hours—and over ninety years.

Chapter Four

The North West Mounted Police Post consisted of a two-story log cabin situated beside a stream. Office, jail, and barracks took up the large, main floor room, with the members' sleeping quarters upstairs.

Like the town itself, the cabin huddled close against the steep side of Turtle Mountain, in a clearing punctuated with tall pine trees and poplars still naked from the winter.

Several large tents were pitched nearby, sheltering food supplies and equipment, and two long clotheslines strung between trees held an assortment of long underwear, pants, shirts, and blankets washed and hung to dry. A corral with an open-sided lean-to provided shelter for the horses.

Constable Liard dismounted and tied his horse in the shade. He loosened the cinch and untied the lariat, herding Tom and Jackson into the cabin and directly into one of the two crude but sturdy cells at the back of the main room. He undid their handcuffs and locked them in, turning a huge key in the lock on the cell door. It was a thick slab of wood with a small barred opening that looked into the main room. Another barred window, even smaller, allowed thin sunlight to stream into the dingy cell.

"Corporal Allan will be back shortly. He'll want to ask you some questions." He hung the key on a nail and went outside.

Jackson collapsed on one of the narrow beds, leaning over to rub the calf of his injured leg. "You figger they've even heard of cars yet, Tom?" He sounded both weary and plaintive.

Tom slumped down on the other bunk, eyeing the high, barred window. There didn't seem much chance of breaking out if they couldn't beat the robbery charge. Neither his shoulders nor Jackson's would ever fit through there, even if they managed to dislodge the bars.

"Cars? It's way too early for cars. I don't think there were any around until the late twenties, when Henry Ford started making the Tin Lizzie."

Jackson groaned. "Swear to God, if we can't get back to normal times in a hell of a hurry, I guess I'm just gonna have to learn to ride a horse. All this walkin's gonna kill me years before I was ever born."

"That's if they don't hang us first."

"Naw, they won't do that. Hell, no. Canadians are noted for being fair. The Mounties have always had a good reputation, even this North West lot. Way I see it, they don't have a whole lot of evidence to charge us with a single damned thing anyhow, although it's going to be tricky explaining where the blazes we were before we got here."

Jackson lay back on the bunk, gave a huge sigh, and closed his eyes. "No point stewing over it, might as well get some sleep. There's not a blessed thing we can do until this Corporal Allan gets back from wherever he's gone. Damn, it feels like I've been up for ninety years." He sighed deeply again, and in moments he was snoring.

Tom had always envied Jackson's ability to fall asleep under any circumstances. He was tired himself—way beyond tired—but he was too geared up even to think about sleeping.

His brain went over and over the events of the past hours, like a rat in a maze that always ended up back at the beginning.

There simply was no rational explanation for what had occurred. Through some unexplainable fluke, they'd been hurtled into the distant past, and now it seemed they were stuck there whether they liked it or not.

And just as Jackson said, there was nothing they could do about it.

At last Tom closed his eyes and in moments he, too, was asleep.

It was a woman's voice that woke him. Unusually husky and vibrant, it was filled with outrage and more than a touch of venom.

"Explain to me, Corporal Allan, if you will—if you can—exactly which law you believe I was violating?" The voice had an appealing resonance, each word clearly articulated. "As far as I know, there's nothing that prohibits a woman from giving a speech in a public place or from carrying placards, as long as she doesn't engage in or encourage violence. Have you never heard of free speech? Do they not cover the rights of individuals in whatever scanty training they offer you lawmen?" Her tone was both sarcastic and scathing. "Although I'm quite certain you've never heard of women's rights, sir. Under the present laws, it seems we have none."

The policeman had a gravelly voice and an English accent, and he sounded exasperated. "You know Hugo Bateman laid a charge against you the last time you did this, Miss Ralston, and I warned you myself that if you continued to protest outside of his establishment, I would have to arrest you. He has a legal license to sell liquor in this town."

Tom sat up and swung his feet to the floor, rubbing his hand over his face. He needed a shave. Jackson was still asleep, snoring softly. The sun was pouring in through the tiny window, and it felt to Tom as if hours had passed since he'd fallen asleep.

Intrigued by the battle going on in the cabin, he got up and walked to the small barred opening in the cell door.

Through the bars Tom saw a Mountie, not Liard, but a barrel-chested, ramrod-straight, middle-aged man in uniform, standing facing a tall, thin, young woman in a floor-length black coat.

Her fiery red curly hair was escaping in all directions from under her straw hat. She had a generous sprinkling of freckles across her nose and cheeks, and she was facing the policeman, her hands on her slender hips, her chin tilted at an aggressive angle.

It was obvious she was very angry. "Hugo Bateman," she snorted. "Don't you dare talk to me about that—that *criminal* having a license. Or about him laying a charge against me, Corporal."

"Hugo has a license to operate a drinking establishment, Miss Ralston," Allan repeated in a weary tone, sounding as if he'd been over this many times before.

She glared at the policeman. She was as tall as he, and she stamped her booted foot in absolute fury.

Tom grinned. He liked her spirit.

"Hugo Bateman knows perfectly well that each time he sells spirits to Nestor Vandusen it's Mrs. Vandusen and the children who suffer!" she yelled.

She had good volume. Maybe she shouted a lot, Tom mused.

"You know perfectly well that Nestor came home at two A.M. this morning, once again inebriated, and beat his wife most viciously." Her voice was even louder. "My brother ran all the way out here and brought Constable Liard, who took Nestor off and then released him at six this morning to go to work. And mark my words, tonight he'll do the same thing all over again. It's Hugo Bateman, for selling spirits, and Nestor Vandusen for drinking them, whom you should be arresting, sir, not *me*."

Corporal Allan sighed, a long, deep, martyred sigh. It was plain that he, too, was losing his patience. "You know we can't arrest Nestor for any length of time unless his wife lodges a complaint, which she refuses to do."

"Of course she refuses, you—you absolute ninny. She can barely speak English, for heaven's sake. She's totally dependent on that worm of a husband for food and shelter for herself and her children, and you do nothing to prevent his cruelty. For shame, Corporal. For shame."

Miss Ralston was losing it in earnest, Tom decided. He felt anxious for her. The law around here seemed all too eager to throw innocent people behind bars. Would they treat a woman any different?

"She knows full well if she lays charges against him, he'll lose his job," she bellowed. "And just who's going to hire Isabella, worn down as she is with beatings, even though she'd be a much better worker than that sodden excuse for a husband? It's the men who are at fault here, Corporal, not the women. A chimpanzee could figure that out."

There was a charged silence. Corporal Allan's rather florid face went from pink to purple. "Are you calling me a chimpanzee, Zelda Ralston? His voice had dropped to an ominous purr. "Let me remind you, you've already kicked me soundly in the shins this morning. Attacking an officer of the law is a serious charge, and I warn you, one more outburst of this sort and I shall put you behind bars where you belong."

"Go right ahead, Corporal. I assure you that when I contact them, the Women's Temperance Union will find me a lawyer, and the details of this disgraceful situation will be spread across the pages of *The Frank Sentinel,* as well as in newspapers throughout the West. You and the entire North West Mounted will look like the fools you are."

She was a dirty fighter if not a cautious one, Tom thought with admiration. He watched the play of emotions on her expressive face.

She wasn't exactly pretty. She was too thin, and

her features were strongly drawn, but there was an electricity about her that seemed to light up the dingy cabin. She had sex appeal, and that hair was like living fire.

Jackson was awake, too, and he came to stand beside Tom, peering out at the scene playing itself out a few feet away.

Evidently her words were enough to drive the corporal over the edge. He grasped her by the upper arm and hustled her to the unoccupied cell beside Tom and Jackson. She took several good whacks at him with her other arm, and he grunted and held up a hand to ward them off.

They couldn't see him thrust her inside, but they heard the barred door slam and the key turn in the lock.

"Whoooeee." Jackson whistled softly and shook his head. "Spitfire," he whispered softly.

"I advise you to sit down in there and collect yourself, Miss Ralston," Corporal Allan advised in stentorian tones. "I've sent for your father. I plan to have a word with him, man to man. Surely he has some control over your disgraceful behavior."

"I'm an adult, Corporal; I happen to be twenty-eight years of age." Her voice was muffled by the cell door, but her outrage came through as powerfully as ever. "My father wouldn't dream of trying to control me. He, at least, has respect for the individual, be they male or female."

"More's the pity." Allan walked to a desk and plopped into the chair, removing his Stetson to reveal a balding head. He used a large white handkerchief to blot at his shiny skull and his brow.

Tom and Jackson looked at one another and

grinned. They could hear the woman in the next cell making small exclamations of contempt and disgust, muttering under her breath. Her long skirts swished and rustled as she moved.

The door of the building opened just then and Constable Liard appeared. The two policemen conferred for several minutes in low voices. Then Liard withdrew the cell key from its nail and unlocked the door to Jackson and Tom's cell.

"Word's just come on the telegraph that the bank robbers were apprehended an hour ago outside of Pincher Creek," he announced. "I guess you two are free to go, soon as you pay me the money you owe Gertie for breakfast this morning. Fifty cents each, she said."

Tom grabbed the coat he'd left on the end of the bunk, and he and Jackson hurried out of the cell. Freedom had never felt as sweet. He drew out his wallet and withdrew a five-dollar Canadian bill.

"Give this to Gertie," he said, handing it to Liard. "Tell her to keep the change."

The constable glanced at first one side of the money and then the other. "Says Canada on it, but this must be some newfangled kind of money. I've never seen its like before, and I'll wager it's no good around here. Don't go trying to pass it off in town, or I'll arrest you all over again." He gave Tom a stern look and handed the bill back. "That the only money you have?"

"Constable, let me have a good look at that bill. It could possibly be counterfeit." Corporal Allan began to get to his feet, and Tom's heart sank.

Until that moment, he hadn't given a thought to the fact that along with everything else, money had probably changed drastically since 1902. Not only were he and Jackson stranded at the wrong end of the century, he now realized, they were also marooned there without usable cash. And if this Corporal Allan got it into his head they were counterfeiters, they could spend a lot longer than a few hours in this barracks.

Tom had no choice but to hand over the money.

Corporal Allan took it and sat back down at his desk. He laid it flat on a piece of paper and opened the desk drawer, retrieving a large, round magnifying glass with a handle. He peered through the glass at the five-dollar bill for what seemed to Tom an endless time, turning it over and over.

"Come here and have a look at this, Constable," he ordered.

Liard moved quickly and took the magnifying glass.

"This can't be right, Corporal Allan," he said in a puzzled tone. "The date on this bill is 1986."

"Let this be a lesson to you, Constable, to pay more attention to detail. You were about to release these men far too hastily."

Jackson was standing beside Tom, shifting uncomfortably from one foot to the other. They exchanged a despondent look.

Liard shot them an accusing look, and Allan peered at them suspiciously from under his bushy eyebrows. "Now, gentlemen. What were your names again?"

"Tom Chapman."

"Jackson Zalco."

"Yes, quite. Well. There's something amiss here, all right, and you both know it. This bill is unlike any I've ever seen. 1986, indeed." He glared at them. "I intend to get to the bottom of this," he said in the same quiet, lethal tone he'd used to address Miss Ralston. "And neither of you is going anywhere until I do. I think your best recourse at this point would be simply to tell me the unvarnished truth. Constable Liard, sit down over there and take notes on these proceedings."

"Damn," Jackson swore.

"I'll thank you to watch your language, sir," Allan snapped. "There's a lady over there, in case you haven't noticed."

Tom had almost forgotten Miss Ralston. He turned to the cell. She was standing with her face close to the bars, watching the scene with the same avid attention as he'd watched her a short time before. Through the bars, she wiggled her fingers at him in greeting.

"Apologies, ma'am," Jackson drawled.

"I believe I've heard the expression before," she purred. "And if the good corporal truly believed I was a lady, do you honestly think he'd have thrown me in here?" Her voice rose an octave. "And by the way, Corporal, this cell is a disgrace. It needs scrubbing down with lye and soap powder. I'm quite sure you have bugs in the bedding."

Corporal Allan rolled his eyes and did his best to ignore her.

Tom was sick of standing and being interrogated while the corporal sat. "This is going to take awhile, Corporal. Mind if we sit down?"

Allan nodded grudgingly, and Tom snagged a nearby chair and handed it to Jackson, then dragged one over for himself, trying to figure out how and where to begin.

Jackson wasn't being any help. When Tom shot him a questioning look, his partner just shrugged elaborately and made a motion with his hand that indicated the stage belonged to Tom.

"We're strangers here," he finally began, trying to ease into it gradually. "We're from another time and place, and I'm not too sure myself exactly how we got here, but I'll explain it as best I can. See, we were watching this movie—"

"Movie?" Allan's eyebrows were near his nonexistent hairline. "What, pray tell, is a movie?"

It began to dawn on Tom just how difficult this was going to be. "A motion picture, a moving picture, a—" He stopped, unable to think of a way of explaining.

"I believe it might be something like a stereoscope, Corporal, except the picture moves," Miss Ralston offered in a superior tone. "I've recently read about a photographic gun that records motion photographs," she went on in her husky voice. "It was devised by a French scientist named E.J. Marey."

She smiled straight at Tom through the bars. "You see, I'm a photographer when I'm not being unfairly incarcerated by the North West Mounted," she explained just as if she was at some tea party instead of in a lockup. "In some of my publications, other photographers have mentioned this technique of making moving photographs, and it very much interests me. If you've actually witnessed this process, I'd like to discuss it with you, sir. Under more pleasant circumstances, of course."

"My pleasure, ma'am." She had a wonderful smile, mischievous and winsome and wide. Tom grinned back at her, forgetting for a moment the gravity of the situation.

"Well, Chapman? Are you quite ready to proceed?" Corporal Allan wasn't long on patience.

"Well, it was the 1990s, and we were watching this movie about the Frank Slide, and something went wrong."

"1990s?" Constable Liard looked up from his note-taking to stare at Tom.

"Frank Slide? What Frank Slide? What kind of balderdash is this, young man?" The corporal was losing his temper.

Tom drew a deep breath. "I know it must sound nutty, but, believe me, there's going to be a Slide, Corporal, a big one. In exactly a year, one year from today, the top of that mountain outside, Turtle Mountain, is going to fall off and half bury this place. This whole valley will be covered in limestone boulders. That's the movie we were watching when we were somehow transported here to 1902."

The corporal and the constable were giving him a look that clearly indicated they had a looney on their hands. Tom glanced at Miss Ralston. She was frowning at him and shaking her head in warning.

Obviously she believed he was spinning a tale to make a fool of the corporal, and was afraid it would backfire on him.

Exasperated, Tom turned to his partner. "Jackson, you tell them what happened. I give up."

Jackson leaned forward, speaking confidingly to Corporal Allan. "He gets like this sometimes, sir. He's my best buddy and he's harmless, but he gets these spells. I sort of just humor him through them. The family thought travel might help, and so . . . It's an old war injury. He took a bullet to the head in combat."

Tom gaped at his partner, speechless at such duplicity, but Jackson wouldn't even look at him.

The corporal and Constable Liard were both staring at Tom with a mixture of understanding and pity on their faces.

Tom sprang to his feet, intending to pop Jackson a good one in the ear for being a lying son of a bitch, but the door behind him opened and a quiet voice interrupted them.

"Afternoon." A tall, middle-aged man came in the door, his body bone-thin but muscular, his shoulders stooped.

He removed his tweed cap, revealing a thinning head of hair a few shades darker than that of the woman in the cell. He glanced at Tom and Jackson and nodded in a friendly way before he turned his attention to the corporal.

"Understand you arrested my Zelda this mornin'."

"Afternoon, Mr. Ralston." Corporal Allan cleared his throat several times and got to his feet. "I see you received my message."

The newcomer had diverted the corporal's attention from Tom and Jackson, and Tom caught Jackson's eye, gave him a dirty look, and made a threatening gesture with his fist. Jackson frowned and shook his head as if he actually had a plan.

"Mr. Ralston, I'm afraid I was forced to, ummm, incarcerate your daughter in one of my cells. She was being most obstreperous," Corporal Allan was saying in a portentous tone. "It pains me to have to tell you this, but she, ummm, ahhhh, she assaulted me. Kicked me in the shin, and then, ahhh, used most objectionable language."

Tom glanced at Miss Ralston. She had her finger pressed to her lips, urging that he be as silent as she was. To Tom's amazement, she also gave him a wink. She had dark eyes. Tom thought they were brown.

"Ah, I'm sorry to hear that, Corporal Allan." Ralston shook his head, a pained expression on his gaunt features. "I've tried to raise her to have respect, but a man alone with a lass . . . It's not easy." He shook his head and sighed. "You'll not be keeping her in jail, surely? She's sorely needed at home, what with me working and Eli still only a lad in school."

Corporal Allan seemed to think it over for an inordinately long time, stroking his moustache as he deliberated. "Well, I'll let her off again with a fine, sir," he finally proclaimed. "But we can't condone this type of behavior. This is the second time this month. If it happens again, I'll be forced to take further action."

"Thank you, Corporal. How much will it be?" He dug a wallet out of his pocket.

"Five dollars."

Tom glanced at Zelda. Although the fine sounded ridiculously low to him, it was obvious that to her, five dollars was an exorbitant sum. She was biting her bottom lip, and there was no trace of humor now in her expression. Her face was flushed with anger.

"And," Corporal Allan was saying, "she's released

in your custody. You're responsible for her actions. Try and keep her under control, won't you?"

Tom noticed that Ralston didn't answer that. Instead, he took two worn bills out of his wallet, dug in his pocket for change, counted it all out carefully, and handed it over.

"Constable Liard, release the prisoner."

Liard came to attention, retrieved the key, and unlocked the cell. Zelda Ralston strode out, her chin high, her eyes flashing dangerously.

"Dad, give me another dollar, please. If you have it." She held out her hand imperiously, and Ralston again dug in his pocket and without a word, handed her a crumpled bill.

She plunked it down on the desk. "That's for the breakfast these gentlemen ate at Gertie's," she spat. "As far as I can see, you've no further reason to hold them. Being mentally deranged isn't a crime, is it, Corporal?" Her tone took on the saccharine sweetness Tom was beginning to recognize. "Because if it's a crime to be mentally deranged, then you know as well as I that half the male population of Frank should be arrested."

Allan's face again turned a dangerous shade of magenta, but it was obvious now that he just wanted to be rid of all of them.

"See that your friend here is closely watched at all times," he barked at Jackson. "It wouldn't do for him to go spouting off his mad fantasies all over town."

Tom felt his blood pressure rise, but he kept his mouth shut. There'd be time enough later to beat the stuffing out of Jackson, when they were safely out of here.

"Yes, sir, I'll keep him under control. C'mon, old buddy," Jackson said in a solicitous tone, taking hold of Tom's arm with a grip like steel and propelling him toward the door.

It closed firmly behind them. The sun was warm. Birds were singing. The sky was intensely blue, the brook trickled nearby, and the fresh air smelled sweet as wine in Tom's lungs. It was hard to stay furious at Jackson now that they were outside the police barracks, but he did his best.

They walked along the rutted road they'd followed earlier, and Tom waited until they'd gone a short distance before he spoke.

"You bloody traitor," he gritted out between clenched teeth, keeping his voice low so that Zelda Ralston and her father wouldn't hear.

Father and daughter were climbing into a buggy parked beneath some pine trees a short distance away from the barracks.

"You want to spend your time in that jail, you go back in there and try to tell them some more of the truth," Jackson answered hotly. "Me, I'd lie and cheat and steal to stay out of there."

"As well as make out I'm three pickles short of a jar!" Tom raged. "How could you do a thing like that? I swear, I'll get you for that one, Zalco."

"Would you gentlemen like a ride back to town?" The horse had overtaken them and Zelda Ralston was smiling down from the high seat of the buggy. Her straw hat was crooked, tilted at a zany angle over one ear. Her fiery hair poked out in all directions, and her huge brown eyes twinkled at him, as if the two of them shared a delightful secret.

He could see she had a dimple high on one cheek.

And Tom suddenly found himself smiling back at her.

Chapter Five

"A ride? Yes, ma'am, we would like a ride," Jackson said before Tom could answer. "I've had all the workout I need for one day." He gave a courtly little bow to both Zelda and her father. "And we do thank you, too, for payin' off our debt back there, Mr. Ralston."

"You gents got off cheap compared to this gal of mine," Virgil Ralston declared with a resigned shake of his head. "'Tisn't the first time and likely won't be the last I'll have to come and bail Zelda out."

"I've a good mind to visit the barrister and charge Corporal Allan with wrongful arrest," she answered. "Perhaps we could get our money back if we sued him, Dad. He's absolutely unreasonable. I was simply conducting a peaceful demonstration in front of Hugo's saloon when he arrived and began to harass me."

"Ah, lass, if I've told you once I've told you a million times that your notions about temperance don't go over in a mining town. Miners are drinkers, and that's that. You'll not change them."

Zelda didn't answer, although it was plain from the stubborn set of her chin she didn't agree.

"Call me Virgil," the older man said to Tom and Jackson. "Climb up here. You'll have to sit on the backboard, but it's better 'n shank's pony. Didn't catch your names in there, either."

Tom and Jackson introduced themselves and swung up on the backboard of the buggy. Virgil clucked to the horse and soon they were jouncing along.

"Using horses sure cuts down on exhaust fumes," Jackson remarked. "Environmentally friendly, huh, Tom?"

Tom didn't answer, but Zelda Ralston overheard and turned to give them both a long, speculative stare.

"Where are you two really from, Mr. Chapman?" she asked in a suspicious voice.

"Why don't you explain it this time, Jackson?" Tom urged with more than a little venom in his voice. "You're the sane one of us, remember?"

Jackson heaved a sigh. "What Tom said back there at the cop shop was the God's honest truth, Miss Ralston," he acknowledged. "But I figured if I agreed with him, we'd be cooling our heels in those cells for who knows how long. So I lied to save our skins and get us out of there fast. And you helped no end, ma'am. I figure if the corporal got back on the money situation, he'd have decided for certain we were counterfeiters and locked us up again."

Jackson still hadn't said exactly where they were from, Tom realized. He could be as slippery as ice when he wanted.

"And are you counterfeiters?" Virgil's voice was filled with interest and amusement rather than alarm.

"Nope, we sure aren't," Jackson said firmly. "We're law-abiding citizens of the U.S. of A., come here to Canada to research a project for our business. Like Tom said back at the police station, somethin' went wrong and we ended up here through no fault of our own."

"I didn't hear your story, but it sounds like a good one," Virgil said. "I'm a sucker for a good story. You two have someplace you have to go in town, or do you want to come home with us and have a bite of supper and talk awhile?"

Not only did they have nowhere to go, they had not one usable cent between them, Tom pondered. After forking out a dollar for them at the police barracks, Virgil knew that.

"Won't be nothin' fancy. It's my turn to cook," Virgil warned. "Zelda here don't only have notions about liquor, she's also got it in her head that Eli and me should share the cookin'. Now if Corporal Allan got wind of that notion, he'd think I was touched in the head, for sure, lettin' the lass get away with it."

Zelda laughed aloud, a musical, infectious sound that brought an answering smile to Tom's lips. "Corporal Allan has a lot to learn about modern women, Dad, and we'll certainly never ask him to supper, so don't fret over it. But you two gentlemen are welcome, if you care to come."

"Thank you, we'd be honored," Tom replied.

As they approached the village of Frank, Tom tilted his head up to look at Turtle Mountain, just south of the town and looming over it. In his mind, he compared the shape he saw with the much different configuration he remembered the mountain having after the Slide. He tried to detail in his mind exactly which part of the lowering giant would come tumbling down and cover this valley, and the knowledge was terrible.

Zelda noticed his intense study of the mountain. "The Turtle's magnificent, isn't it, Mr. Chapman?" she remarked. "It's also a drawback, however, because it puts the entire town in shade very early in the day. In the winter, the sun sets as early as half after one. We truly live in its shadow."

Jackson gave him a warning nudge in the ribs, and Tom could only nod.

"Supplies us with a livin', though. She's rich with coal, the Turtle," Virgil remarked.

"Are you a miner?" Tom was still looking up at the mountain.

"Aye, lad, that I am. Been underground so long, I got coal dust in my blood," Virgil said with a smile.

They trundled through town, and Zelda identified the major businesses as they passed them. "That's the Hall. There's a piano and a good stage where theatricals are performed. Dances are held twice a month, and every Sunday evening Pastor Ward holds church services there as well."

They passed the Palm restaurant, Meals At All Hours, and Tom and Jackson exchanged glances, vividly remembering that morning and the series of events that had begun with them walking into the Palm and ordering breakfast from Gertie.

"That's the newspaper office," she said next. "The editor means well, but he can't spell worth beans and he won't print anything the least bit controversial."

Virgil turned to the two men and winked broadly. "What she means is Harry won't put his neck in a sling printing the hotheaded letters she writes. He's a wise man, is Harry."

"Each and every letter is about issues that badly need addressing," Zelda declared, going on with the travelogue as they continued down the street.

"That building under construction over there is going to be the new CPR train station. That's the Union Bank, of course, and there's Mr. Leitch's grocery and furniture store, and further along is the post office."

Beside the post office was a small building fronted by a large sign that announced, "Beaseley's Studio, Our Photographs Will Always Whisper, Come Again."

Tom remembered what Zelda had said about being a photographer.

"Is that where you work, Miss Ralston?"

She turned and gave him a look of disdain. "Me, work for William Beaseley?" She sniffed, her chin tilted skyward. She snapped, "Certainly not! Mr. Beaseley and I have very different ideas about what constitutes good photography. Strange as it seems to most men, I happen to have my own studio and my own business, Mr. Chapman."

She turned away and Jackson rolled his eyes at Tom. Zelda Ralston had both a temper and an attitude, that was obvious.

"Over there's the tipple and the mine buildings," Virgil indicated. "We live along here, on Alberta Avenue. That's our street next."

Tom had been envisioning the map he'd studied of the path of the Slide, and his heart sank. He was certain that all the houses along Alberta Avenue had been buried.

Today, however, they stood in a neat and tidy row. The Ralstons lived in a white two-story frame house, identical to others set in a line only a short distance from the center of town, near the CPR tracks. In front of the house was a tasteful notice that said, "Ralston's Photography Studio, Portraits a Specialty."

Around the tiny front yard was a green painted picket fence, and in a flowerbed close to the house purple crocuses were already in full bloom. Next door, several ragged children waved and called a greeting, and Virgil and Zelda smiled and waved back at them.

Virgil guided the horse around the back and in through a gate, stopping to let them climb down. Then he steered the animal into a small barn painted the same green as the front fence. An outhouse at the far end of the yard also sported a coat of the same green paint, and a chickenhouse with several white hens and a rooster scratching in the dirt was neatly surrounded by a wire fence. A water pump stood near the house, a bucket under its spout.

"Come on in," Zelda invited Tom and Jackson, opening a door that led into a small, screened porch. A rocking chair with a worn, brown pillow indicated that someone often sat there. A second door led into a warm kitchen, a large, bright room with walls papered in a pattern of cheerful yellow daisies.

"Take off your coats. There's hooks behind the door," Zelda instructed, slipping out of her own coat and reaching up to pull two long, lethal hatpins out of her straw boater. She lifted it off and hung it beside her coat, absently patting at her hair. Curling strands had come loose from the sloppy knot on the top of her head, and she tucked them up, only to have them fall back down, trailing over her ears and down her neck.

She was even thinner than she'd appeared with her coat on, but there was nothing gaunt or shapeless about her. She had delicate but definite curves. She wore a white cotton blouse with puffy sleeves, and a long, plain navy-blue skirt that came well past the tops of her sturdy black boots. Her waist was minuscule; Tom was sure he could span it with his two hands. She had nice ears, too, he noticed, delicate and pinned flat to her skull.

She saw him looking at her and color flooded her face as she spun away across the room. "I'll just get this stove going so Dad can start supper." She fiddled with a damper on the large iron cookstove that dominated the room. She opened the stove lid with an iron lifter and expertly shoved in several lengths of wood.

When the flames burned high, she bent over the coal bucket, shoveling several scoops of coal on top of the wood. Oily smoke billowed out, and she waved it away, muttering under her breath. She replaced the stove lids with a bang, dusting off her hands.

Fascinated, Tom watched her and took in the details of the kitchen. A wooden table and four chairs were in the middle of the room, and a washstand with an enamel basin and a bucket of water was tucked into the corner near the back door. Another water bucket stood on the narrow counter, with a long-handled dipper hooked to its side. Above the counter, open-fronted cupboards held neatly stacked dishes. The bottom cupboards had no doors; instead, they were skirted in gathered, yellow-checked fabric. A lamp on a shelf attested to the fact that there was no electricity.

"I'll make us some tea. You do drink tea?"

She blew a strand of hair out of her eyes and peered into a large, black iron kettle, adding several dipperfuls of water from the bucket before replacing it on the stove. "I don't think Dad would survive a single day without his tea."

Tom and Jackson assured her they'd love some.

"My brother, Eli, isn't home yet. He delivers groceries after school for Dypolt's Store. He's fifteen." Her freckled face rosy from the stove, she beamed at them like a proud parent. "Eli's very clever. He's going to be a doctor or perhaps a lawyer. He's going East to university in a year or two."

The back door opened and Virgil came in. "Gettin' right nippy out there again. Sun's gone behind the mountain and the temperature's dropping fast. Gonna be a cold night."

He took off his coat and hung it up, unfastened

the sleeves of his worn, white shirt and rolled them past his elbows, revealing gray-flecked underwear. He poured water into the chipped enamel basin and scoured his hands with the bar of yellow soap, then dried them.

"Now, Zelda, I'll make a stab at the supper, seein' as how it's my turn. You take Tom and Jackson in the front room and show them some of your photographs, why don't you? She takes good pictures, does our Zel."

"Holler if you need help, Da," she instructed, smiling at the older man and giving him a pat on his weather-beaten cheek.

"How about I stick around here and give you a hand, Virgil?" Jackson was already shoving up the sleeves of his sweatshirt and scrubbing his hands in the basin the way Virgil had done. "I like to cook. Worked in lots of greasy spoons in my time doing short order."

"Much obliged, son. You start on these spuds and I'll get the pan heatin' for the sausage," Virgil agreed with enthusiasm.

"The water's on for tea, Dad. Give us a call when it's ready."

Zelda obviously had no qualms at leaving Jackson to help in the kitchen. She led Tom way down a narrow hall where a staircase rose steeply to the second floor. She opened the door to a small room which held an assortment of framed photographs, an immense camera on a tripod, and another, smaller box camera on a cluttered table. Several screens rested against the wall, with scenes painted on them, one of a sunny garden, the other a bubbling stream under oak trees. There was an ornate sofa, an overstuffed armchair, and an outer door with a bell to warn of customers.

"This is my photographic studio, Mr. Chapman," she said, sounding both shy and proud. "I have a developing room in the cellar."

"Why not call me Tom?" He smiled down at her. She came just past his shoulder.

She gave him a long, level look and then nodded. "If you like. I'm Zelda, as you know."

"Zelda's a beautiful name. Same as F. Scott Fitzgerald's wife, right?"

She gave him a puzzled look. "I've never heard of her. Who is she?"

Like a thunderbolt, the realization again came to Tom that it was only 1902. Fitzgerald hadn't even begun to write his fictional masterpieces yet. The world wars hadn't been fought; there were no computers; and the clumsy cameras in this room were vivid proof that even photography was in its infancy.

There'd been so many urgent and immediate concerns during the past hours that the full import of this time period and place hadn't fully dawned on him until this moment. His stomach lurched. It was almost impossible to believe what had happened.

"Tom? This other Zelda?" She was looking at him with a puzzled expression on her face.

"Oh, she was—just a sad woman I read about once," he managed.

"My name is actually Griselda," she confessed, blushing again and wrinkling her freckled nose. "Awful, isn't it? It was my mother's grandmother's name. Thank goodness Dad didn't care for it, either. He shortened it to Zelda." She reached for a silver-framed photo on a small desk and handed it to him. "This was Mother, holding me. She died when I was thirteen, when Eli was a baby."

Tom recognized the picture as a daguerreotype. It depicted a lovely young woman cradling a fat, smiling baby.

"I see where you got your beautiful eyes." Tom was far too aware of her nearness and uncomfortable with all this talk about families and mothers. He set the photo back on the desk quickly and moved away to study the framed photos that covered the walls.

Almost without exception, they were scenery and wildlife studies of mountains and woods, deer, a raccoon holding a piece of bread, even one dramatic enlargement of a black bear, standing on his hind paws and looking into the camera as if posing.

"You're very good at what you do." Tom was both surprised and impressed by the clarity of detail and the content of the photos. They were black and white, of course, but except for the lack of color, they could have been done by a photographer from his own time. "You must have a good business going here."

"Thank you," she said. "I do believe I'm a good photographer," she added without a trace of vanity. She paused, then remarked, "As for my business, it's unfortunate, but the majority of the town's residents patronize Beaseley, I'm afraid."

Tom frowned. "I don't see how they could fail to recognize how talented you are, Zelda."

She waved her hand disparagingly at her photographs. "Pure frivolity. No one in Frank is interested in purchasing scenery and wildlife photographs. I do them to please only myself. The way a photographer in a mining town like this makes a living is by doing portraits, pictures of weddings, funerals, christenings."

Tom recalled the sign outside the house and the conspicuous absence of any portraits in this room. "You're saying your business isn't doing too hot?"

"Too hot? That's an unusual way of phrasing it, but I think it's very descriptive all the same." She smiled, a mischievous smile but rueful as well. "Mr. Beaseley is the photographer of choice in Frank. Even the North West Mounted hires him to take pictures of their criminals. Why, if Dad hadn't rescued us today, all three of us might have had to pose for him." She shuddered.

"Couldn't you advertise?" Business problems intrigued Tom. God knows, he and Jackson had gone through enough of them.

She shook her head. "I tried running an advertisement in *The Sentinel,* but it was throwing good money after bad. Business here relies on word of mouth, and being arrested isn't the best thing for a spinster's reputation, even when she's known to be a hopeless eccentric."

"You're not a spinster, Zelda. You're not exactly over the hill. How old did you say you were? Twenty-eight? Hell, in my time, most women are just getting established in their careers at that age."

She frowned at him, looking as though she suspected he was making fun of her. "What do you mean, in your time?"

There it was again, the whole unbelievable time-travel thing. He kept coming up against it, like a wall he'd have to scale sooner or later.

"Zelda, you in the studio?" a young male voice bellowed from the hallway. Then a half-grown boy appeared in the doorway, precariously balancing a tray with a teapot, two sturdy mugs, a jar of cream, and a pot of sugar.

He had Zelda's fiery hair, but his was straight, not riotously curly. Instead of just a sprinkling of freckles like she had, his face was matted with them. His eyes were the same blue as Virgil's, and his clothing didn't quite seem to fit. His wrists hung out of his shirt cuffs, and his pants were a little too short, as if he'd grown while wearing them.

He shot a curious look at Tom and grinned. Even his teeth had grown too quickly for the rest of him. "Dad said to bring in this tea."

"Thanks, Eli. Set it down there on the table before you spill it. Eli, this is Mr. Chapman. Tom, my little brother, Eli."

"I wish you'd stop calling me little, Zel." Eli's voice was exasperated, and it was in the process of changing. It squeaked into the upper registers and fell again to a deep bass. "I'm nearly as tall as you are."

"Hi, Eli." Tom smiled at the boy and held out his hand.

After a moment's hesitation, Eli shook it, and Tom was touched at the boy's effort to produce a strong, manly handshake.

"How'd'ya do, Mr. Chapman?" His wide-eyed gaze took in Tom's roomy green sweatshirt and close-fitting jeans, and then lingered wide-eyed on his watch.

"I'd rather you just called me Tom."

Eli shot a questioning glance at Zelda, and after

a second she nodded. "If Mr. Chapman finds it acceptable for you to call him by his first name, then you may," she agreed. "Now go and wash up and then set the table."

"There's a ball game after supper. Can I go play, Zel? Please?"

Tom watched as Zelda fell naturally into a motherly role with her brother.

"Don't you have lessons to study?"

He shook his head, making his red hair fly. "No, ma'am. I finished everything in school today."

"Even your grammar?"

"All of it. Every paragraph. You can check if you want."

"Very well then. But not later than nine–thirty, remember."

With a last look at Tom and a shy nod in his direction, Eli was gone in an awkward flurry of elbows and knees, bumping against the doorframe and sliding on a small scatter rug in the hall.

"He's so clumsy since he's begun growing taller," she said fondly. "And he's far too apt to skimp on his lessons in order to play ball." It was obvious that Zelda adored her brother.

"Let's take this into the sitting room," she suggested.

Tom brought the tray, and they crossed the hall into a cramped, homey little room with a potbellied heater giving off welcome warmth, a horsehair sofa, and two comfortably worn chairs, as well as several small tables and wooden stands holding numerous plants. There was also a small bookcase with an assortment of well-worn volumes. Tom knelt to inspect these before he took a seat in one of the armchairs.

There were several volumes of poetry, a collection of Shakespeare, a dictionary, *Jane Eyre, Twenty Thousand Leagues Under the Sea,* several books by Robert Louis Stevenson, and a stack of magazines.

Zelda moved to the stove and, as she'd done in the kitchen, automatically shoveled in a scoop of coal from a bucket before she, too, sat. Then she poured them each a cup of tea, adding cream and sugar. For a time, they sipped the strong brew in silence as a peculiar and uncomfortable awareness grew and intensified between them.

Chapter Six

Zelda felt the silence stretch like good pastry dough—the kind she could never quite manage to achieve. She struggled and failed to find something to say that would dissipate the tension that had suddenly crept into the cozy room.

Zelda, you surely aren't fool enough to begin entertaining notions of any sort of flirtation with this man, she cautioned herself sternly. Don't allow yourself to become one of those silly, vapid spinsters who embarrass themselves and everyone else with their giddy fluttering whenever they find themselves alone with an attractive member of the opposite sex.

Acknowledge the fact, if you must, that Mr. Tom Chapman is most engaging with his thick, black curls, and midnight-blue eyes, and that lean, raw-boned face. Admit, if you have to, that you find his lopsided grin endearing, that in spite of his occasional strange usage of the language, he appeals to you because he is intelligent and educated, very obviously not a miner, and a good bit taller than you are. And face up to the fact, she reminded herself, that under normal circumstances a man like him would never look twice at a skinny, freckled redhead fast approaching thirty years of age.

"Do you—" he began.

"What do you—" she said.

They each stopped speaking, met each other's eyes, and laughed.

"Ma'am?" He made a courtly gesture with his hand.

"I was just going to ask what you like to read. I noticed you looking at our books."

As she'd hoped it might, the tension dissipated and he relaxed. "Oh, almost anything," he replied. "Everything," he amended. His eyes sparkled and his face became animated. "I read a lot of history, because of my job, and I enjoy historical fiction, too, James Clavell, Larry McMurtry."

How could she have been so self-centered? She'd talked about her photography and hadn't even asked him what he did for a living.

"And I love to read action-adventure tales, like James Bond—" He stopped abruptly and the confused look she'd seen before came over his rugged features. "But then, I guess you've never heard of James Bond."

"Actually, I'm not acquainted with any of the writers you've mentioned, but they sound fascinating," she said in a polite tone. "Personally, I enjoy a writer called Jules Verne. He wrote a wonderful tale called *Journey to the Center of the Earth.* I liked it so much I read it aloud to Dad and Eli last winter. Are you familiar with it, Tom?"

He shook his head. "I know of Jules Verne, but I've never read his books. It's sort of science-fiction stuff, isn't it?"

"Science fiction?" There it was again, his peculiar use of the language. "What is science fiction?"

"Damn." He tipped his head back on the sofa, closed his eyes, and grimaced. "This is tough. There's so much that hasn't happened yet."

The feeling came over her that she'd experienced earlier, when she first saw him at the barracks today. It was as if she were encountering a foreigner, someone from a very strange land she'd never heard of, much less visited.

It was disquieting. He'd admitted he wasn't Canadian, but neither were most of the people in Frank. This was a very new community, barely two years old. Zelda and her father and Eli had only moved there themselves the year before. But Zelda had met a number of American settlers and found their ways comfortably similar to those of Canadians.

Tom was different in some way she couldn't define. His clothing was strange, and his haircut. His jacket was peculiar, and he wore that strange timepiece on his arm.

Of course she remembered his outrageous tale about being from some unimaginable time in the distant future, and she wondered again why he'd related it to Corporal Allan.

At first, she'd been amused; she thought Tom was poking subtle fun at the corporal, which was no more than the stiff-necked lawman deserved. But then she'd become uncertain when the business of the five-dollar bill began. Where had the strange money come from? It had been obvious that neither Tom nor Jackson had currency that was usable, and yet she'd seen that Tom's billfold contained what looked like a large amount of money.

And what he'd said about Turtle Mountain had sent icy shivers down her spine. Of course there were tales about the mountain. Everyone knew that the local Indians refused to camp near it. They called it The Mountain That Moves. But, of course, Tom's far-fetched tale about the whole top of the mountain falling down on the town was nothing short of absurd.

And what about Jackson's subsequent claim that Tom wasn't right in the head? It explained his delusions, but it didn't seem to her that Tom was mentally unstable.

Mind you, Zelda mused, she'd never encountered any true lunatics, so how would she know? And Dad certainly didn't seem to think anything was amiss with Tom. But then, Dad hadn't heard the conversation about the money and the mountain.

Tom just had a good imagination, and he was mischievously duping the corporal, she concluded.

Still, there were other puzzling things about the two men. What, for instance, was the peculiar device that held both Tom and Jackson's coats together in the front without the aid of buttons? She'd watched them fasten their coats in the wink of an eye. The edges seemed to knit together and stay that way.

And what vocabulary were they using that included so many terms she'd never heard before, like "science fiction" and "too hot"?

"Dad says come eat. Supper's on the table." Eli stuck his head around the corner of the door and was gone again.

Tom got to his feet quickly, as if he were relieved at the interruption, and Zelda smiled a bright smile and scolded herself for feeling intense disappointment at his eagerness to join the others.

She still hadn't asked him what job he worked at, either.

Dinner was surprisingly tasty, Zelda concluded. For once, Dad hadn't burned the sausages, and instead of being lumpy, the potatoes were mashed creamy smooth with milk and butter. The beans she'd cooked the day before were heated exactly right, and both Virgil and Jackson were inordinately proud of themselves as the others complimented them on the simple meal.

"Jackson's a right dab hand with the gravy," Virgil announced, and Zelda had to agree that it was better than either she or Virgil could produce.

"But you make great biscuits, Virgil. I couldn't turn out biscuits like these to save my soul," Jackson objected, buttering one and popping half of it in his mouth.

"That's Zelda's doin'," Virgil claimed, giving her a snappy salute with his hand. "She's the one taught me to make biscuits." His blue eyes twinkled with mischief. "Guess she kinda figgered seein' as how she'd be in jail off and on, 'twas best I learned how to cook lest Eli and I starve."

"Hush, Dad." Zelda frowned at him, indicating

that Eli was present, but it was plain her brother already knew about her day's experience.

"Dad says you got put behind bars today, Zel. What was it like in there? What did you do this time, anyhow? Was it over Mr. Vandusen getting drunk last night?"

"We'll discuss it later, Eli. Eat your supper or you'll be late for the game," she admonished, frowning again.

They ate, and Zelda was relieved that the talk after that was of everyday matters, the coal mine, the softball game Eli was eager to join after supper. While Zelda served bottled wild strawberries for dessert, Virgil launched into a short history of the town of Frank.

"This is a reg'lar boom town," Virgil explained, spooning up a mouthful of the tart red berries Zelda had gathered and preserved the previous spring. "Barely two years old, already six hundred people hereabouts. Named after a countryman of yours, Tom, a gent called Henry Frank, from Butte, Montana. Him and this Sam Gebo feller formed the Canadian American Coal and Coke Company, opened the mine, built this town from scratch in a matter of months. Attracted miners the likes of me from all over the place. Fair wages, and this is said to be the world's richest coal mine," he boasted.

Tom asked, "Where did you come here from, Virgil?"

"Carbonear, Newfoundland, was where I was born. My da, he was a fisherman, but I left home early, went to work in the mines in Springhill, Nova Scotia. Met my Hilda there, and after Zelda came along, we moved back to Newfoundland fer a while, wanted to be with family." Virgil shook his head. "Times was bad and fishin' just wasn't up my alley. Moved around a fair bit, tried my hand at farming, but always went back to the mines. Like I always say, it's in my blood. It's what I know best, mining. Dirty work, clean money." He chortled at his joke, then started to cough, a deep, racking sound that shook his thin frame and brought tears to his eyes. He got up from the table and staggered into the hall, unable to get his breath.

Zelda shook her head with chagrin. She'd hoped Dad might make it through the meal without having an attack, but he seldom did these days. A deep and unnamed fear twisted her insides, and she got up quickly and took the brown medicine bottle from the kitchen shelf, found a spoon, and followed Virgil. When he was able to swallow, she spooned in the cough medicine. After a few moments, his coughing subsided and they both returned to the table.

Tom and Jackson stopped eating. They watched, alarmed at the ferocity of the attack.

"Sorry, gents," Virgil wheezed when he sat down again. "Damned coal dust gets in a man's lungs and sticks there." He took a long, deep swallow from his teacup. "Now, enough of me and mine. What's this yarn of yours that got under the corporal's skin today, anyways? What made him think you two were counterfeiters?"

"Counterfeiters?" Eli's eyes widened and he stared, awe-struck, at first Jackson and then Tom. "Are you really counterfeiters?" His voice was reverent.

"Don't be ridiculous, Eli. Of course they're not."

Zelda felt herself tense. For some reason, she didn't want to hear what Tom and Jackson had to say.

She looked at Tom. His dark blue gaze met hers for a long, intense moment.

"Corporal Allan got the wrong impression of us, Virgil," he said finally, carefully evasive as if he had read her mind. "We happened to have some"—again Tom's eyes locked with Zelda's, and she was aware of a message sent and received, a silent reassurance—"some foreign money that he'd never seen before, and he jumped to the wrong conclusions. Jackson and I aren't criminals of any sort. I guess you could best say we're—vagabonds. We travel around looking for work, and we follow up on whatever honest opportunity presents itself."

"Well now, I did that myself as a young man." Virgil nodded.

The excitement faded from Eli's eyes. "Can I be excused now, Dad? I'm gonna be late, and we're up to bat first."

"Go ahead, son."

Eli jumped up and knocked over his chair, set it back on its feet, and left in a hurry, slipping on a scatter rug before he made it out the door.

Zelda shook her head and clucked her tongue.

"I take it this foreign money you two got ain't much good hereabouts?" Virgil waited to ask the question until after the back door slammed and Eli was gone.

Zelda saw Tom and Jackson exchange a look.

"No good at all." Tom sighed. "We're going to have to find work fast and earn some money. But I'm afraid until we do, we'll have to owe you the money you paid to the Corporal on our behalf."

"Oh, say now, that ain't why I was askin'." Virgil shook his head. "No, sirree, a measly dollar ain't gonna break us Ralstons."

It was a chivalrous thing to say, but not entirely true, Zelda reflected. She mentally tallied up how much money was left from Dad's last mine check. Minus the six dollars he'd handed to the police today—how could that beastly corporal fine her the unheard of sum of five dollars?—there was probably not more than two dollars left. Payday wasn't for another week, and Dad had missed three shifts from illness, so his check wouldn't be much. And she'd made only two dollars in the last month with her photography.

She owed the milkman, and she already had a bill at the grocery. Rent on the house was due the first of May, and Eli needed new trousers in the worst way. And always, there was the savings account at the bank for Eli's education. Regardless of how short of money they were, Zelda religiously put a dollar from each check into the account.

Worrying about money was familiar to Zelda. She tried to be philosophical about it, but it nagged at her all the same, waking her even at night and making it difficult to sleep again.

Virgil said, "What came to me was, you two got nowheres to stay and no money to eat with. I've been in that spot myself, now and again." He shot a quick, guilty look at Zelda, and her heart sank.

She knew what was coming. Dad was softhearted, he couldn't bear to think of these two without a place to sleep or a hot meal to eat, and it wouldn't matter one whit to him if she had to spend his last dime buying food to feed them. If they stayed long, that's what it would come down to, too.

She glanced at Tom, and realized she didn't want to think of him cold and hungry, either. But even apart from the strain on the budget, how would she fare with him living right there?

Jackson Zalco didn't bother her in the slightest, in spite of the fact that he, too, was an extraordinarily handsome man, as blond as Tom was dark, and just as muscular and tall.

There was something about Tom Chapman that affected her in a fashion she didn't need or want, one she couldn't explain. She didn't have the slightest idea how to deal with it, because she'd never felt exactly this way before.

"I thought mebbe you'd stop here with us, till you get on yer feet, so to speak," Virgil said. "No room in the house, but there's a big, dry loft out in the barn filled with hay, and we got plenty extra quilts you can borrow. Ain't fancy, but it's a roof over yer heads, and I make a good pot of mush in the mornin'."

The two men looked first at Virgil and then at one another.

"As you know, we haven't a usable cent to our names, and nothing but the clothes on our backs," Tom confessed. "I realize this is an imposition, but we'd be very grateful for your hospitality, even just for tonight."

Zelda could tell how difficult it was for him to accept Virgil's offer, and it touched her. Tom was a proud man; it obviously galled him to be in the position he was in.

He went on in a firm voice, "With the understanding, however, that the moment we get a job, we'll pay you back. And you can rest assured we'll be out looking for work bright and early tomorrow morning."

Virgil nodded. Zelda knew her father would make the two men welcome for as long as necessary. Apart from the mines, jobs weren't all that plentiful in Frank, due to the vast number of immigrants arriving daily, all of them eager to settle and make a living. The men could be in the hayloft for quite some time.

Part of Zelda insisted it would be better if Tom walked out their door tonight and disappeared. But another traitorous part of her was glad he'd be around for at least a little longer.

"That's all right with you, is it, Zel?" Virgil's question came a bit late, she reflected wryly, now that the arrangement between the men had already been reached.

"Yes, it's quite all right, Dad," she agreed, giving him a reassuring smile and noting the high color in his cheeks. It wasn't natural, that color. She'd have to somehow convince him he had to see Doc Malcolmson again.

She rose and began to collect the dishes, and in an instant, Jackson and Tom were on their feet, helping her.

"I'll do these," she insisted. "Dad, you three go on into the other room and relax now. You've earned it. Sit and have your pipe." Zelda knew her father lived for the pipe he smoked each night after supper, and she made certain, no matter how short they were, that there was always tobacco for him. He never spent a cent on himself, otherwise. "You cooked, I'll do the dishes. We'll catch up with our

Eli tomorrow night. It's actually his turn."

"I'll be happy to help," Tom insisted, but Zelda refused.

"Go on in and talk with Dad. He enjoys company."

The truth was, she wanted to be alone for a while. She needed to be alone, to think through the day's happenings, to examine the emotional reaction this Tom Chapman roused in her. She had to try and put a stop to it before it became even more intense.

She couldn't do that with him right beside her. She wasn't sure she could do it at all, and that troubled her deeply.

There'd never been a man to whom she'd felt this attracted, and that was absurd, because she'd known him for only a few hours. But for some reason, time didn't seem relevant. She felt as if she'd known him forever.

She waited until the soft rumble of male voices and the smell of pipe tobacco issued from the sitting room down the hall. Then she tied an apron around herself, filled the dishbasin with hot water from the reservoir on the side of the stove, sprinkled in soap flakes, and attacked the dishes.

Was this—this peculiar sensation she felt around him just some traitorous physical need, come on her because she was nearing her thirtieth birthday and still a virgin?

But she had chosen to remain a virgin, she reminded herself, scrubbing a pot with excess zeal. In spite of the fact that she wasn't pretty, she was still a spinster by choice. She wasn't one of those sad women who'd never even been asked for their hand in marriage or never felt desire burning in their loins. A flush rose when she thought of those bodily needs, and the vivid dreams that eased them, however temporarily.

She doused plates and cutlery and scrubbed them with unnecessary vigor.

Before moving West, she'd had two serious suitors in her life, and she'd sent both of them packing without a qualm. She wasn't attracted to either, and her uncompromising honesty forced her to acknowledge that behind their attempts at wooing her lay not love, but the stark, desperate need for a woman—any woman.

Edgar had been a widower with a two-month-old baby and three other small children. Zelda had loved the little ones and pitied their father, but never enough to accept his hasty proposal of marriage.

Bert, too, had needed her. He'd been a kind, honest man, already middle-aged and settled into a routine. His mother was bedridden, requiring a woman's care. Zelda had visited the pitiful old woman regularly, but she'd gently refused Bert's offer of marriage when it came, although she'd thought that Bert might represent her last opportunity for a home of her own and a family.

But really, she thought in disgust, how could she think of marrying either man when neither one had even attempted to make any sort of love to her? She'd done enough reading—she had those certain feelings—that told her that there was a physical side to marriage that was equally as important as the business part, and the thought of engaging in intimacy with either man had set her teeth on edge.

Here in the West, of course, there were untold

numbers of single men hungry for a woman. Zelda was well aware of the fallen women who lived in the houses on the outskirts of town, the area men called the Tenderloin, and of how popular their establishments were.

She was also aware that if a husband was what she wanted, she could probably find one in Frank without too much trouble. The men outnumbered the women to an astonishing degree, and great numbers of them were single and young.

And, she reminded herself, snatching up a clean dishtowel and beginning to dry the stack of clean dishes, she didn't have to look far to see what her life might be like, married to a miner in the town of Frank.

There was Isabella Vandusen next door, several years younger than Zelda, the mother of two babies, with a life that was nothing short of dreadful. Isabella was in danger of a beating each time Nestor drank too much, but she was also totally dependent on him for every morsel of food and scrap of clothing.

There was Lydia Kovich, worn out from being pregnant for the third time in four years. She'd been Zelda's friend until Zelda gave her some information on birth control from the Women's Temperance Union. Lydia's husband, Guido, had found the pamphlets and told Lydia that he'd throw her out into the street if she dared use any of the devices, and that Zelda was no longer welcome in their house. He'd torn up the pamphlets and scattered them all over the Ralstons' front yard, and to the day the Koviches moved to Calgary, Lydia had never spoken to Zelda again. She hadn't even said good-bye.

There were plenty of other examples of married life. Zelda knew numerous women whose husbands drank away badly needed cash in the pubs and frequented the house of ill repute, and the wives were helpless to do anything about it.

It was perfectly obvious that a man had altogether too much power over a woman once he married her. Zelda had long ago decided she would rather go to her grave a frustrated virgin than relinquish her freedom of thought and action just for the pleasure of having babies and her own home.

She dried the last pot and hung the towel neatly on the rack. The image of Tom Chapman's midnight-blue eyes and lazy grin imposed themselves on her mind and sent an involuntary shiver down her backbone.

Going to her grave a virgin hadn't seemed such a great sacrifice when she'd never actually met a man who tempted her to do otherwise.

Unfortunately, Tom Chapman did.

Tom finished arranging his blankets on the stack of sweet-smelling hay. It was cold in the loft, but Zelda had given him and Jackson each a thick, goose feather-stuffed quilt as well as sheets and pillows, so he had no doubt they'd sleep warm and comfortable.

Jackson's head and then his shoulders appeared in the square opening where a wooden ladder nailed to the wall led down to the barn proper. He hoisted himself up into the loft.

"That outhouse sure isn't the place to linger on a

cold night." He shivered. "Those contraptions are enough to make a guy anal retentive forever." He looked around, squinting in the pale light of the lantern Virgil had given them. "Hey, Tom, this reminds me of that job we had for that Texas millionaire who was certain there was Mexican gold buried in the desert. Remember how we ended up bunking in the hayloft of that barn?"

"Yeah. Except for thermal sleeping bags, flashlights, freeze dried food, and our Jeep parked outside, it's nearly the same. Get your bed made up. I'm gonna blow out this lantern. I think Virgil was a little afraid we'd burn the barn down with the damned thing. He told me three or four times to be careful."

Jackson hastily chose a spot several yards away from Tom and made his bed, then sat down on the blankets to tug off his boots and his jeans. He left his underwear and his sweatshirt on and crawled into the nest of blankets, wrestling the quilt into a cocoon around himself as Tom undressed, climbed into his bedroll, and carefully blew out the light.

"It's freezing in these damned mountains," Jackson complained. "I've forgotten what that sign said the elevation was when we drove through the Crowsnest the other day, but I do remember it was high. No wonder it's so damn cold here. We're way to hell and gone up in the Rockies." He paused and then added, "Was that just the other day?" His tone of voice changed. "It feels like a year ago, and God knows when it really was, considering what's happened to us since." He was silent a long moment. "You figger we got a hope in hell of getting back where we belong, Tom?" he then asked quietly.

"I don't know. What with one thing happening right after another, I haven't had time to give it much thought today."

"Well, we're gonna have to try," Jackson declared. "I don't know about you, but I surely don't relish freezin' my ass off sittin' in an outhouse for the rest of my life. I like central heating and electric razors and showers with lots of hot water."

Tom did, too, particularly now that they weren't available. "How do you figure we oughta go about it?"

Tom could almost hear Jackson shrug. "Got me," he said, and Tom did hear the frustration in his partner's voice. "There wasn't a thing up on that hillside to indicate how we got here in the first place. It must have had something to do with that movie we watched."

"Yeah. *In the Shadow of the Mountain,* wasn't that what it was called?" Tom gave a humorless chuckle. "Damned if we didn't end up right here in its shadow all right. Doesn't make me too comfortable, looking at that sucker in the moonlight, knowing it's planning to blow its top right off."

"But not for another year, right? This is April of 1902, the Slide was April of 1903. So we got time to maneuver, even if we're stuck here awhile, God forbid. And there's not a thing we can accomplish tonight, anyhow. Ask me, we're damned lucky to meet people as nice as these Ralstons. They sure saved our sorry asses in that lockup today."

Silence fell. Tom thought Jackson was already asleep, but after a time his voice sounded again in the darkness. "Tom, they're poor, these Ralstons. You can tell by their clothes, and there wasn't a whole hell of a lot in the cupboards to eat, either. And that cough of Virgil's sounds serious to me. He had an attack when we were cookin', and the kid, Eli, let it slip that Virgil's missed work because of it.

"He indicated Zelda's been on her father's case to go to the sawbones, but I'd lay you odds Virgil figures they can't afford a doctor's bill. Way I see it, we owe these people big-time, Tom." He gave a frustrated snort. "Can you believe we've got probably four hundred bucks cash between us and every gold card known to man, and not one bit of it any good?"

The irony of it hadn't escaped Tom. "First thing in the morning, we'll find work, anything that'll let us reimburse the Ralstons right away." Zelda's face was clear in his mind, and it disconcerted him to realize it wasn't only compassion he felt for her. "There's always the possibility we'll get slam-dunked back into the nineties with as little warning as we arrived, so we'll make paying them back our first priority."

"Right on. All I can say is, slam dunk can't come too soon for this cowboy." Jackson yawned aloud. "Well, tomorrow's gonna be busy, so guess I'll get some shut-eye." In another moment, he began to snore, and soon Tom, too, fell into a restless sleep.

The long-forgotten sound of a steam train whistle penetrated Tom's dreams, the sound of an engine straining, grinding slowly up a steep grade with its load of overflowing coal cars strung along behind.

In his dream Tom was a child again, crammed three in a bed with his little brothers in a dingy row shack in a coal mining town.

Was his stepfather home? Was he drunk? Was he

fighting with his mother again?

With a smothered cry, he bolted upright and dragged himself fully awake, unable to figure out at first where he was, not even caring. Instead, he was grateful beyond all imagining that he was a grown man, far away from that coal town of his birth.

Jackson's soft snores punctuated the darkness.

The loft was in almost total blackness, but through a small, high window cut into the wall up near the rafters, Tom could see a lighter patch, a smidgen of night sky.

Through the frosty air came the sound of the train, at the top of the grade now and gaining speed. Its distinctive, throbbing rhythm faded gradually into the far distance.

Muted then, was a sound Tom recognized from his childhood, the sharp, piercing summons of the mine whistle, calling the night-shift crew into the bowels of the mountain.

Despite the frost-laden air, sweat broke out on his forehead.

He seldom loosened the tight knot he kept on the sack of his memories, but now it came undone in spite of him. He was with those miners again, a gangly, frightened teenager, walking with the others on his first shift, up the spur line to the mine entrance with his heart hammering so hard he thought it might leap out of his chest.

He felt again the sickening terror that had gripped him all those years before when he stepped into the cage and, along with the other miners, plummeted six hundred feet straight down to the coal face.

He felt again that choking, trapped sensation when he realized he was deep underground with only a feeble lamp to pierce the darkness. Again he was seized with the terrible despair that had filled him, and the knowledge that his stepfather had thought that this was where Tom would spend all the long hours of his working life.

He'd been fifteen years old.

Chapter Seven

For two months, Tom had kept at it, his days filled with drudgery, work, sleep, and hunger.

Because of his stepfather's drinking and his mother's as well, there had never been quite enough food to satisfy the raging hunger of a growing boy forced to do a man's work. Despair had grown in him.

Then one Friday morning, he'd picked up his pay packet, walked to the highway, and stuck out his thumb. A truck had come along and given him a ride, the first of many such rides. He'd been cold and frightened, penniless and alone more often than not in the months and years that followed, but he'd never gone back. After a time, he'd even stopped hearing the mine whistles and the freight trains in his dreams. Over the years, he'd trained himself not to remember.

Ironic, that now he should be trapped in a place and time where those trains, those whistles, were part of the very fabric of everyday life—sounds that he'd hear over and over again, as long as he stayed in Frank.

He convinced himself that wouldn't be for long, and after a time he slept again. When he awakened, it was to Virgil's cheerful whistling as he made his way out to the privy in the gray light of dawn. Tom threw the quilt aside and gasped at the icy coldness of the morning air.

"Rise and shine, partner." He shook Jackson's shoulder. "Let's go find ourselves a job."

By that afternoon, it was obvious jobs were neither plentiful nor easy to find in Frank.

Tom and Jackson had eaten bowls of Virgil's porridge and set out, confident that two strong men would have no problem finding work. At noon, with no success at all, they had decided to split up the town and each canvass half, taking whatever menial work they could find, agreeing to meet late in the day at the foot of Dominion Avenue.

"Any luck?" Tom leaned back against an empty hitching post, tired and discouraged.

Jackson shook his head. "Nothing steady, that's for damned sure. The grocer paid me fifty cents to move about seventy boxes of canned goods into the storage room." Jackson groaned. "He didn't let on that the storage room was down in the cellar, fourteen twisting, narrow steep steps down. Didn't do my bum leg any good, I can tell you. Then I made another dollar serving beer at the Imperial Hotel while the regular barman had his lunch. Never thought I'd have to sling beer again," he said with a shake of his head and a rueful grin. "I can't believe how hard a man has to work these days to earn a dollar."

"I know what you're saying," Tom agreed. "Makes you realize how generous it was of Virgil to fork out a buck on our behalf."

"They're paying the royal sum of $2.75 a day to laborers at the construction camp on the edge of town," Jackson reported. "It's backbreaking work. I put our names in, and the foreman said if we get there at daybreak tomorrow he might hire us on, one day at a time. He isn't hiring steady just now."

"Neither is the mine. I put our names on a waiting list, but there's a dozen men ahead of us."

Jackson gave Tom a curious look. "Thought you told me once you'd never set foot in a mine again, as long as you lived, no matter what."

"Yeah, well, beggars can't be choosers, and maybe something else will turn up before we're forced into going underground." Tom tried to keep the despondency he felt out of his voice. "The mine's about the only place there is to get a steady job around here. Miners are making $3.50 a day, which I now figure is a pretty good wage." He gave a rueful grin. "Shows you how fast a person adapts. A month ago, I turned down that contract in South America. Would have netted us a cool ten grand for three weeks' work."

"The wages here make sense when you check the prices being charged for things, though," Jackson replied. "Fancy hotel rooms are two bucks a day, you can get a fair meal for twenty-five cents. That breakfast we had was overpriced, I figure now. Gertie saw a chance to make a profit on two dumb strangers."

"You're right," Tom agreed. "I checked the menu at the Frank Cafe. Most breakfasts are around a quarter." He held up his hands, bleached from strong soap and dishwater. "In fact, I washed dishes there most of the afternoon, and they paid me a buck fifty. Haven't washed dishes at a cafe since I was a kid on the run. Well, at least we've got enough between us to pay Virgil back the dollar we owe him and maybe buy some groceries to help out with supper."

Virgil, and Zelda, too, had insisted they come back if they hadn't managed to find work that included room and board.

"C'mon, Tom. Let's head on over to Dypolt's Store and see what we can get for a measly two dollars. Sounds insane, if you figure what things cost where we come from, huh? But I checked out prices when I was carrying boxes, and I figure we might just do okay."

Half an hour later, with an overflowing bag of groceries, they made their way back to the Ralstons, feeling better about their efforts.

"Didn't realize at first that mincemeat meant hamburger," Jackson said gleefully. "At fifteen cents a pound, it's a bargain. And how about cabbage at three cents a head? And milk, a dime a quart? With those onions and carrots, I'm gonna make up a big pot of hamburger hash. Old man Dypolt was generous, too. Threw in that soup bone and only charged us ten cents for the spuds, and we each have a razor of our own now, so we don't have to borrow that lethal weapon of Virgil's like we did this morning. Damn, these straight razors are somethin' else. Thought I'd cut my throat with his for sure. Now I get to practice with my own. Y'know, I'm glad now I didn't say a word to Dypolt about those damned cellar stairs. The old goat was more than generous."

"He probably took pity on us because we look scruffy and half-starved. God knows, I feel it. They gave me a bowl of soup and a hunk of bread at the cafe, but that was hours ago. I'd give a lot right now for a cheeseburger and fries, with a double malt and an apple turnover." Tom's mouth watered just thinking of it, and Jackson groaned in sympathy.

They turned into Virgil's yard, waving and calling a friendly "hi" to the kids next door. They made their way around the back of the house, where Eli was bouncing a softball against the barn and catching it on the rebound. His face lit up when he saw them.

"Hey, you came back. Zel said you might. She's in the house. You want to toss a ball with me?"

It suddenly dawned on Tom that every step of the way home, he'd been looking forward to seeing Zelda again. She hadn't been up yet when they left the house that morning.

What was going on here? He'd never let a woman get under his skin this way. The last thing he needed right now was even more complications.

"You go ahead in, Jackson. I'll test this fellow's throwing arm awhile." He caught the ball Eli slung at him and sent it back hard, putting a curve on it that forced the boy to run, then leap high in order to catch it.

Tom backpedaled so there was the entire width

of the yard between them, stretching high to catch the throw Eli sent his way. He was close to the fence that divided the Ralstons' yard from the one next to it, and the small boy and girl came running to watch the ball game, peering through the wire.

Tom and Eli had been throwing the ball back and forth about fifteen minutes when the hollering began in the house next door, a man's deep voice raised in anger, a woman answering in a softer, pleading tone. The words weren't in English, but it was obvious from their volume that the Ralstons' neighbors were having a brawl.

Tom's stomach tensed. He hated domestic quarrels. He tried to tune out the angry voices, keeping up a steady banter with Eli.

"Look out, look out. Here it comes. Stretch . . . Aaaahhhhaaaa, missed it. So that's your weak spot. . . ."

There was a frenzied exchange of words from the other house, and then a male voice cursing in a steady stream. The outside door slammed.

Tom turned to glance over his shoulder. A stocky, muscular man in workman's clothes was coming down the steps, pulling on a brown coat. The little girl and the boy, who'd been watching the ball game, cowered against the fence, their faces anxious.

The door burst open again and a plump, little fair-haired woman came running out after the man, sobbing something in a language Tom didn't understand. But the appeal in her voice was plain.

She was obviously begging him not to leave. She lifted up her long skirts and rushed toward him, catching him by the arm halfway across the yard.

Tom, embarrassed at being a witness to such an intimate scene, turned back to the ball game, but the woman's voice brought him whipping around.

The crud had hit her. She was sitting on the muddy ground, her long hair loose around her shoulders. One hand nursed her ear, the other held up to ward off what she obviously thought were more blows about to descend on her. The man was standing over her, his fists raised.

Tom didn't remember hopping the fence. The man's back was to him, and he caught him by surprise and whipped him around. Tom had a fistful of coat and one arm drawn back to deck the punk when he remembered the two kids, cowering against the fence, scared out of their minds. And this was their father.

Damn. Tom couldn't bring himself to beat the man to a pulp with his own kids watching. With a muttered curse, Tom unclenched his fist, but he retained his grip on the man's coat.

The coward didn't seem eager to fight with a man, Tom realized with disgust. He was holding his hands up, palms out, abject fear on his face.

Eli, too, had jumped over the fence. He was helping the woman to her feet, his eyes bulging as he watched Tom.

"Take her over to your sister, Eli, and the kids, too," Tom instructed.

As Eli shepherded the weeping woman and the children through the back gate and into the Ralstons' yard, Tom gave the man a vicious shake, still longing to plant a fist in his jaw. He had bloodshot eyes and a red nose, and he reeked of liquor.

"What's your name, you drunken slimeball?"

"Vandusen." The words were accented, but it was plain he understood some English. "Nestor Vandusen. Don't punch me. I am sorry for hit Isabella," he whined.

Tom suddenly remembered the scene at the jail the previous day. Zelda had mentioned Vandusen and the fact that he regularly drank and beat his wife. Tom was sorely tempted to give him a taste of his own medicine, but the man was such a cowering wimp, he couldn't bring himself to do it. Instead, he deliberately tightened his grip on the coat, which he knew was cutting off oxygen.

Nestor began to struggle, and his face turned deep red. When he began making gasping sounds and started to claw at Tom's hand, Tom shook him again, long and hard.

"I'm gonna be right next door from now on, Nestor," he lied, his voice low and lethal. "And I'm going to pay regular visits over here, understand? If I see one single indication that you're drinking and that your wife is having a bad time with you, Mister, or I find out that you *ever* again lay a hand on her or on those kids, you better clear out of town before I catch you, because I'm gonna beat you to a sodden pulp. Got it?"

Nestor's face was turning blue. He nodded vigorously, and after a long moment, Tom dropped him. The man sank to his knees, dragging in deep lungfuls of air, and stayed there, his head down, as Tom turned his back and walked to the fence. He vaulted over and headed for the back door, his muscles quivering in the aftermath of the ugly scene. He turned to look back at the other man, just in time to see him get to his feet and scuttle out the gate, setting off down the street at a determined trot.

Probably going straight to the Mounties to charge me with assault. I'll be back in lockup before nightfall, Tom thought wryly.

Jackson was in the kitchen stirring an iron pot on the stove, his sweatshirt sleeves rolled high and one of Zelda's gingham aprons tied incongruously around his hips. "Eli gave me the headlines on what was going down, so I figgered you could handle it just fine alone," he said laconically. "Everything turn out okay?"

"Fine," Tom said tersely.

At the table, the little boy and girl from next door were eating jam sandwiches and drinking milk. The boy shot a look at Tom, his small face pinched and frightened.

Jackson jutted his chin toward the hallway. "Zelda took their mama in there. I sent a pot a' tea in with Eli. They seem to use the stuff like valium around here. Virgil's at work, afternoon shift, Eli says. I'm addin' some stuff to this hash so there'll be plenty for all of us."

Tom hadn't had much to do with little kids, but he didn't want these two afraid of him. They'd seen him threatening their father, and much as Vandusen deserved to be threatened, it must have been terrifying for them. Awkwardly, he crouched down beside the table and smiled at them.

"What's your name, big fella?" he asked the boy, wondering if the little guy spoke any English. His tawny hair was cut in a perfect bowl shape, and he was chewing methodically on a bite of sandwich. His dark brown eyes were wary.

The child swallowed hard, and said, "My name Eddy." He pointed a grubby finger at his sister. "Her Pearl."

"How old are you, Eddy?"

The boy promptly held up four fingers.

"Four years old? Hey, are you ever a big fella for four. And how old's your little sister?" She had a tangled mass of golden-brown curls, and there were tear tracks down her cheeks. Her button of a nose was running. She dipped her head and wiped it on her sleeve, looking up at Tom through long, wet lashes, and his heart constricted with pity.

Eddy was holding up three fingers now.

"So Pearl's three. Well, whad'ya know about that." Tom had no idea what to say next. In his entire adult life, he'd probably said less than ten sentences to any child. His and Jackson's lifestyle wasn't one that included much contact with children.

Jackson solved the problem. "Hash is all done here. Wash up and set this table, Tom, my friend. Then big Eddy here can go tell the ladies to come and eat. Eli," he bellowed, and when the boy came hurrying down the hall, Jackson ordered, "go bring in that bench that's out in the barn, soldier. It'll do for extra seating."

Eli grinned, snapped off a salute, and hurried away. Jackson jerked a thumb at a napkin-covered mound on the cupboard. "Zelda made bread today and some cookies. We can eat them for dessert."

He grinned at Tom, his wide, wicked pirate's grin. "I always figgered I'd open a little pub someday, Tommy boy, when I got too old for the adventurous life," he drawled. "This here is real good practice. All that's missin' is the draft beer. And, man, do I miss it," he added in a stage whisper.

He whistled and broke into snatches of a Western song as he served up the meal, and Tom was suddenly envious of his partner's ability to adapt like a chameleon to whatever circumstance sent his way.

Tom filled the washbasin with hot water and stripped off his grubby shirt, doing his best to scour away the sweat and grime of the day. More than almost anything else, he longed for the comfort of a long, hot shower, the simple luxury of having clean clothing to put on afterwards. After two full days wearing them, his jeans were grubby, his shirt sweaty and stained, and he'd have to wash out his underwear and socks tonight for sure.

How did people stay clean in this day and age? When the hell were laundromats invented, anyhow?

Virgil had loaned them a comb, and Tom raked it through his unruly curls. He was pulling his shirt back on when Zelda walked in. He shoved the sleeves high.

"Tom, I must thank you for what you did for Isabella." She came over and stood close to him, speaking in a low voice so the others couldn't hear. She smelled good up close, a homey smell, of fresh bread and cinnamon. "Eli said you gave Nestor a taste of his own medicine. Goodness only knows, he richly deserves it." Her forehead creased in a frown. "I only hope he doesn't retaliate by being even more brutal when Isabella goes home tonight. I've tried to convince her and the children to stay here, but she insists she has to go back."

"Don't worry about that." She was wearing a blue

dress today, Tom noticed, and her hair was rolled into a loopy ring around her head. As usual, it wasn't staying put, and curly bits were floating over her ears and forehead. He liked the clean, scrubbed look her face had, devoid of the makeup he was so accustomed to women wearing.

"I'm going to keep an eye on things over there," Tom said with grim determination. "I warned that bully what would happen if he tried anything like this again."

Zelda's brown eyes were eloquent with gratitude. She reached out and put her hand on his bare forearm, giving it a grateful squeeze with her long, warm fingers.

Tom's reaction to that innocent touch amazed him. Heat shot through his body, and he had the insane urge to reach out and draw her close to him, just so she'd have to touch him again.

Lord, Chapman, what the hell's wrong with you? You been altogether too long without a woman, that's what it is.

"Sit down. Supper's gettin' cold," Jackson ordered, and Tom drew a deep, relieved breath when Zelda moved away. He ignored the knowing wink Jackson shot him. Very little ever escaped Jackson's lazy gaze.

Dinner was pleasant in spite of the flaming red mark that blazed like a flag on Isabella's cheek. She was quiet and very shy, and she was good with her children, strict, but loving.

When Zelda introduced her to Tom, she looked up at him through her long lashes in the exact way her small daughter had done.

"T'ank you," she whispered, her hazel eyes flooding with tears. "I am sorry for cause you trouble."

Tom awkwardly patted her shoulder, again at a loss for words.

After they all finished eating, the women cleaned up, and Tom and Jackson went out to the barn with Eli to feed the horses and throw grain to the chickens.

"Did you beat the living tar out of Nestor, Tom?" The moment they were alone, Eli was full of eager questions. "Did you punch him good? He deserves it. My dad says he's nothing but a common bully. I think my dad hit him one time, too, when he caught him punching Isabella. I went for the police so I didn't get to see what happened, but Dad had a real sore hand for a while," Eli said, almost bursting with pride. "My dad says Nestor Vandusen is a sorry excuse for a man." The boy was suddenly vehement. "One of these days I'm gonna knock his lights out for him, 'cause Isabella is a real pretty lady. It's too damned bad she's married to such a bastard." His face turned magenta.

Busily forking hay for the horses, Tom and Jackson exchanged amused glances. It was obvious that Eli was doing his best to convince them he was a tough guy.

Tom explained exactly what had taken place, emphasizing there'd been no bloodshed, but repeating the dire threat he'd made. He added that the last he'd seen of him, Vandusen was scuttling off down the street.

When Eli went to bring a bucket of water for the horse trough, Tom said quietly, "We'll need to keep a keen eye on that place tonight, Jackson, in case

Vandusen comes back drunk and meaner than ever."

"I sorta hope he does." Jackson's voice was grim. "If it happens, I get first licks. One thing I can't abide, it's a man hittin' on a helpless female."

A little later, Tom and Zelda escorted Isabella and the children home. Tom carried a sleepy Pearl, her tiny arms linked trustingly around his neck. They helped Isabella light lanterns and stoke fires, and while Zelda and Isabella settled the tired children in their beds, Tom went out to the woodshed behind the house and chopped kindling and carried in buckets of coal for morning. He was catching on to the system.

They lingered with Isabella as long as possible, but there was no sign of Vandusen, and at last they left.

It was very dark outside. Tom reached out and took Zelda's hand in his as they made their way down the back path and into the Ralstons' backyard. The skin on her hand was chapped, and he ran his thumb over it tenderly, feeling again the intense physical attraction she roused in him.

He opened the back porch and drew her inside. Lantern light was seeping from under the closed kitchen door, and he could hear Jackson's deep drawl and then Eli's voice answering from the kitchen.

She reached out to open the inner door, but Tom stopped her. Temptation overwhelmed him. He blocked her way to the door, and without a word he gathered her into his arms.

She felt both bulky and fragile, bundled as she was into her voluminous skirts and long, heavy coat. She didn't object to his embrace, but at first she was stiff and unyielding in his arms.

He heard her breath catch in her throat. His heart was hammering. Her hands came up and rested on his upper arms, not pushing him away, but not holding him close, either.

He brought his hand up to her face, stroking his finger across the velvety softness of her cheek, rubbing his thumb across the fullness of her lips, gentling her before he cupped her chin and tilted it up so he could bend down his head and kiss her.

It was obvious to Tom that she hadn't been kissed often, and that realization both shocked and excited him. Not since his early teens had he kissed a woman who wasn't knowledgeable about how to kiss back.

At first, her lips remained tightly closed, and with infinite patience, Tom coaxed them open.

She gasped again, and a convulsive shudder ran through her. Her arms slid up and around his neck, and the tip of her tongue shyly touched his, once, and then once more, confidently this time.

That single, shy contact was like gasoline poured on the fire burning within him. His arms tightened around her, drawing her closer.

Her head tilted to a better angle, and she moaned deep in her throat, inflaming him even more. He slid his mouth over her swollen lips, enthralled with the sensations she created in him. He drew her closer still, frustrated with the layers of clothing between them, aching to feel the thrust of her breasts against his chest, the hollow between her thighs pressing against his heat and hardness. Without conscious thought, he slid his arm down and cupped his hand over her buttocks, moving his legs apart to accommodate her, pulling her tight against him.

His heart slammed against his ribs. He wanted her with a suddenness and an urgency that scared the living hell out of him.

He forced himself to draw back, put distance between them, struggle to regain some semblance of control.

What in God's name was he doing? Zelda was undoubtedly a virgin. Women weren't sexually active in this day and age as they were in his time. He was taking advantage of her innocence, and he was a guest in her father's house.

He had no future there. He certainly had no past.

He had no job, no money, no clothing, not even a clean pair of briefs to his name.

He had no business standing in the dark, kissing her and fantasizing about pushing her up against the nearest wall, shoving those long skirts up, sliding himself into her.

But, God, he wanted to.

Oh, how he wanted to.

He drew back, putting the necessary distance between them, and it seemed one of the hardest things he'd ever had to do.

Chapter Eight

"I should go in now, Tom," she whispered, her voice not quite steady. "Eli needs to be sent to bed and Dad will be home right away. I always make him a pot of tea and something hot to eat after his shift."

"Yeah." His own voice was thick, his throat tight. "Yeah, it's getting late."

"Tom?" Her voice was barely audible.

"I'm here, Zelda." Control was slow in coming. Unable to help himself, he reached out and ran his hand over her hair. Most of it had tumbled down while he was holding her, and he marveled at how long and soft it was, silky to touch, alive. It clung and curled around his fingers.

"I'm pleased you kissed me, Tom." Her words came out in a fierce low rush. She fumbled with the door, then bolted into the kitchen and on through the hall, not pausing even to take off her coat.

Jackson and Eli, sitting at the kitchen table with glasses of milk and cookies, stared first after Zelda, then turned to Tom as they heard her feet pounding up the stairs. Both of them looked at him, Eli curious, Jackson speculative.

He returned their gaze and forced himself to give an expressive shrug, holding his hands out to indicate he had no idea what was with her.

"Think I'll turn in," he managed to say in a casual tone. "We have to be out at the construction site at six in the morning to see if we've got a job for the day. Night, Eli." He turned and went back out the door, walking slowly to the barn, cursing himself for being a fool.

Kissing Zelda hadn't been a smart thing to do. She wasn't at all the type of woman he usually kissed, he reminded himself. He'd always made it his policy to stick to women who were as footloose and fancy-free as he was, so that when he moved on, nobody ended up hurt.

And in this instance, he definitely planned to move on, so he'd do well to stay away from Zelda Ralston and concentrate all his energies on finding a way back to his own time.

Trouble was, apart from her, everything about this place and time depressed him. The very thought of spending the rest of his life at this end of the twentieth century made suicide sound reasonable. Mind you, suicide wouldn't be necessary if he stayed in this house for another year. The Slide would bury the building and everyone in it.

He looked up at Turtle Mountain and shuddered.

* * *

At daybreak the next morning, Tom and Jackson were hired on as laborers at the McVeigh construction camp, but only for one shift. Two of the regular workers had got in a brawl the night before, and were in no shape to do a day's work.

It was the toughest physical labor either Jackson or Tom had done for years. Their job was to help clear away brush and timber for the laying of a branch line of the railroad to a nearby small town, and the work was both backbreaking and dirty. To make matters worse, a storm came up in the afternoon and rain pelted down, soaking them to the skin, but at the end of the day, they'd each earned $2.75.

Tom worked side by side with a young blond giant named Lars Olsen who'd emigrated from Sweden two years before. He'd only been in Frank a few weeks, and he told Tom that although he was trying to get on at the mine to earn some money, his dream was to buy land and to farm. Lars had come to Canada with very little cash and he knew exactly how to make each day's wages stretch like good elastic.

Tom listened closely to what Lars told him, and the moment he and Jackson were paid, they raced down the muddy street to Murphy's Ready To Wear and each bought a change of clothes. The rather baggy denim jeans Lars had recommended as cheap and good wearing, cost all of eighty-five cents, underwear, twenty-five cents, and of a design that set Jackson laughing so hard the stuffy clerk took offense and almost refused to serve them further, and serviceable heavy cotton shirts for seventy-five cents.

Carrying their new clothes in a paper, string-wrapped bundle, they hurried to the washhouse at the mine that Lars had also recommended. For a euphoric half-hour and the princely sum of twenty-five cents, they soaked and scrubbed and rinsed in steaming hot water. Then, feeling almost human again, they put on their fresh—decidedly quaint—clean clothes and headed for the grocery. By pooling their remaining sixty-five cents each, they managed to buy enough food to supply themselves and the Ralstons' with the raw ingredients for a good dinner.

"I reckon we owe Lars a beer, if we ever manage to get enough money ahead to afford one," Tom remarked as they walked up the street toward the Ralstons' house. "At least we've got work for another day. The foreman said if we turned up sober at six tomorrow morning he'd hire us on again."

A buggy passed them, drawn by a team of lively gray horses. A young woman in a brown coat trimmed with fur and a hat that appeared to have an entire nest of birds on its crown shot a provocative look at Jackson, and smiled coyly as she passed him.

"You ever get thinkin' maybe we're only dreamin', Tom? That given enough time, we'll just wake up in some nice motel with an X-rated movie blaring on the TV and laugh over this nightmare we both had?" Jackson's tone was wistful. "I mean, look at this confounded place. Horses and buggies and ankle-deep mud everywhere. Women in fifteen layers of clothes. Me wearin' underwear that would give ole Calvin Klein a coronary, workin' my guts out just to afford a change of clothes and supper."

"I think of it all the time. I wish to God it *was* only a dream. But the longer it goes on, the more I get thinking we're stuck here, Jackson, at least for the time being. I can't see anything for it except to bide our time and make the best of it."

Jackson nodded. "Ask me, the best of this sorry mess we're in is the Ralstons," he declared. "It's mighty good of them to take us in the way they have. I only hope we're not puttin' them out too much."

Tom didn't say so, but it had crossed his mind that after Zelda had time to think over the way he'd kissed her the night before, she might get spooked. She might give him and Jackson their walking papers—and that could be the best thing that could happen.

Besides his concern about being a burden on the family, part of him was beginning to think he'd be better off far away from Zelda Ralston and the temptation she provided.

"As soon as we can afford it, we'll move into the rooming house Lars talked about," he said. "There's a waiting list, so we better get our names in fast."

"Good idea," Jackson agreed.

Tom thought so, too. He needed to put distance between himself and Zelda before things went any further, he knew that. The only problem was, right this minute, he couldn't wait to see her again.

Zelda's first waking thought that morning had been of Tom, longing to see him but dreading it as well. She felt nervous as a cat at the prospect, worried about how she'd ever be able to look him in the eye and talk normally again after that searing kiss.

She'd awakened often during the night, her mind blissfully replaying every single instant in his arms, and for once, the voice of reason that always reminded her she was being ridiculous had been strangely silent.

She washed and dressed in her usual plain white blouse and dark skirt, wishing she had a larger wardrobe, a bigger bosom, more manageable hair. But in spite of those serious drawbacks, Zelda Ralston, she told herself in the mirror, grinning like a fool, you've been well and truly kissed.

"You're sure in a good mood this morning, Zel," Eli commented as she hummed a tune and ladled out his porridge. "Is someone finally coming by for a portrait?"

Normally, the reminder that her photography business was practically nonexistent would have been enough to dampen her spirits, but today Zelda refused to be downcast. "It's spring. It's going to be a lovely day when the sun comes up, and I'm going to wash clothes this morning and then go outdoors and take photographs all afternoon," she answered gaily, pouring herself a cup of coffee. "Hurry up and finish your breakfast, I want you to fill the boiler on the stove for me before you leave for school."

Eli eyed her curiously. "Boy, I never saw you in this good a mood before when you was gonna wash clothes," he remarked. "I thought you hated washing."

"*Were* going to wash clothes," she corrected. "You must watch your grammar, Eli. You don't want to sound like a bumpkin when you go East to university."

He stopped shoveling porridge into his mouth and toyed with the spoon, banging it against the table and sending droplets of milk shooting everywhere. "I'm not sure I want to go to university, Zel. I don't think I do."

Zelda refused to let even this old, familiar argument with Eli irritate her this morning. She sipped her coffee and smiled at him. "Oh, of course you do. You certainly don't want to end up working in the coal mines, and university is the best way to avoid that," she reasoned.

"Dad works in the mines. He likes it fine," Eli said in a rebellious tone. "Maybe I would, too."

Zelda had heard her father coughing again in the night, and her ever-present uneasiness about his health surfaced. "Dad never had the chance to go to school, you know that," Zelda said reasonably. "He's a naturally smart man. There's no telling what he might have been if he'd had an education."

"Jackson says he never went to university, either," Eli said in a sullen tone, not meeting her eyes. "He told me Tom never did, either."

In spite of her good intentions, Zelda's temper was rising. "They probably never had the opportunity, and look where it got them!" she snapped. "Neither of them have a penny to their names."

"They do, too." Eli's defense of his new friends was vehement. "Jackson says they have piles of money, but they can't get at it right now. Him and Tom are adventurers. They go looking for buried treasure and pirate's gold and everything, and they found enough of it to make them wealthy men, Jackson says."

Zelda was shocked that Jackson Zalco would fill her brother's head with such utter rubbish. She was going to have to have a serious talk with him. "Eli, I'm quite sure if you asked him, Jackson would also tell you that he'd much rather be a doctor or—or a lawyer, than an—an adventurer. At the moment, he's not doing too well, is he? An adventurer must wait for opportunity, but a man with a career always has his training to fall back on in difficult circumstances."

Eli was shaking his head. "Nope, I asked him, and he says he never wanted to be anything but what he is. He used to be a kind of soldier. That's how he got his leg hurt, and he said that since he got out of that pile of shi—that mess, he never looked back. Him and Tom were self-made men, living the good life until they ended up here. That's what Jackson says."

Self-made men? Living the good life? Zelda frowned at her brother. He was picking up some of the strange terms Tom and Jackson used. And he was also picking up ideas she didn't agree with at all, ideas that she didn't want Eli entertaining. His future was planned, the future she wanted for him, the future they'd all saved for.

"Finish your breakfast, young man, you're going to be late for your lessons. I've packed extra sandwiches so you won't get hungry delivering groceries after school."

"Delivering groceries for ten measly cents a week." He sneered, contempt in his tone. "Zeke Penman is the same age as I am and he's making big money working at the mine already." He gave Zelda a beseeching look. "I want a bicycle and a good catcher's mitt, Zel. I hate school. I want to quit and get a real job, so I can help pay the bills around here and have some money left over to buy things I want." His voice had risen. It fluctuated from a boy's falsetto to the deep bass of a man, reminding her that it wouldn't be long before he was fully grown.

"Lower your voice, Eli, you know Dad's sleeping," she warned in a scandalized tone. "And not another word about quitting school. I won't listen to any more of this nonsense. Now off you go." She handed him his satchel and the packet of lunch, entirely forgetting about the wash water.

He gave her a nasty look and slammed out the door, and Zelda collapsed into a chair, her coffee forgotten, her joy in the day tarnished.

Eli had always been headstrong and impulsive, but she'd managed to control him with reason and patience and plenty of love. Their mother had died when he was a tiny baby, four months old, and Zelda had raised her brother, lavishing on him all the love and devotion she would have given her own child, had she been lucky enough to have one. And until recently, Eli had never defied her like this. His rebelliousness troubled her.

She stoked the fire and remembered the wash water. Muttering under her breath, she pulled on an old jacket. She took the water pails out to the pump and filled them, pouring the water into the stove's reservoir and also into the big copper tub she'd set on the kitchen stove to heat.

On her third trip, Isabella called her from the

fence. She had Pearl on her hip, and she was clutching Eddy by the hand. She looked panicky and totally distraught, and with a sinking feeling in her stomach, Zelda wondered if Nestor had come home and was again causing trouble.

Isabella poured out a garbled torrent of words in some mixture of her native Dutch and what she thought was English, not one syllable of which Zelda understood.

"Eddy, can you tell me what your mama is saying?"

The solemn little boy nodded. "She say my papa, he is not come home all night."

"Oh, I see." It wouldn't do to discuss this in front of the children. "Eddy, there are cookies in my kitchen, in a bowl on the counter. Take Pearl with you. Go through your back gate and into our yard, and you can each have a cookie. Close the door quietly. Mr. Ralston is sleeping."

Eddy held up two fingers questioningly, and Zelda smiled and nodded. "All right, two cookies each." The poor little rascal deserved all the cookies he could eat.

He said something to Isabella, and she set Pearl down. Eddy grabbed his sister's hand and towed her away.

Zelda watched them for a moment, thinking it would be a blessing for all of them if Nestor had indeed disappeared. But Isabella was now wringing her hands and weeping.

"Gone," she proclaimed, her huge eyes swimming with tears. "Nestor, he is gone, not come back, maybe." She struggled with the language, and then added, "Me, I have no money. Nossing."

Zelda understood all too well. Isabella was an immigrant, without friends or family, totally alone and dependent on her husband.

"Maybe he's gone straight to work, Isabella," Zelda suggested, but Isabella shook her head. She made Zelda understand that she'd already walked to the mine office and asked. She'd just gotten back. Nestor hadn't appeared for work.

"Then he's probably at the Mounted Police barracks," Zelda declared with an exasperated sigh. The miserable man had probably gotten himself locked up for one reason or another—and well he deserved it, she thought with righteous indignation.

But whatever her own feelings about Nestor, Isabella was beside herself with worry. Well, Zelda thought, there went all her own plans for the day.

"Let's hitch up the buggy and go see if he's at the jail." She sighed, absolutely dreading another encounter with Corporal Allan, but unable to turn her back on her neighbor. Her reward was the look of gratitude on the other woman's face.

They rode to the jail, where Zelda learned to her enormous relief that Corporal Allan had gone to Lethbridge for several days, leaving Constable Liard in charge of the detachment. Liard hadn't seen anything of Nestor.

"I did regular patrols of the town late last night and early this morning," he told Zelda and Isabella. "If Vandusen had been anywhere around, I'd have probably seen him, I visited all the saloons and gambling halls, and, ahhh—" the young policeman's face reddened. "All the other establishments Nestor might be likely to frequent," he added discreetly. "You ladies go on home, I'll check around and see what I can find out. I'll come by later and let you know what's going on."

Back home again, Virgil was still not up, which wasn't like him at all. Zelda set Isabella to making some jam sandwiches for the children's lunch. She brewed her father a mug of strong tea and took it up to his room.

"Dad?" She knocked softly on his bedroom door, then pushed it open. "Dad, are you all right?"

"Come on in, lass. I'm just bein' a mite lazy today." His voice was hoarse. He opened his eyes and smiled at her, but it was immediately obvious to Zelda that he was ill. The bedclothes were tumbled and damp from sweat, and his face was flushed. He made an effort to sit up and immediately began to cough, the deep, rattling, endless cough that had troubled him off and on for the last six months.

Zelda set the tea on the bedside table and put the back of her hand on her father's forehead. "Heavens, Dad, you're burning up with fever. I'm going to send for the doctor." She turned to go, but he caught her hand and held it.

"No doctor, Zelda. It's just a chill. I'll be well again in no time." He coughed again and when he recovered enough to speak, he added, "We've no money for the doctor, lass, you know that. And it looks as if I'll be missing work again today, so that means even less to go on." The coughing began again, and he sank back on the pillows, unable to get his breath.

Zelda rubbed his back and waited out the seizure, holding the mug for him so he could sip the hot tea when he was able. When he seemed to be resting easier, she straightened the bed and hurried downstairs, worry about her father now uppermost in her mind.

Isabella had settled the children at the table with their lunch, and she was washing the breakfast dishes Zelda hadn't gotten around to.

"My father's sick, Isabella. I'm going to go for Doctor Malcolmson." She pulled on her coat and plopped her straw hat on her head.

"I vill make soup for him," she declared, and immediately began gathering vegetables. At least her announcement seemed to have taken Isabella's mind off her own problems. "I vill stay here with him until you come back. I vill take good care."

Wondering how many more things could go wrong in one day, Zelda hurried across the flats to Dr. Malcolmson's small hospital.

She was walking back home again with the doctor's promise that he'd come by as soon as he could later that afternoon when she met Constable Liard.

"Miss Ralston, I'm afraid I have some bad news for your neighbor," he told her. "Nestor Vandusen was seen climbing into a freight car on the westbound train last night. It seems he's skipped town."

"So he has deserted Isabella and the children," Zelda exclaimed.

"It looks that way. He may very well come back, but it's not too likely," Liard said. "You see, I've asked questions around town, and it seems Vandusen has been gambling as well as drinking and, uhhhh—womanizing. He owes a tidy sum of money to a certain unsavory character."

"How much does he owe?" Zelda knew of men who'd lost everything they owned gambling. Their families suffered horribly for their stupidity.

"I'm not sure exactly. It seems to be in the neighborhood of two hundred dollars."

Zelda gasped. It was a small fortune. "Surely this—person—won't come after Isabella for the money?"

"I doubt it." Liard shook his head. "I'm coming now to talk with Mrs. Vandusen. If this man should bother her about the money, I want her to come to me and lodge a complaint immediately. You're her friend, can you help me make her understand that?"

"She's at our house right now," Zelda told him, her heart sinking at this new disaster Isabella would have to face. "I'll certainly try."

The wonderful smell of homemade soup floated out to meet them. Eddy and Pearl were playing in the backyard, and Zelda invited the young Constable in for a bowl of soup and coffee, so they could both try and explain everything to her unfortunate neighbor.

Isabella didn't weep this time. Instead, she turned paper-pale when she finally understood that Nestor was gone, probably for good.

Constable Liard looked miserable at having to explain about the gambling. Isabella kept shaking her head in confusion, and Zelda had to go over and over it.

Even then, Zelda wasn't at all sure Isabella understood. She seemed dazed.

The doctor arrived while the constable was still there, and Zelda took him up to her father's room, waiting anxiously in the hallway until he was done examining Virgil.

"I'm afraid your father's lungs are sadly weakened from working all these years underground," the old doctor said with a sigh. "He's caught the grippe, and he's running a high fever. He's to stay in bed at least ten days. I've left some medication for him, but I want you to send your young brother to my office later this afternoon to pick up another preparation that might help."

He hesitated, and then added, "You know, your father shouldn't be working underground at all anymore, Miss Ralston. His lungs are very bad. It's time he retired from the mines. I told him that quite some time ago."

Zelda stared at him, shocked almost speechless. "But Dad's young, only fifty-five. He never told me that," she whispered.

"Well, he probably didn't want to worry you, but you should know his lungs are seriously compromised by years of coal dust." He sighed. "I see it all the time. We call it black lung."

Black lung. The words struck terror in her heart. With trembling fingers, Zelda paid him for the visit and the medicine with what was left of the food money.

Downstairs the constable was gone, and after showing the doctor out, Zelda sank into a chair at the table, across from Isabella. She felt battered by the doctor's words, exhausted by the happenings of the day.

"I must find, somehow, a way to make money," Isabella said in a desperate tone. "Zere is rent, and food, and coal for za fires. Zere is clothing, and—" The list seemed to overwhelm her.

Ironically, it was the same list that was racing

through Zelda's mind. She, too, would have to find a way to earn enough money to feed her family—and to send Eli to university, she added grimly. And it was obvious her dream of earning good money as a photographer was just that—a dream, without substance.

Virgil had always encouraged her photography, insisting that it just took time to find a clientele, but the time for such fantasies was over. No matter how good a photographer she was, it didn't bring in cash without customers.

"There must be *something* we can do," she pondered, frowning across at Isabella. "We're both intelligent, hardworking women."

There were jobs in the town that women could perform, maids at the hotel, cooks at the restaurants, but Zelda knew only too well that the wages were pitifully low, certainly not enough to support a family. Ironically, she'd led four women on a protest march just before Christmas because their wages were so low they could barely live. That act of bravado had resulted in a reprimand from Corporal Allan, and two of the women had lost their jobs, for which they blamed Zelda.

Besides, cooking or cleaning professionally was the last thing she should attempt. She hated housework. Isabella certainly seemed proficient in the kitchen—witness the soup Constable Liard had bolted down. But hiring herself out as a cook was nothing more than a joke, Zelda concluded. She was barely able to wrestle up satisfactory meals for herself and her father and Eli.

It had been wonderful the past two days, having Jackson Zalco do most of the cooking. . . .

"That's it," she exclaimed, startling Isabella. "Room and board. We'll offer Tom and Jackson room and board, Isabella, as a business venture."

It took a moment or two to translate it into terms Isabella understood, but when she did, she began to nod, and a little of the desperation faded from her expression.

"They're sleeping in the barn because I haven't space for both of them in the house, but if I clean out the attic and move up there myself, then my room would do for Tom, and you can board Jackson. It won't pay all the bills, goodness knows, but it's a beginning."

Zelda had to slow down and repeat herself, but Isabella soon grasped what she was saying.

"You'll have to be careful who you take in besides Jackson, though. We'll see to that when the time comes. For now, at least we know Mr. Zalco is a gentleman."

And the reason for sending Jackson next door was simply because she didn't want him filling Eli's head with any more of his nonsense, Zelda assured herself. It would be wiser for him to move next door with Isabella, and for Tom to stay there.

That arrangement had nothing whatsoever to do with how Zelda felt about Tom, she was certain of that. Well, she was almost certain.

"They haven't steady jobs yet, but they're very ambitious. I know they put their names down at the mine. They'll get on soon," she reflected, more to herself than Isabella. With Nestor gone, the waiting list at the mine was already one less than it had been that morning.

Two less, she forced herself to acknowledge. Dr.

Malcolmson's warning echoed in her brain. "Your father shouldn't be working underground. It's time he retired."

For a moment, utter panic overcame her. How would they live with Virgil not working? They had no savings, apart from the sum set aside for Eli's education. If only she had some training. If she was a nurse, or a teacher, or a secretary . . . But her formal schooling had been cut short when her mother died and Zelda had taken on the full care of her baby brother. And she'd never regretted that or considered it a loss. Eli had become the child of her heart, the son she most probably would never have. She'd fight tooth and nail to make certain he had the opportunities he deserved.

"Come and give me a hand, Isabella. We'll have to shift furniture around and move all my clothing."

The attic was drafty, unfinished, and undoubtedly full of spiders.

Moving up there was an easy sacrifice if it helped pay the bills and keep Eli in school.

Chapter Nine

It wasn't as if he and Jackson had much choice in the matter, Tom reflected later that night.

It was plain as the nose on your face that the two women were desperate, and even if he and Jackson had the means, it would be unthinkable to move somewhere else after the Ralstons had been so generous to both of them.

So Jackson had gone off with Isabella, holding Eddy's hand and chatting away to the little boy. But Tom had seen the flash of absolute panic in his partner's eyes. Like Tom, Jackson had no experience with family life, with living in close quarters with women and children, and Tom knew that about the last thing his friend wanted was to be marooned with Isabella and her two kids.

Not that Jackson minded kids any more than Tom did. It was just that neither of them knew the first damn thing about them, and even less about how an ordinary household operated on a day-to-day basis. Sleeping in the Ralstons' barn for a couple nights, helping out with the cooking—that was one thing.

Moving into a household on any sort of a permanent basis was quite another. Tom was as apprehensive about it as his partner.

Theirs had always been a bachelor's existence, his and Jackson's, first in the army, and in latter years, by choice as well as by the nature of their work.

They'd eaten and slept when and where they chose, relying on laundromats and restaurants and motels and dry cleaners. No one questioned or cared or knew when they came or went, or with whom, and they'd liked it that way.

But, Tom reflected, punching the pillow on the narrow bed in the small upstairs room, that was in his former life. He seemed to have been born again, reincarnated, and now the rules were different.

He'd watched programs on reincarnation, listened to people like Shirley Maclaine go on about it. He'd always reserved judgment, not caring one way or the other. Who gave a damn what happened after you were dead? It was living that counted.

Now, he figured those gurus were at least partially right about people having other lives. The only area they were way off base about was the dying part. Tom could have told them with absolute certainty that a person didn't have to die to be reincarnated.

He rolled over onto his stomach, trying to get comfortable enough to sleep. The entire bedroom smelled faintly of Zelda's perfume, and now his nostrils filled with the lemony scent of her hair, clinging to the pillow underneath the embroidered cotton cover.

He fantasized about what she looked like naked, underneath all those clothes. Like a colt, he decided, or a fawn—long, slender legs, narrow hips, concave belly, with a nest of soft red curls shielding unexplored secrets. His groin swelled and hardened, and he groaned and turned over on his back.

Idiot. For all you know, she could have hips as wide as the skirts that hide them, and legs and ankles like tree stumps, he chided himself.

What brought his eyes wide open in the darkness and kept him from sleeping for another long, worrisome time was the revolutionary realization that even if all of that was true, it still wouldn't for a moment stop him from desiring Zelda Ralston.

A day, and then two, and finally five days passed in a blur of work and sleep and simple gratitude for having a job, however temporary. Tom's body slowly adjusted to the hard labor demanded of it, although muscles he hadn't used in years were stiff and sore.

Each afternoon, he and Jackson were paid for their day's labor on the construction crew and told to appear the following morning.

Friday arrived at last, and Tom longed for the weekend, only to learn that the forty-hour week hadn't been invented yet, and everyone took for granted that Saturday was a workday like any other.

By the time their shift was finished late that Saturday afternoon, both he and Jackson were bone-weary and fed up. The only slight consolation was they'd been able to pay Zelda and Isabella for two weeks' room and board—the princely sum of eight dollars each—and they'd bought themselves a few more clothes and some sturdy work boots.

They'd fallen into the habit of bringing a fresh change of clothes and a towel to work each morning so they could visit the bathhouse before they headed home at night. They'd both learned quickly that bathing at the Ralstons' or at Isabella's was a production. Buckets of hot water had to be heated on the range and dumped laboriously into a large tin tub behind sheets draped across chairs for privacy.

One session like that had been more than enough. The bathhouse at the mine was both convenient and refreshing after a day's hard labor, and well worth the quarter it cost.

Besides themselves, Lars Olsen was the only other worker who bathed every day. Tom had learned from overhearing conversations among the construction crew that most of them considered a daily bath not only unhealthy but also downright dangerous. He had to wonder how their poor women put up with the smell. Tom figured he had a pretty strong stomach, but even in the open air, he'd learned to stay upwind of most of his fellow workers.

Lars, his blond hair wet and his tanned skin shining from hot water, was coming out of the bathhouse at the same time as Tom and Jackson late that Saturday afternoon.

"Hey, Lars, care for a beer? I'm buying. We owe

you one for all your good advice," Jackson suggested.

Lars's handsome features split in a delighted grin. "Yah, sounds goot to me," he agreed, and the three of them headed for the Imperial Hotel.

The bar was smoky and the noise level deafening. The room was crowded with coal miners and laborers, men weary from the long week's work, celebrating the end of a hard week's labor.

Tom glanced around. There were three or four women in the room as well, but it was obvious that they weren't the same sort of female as Zelda or Isabella. These women wore their bright dresses tight and dangerously low cut. Their manner was flirtatious and provocative as they moved from table to table soliciting business.

Their clothing might be a little more subdued than the hookers from his own time, Tom decided, but the way they went about their work was the same.

"Hello there, handsome," one of them greeted Olsen as they moved across the room looking for a table, and the young man blushed to the roots of his hair.

"Goot evening, Susie," he responded. She came over and stood on tiptoe, holding his arm in a familiar grasp and whispering in his ear. Lars shook his head. With a good-natured shrug and a pat on his cheek, she moved away.

Tom smothered a grin. It was obvious that Lars could recommend other services besides bathing and what coveralls to buy.

They finally located an empty table and ordered beer from the harassed waiter. They waited and waited, but no beer arrived.

"The hell with this," Jackson finally declared. "I'm gonna go see what the holdup is." He shouldered his way through the throng and over to the bar. After a short time he returned with two foaming mugs of beer on a tray and set them in front of Tom and Lars.

"One of the bartenders just quit. The owner remembered me from the other day, and he wants me to help out for a while behind the bar."

He winked at Tom and Lars and grinned his wide, white grin. "Said if I pitched in for an hour or two, all three of us get free beer all evenin'. Not that I'll have time to drink it, but I'll make certain you lucky dudes get my share."

"Not a selfish bone in your body, Zalco," Tom teased.

"Hate to disappoint you, Tom, old son, but I'm not doin' it just to get you deadbeats free beer. See, I've come to the conclusion I'd dearly love a steady job here." Jackson nodded around at the smoky, stuffy bar. "Man's only gotta work on that killer construction crew a week with a game leg like mine to really appreciate the good life." He winked and went back to the bar.

Tom and Lars toasted one another and drank. It seemed that half a lifetime had passed since Tom had last tasted the bitter, malty goodness of beer, and he appreciated every single drop.

"So ver are you from, you and your friend?" Lars leaned his elbows on the small table, his open face affable and curious.

Tom had learned discretion at the hands of the North West Mounted. "We're traveling men," he temporized. "I guess you could say we've been almost everywhere. How about you, Lars? What brought you here from Sweden?"

"Ach, I vanted a place of my own," Lars replied. "Back home, there ver too many boys in the family, five big men and my parents and two little sisters, on vun small acreage. It vasn't enough to support all of us, so I came to Canada. See, there isn't land to be had back home for the asking, the vay there is here." His broad face grew pensive. "But I am lonesome here in Canada. I miss most of all my little sisters. Ven I came first I vorked on a farm in Saskatchewan. The family was goot to me, but I didn't like so much space. I'm a mountain man, and ven I have made some money, I vill go further Vest, closer to the sea, and I vill find land and a vife and make a home of my own." There was absolute determination in his tone, and Tom envied him. Lars had a definite goal in mind, an attainable goal. In comparison, Tom's own overwhelming desire to return to his own time seemed more than ever unattainable.

"Out toward Vancouver there's beautiful farming land," he told Lars. "You'd like it out West."

Lars drank again, looking at Tom curiously from over the rim of the beer mug. "So you've been there, to this Wancouver? Out Vest?"

"Oh, yeah." Tom envisioned the sprawling, beautifully modern city, wondering with an ache of nostalgia what it looked like now, in its infancy. "We spent some time on the West coast, Jackson and me. Had a job there once."

They'd been hired to try and locate a cache of gold rumored to be lost in the mountains near

Hope. They'd enjoyed the search, but it was unsuccessful.

"So vat brought you here, to this coal mining town?"

Tom knew Lars was too polite to ask how two men who'd traveled as much as Tom claimed could possibly be as ignorant of everyday things as he and Jackson were. Suddenly a great and overwhelming loneliness came over him, a longing for someone besides Jackson to accept him for what and who he really was.

Jackson was a good friend, but as Tom looked across at the open, sunny face of the young Swede, he had a sudden desire to confide in Lars. He wanted to explain how he'd come to be here, in this hotel bar, at a time in history when technically, he hadn't even been born yet.

And so he tried as Jackson plunked a steady supply of beer down on their table. Tom did his best to convince Lars that he and Jackson came from far in the future. He leaned close to the other man and spoke in what he thought was a clear, convincing manner, outlining the highlights of the world he knew so well.

Two hours later and halfway through his explanation, he knew it was a hopeless endeavor.

Lars laughed hugely at the very idea of such things as cars and airplanes and computers. Even when Tom detailed exactly what was going to happen to the town of Frank the following year when the mountain slid down, Lars didn't believe for a moment he was telling the truth.

"So, you had been listening to Indian stories," he chided Tom. "They are superstitious, these Indians.

They think the mountain moves, and they von't camp here at its base. It is a big yoke around here. Ve have back home men who can tell such tales as you, also," he added with admiration. "They go from willage to willage, entertaining the people, but none are as good as you, my friend."

He reached over with his huge fist and tapped Tom good-naturedly on the shoulder.

Feeling utterly frustrated and misunderstood, Tom finally gave up and concentrated instead on emptying the overflowing mugs that kept appearing like magic in front of him.

The moon was up, high and cold in the starry sky when he and Lars left the saloon. Jackson was still busy pouring drinks, and he waved cheerfully at them from behind the bar. It was past eleven.

"Good night, my friend." Affectionately, Lars wrapped his arm around Tom's shoulders and drunkenly thumped his back in a friendly manner once or twice, endangering Tom's ribs. "Thank you for a good evening. See you Monday morning." He set off, a trifle unsteady, heading for the construction camp where he slept in a tent with two other men.

Tom made his way to the Ralstons, aware he'd had a little too much to drink and not caring a good goddamn. He felt fine, he decided.

He and Lars had talked easily once Tom stopped trying to burden him with the truth. But even knowing that Lars hadn't believed him hadn't seemed to matter after a few more beers.

The liquor had released the tight knot of anxiety that had been with him since he'd arrived in Frank.

For the first time, he felt almost happy. He whistled a haunting Western tune under his breath as he made his way through the dark streets of the now-familiar town. He was hungry; the last he'd eaten was the lunch Zelda had packed for him, and that was a long time ago. Maybe he could raid the cupboards and make himself a sandwich when he got home.

It would be nice if Zelda was up, he fantasized. They could make a pot of that infernal tea and sit and talk. There never seemed a chance these days to be alone with her, to have a private conversation. She was always busy, cooking, cleaning, ironing clothes, helping Eli with his homework. Maybe if they had a chance to talk, he could tell her some of the same things he'd tried to tell Lars.

Zelda would believe him, he assured himself. She was an intelligent woman; she had imagination and foresight.

She was a desirable woman. For the rest of the short distance, his brain insisted on creating X-rated fantasies that involved his adept removal of the intriguing layers of clothing she habitually wore.

There was lantern light shining through the kitchen windows of the Ralstons' house, and Tom opened the back door and smiled with delight to find Zelda sitting with a cup of tea at the kitchen table.

"Hey, pretty lady. How're things?"

She didn't answer, and Tom's smile quickly faded when the ominous look on her face signaled that all was not well.

"What's up, Zel?" He took off his coat, missing

the hanger on his first try and depositing the package with his dirty work clothes on the floor underneath the coats. He frowned, suddenly concerned. "It's not Virgil, is it? He's not worse?"

Virgil had stayed in bed for several days, but yesterday morning he'd gotten up and made his special porridge before Tom left for work, insisting he was feeling much better. Tom had been immensely relieved.

She shook her head, a single, definitive shake. Tom noticed that she was wearing one of her long-sleeved white blouses and her usual long dark skirt. It was really too bad, he mused with a pang of real regret, that nobody had yet thought up those nice, tight leggings that women in his own time wore. She'd probably be a lot more comfortable in something like that, and he'd certainly enjoy them one hell of a lot more than these floor-length jobs.

Come to think of it, he could also envision her in a little miniskirt, not too short, just mid-thigh, made of denim. With pink satin panties—

Her voice snapped him out of his pleasant reverie. "You've been *drinking,* have you not?" The words were spoken in such a horrified, hushed tone that Tom was sure at first she was joking with him. "You're *inebriated.*"

He grinned at her and winked, pretending to be much worse off than he really was. "Jus' a few little beers, pretty lady," he said, deliberately slurring his words and then staggering a bit as he sat down across from her at the table. "Had a few beers after work with good ole Lars."

Her full lips pressed together in disgust, and her chocolate-brown eyes all but shot sparks at him.

Her curly hair, escaping in all directions from the bun she'd tried to stuff it into, was a nimbus of fire in the lamplight. "I might not have made myself clear when we arrived at this agreement about room and board, Mr. Chapman, and for that reason I'm going to overlook this transgression," she began in a voice that quivered with anger and outrage.

"Imbibing in spirits is simply not allowed in this house." Short of breath, her words came out in spurts. "I will overlook tonight's spectacle for the sake of fairness in case I didn't previously spell this out. But if you choose to succumb again to demon rum, you will have to find other accommodations immediately."

Her chest was heaving with emotion, and color had stained her cheeks a deep rose. She'd never looked more desirable—or sounded more ridiculous.

Still mellow and loose from the beer, Tom didn't take her words too seriously. Highly amused by actually hearing her say such things as "imbibe" and "demon rum," he didn't know whether to burst into laughter or gather her into his arms and make better use of her passion.

"Hey, Zelda, calm down," he said with a smile, reaching across to touch her hand. "A couple of beers doesn't turn me into an axe murderer. I'm not even drunk, or at least not much. I was just putting you on a little."

She snatched her hand away from his touch and leaped to her feet, wrapping her arms around her torso, her breasts heaving.

"You may think this is amusing, but I assure you, I do not!" she spat at him. "I will not have my brother exposed to the evils of alcohol in his own home. There are enough examples of what spirits can do in this town, without Eli witnessing it here."

Tom realized that she was actually trembling, and he felt a pang of remorse. He'd forgotten for the moment about Isabella. Zelda had probably only seen the really wicked side of liquor. As far as he knew, Virgil didn't drink at all, so she likely wasn't even aware that a man could have a few beers once a week without turning into a raving alcoholic.

"C'mon, Zelda, sit back down and we'll talk about this. The odd beer just relaxes a guy a bit." He leaned back in the chair, trying to look both sober and unthreatening. "You're overreacting just a little here. I'm a long way from being soused."

To his utter amazement, his words seemed to push her over the edge. Angry tears glistened in her eyes. "Over—overreacting, am I?"

She moved swiftly to the range and flung the oven door down, grabbing a pot holder and pulling out a heaping plate of scorched food. "This was your dinner, ready exactly on time, but you chose not to come and eat it." She upended the plate and dumped the whole mess on the oilcloth-covered table in front of him. Bits of gravy spattered on his shirt, and an ugly glob of greasy sausage dropped into his lap.

"I refuse to be taken advantage of in such a manner." Her voice rose to a near shriek. "I assumed you'd had an opportunity to work late, and I waited supper for you. I never dreamed you were in—in one of those dens of iniquity, succumbing to temptation. As far as I'm concerned, from now on you can cook for yourself. I'm through struggling to provide meals for a man who hasn't the common decency to come home and eat them."

Tom was too flabbergasted even to get angry. He sat in shocked silence as she turned on her heel and flounced out of the room, her back ramrod straight, her hair bouncing and tumbling in tendrils over her shoulders. He heard her booted feet pounding up the stairs, then scurrying up the narrow ladder to her attic room.

Tom had most of the food mess cleaned up by the time Virgil crept quietly down the stairs and into the kitchen.

"Couldn't help but hear the rumpus," he said, lowering himself into a chair and lifting the lid of the teapot to see if there was any left. "Reach me down a mug, would you, son?"

Tom did, and Virgil poured himself some tea, stirring in three spoons of sugar and then adding a dollop of milk. He stirred again and took a long, deep draught. He swallowed and sighed with pleasure. "Nothin' like a good cuppa tea," he said, the way he always did. "Y'know, I think I'd fancy a sandwich. There's a bit of cheese in the cupboard there and fresh bread. Mebbe you'd join me, Tom?"

Tom cut thick slices of bread for both of them, adding the cheese. Then, with Virgil directing him, he toasted the sandwiches on top of the range in the wire contraption that substituted for an electric toaster.

The result was ambrosia. Tom devoured his, and Virgil silently proffered another half. "Not as hungry as I figgered," he remarked, and Tom understood that Virgil hadn't been hungry at all, but he'd realized Tom was ravenous.

When Tom was done, Virgil looked at him and grinned, exposing several gaps where teeth were missing. "So our Zelda's riled up at you fer havin' a few beers," he commented. He took several more gulps of tea, and his faded blue eyes twinkled at Tom over the rim of the mug. "I should'a warned ye. She's got a right snappy temper, has our Zelda."

Snappy wasn't the word for it, Tom concluded. His pants had a huge grease stain across the front, and the gravy hadn't done his shirt much good, either. "I think she was upset because I didn't make it back for dinner," Tom remarked in a mild tone.

Virgil nodded. "Likely. She's a good lass, but she sorely hates cookin', ya see. Puts her in a foul mood. And she's got this here bee in her bonnet about boozin'. It's to do with that Women's Temperance Union she joined before we moved here." He leaned across the table. "Don't let her get under yer skin with all that carryin' on, Tom," he added in a whisper. "She's a fine lass, but she's too serious by far. What she needs is to get out a bit more, have some fun for a change, see how the other half lives, so to speak. She's had too much responsibility in her life, what with raisin' Eli, and now me takin' poorly isn't helpin' none. Not much of a life for a young lass."

"If my having a beer now and then is going to upset her like this, it might be best if I found another place, Virgil." Tom spoke with reluctance. It wasn't what he wanted, but the cautious part of him kept urging that he put distance between himself and Zelda, and this was the perfect opportunity. After all, she'd all but kicked him out.

Virgil's shoulders slumped, and he suddenly looked shrunken and old. "It'd likely be easier someplace else, I can see that," he said with dignity. "But I'd be much obliged if ye'd stay, Tom. Truth is, with me not workin' steady, money's a mite short, so your board is much appreciated."

He looked down at his tea, embarrassed at having to admit his own frailty. After a moment he added, "There's another thing, too. That boy of mine could use a young man's guidance now and again. I know fer a fact he's right fond of you." He sighed and shook his head. "Zelda don't realize it, but Eli's been skippin' outa school lately. Hirin' himself on as gofer boy around the mines, real secret like, not realizin' I'd hear of it straight off." His craggy face was sober and worried. "I've not told Zelda. She'll take a strip off the lad when she hears. She's dead set on him gettin' an education, see, but you can't force a boy that age. He's growin' up fast, and some of her notions don't sit any too well with him." He waggled his head and sighed. "We've always gotten on, Eli and me, but lately he ain't sayin' much. Mebbe he'll talk to you, long as you're here."

Tom felt as if he'd stepped into quicksand. The last thing he was suited for was advising a teenager about anything. But Virgil looked frail and old and ill, and Tom's own chest ached in sympathy when Virgil coughed on and on in the night.

"Sure, Virgil. I'll do what I can," he heard himself saying, and his reward was the relief and gratitude in the older man's eyes.

Chapter Ten

Breakfast the next morning was strained, despite Virgil's valiant efforts at small talk.

Zelda fried the eggs until they were like rubber and methodically burned the toast. She was exquisitely polite when she had to speak to Tom, but she avoided his eyes and was careful not to so much as brush against him when she served him.

Eli had gotten up at dawn to go fishing with his friends, so there was only Tom and Virgil and Zelda at the table. By the time he'd managed to swallow his first bite of breakfast, Tom wished fervently that he'd stayed in bed and nursed the hangover that was making his head pound and his stomach roil.

When the knock sounded at the back door and Jackson came in, Tom felt enormous relief.

"Thought you might like to take a stroll along the river, Tom," Jackson suggested after he'd greeted

Virgil and Zelda and accepted a cup of coffee.

Tom raised his eyebrows. Jackson detested walking.

The sun beat down on the valley, and the town lay basking in the first real warmth of spring. The surrounding Rockies had snowcapped peaks all year, but the snow on Turtle Mountain was disappearing day by day.

"Thing I hate worse than almost anythin' about bein' in this place is not havin' a truck to ride around in," Jackson grumbled as they made their way through the quiet Sunday streets. "Let's just find us a bench or somethin' to sit down on."

There were no benches, but a wide, flat rock near the river provided a seat.

"Last night—this mornin', more likely, the owner of the Imperial offered me a steady job as bartender," Jackson began after they were settled. "Room and board at the hotel goes with the job, and the pay's almost enough to live on."

"So you're moving over there?" Tom felt a peculiar sinking in his stomach. He and Jackson had lived and worked together for years. This was the first time either of them had taken a job that didn't involve them both.

Jackson nodded. "Can't afford not to." He sighed and shifted to a more comfortable position. "Y'know, Tom, living at Isabella's is makin' me crazy. I like her well enough, and the kids are cute little shavers, but, hell, I know myself. There's gonna come times when I want to bring a woman to my room, or to spend the night at hers, or get pissed and not go home at all, and there's no way I can do any of those things, living there. Hell, Isabella was waitin' up when I got in at two this mornin', not that she said a word about it, but I felt guilty as hell for keepin' her from sleepin'." He blew his breath out in a rush and shook his head. "It's just too much like bein' married, Tom, with none of the perks."

Tom gave a rueful grin. "Zelda was waiting up, too, and she took a strip off me, gave me a lecture about the dangers of demon rum. I thought I was going to have to move back out to the barn for the night."

Jackson chortled. "Serves you right, downin' all that free beer. I figured she was kinda huffy this mornin'." He sobered and added, "Only thing that really bothers me about this job is leaving Isabella and those kids in a tight spot. I told her I was movin', and her face fell a mile. I know she needs the rent money real bad, and I wouldn't want to see her get some bad-ass guy in there who'd maybe take advantage of her.

"She's a real sweet little lady, and she's smart, too. She's learning English real fast. So I got to thinking. You figure maybe Lars Olsen might want to move in? He seems a decent sort, the kind you'd trust with your sister. If you had one. I sorta sounded Isabella out at breakfast about him, and far as I could see, she's willin' if he is."

Tom considered it. "It would be one hell of a lot better for him than living in that tent. You could put it to him and see what he says."

Jackson looked uncomfortable. "Well, see, I kinda figured you know him better than me, what with drinkin' all that beer I brought over last night. So I thought maybe we'd both go over there now and you could sort of put it to him?"

Tom grinned at his partner. Jackson would fight a half-dozen men bare-handed rather than have anything remotely resembling a business discussion with them.

The camp was just waking up when they arrived. Lars, with no trace of a hangover, sat cross-legged in front of his tent, shaving with his straight razor and a small basin of water he'd heated on an open fire.

"Coffee?" He rinsed out two tin cups and poured an inky brew from a fire-blackened pot.

Tom explained why they'd come.

"Yah," Lars said slowly when he'd heard all about Isabella. "Yah, I think that would suit me yust fine. This camp, it is not so goot."

Tom figured that was the understatement of any year. The wind had shifted, and the smell from the latrines blew over them, making his stomach heave. A short distance away, someone who'd drank too much the night before vomited in the space between two tents.

Nervous at the thought of meeting Isabella, Lars dug through his trunk and put on a clean, wrinkled white shirt, an equally creased pair of good trousers, and a worn, green suit jacket he'd somehow outgrown. It was in danger of splitting down the back if he so much as drew a deep breath.

In spite of the jacket and the difficulty Lars and Isabella had communicating, that first meeting was a success. Isabella was nervous, and most of her English deserted her, but Lars was sympathetic; he'd gone through the same struggle with English himself, he told her, his own Swedish accent more evident than usual.

His kind face split in a delighted grin when he met Eddy and Pearl. It was obvious he considered them a bonus. Within moments, he'd shed the constrictive coat and was down on his knees helping Eddy construct a house with wooden blocks.

By noon, it was all settled.

"Come on over and inspect what's advertised as the best two-dollars-a-day room in Frank," Jackson urged Tom. "Steam heat, electric light, and plastered throughout. Fodor'd be downright fired up over this baby."

"Guess the plastered part refers to the bar," Tom quipped. "I'll come visit in a day or two." He knew it was ridiculous, but he'd never felt more alone in his life. He watched Jackson, carrying his meager belongings in one small paper bag, limp off down the road toward the hotel and his new job.

Zelda was just coming out of the house, her ragged old straw hat perched on her head and a spade in her gloved hands.

"Is there a problem at Isabella's?" She was still formal and distant with him.

Tom explained about Jackson's job and Lars moving in. Zelda listened and nodded, thawing a little.

"It's kind of you and Jackson to find someone else suitable to board with Isabella." She hesitated a moment, then tilted her chin up, and looked him straight in the eye.

"And will you be moving out as well, Tom?" The words were challenging, but he could detect the uncertainty in her eyes.

He held her gaze and said softly, "Is that what you want me to do, Zelda?"

She dropped her eyes and shook her head. "No, I don't," she said in a stiff voice. "Dad insists I was too harsh last night. I—I apologize."

Tom could tell that the words almost choked her, and he found himself relishing her discomfort. After all, he still had to try and clean the gravy off his pants and shirt.

But he might have known Zelda wouldn't eat crow for long.

"You realize, however, that I still have strong feelings about liquor," she added immediately, her chin tilted skyward, her brown eyes flashing.

He had to laugh. She was indomitable, and for some reason that delighted him. "I sorta gathered that. You were pretty vocal about it last night."

She flushed, transferring the shovel from one hand to the other.

"What are you planning to do with that?" Tom pointed his finger at the spade.

"This?" She glanced at it as if she'd forgotten all about it. "Oh, this. I'm going to dig the garden. Dad always plants early in May. He's having a sleep, and I thought I'd get it done before he woke up. Otherwise, he'll be out here digging, and the doctor expressly said he's not to do anything physically demanding."

"Let me do it." Tom took the shovel from her and headed over to the garden area. He'd never dug a garden, but the soil had been carefully prepared the previous fall, and turning over the rich black loam proved easy and enjoyable.

Zelda joined him, picking out stones and roots

and using a rake to smooth the earth after Tom turned it over. The sun was hot, and the yard was peaceful, filled with the songs of birds and the laughter of Eddy and Pearl, playing in Isabella's backyard.

First he rolled his sleeves high and pulled his shirttail out of his pants. Finally he shucked it off altogether, enjoying the sun on his bare flesh almost as much as the glances Zelda shot at his naked torso whenever she thought he wasn't looking.

He was as bad as she.

"Do you like to garden, Tom?" She was bending over, her bottom stuck in the air and a layer of white petticoat showing beneath the hem of her skirt. He studied her from the back, trying unsuccessfully to assess her exact shape and size through the maddening layers, longing for the advent of short shorts.

"Never done any. Never stayed in one place long enough to plant a garden." One thing about it, the outfits women wore here left absolutely everything to the imagination. It was depressing.

"Not even when you were a child?" She straightened and turned quickly, and he pretended to be obsessed with the clods of earth he was turning.

"We had no backyard to plant anything in, and even if we had, my parents weren't exactly the gardening sort."

"Where did you grow up?" She leaned on the rake, her chin propped on the back of her hands, unaware that this was a subject he definitely didn't want to talk about. But short of outright rudeness, there wasn't any way around it.

"In Idaho, in a coal mining town not too different

from this one." The similarities haunted him. "My stepfather was a miner." *What had made him volunteer that?*

Her surprise was evident. "You never said a word about coming from a mining family. Dad'll be beside himself. Did you ever work underground?"

He grunted. "Oh, yeah. For all of a month, when I was fifteen. I hated it. I left home and hit the road, never went back."

"Fifteen?" Her expression was troubled. "Oh, Tom, that's so young. That's Eli's age. I can't imagine a child of fifteen being on his own. Your parents must have been sick with worry."

Tom shook his head. "Not likely. They were probably relieved as hell to see the last of me. I'd started having some terrific fights with the old man before I took off."

He upended a particularly stubborn chunk of soil and chopped it to bits with the tip of the spade, putting a lot more energy into it than the job needed. "They fought, they drank. They were the kind who should never have had kids in the first place." He put his foot on the shovel and pushed hard, welcoming the strong resistance of the earth.

"Did you have sisters and brothers?" Zelda's rich voice held a world of compassion, and it annoyed him. He didn't need pity. He'd made out just fine on his own.

The questions were becoming more difficult for him to answer, and he wished she'd just drop it. "Two stepbrothers, both quite a bit younger than me." He didn't have to answer, but for some reason he couldn't stop himself. "Ryan was seven when I left. Billy was four."

Sometimes he still remembered exactly how they looked, but sometimes their features were blurred in his memory. Right now, he could see them as clearly as if they stood right there in the garden—Ryan with his gap-toothed grin, Billy's chipmunk cheeks. Weird how in his mind they never got any older, when in reality they'd been adults for years now.

He drove the shovel viciously into the earth.

"Are you close to them?"

"Nope." His voice was curt. "I've never seen them since the day I left. I don't know where they are." It was an old sore, one that he tried never to think about, and he resented her for making him do so now.

He glared at her, daring her to comment. She looked shocked, and again he felt compelled to explain. "I've tried to locate them, but my parents died in an accident shortly after I left home. The boys were taken by a social agency and adopted. Their names were changed, the agency went out of business, and all their records were lost." He dug still faster, sweat dripping off his nose and running down his chest.

He'd tried. He'd hired a private investigator a few years back, but the records were sealed. "Wherever they ended up had to be better for them anyhow." It was his only consolation. He couldn't believe it when he heard himself blurting out, "I've always blamed myself for walking out on them."

"Oh, Tom." She moved close and stripped off her glove, then put her hand on his arm. "I'm so sorry." Her big chocolate eyes were shiny with tears, her fingers on his bare skin seeming to burn a pattern where they touched. "I only have Eli, but if I somehow lost him, I don't know what I'd do." The emotion she felt made her voice tremble.

He looked down into her face, studying each feature as though it were a puzzle he was going to be tested on—sunkissed cheeks, straight, freckled nose, wide mouth, long, graceful throat, uneven hairline. What made this particular face so special to him? What made him look at her and suddenly find her heart-stoppingly beautiful?

She had a smudge of dirt on her temple where she'd shoved her hair back, and there was a fine beading of sweat on her forehead. Her special scent, sweet and intimate, filled his nostrils and he wanted more than anything to gather her into his arms and hold her tight, crush her against his chest.

What was it about this woman that drew him so powerfully?

Her breathing quickened, and he could tell that she sensed it, too, this irresistible magnetism that existed between them. His fingers closed over her shoulders, leaving dark smudges on the pristine white cotton of her blouse. But before he could draw her to him and kiss her the way he needed to, she shook her head and moved back, stumbling a little on the clods of dirt.

"Not here, Tom," she breathed. "Everyone can see us." She gestured with her hand, and he realized that Eddy and Pearl were hanging over the fence, watching with somber, dirty little faces and saucered eyes. In the yard on the other side, an old woman with a black scarf tied over her head was bending over her own garden, but it was obvious her attention wasn't on the roses she was pruning.

He swore under his breath. "Where then, Zelda? For God's sake, where?"

In the house, Virgil would awaken at any moment. There was the barn, and Tom was beginning seriously to consider dragging her into its dusky privacy.

With her lower lip caught between her teeth, she studied him for a long, silent moment. Then she seemed to make up her mind.

He had the feeling that something momentous was being settled between them.

"I'm going for a walk in a little while, to take photographs," she said, her husky voice a little breathless. "Would you care to come along?"

He only nodded, but there was a wealth of feeling in that nod.

There wasn't time to heat enough water for a bath. So she took a steaming kettle, a basin of cold water, and a small container of vinegar up to her attic room.

It was going to be an oven up there when summer came; even now the unfinished space was stuffy and close.

She stripped off her skirt and blouse, undid her petticoats, and let them fall in a heap. She removed her chemise and drawers, grateful that she'd burned her stays several years before after attending a lecture by a female doctor who attributed many of the common ailments women suffered to the cruel stricture of corsets. She'd been much more comfortable ever since, and she tried not to allow the scandalized glances she sometimes received to bother her.

Lathering the washcloth with some of her carefully hoarded lavender soap, Zelda scrubbed herself thoroughly, top to bottom. She emptied the basin in the slop bucket and refilled it from the kettle and rinsed. Then she rubbed herself dry on a rough towel that smelled sweet from the clothesline.

Powder, a touch of rose perfume on her throat, behind her ears, at her wrists . . . The next part was difficult, but very necessary.

Her heart was hammering and her hands trembled as she retrieved the tiny box she'd kept hidden for over a year in her underwear drawer. She withdrew one of the small sponges with its attached string and doused it with vinegar. She'd read the instructions so many times she had them memorized, but she'd never attempted to insert it before. She'd never had reason to. One didn't need birth control when virginity seemed a terminal condition.

She squatted, feeling awkward and a trifle hysterical as she lectured herself about false modesty, female emancipation, and experiencing life to the fullest when opportunity presented itself. With trembling fingers, she did her clumsy best to position the device properly.

Zelda had discovered the little cave the autumn before, when she was climbing up Turtle Mountain to photograph the village. It wasn't far up the hillside, just high enough to allow a view of the valley below. It was small, only about four feet high and the same deep, little more than a hollow on the side of the mountain. But it was private, dry and comfortable, its floor a soft drift of autumn leaves. She'd gone there several times just to be alone, to sit and dream.

As she walked with Tom that afternoon she remembered exactly where it was, and she deliberately steered them in that direction.

The pathway led first through poplar trees and then into heavier evergreen growth at the base of the mountain and up the slope. The earth was mushy in places, still thawing from the winter's frost.

"How did you get interested in photography?" He'd taken the strapped canvas bag she'd sewn for her camera and slung it over his shoulder. As soon as the village was behind them, he'd reached for her hand as well. Every so often he'd rub his thumb across her palm, sending delicious shivers racing through her.

"Back East I worked as a governess, caring for three children. The mines were slack, and when Dad decided we were coming here, my employer gave me a box camera as a parting gift. I struggled to learn how to use it and even more to learn to develop my own photographs. I'd always been interested in art, but I'm afraid I lacked talent with a brush. Then I found a book detailing a photographer named Julia Margaret Cameron. Have you ever heard of her?"

"Nope, but I'm not up on photography at all. Ansel Adams, that's about it. What kind of pictures did this Cameron woman take?"

She'd never heard of anyone named Ansel Adams. "Julia Margaret Cameron was a portrait photographer, but she also transformed real people into scenes from Tennyson's *Idylls of the King*. She was wonderfully creative, and looking at reproductions of her work, I began to realize the potential of the camera. During our journey from the East, I photographed many scenes that I found interesting, and I managed to sell some of them to the newspapers. That small amount of success went straight to my head and I decided to make photography my career. Unfortunately, when we arrived in Frank, Beaseley had just opened his studio, so mine wasn't the novelty I'd hoped it might be."

"Still, there ought to be enough work for both of you. Lars was telling me how many immigrants just like him there are in Frank. You'd think most of them would want photos made to send to their families back home."

"One would think so," she said, hiking her skirt up to her knees to navigate a marshy section of the path, fully aware of Tom's eyes on her stockinged legs. "I don't attract any of their business, although from what I understand, Mr. Beaseley is overwhelmed with work. Of course Dad says it's because I'm too vocal in my beliefs about emancipation for women, and the need for unions in the coal mines. The residents of Frank are disturbed at a woman speaking out on such issues." She stopped and looked around. The cave was just over there, behind that bush. He'd see it in a moment, and then she'd suggest they sit there and rest, and then . . . then. . . .

"Virgil's probably right about you scaring them off." He turned his head and grinned down at her, the crooked, engaging grin that tugged at her heartstrings. "You're ahead of your time, Zelda. You'd fit right in where I come from. In the nineties, it's taken for granted that women are equal to men, and as for unions, they've become so powerful they control the companies."

Zelda frowned and shook her head at him. She deliberately extricated her hand from his and turned her back, moving ahead of him toward the cave, disappointed that he was spoiling things this way. She hated hearing him lapse into his fantasy world again, for she'd hoped he'd forgotten all about it. It troubled her more than ever now that she'd made up her mind to commit her body to him.

She gasped and nearly lost her footing when suddenly his hands grasped her shoulders and swung her roughly around to face him.

"You just don't want to hear the truth about me, do you, Zelda?" His voice was quiet, but his fingers dug painfully into her shoulders, and the expression on his face made her swallow hard.

He was furious, and it frightened her.

Chapter Eleven

She'd never seen him really angry.

Even when she'd berated him for drinking, there'd been that wicked gleam of humor lurking in his eyes, the suggestion of a smile on his lips. There was none of that now. His blue gaze was cold and contemptuous, his jaw set.

"You think if you refuse to listen to me, it'll all go away, Zelda? You want to go on pretending that I'm not quite right upstairs, the way Jackson told that Mountie? Well, that's bull, lady, and somewhere in that fine mind of yours you realize that."

"You let me go this instant, Tom Chapman." She struggled, shocked at how strong he was, how easily and effortlessly he trapped her within his grasp. She jerked away, trying to get loose, furious at being held captive. "Let me go, I say. How dare you?"

He grinned, but it wasn't the friendly grin she was

used to. Now there was something primitive about him. "Sorry, Zelda. That tone probably works real well on Virgil and Eli. Makes 'em snap right into line, but it doesn't cut ice with me." He looked around, never letting up for one instant on the iron grip he had on her arms.

"We're going to find a nice place to sit down. Then you're going to listen to what I have to say without interrupting or walking away or giving me that superior glare you're so good at."

He gave her a shake. "Damn it, Zelda, I'm sick of having you look at me as if you think I'm half nuts every time I mention who I really am and where I come from."

She wanted either to weep or else to smack him a good one. Confound him, he was ruining all her plans. She hadn't brought him there to listen to far-fetched fabrications about some imagined life he'd led. She wanted him to hold her, not with anger like this, but with passion. She didn't want conversation—especially not this particular conversation.

Just then he saw the little cave. He released her shoulders and took a firm grasp on her elbows, steering her toward it, checking inside carefully to be certain it was empty.

"Here, this place is as good as any." He sank down and, none too gently, pulled her down beside him on the leaves. "Now, Zelda Ralston, for once in your life, shut right up and listen to me, okay?"

She shot him an outraged look. She huffed and moved several feet away from him, rearranging her skirts and straightening her spine, making certain he knew how affronted she was by his behavior. Tears of utter disappointment welled and threatened to spill over, but she held her eyes wide open and willed the tears away, not wanting him to see such weakness.

He was quiet for so long, she finally sneaked a sideways glance at him. He didn't notice. He was staring out over the valley, lost in thought.

When he did speak, his words took her by surprise.

"When were you born, Zelda? What year?"

She looked at him, puzzled and intrigued by his question, but still put out with him. Her voice was huffy. "In 1868, of course. I'm presently twenty-eight years of age."

He nodded, but when his eyes met hers, they were troubled. "I was born in the late fifties, Zelda. The *nineteen* fifties. Technically, I'm nearly ninety years younger than you are." He held her gaze, and his expression softened into a rueful smile. "It's one hell of an age difference, huh?"

The hair on her arms stood on end. Whatever else he was going to tell her, she didn't want to hear. Something about all this terrified her. She started to get to her feet, but his hand closed around her arm and brought her down again with a thump.

"Sit down, Zelda, please, and listen. I want you to know about my world. It's important to me that you do." He shifted his body and dug in the pocket of his trousers, withdrawing his wallet. Flipping it open, he withdrew several pieces of what looked to her to be celluloid and held them out.

"This is called a photo ID. It's my driver's license. This one is a charge card."

Unwillingly, she took them. Curious in spite of her misgivings, she looked at them. The card with the photograph shocked and thrilled her, and she couldn't stop staring at it. It was a tiny portrait of Tom, an excellent portrait, but it was in *color*. She'd never imagined a photo could be as clear and vivid, or that the actual shades of his hair, eyes, and skin tone could be reproduced so accurately. And how had it been imposed on the tiny card? It was encased in some sort of protective covering, not glass, malleable when she bent it slightly. There were no seams, no indication of how the photo got inside the covering. There were numbers, Tom's name, an address in New Mexico. She ran her finger across the shiny surface and swallowed hard. Whatever this was, it wasn't a technique or a material she'd ever heard of. Photography of this sort wasn't possible, she knew that.

Fingers trembling now, she examined the other card. It, too, was encased in the same strange substance. "MasterCard," this one read, and again, Tom's name beneath a string of numbers. On the right hand side was the image of an eagle, and when Zelda tilted the card in the sunlight, the bird seemed to move. Startled, she dropped it and shrieked, and again Tom smiled, but there was no real humor in it.

"In my world, this card will buy almost anything. We use it the same way we use money," he explained, picking it up and sticking it back in his wallet. " '*MasterCard, don't leave home without it.*' " He shook his head, muttering, "I'm gonna call their head office and tell them a thing or two, if I ever get back." He turned to her, taking her hand in his again, resting it on his thigh, so she was aware of the corded muscle, the lithe strength of his legs.

"Zelda, it's so hard to know where to start, or what to say to make you understand things like television, and microwaves, and airplanes." He reached out and touched the bulky canvas bag that held her camera. "Photography, for instance. Almost everybody in my time owns a camera. Most of them are small enough to fit in the palm of your hand. Or you can buy an instant camera, a cardboard thing that shoots a roll of film, then gets thrown away. Color film is used far more than black and white, and there's different speeds of film, so you can take pictures in the dark, or stop a bird in flight. Most people have camcorders. . . ."

On and on he went, and Zelda listened, drawn into the magic world he described in such intimate detail. Astounded and still skeptical, but slowly, against her will, she became convinced he was telling the truth.

He wasn't mad. He wasn't suffering from delusions. He was exactly what he claimed to be, a man from another time, stranded, incredibly, in her era.

Perhaps a part of her had known from the very beginning, in the jail when he'd first tried to explain about his strange money. She'd seen his watch every day, and refused to acknowledge what it indicated. She'd told herself it was European, because she hadn't wanted to believe him, any more than she wanted to now.

"We were searching for lost gold, Jackson and I." Detail by detail, he went over the incredible events that had brought him to Frank, to 1902—there, to her. He explained again about the Slide, and her blood ran cold. He was talking about the mountain they were sitting on, about the town below them, about the people she knew. He knew the exact date, the hour, and minute when the disaster would occur, and she couldn't disbelieve him any longer.

"We ended up on that small hillside northwest of the town." He made her stand up, and he pointed it out to her. He described how he and Jackson had made their puzzled way down to Frank, into the cafe, and how they'd ended up in jail.

At last there was no more to tell, and he sighed and fell silent.

"What can we do, Tom?" The images he'd drawn in her imagination were vivid and horrible, of the peaceful town below them half-covered by boulders, of bodies strewn across the rocks. She felt sick. "How can we warn everyone without having them think we're lunatics?"

He gave her a tired, knowing smile, and she felt ashamed. That was exactly what she'd almost believed about him—that he was a lunatic.

"I didn't, you know," she said earnestly, touching his arm with her hand. "I didn't believe, Tom, ever, that you were truly demented."

He laughed and shook his head. "Demented," he repeated softly.

"I was frightened," she explained. "You must admit it's a difficult thing to accept, this—this time-travel idea." He'd told her so many things her brain felt close to bursting. "Do you think you'll find a way to go back, Tom?" It was the question she'd wanted to ask during his entire monologue. Her chest felt tight with foreboding as he frowned, staring past her at the doomed town that lay at their feet.

"I don't know." He sighed, and there was such a

wealth of sadness in his tone that she felt like crying.

"I don't know if there is a way to go back. I've thought about it." He laughed, a harsh, unhappy sound. "Those first days here, it was almost all I thought about. I've talked it over with Jackson, and we think our only chance might be on the night of the Slide. Something happened when we were watching that movie that depicted the actual event. Maybe when it really happens next April, some doorway might open and we'll make it back again. It's the only plan either of us can come up with, and it's probably one hell of a long shot."

She swallowed hard, trying to clear the thickness from her throat, trying to sound interested instead of desolate. "Is it so much better then, that—that future world of yours? I mean," she went on hastily, "I understand that everything here must seem strange and—and old-fashioned, as you said. But—but don't you think that perhaps as time goes by, you'll get used to it, Tom?"

She fought the quaver that threatened to reveal her vulnerability. "Don't you think that maybe this place—not Frank, necessarily, but somewhere else, in this era—might become home to you?"

He didn't even wait until she finished speaking before he began to shake his head. "Zelda, I'm flat broke." His voice was harsh and passionate. He dug in his pocket, pulled out his wallet again, and shook out a dollar bill and two dimes. "That's it. That's every cent I have access to here. I detest being poor." There was fury in his voice and passion.

"I hate it more than anything else in the world. I grew up penniless, not even having enough to eat at times, and I've struggled and planned and saved my entire adult life to amass enough money so I'd never be poor again." He smashed his fist down on his own leg, startling her.

"Damn it, back in my own time, I've got bank accounts, investments, real estate. I studied economics. I hired a man to teach me about money markets just so I'd know how to go about investing the money I made. I was fast approaching a time when I'd be free of all financial worries, a time when I could go live in Hawaii, or Palm Beach, or New Zealand—anywhere I wanted. I could work if and when I chose."

His deep blue eyes burned with an almost fanatical light, and the lines in his face deepened. "If I stay here, Zelda, that's all gone. I'd have to start all over again, and from what I can see about this time in history, this place, it's tough even to earn a decent living, never mind amass the kind of money I have." He shook his head. *"Had."*

There was bitterness and infinite despair in his voice. "Zelda, I'm almost forty. I don't know if I'd even have the energy to start all over again. It takes money to make money, and I'm not even earning enough to take you out for a decent dinner."

She looked at him, and she realized he wasn't the man she'd thought she knew at all. With each new revelation, Tom became a stranger all over again. The person she'd wanted to believe was prone to spells of fantasy was instead a man out of his time, from a world far in the future, a world even her rich imagination couldn't begin to grasp. She'd believed him to be as penniless as she was, and instead he'd been wealthy. Their differences were too great for her even to absorb their full import.

Most disturbing of all, he was committed to leaving . . . not just Frank, or these North West Territories, or even Canada. If he could find a way—and it was obvious he would try his level best to find one—Tom would leave her and her entire world behind, entirely and forever, without a moment's hesitation. And he was set on going where she could never follow, even if she wanted to—into the distant and unimaginable future.

She drew her knees up to her chest and hugged them with her arms. Trembling, she tried to absorb everything he'd said, to fit it into the context of her life, her reality, the silly dreams she'd dreamed this past week in spite of her common sense.

"I see," she finally said in a flat tone. "So it's actually about money."

He frowned at her, but he nodded. "Yeah, it is, pretty much. I could live without computers and airplanes. I used them but I never liked them much. I could live without my vintage motorcycles, even though I miss them. But money, Zelda. Money's absolutely essential."

A tight fist squeezed her heart, and for an instant she wished she had enormous riches, more than enough for both of them.

In the next instant, she realized the folly of that. She already knew Tom would never accept money from her, even if she had it to offer. He was far too proud, too independent.

She looked at him, assessing every feature. His black curly hair had grown longer, and it hung down over his forehead, thick and rich. His face was both strong and weathered, each spare, handsome feature clearly drawn. There was an inherent toughness about his looks that spoke of hard living. She watched the play of muscles in his arms and shoulders as he shifted beside her, noted the tall, elegant leanness of his hard body. Yet in spite of everything he'd told her—because of everything he'd told her, perhaps?—she knew she still wanted him to be the one to love her.

But he was getting to his feet, absently brushing off the seat of his pants, reaching down to pull her up as well.

"We'd best be heading back, Zel," he was saying. "It's getting—"

She'd wrestled with Eli enough to have learned a few tricks. She caught him off balance, pulling him back down almost on top of her, their arms and legs in a tangled heap.

"What the—"

She felt ridiculous, shy and silly and absolutely stupid about whatever it was one should do next in the game of seduction, but she was determined. Even before Tom appeared in her life, she'd decided she was not going to go to her grave a virgin, but neither was she going to bed just anyone.

She'd known from the moment he kissed her that this was the man to remedy the situation, and she'd decided that it would happen today, and when she made a decision, she stuck to it. Her skin grew warm and her breath came fast. It was now or never.

She reached up and grasped his head, just behind his ears, and pulled him down until her lips were under his. He'd taught her how to kiss, and she prided herself on being a fast learner. She parted her lips and touched them to his, her tongue outlining the shape of his mouth in exact mimicry of the way his had done.

For a long moment, their mouths joined, but instead of taking control the way she hoped and longed he would do, he raised his head and looked down at her. His forehead was creased in a frown, his dark blue eyes puzzled and somewhat shocked.

Tom, please, please don't say anything. Don't make me say anything—just do whatever it is men and women do. Do it now.

Surely, oh, God, surely this desirable imbecile of a man would realize what she wanted without her having to put it into words?

He'd done everything in his power to drive her away.

He'd told her brutally that he wouldn't be staying, that he didn't even want to stay in her world.

In spite of the fierce response she aroused in him, the slow banked fire that burned between them, he'd believed he was doing the right thing in forcing her to listen, to acknowledge the facts of his presence there. He was doing the only thing that was right by making it painfully clear that there was no future for her with him, that whatever this explosive thing was between them, it would have to go unexplored. Casual sex in this day and age wasn't accepted.

Tom knew that, just as he knew that Zelda was a virgin in an age when virginity was the only option for a respectable young woman.

So why was she teasing him like this? What game was she playing, pulling him down, kissing him, squirming so that the entire length of her tall, slender body pressed against him, and his own hardened painfully in response?

She kissed him again, and it was all he could do to pull away.

"We'd better go easy here . . ." His whisper was rough yet gentle.

She didn't answer. Instead, her arms wound more firmly around his chest and she pulled him even closer.

"Damn it, Zelda, you're playing with fire, a man can only take so much!"

He drew back, scowling at her, and like a thunderbolt, the truth struck him. It was clear by the expression in her eyes, the look on her face, the slight trembling of her arms around him, that she wanted him to go on. Wordlessly, she was asking him to make love to her.

He froze for a long moment. Then he relaxed and gathered her close against him. "Are you absolutely sure, Zelda?" In spite of her body language, he needed the commitment of words, but she still didn't speak. Instead, she nodded shyly and then again with more vigor.

A shudder went through him, and with it came exaltation.

She was asking him for what he'd longed to give from the first moment he'd met her.

"Come here." He sat up, drawing her across his lap. It was his turn to take her head in his hands. Her hair was already tumbling around her ears, and with swift fingers he found the last of the pins that held it and freed them, combing the long, wild mass down around her shoulders. Loose, it reached far down her back, spilling over her shoulders in a thick, curling, fiery mass to cover the white fabric of her blouse.

"Your hair, Zel. You have the most beautiful hair I've ever seen." He threaded his fingers through its silky strands, cupping her head in his palms and drawing her face to his. His lips closed over hers in a lush, deep, luxurious kiss, the sort of kiss he'd ached to share with her. She tasted like sunshine.

Her arms encircled his neck, shy at first, her fingers exploring his shoulders, circling his ears, tangling in his hair.

The luxury of being able to hold her close and kiss her in all the ways he wanted was both heady and agonizing. Sitting on his lap, her warm buttocks pressing against his crotch, she unwittingly made it difficult for him to maintain the control he needed.

With a groan, he once again rolled them to the ground, body to body, mouth to mouth, pinning her half beneath him. He slid his hands from her shoulders slowly down to her breasts, cupping their warm, slight fullness, thrilling to the hard rise of her nipples pressing against his palms through the cloth. Slowly, deliberately, he circled them with his thumb, once, and then again and again, at the same time kissing her with deep, drugging kisses.

She went utterly still in his embrace. Her breath stalled, and when he raised his head, her eyes met his, wide, dark brown pools of wonder. "Oh, Tom," she breathed. "That feels. . . ."

She shuddered in his arms, and he moved to cover her with his body, gently separating her legs with his knee, making a cradle so he could fit himself against her. She groaned as her body bucked against him, innocently demanding what he was so willing to supply—but slowly, he reminded himself.

With trembling hands he tugged her blouse out of the waistband of her skirt, but his fingers were unbelievably clumsy on the tiny buttons that closed it. He managed three, four, six, before she took over the task. In moments the fabric parted, revealing another garment, a snowy-white camisole edged in delicate white lace—and fastened just as securely as her blouse had been down the front, but with even smaller round pearl buttons.

He groaned with frustration, but he valiantly began the task of undoing them. There must have been two dozen or more, and his fingers felt three times too large and unbearably clumsy. He thought ruefully of the single, easy hook he'd become adept at undoing on the bras of his own time.

Once again, Zelda came to his assistance, her quick fingers making short work of the chore. The front of the garment parted, and to his intense relief there was nothing more under it. At last her creamy skin lay bare to his eyes and his touch.

As he'd suspected, she was delicately made, her collarbone fragile, her breasts small but beautifully formed. He leaned over her, supporting himself on his elbow, and beginning at her chin, he trailed his lips over every inch of her neck and shoulders. He took his time, breathing in the delicate, faint perfume that seemed to emanate from her very pores. He could feel her heart hammering against her ribs like a wild thing demanding freedom. Its rhythm increased as his lips nibbled at the tender skin at the side of her small breast and then at last closed over the hard copper-hued nub at its center, suckling, wetting, teasing her nipple to full arousal.

Small sounds escaped her, wordless sounds that signified her pleasure, her surprise, her delight in what he was doing, and they inflamed him. He sat up and undid his shirt, stripping it off and raising her so he could slip it beneath her. Then he gathered her to him once again to revel in the delicious sensation of her soft, smooth skin touching his hair-roughened chest.

"You're strong, Tom." Her hands touched his bare shoulders, stroking, sliding down, exploring him for the first time, coming as far as his belt and scurrying up again, inflaming him.

He slipped his hand down between them, under her skirts to the damply hot fabric of her underwear. He sought the part of her that fit his cupped hand, pressing and rocking against it until her buttocks moved in automatic response.

"Tom . . . oh, my heavens, Tom . . ." Her whisper was full of wonder, choked with the rising passion that made her skin seem to burn beneath his mouth and hands.

After a time he took her hand and guided it down to the front of his jeans, teaching her the shape and hardness of him. He groaned at the pleasure of her warm hand on him.

It was unbearably good, having her touch him. He unzipped his pants, shucking them and his underwear off, and she gasped as her fingers reached out and touched his naked sex. Then, with him guiding her hand, she found again what pleased him.

She learned quickly and all too well.

"Stop, love—stop—" He teetered on a dangerous edge and drew back, holding her hands in his to restrain them, his eyes shut tight. He breathed as if he'd labored long and hard, struggling for control.

"Did I hurt you?" Her agonized whisper brought a tortured smile to his lips, and he shook his head.

"It's just that I want you, Zelda, so much that you're making me crazy."

"Love me, then. Please, teach me how, Tom. It's so awful, not knowing what to do." She drew in a shaky breath and let it go. The utter trust and innocent passion on her face and in her eyes struck at some deep part of him he hadn't known existed until then.

With the last remnants of reason, he whispered, "You could get pregnant. I haven't anything to protect you."

Her eyes met his for an instant, then flickered away, and the rich color in her cheeks deepened. "It's all right, Tom. I've taken care of that. I'd never try to trap you with a child."

He was astounded, then grateful, and all he could think of now was getting the rest of her clothing off. He reached down, searching for the zipper at her skirt waist and encountering buttons. With a maximum amount of fumbling, he managed to undo them and slide the dark garment down her narrow hips and off. Then he searched again, trying to find his way past the intricate closures, the maddening layers of fabric to release everything else underneath.

She wore what he identified as a long, cotton slip, and beneath it her underpants seemed to reach all the way to her knees. She had high-laced boots, and her dark stockings disappeared into the legs of her—bloomers? Knickers? He'd never encountered anything quite like these panties before. He searched for elastic at her waist, and his heart sank when his fingers once again encountered rows and rows of buttons.

He cursed under his breath, and sweat broke out on his forehead. "Sweetheart, you're going to have to help me out here."

She giggled, and with a few deft movements, the problem was solved, the buttons free, her boots and stockings off.

Incredibly relieved, trembling with anticipation and intense desire, he was finally able to slide the remaining garments down her long, shapely legs, and finally, finally she was naked. Long and slender and fragile and so soft, her skin was the color and texture of rich cream, her long red hair a startling contrast to her pale nakedness.

He'd fantasized about her, dreamed about her, thought of her body and how it would look unclothed, and now his eyes devoured her.

"My God, you're so beautiful," he breathed.

She frowned at him. "You don't have to say such things to me, Tom."

He was puzzled. "I can't help saying them. You are beautiful."

Her skin flushed, and the anxiety in her eyes faded a little, and he realized that she was infinitely more responsive, more vulnerable, more insecure, more self-conscious, than he'd ever imagined.

He must be careful, so very careful, not ever to hurt her in any way.

Chapter Twelve

Nothing in her life had prepared Zelda for the sensations that flooded her body as Tom's fingers slid into her most intimate parts and his mouth and tongue danced with her own.

She shivered and her mind filled with color as he kissed and caressed her. At first, through her closed eyelids, she could sense the spring green of the surrounding foliage. But as each breathtaking plateau gave way to another, still higher, color became a vortex that spun and throbbed. Green became yellow, hot orange, and finally, a burning, throbbing red heat that engulfed her.

Her body moved instinctively against him in a rhythm that only increased the agonizing need spreading in a hot liquid wash throughout her abdomen, deep in her belly. She whimpered with frustration and delight.

He slid his hand down between them and a cry escaped her. Her eyes flew open, riveted to his face.

"Go with it, sweetheart," he whispered hoarsely, his blue eyes burning with an intensity that seemed to carve his features sharp and clear and hard. "Let the feeling take you."

His fingers knew exactly where to touch and how to intensify the fever that gripped her, but the pleasure was so intense it bordered on pain. She shook her head from side to side, wanting him to stop, frightened now.

But he refused, and the exquisite sensation grew and grew. Suddenly she writhed against him, and something in her lower body clamped and held, then exploded into an ecstasy that went on and on, bringing a wild, hoarse cry soaring from the depths of her being.

He held her, murmuring words of encouragement and praise. When at last the fierce storm subsided, she felt boneless and weak, overwhelmed.

Before she had time to move or to think, he entered her.

The pain was as intense as the pleasure had been a moment before, and again she cried out, this time in acute distress. Her body bucked against his as she instinctively tried to ease the hurt, and for a moment she fought him. He held her immobile with his weight and strength, gritting his teeth, his elbows planted in the soft earth.

"Ssshhhh, love. Easy, sweetheart. It'll pass. Just relax and in a moment it'll feel better." Droplets of sweat beaded his forehead, and every muscle in his arms and chest was clearly defined as he held himself rigid above her, waiting for the worst of the pain to transform itself into pleasure. He watched her face, looking into her eyes until she felt he could see into her very soul.

When the worst of the burning passed and she felt her muscles relaxing, he began to move within her, slowly at first, and then with increasing intensity. She realized that the incredible sensation she'd experienced before was happening again, deeper and even more pleasurable.

Instinct made her wrap her legs tight around him and thrust up, and within moments, that was his undoing.

He threw his head back and his entire body convulsed. A low, guttural cry ripped from his chest as he spilled his seed within her.

"Do you think ordinary people ever talk about this honestly, Tom? Women to women, men to men?" She was wrapped in his arms, her head cushioned on his shoulder. The fabric of her skirt was drawn over their legs to ward off the coolness of the air now that the sun had disappeared over the top of the mountain.

"They sure do where I come from," he said in a languorous voice, his fingers stroking the bare, silky skin of her upper arm. He knew they should get dressed and go home soon. It was getting chilly. But he was putting it off, drunk with the absolute wonder of having her naked, languid, and satisfied in his arms.

Her response, the depths of her natural passion, fascinated him, and if it hadn't been so late, he'd have made love to her all over again. He'd had his share of women over the years, but he'd never encountered a woman like Zelda, wildly passionate, intuitively sensual, and at the same time so very innocent.

"What exactly do they say about it?" It was a subject she was obviously going to explore in depth, and he grinned again, captivated by her honesty as well as her natural curiosity.

"Oh, everything there is to say, and then some. There's so much talk about sex it'd take all the pleasure and magic away if a person listened long enough," he mused. "But things are different there, too. There's problems that don't exist yet in this era."

He remembered television ads for condoms because of the terrible threat of AIDS that hung over his generation like a modern-day plague. He thought of the epidemic of sex crimes reported on the nightly news with sickening regularity; the sexual innuendoes that were so much a part of everyday conversation; the outright pornography available everywhere; the movies and books and magazines devoted to lewd perversions; and the ad campaigns that used sex to sell everything from cars to cigarettes.

Here, now, there was an innocence that was restful.

"Well," Zelda proclaimed in an aggrieved tone, "no one has ever once hinted to me how absolutely wonderful doing this really feels."

She sounded so offended he laughed out loud.

"The occasional romantic novel skirts around it," she went on, pointedly ignoring his amusement, "but now that I've experienced it firsthand, I feel as though I've been the victim of one more conspiracy aimed at single women. There's obviously a code of silence intended to keep spinsters unsuspecting and stupidly innocent of such pleasure. They must think we'd go berserk and accost innocent men in the streets, for heaven's sake."

"I'm very glad you liked it," he said with heartfelt sincerity. He'd never made love to a virgin before, and the responsibility would have weighed on him if he hadn't been half out of his mind with wanting her.

"Is it always this good, Tom?"

"No." The word burst from him, because it was the truth, but also because it dawned on him all of a sudden what could conceivably happen if he said yes.

Being Zelda, she might just search out someone else to experiment with, and that very thought rocked him to the soles of his bare—and increasingly chilly—feet. "It's hardly ever like this," he hastened to explain. "This is like—" He searched for an analogy, and found the perfect one. "It's like winning the lottery. It probably only happens this way once in, ohh, ten million times. A hundred million," he amended, just to be on the safe side.

"Lottery? I've never heard of this lottery."

Damn. The time difference did make vocabulary tough at times. "It's like betting on a horse race, like—like winning the Kentucky Derby."

"I see." She thought for a moment. "And how many times has it been like this for you then?" The question was posed in the same tone as the rest of her queries, but he understood its import.

"Never, Zelda." Again, it was nothing more or less

than the truth, even though that truth rocked him to the bottom of his soul. He wasn't ready to acknowledge the feelings she stirred in him.

She must have sensed his reluctance, because she was quiet for a long time after that.

"C'mon, Zel, it's time to go." He gave her one last kiss. The short spring afternoon was fast becoming evening.

She began the laborious process of dressing, and after pulling on his own clothing he watched her, marveling all over again at both the complications and the plainness of her underwear. He mentally compared it to the bikini panties and scanty bits of lace that passed for undergarments among the women he'd known. These unadorned white garments weren't revealing in the slightest, but somehow they were far more arousing on Zelda than the most provocative of lacy scraps had been on other women.

Still, he wished he could buy her a stack of that other stuff, just to see her shocked delight. And to watch her model it, of course.

He helped her find the hairpins he'd removed, and again he watched as she used a comb from the camera case on her tangled curls. Then she twisted them into a semblance of a knot and did her best to secure it on the top of her head.

She was an unusual woman. Even now, there was no false modesty, no embarrassment at having him see her perform these intimate tasks. That was amazing, considering her virginity and the social restrictions of the age she lived in.

Zelda was far more honest and open than many of the females he'd made love to in his own time.

She'd certainly been more naturally responsive. She was a deeply passionate woman, and his male pride delighted in the fact that he'd brought her pleasure.

He felt inordinately protective and tender towards her because of it. She was feminine and very lovely, kneeling on the cushion of dried leaves inside the mouth of the tiny cave, struggling with her mass of hair.

"Finding this cave was really good luck," he remarked. "It's really something how we just stumbled on it like that."

She was on her feet now, brushing bits of debris from her wide sleeves and her skirt. In the instant before she bent low to remove something invisible from her hem, he caught a glimpse of the guilty scarlet color that flooded her face, and astonishment made his mouth drop open. He caught her arms and drew her into his embrace, taking her chin in his hand and forcing her to look at him, grinning down at her.

"Zelda Ralston, you devil. You knew exactly where this cave was, and you deliberately led me here, right?" Another thought struck him, just as mind-boggling as the other had been. She'd assured him there was no chance of pregnancy. He had no idea what was in common use, but it sure as hell wasn't birth control pills, so she must have made some very careful preparations before they even left the house.

"You actually *planned* every detail, didn't you? You brought me here deliberately to—to seduce me." It was astounding, considering that she'd never done any such thing before.

It was also funny and very flattering to think that she'd thought this through ahead of time and had prepared so meticulously.

He assumed a wounded expression, pressing his hand to his heart and mimicking the formal speech of the day. "Madam, I'm truly shocked at such wanton behavior. And you a single lady of a certain age, too." He was endlessly amused by her conviction that twenty-eight was the threshold of senility.

He was appalled when her eyes registered hurt and confusion. Her face crumpled and tears slowly began rolling down her cheeks. She swallowed hard and her chin quivered. "Please, please don't make fun of me, Tom," she said, her husky voice fierce, throbbing with emotion. "I can't bear having you think of me as just some—some desperate old—old maid, who'd—who'd throw herself at the first unsuspecting man who came along."

He drew her close, disgusted with himself for hurting her feelings. "Zel, don't cry, I was only joking."

He used his finger to swipe at the tears on her cheek, but she wrenched herself out of his embrace and turned her back on him. Her spine stiff and ramrod straight, her arms were folded protectively across her chest. "I know all too well that I'm not pretty, or dainty, or charming, or—or voluptuous, or any of the things men want in a woman," she pronounced in a matter-of-fact tone that tore at his soul because it spoke of a lifetime of hurting.

"Being unattractive"—her voice quavered a little on the word but she recovered quickly—"doesn't mean I don't still have feelings and"—her self-control wavered again and she gulped audibly—"and—ummm, desires, the same as other women."

She swallowed several times and then turned to face him, her color high, her chin held at that impossible angle he recognized so well.

"I understand that you probably feel alarmed now, afraid that I'll—I'll make further demands on you, but I assure you, Tom Chapman, I won't. I have far too much pride and common sense for that. You're perfectly free and unencumbered, just as you were before any of this occurred."

He wanted to roar with laughter at the utter ridiculousness of her words. He wanted to turn her over his knee and beat some sense into her. Most of all, he wanted to strip her *red* naked and take her again and again until she could no longer question how he felt about her beauty.

Instead, he pulled her roughly into his arms, holding her still when she struggled like a wildcat. She was fierce, this Zelda of his.

"Listen up, lady, and listen good." His voice was gruff with emotion, and he wished with all his heart that he could sing as well as Jackson could.

Well, he'd have to just do his best, and this particular song didn't require a lot of range anyway. Besides, she wouldn't have heard it before, so she couldn't be critical of his rendition.

It wasn't yet written, but was a song that he remembered well. The words had always tugged at some deep, lonely part of him. Until this moment there'd never been anyone to sing them to.

In fair imitation of Joe Cocker, the froggy-voiced artist who'd written and recorded the simple, yet elegant tune, he told her how beautiful she was to him. He sang of hopes, of dreams, of need. He allowed the words to convey all that she meant to him.

He sang from the center of his soul.

She shuddered, then went utterly still as he repeated the words, soft and slow and earnest, taking his time, giving them the intensity he couldn't phrase in his own words. He knew he didn't do justice to the final, quavering high note, but sincerity made up for technique. His voice floated off into the twilight, and when she took his face between her palms and kissed him, her brown eyes were soft with sentiment and he tasted the salt of her tears.

Drying glasses behind the bar, Jackson squinted across the smoky room, his attention captured by the woman in the red dress with the smooth coil of light blond hair. She was standing on the tiny, makeshift stage by the piano, crooning a love ballad in a smoky soprano that impressed him with its range and power.

Her body impressed him, too—at least, the visible upper part did. Her ruby satin dress dipped low over her generous breasts, nipped tight at her waist, then flared into a huge expanse of skirt that made him fantasize about her legs.

Were they long enough to wrap around his waist with some to spare? In this place and time, skirts being what they were, a man could only hope. A leg man in this day and age was a real gambler.

"Who's the babe, Silas?" Jackson refilled the beer glasses from the spout and set them back on the tray for the burly waiter.

"Her name's Leona Day."

"She for hire?" Most of the women who ventured into the saloon were hookers. Nice women didn't frequent bars in 1902, and so far, the not-so-nice had stirred not even a flicker of his interest.

But this one did. He'd plunk down his entire night's earnings for a few hours with Miss Day, Jackson decided.

Silas managed to shoulder the loaded tray and shake his head at the same time. "Leona's no whore. Word is she's private property, keeps company with that old dude over there in the corner." He jerked his chin at a quiet, well-dressed old man with a large moustache, sitting alone and nursing a beer.

Jackson looked again at the singer and reached for a seldom-used bottle under the bar. "When you get back, take her this glass of sherry with my compliments."

Silas grinned, exposing his missing front tooth. "She won't thank you for sherry, Zalco. Leona drinks whisky, neat." He set off to deliver his orders.

When he came back, Jackson substituted a healthy portion of the best Scotch the hotel had to offer and watched as Silas threaded his way across the room and handed it to the lovely woman when her song ended. Silas gestured over at Jackson as she accepted the glass.

She sipped it and nodded acceptance. Jackson bowed theatrically and lifted his hand in a snappy salute.

He couldn't leave the bar just then. But when her next break came, he put Silas in charge and walked to the table where she sat with the old man, still sipping the whisky he'd sent.

Jackson had been fast at learning the rules that governed saloons in 1902. He checked the old geezer for visible side arms. The lady was a looker, but he preferred not to end up with a hole in his skull over a woman. A dude as old as this, sporting a woman like Leona, might prove a little touchy about a younger man sniffing around his lady.

"Evenin', folks," he drawled with a disarming smile. "I'm Jackson Zalco, your friendly bartender. Just wanted to compliment you on your singin', ma'am."

The old man half rose in a courtly gesture, a friendly smile on his narrow, weathered face. He held out a hand and Jackson shook it.

"George Edwards. Pleased to make your acquaintance, son." His voice was soft, mellow, and polite. "Sit a spell, why don't you? This young lady is Miss Leona Day."

"Thank you. I'd appreciate a seat for a minute or two." Jackson straddled the chair closest to Leona, breathing in a whiff of the spicy perfume that clung to her like a magical cloud in the midst of the smoke and the smell of beer. Up close she was even lovelier than she'd seemed from a distance.

"This is only my second Saturday workin' the bar in this place. It's pretty busy for a little town like Frank. You sing here often, Miss Day?"

"Whenever I'm invited," she said with a tiny smile.

Hot damn, she was beautiful. Ravishing. Her eyes were huge, an honest-to-God cornflower blue, and she had the most flawless peachy skin Jackson had ever seen. Her mouth had the swollen, pouty look actresses in his own time paid big money and underwent silicone injections to achieve, and her jawline was both strong and lovely, her chin cleft in the center just the way his own was.

He figured it looked one hell of a lot better on her.

She was assessing him openly, her eyes taking in his long, thick club of blond hair, tied back as usual with a leather lace. He knew the snowy-white shirt and bow tie suited him.

"You new in town, Mr. Zalco?"

"Call me Jackson, ma'am, please. Me and my partner got here a couple weeks ago."

"Planning to stay?" She raised the glass again and swallowed. Her neck was long and graceful, and her full breasts swelled out of the rich satin of her dress.

Jackson's hands ached to cup them. It was a damned good thing he was sitting down. Just being near her brought an uncomfortable fullness to his groin, and his trousers were snug to begin with.

"Yes, ma'am, we're here for a while. About a year, I reckon."

He and Tom both figured there might be an outside chance they'd get hurtled back to their own time next April when the Slide came down. Spending the next eleven months in Frank seemed like a life sentence in purgatory. Now, smiling across at Miss Leona Day, Jackson actually thought there might be a little ray of light in the darkness of those months.

"Where you folks from?" Jackson had learned it was better to get others talking about their backgrounds than to have to make up lies about his own.

"Back East," Edwards said vaguely. "No special place. We travel around a fair bit. You?"

"New Mexico, but not for some time," Jackson replied, equally evasive. "Same as you, we travel a fair bit, me and my partner. His name's Tom Chapman."

"He here tonight?" Edwards scanned the room. He was sitting with his back to the wall, in a location that allowed him to keep an eye on everyone in the room.

"Tom's not much for drinkin'," Jackson explained. "Specially lately," he added half to himself. Zelda and her demon rum.

He saw Silas signaling frantically from behind the bar, and reluctantly got to his feet. "Guess I'd better get back to work. It's been a pleasure meetin' you, Mr. Edwards, Miss Day."

He stretched out his hand to her and she laid her long-fingered palm against his for an instant, then withdrew it. The skin contact sent a ripple of awareness up Jackson's arm, and when he met her blue gaze, he saw a reflection of the same banked fires that burned inside of him.

Leona Day sang another two sets before the bar closed. After the final song, George Edwards escorted her out, tipping his hat to Jackson as they passed the bar. Leona nodded in his direction without meeting Jackson's eyes.

"She left this here note fer you, Zalco. Guess you made an impression," Silas said, smirking a few moments later after he'd cleared the table where Edwards had been sitting.

Jackson snatched the folded scrap of paper and opened it.

"Room 210, when you're free tonight," was printed neatly, along with a scrawled "LD."

* * *

Part of Jackson's job was to help Silas clean up after the bar closed. The job had never been done with such speed or reckless abandon, and as he worked Jackson's brain feverishly went over the ramifications of the invitation.

Was it some kind of after-hours party? Would Edwards be present, or—please, Lord—would Leona Day be all alone when he got there? If so, was there danger of a shoot-out at sunrise with the older man should matters progress the way Jackson prayed they might?

Getting shot after a night with Leona Day might just be worth it, all things considered.

At last he climbed the stairs, cursing his aching leg. He went to his own cubbyhole of a room and scrubbed away the smell of beer and tobacco that clung to him. Then, amused by his own nervousness, he tapped softly on the designated door.

It opened and she was there, wearing a soft blue robe, her fair hair loose and tied back with a silk scarf.

"Jackson Zalco, how nice of you to drop by," she said in her throaty voice, just as if it was the middle of the afternoon instead of two in the morning. "Come in." She stood aside so that he could pass.

The room was large, much larger than the cramped, austere closet upstairs that Jackson had been given as part of his job, and Jackson saw at once, with an enormous sense of relief, that there was no sign of Edwards.

As far as he could tell, there was no indication that a man lived there at all. This was getting better by the second.

An ornate sofa and two armchairs were grouped at one end of the rectangular room, and Leona had made the area distinctly her own by putting framed pictures and an assortment of perfume bottles on the low, round table between the chairs. She'd draped a pretty scarf across the top of the window and covered the bed with a pink satin comforter. Her voluminous, jewel-colored dresses spilled out of the wooden armoire and also from a huge, open trunk in the far corner. The air was filled with her perfume, the spicy, faintly oriental fragrance that Jackson had detected in the bar.

"Sit down, why don't you." She'd locked the door, and now she gestured at the sofa. "I have whisky, if you'd like a drink?"

"I'll pass, thanks. Nothin' like bartendin' to put a man off good liquor," he said easily, sitting where she'd indicated.

She seemed entirely at ease, drifting over to the armchair and sinking down into it. Her feet were bare, small, narrow feet, and she tucked them up underneath her. Jackson glimpsed delicate ankles, slender calves.

Wordlessly, she picked a flat silver cigarette case from the low table beside her, snapped it open, and held it out to him.

He shook his head. "Gave that up, too, a couple years ago now. A young fellow Tom and I knew died of cancer, so we both swore off the butts after that."

She frowned, obviously puzzled, and he silently berated himself. Like a million other things in 1902, no one had yet made any connection between cigarettes and cancer. She closed the case without taking one herself and laid it back on the table.

"Well, I'm afraid I can't offer you tea and biscuits," she said with a mischievous twinkle in her blue eyes.

"I've had enough tea to last me a lifetime."

Jackson had never been long on subtlety. He felt it wasted a whole hell of a lot of valuable time. He lounged back on the stiff, uncomfortable sofa and rested one booted foot on the other knee, making up his mind that it was time to separate the bull from the buckwheat. The night wasn't getting any younger.

"So, Leona, what's the drill with you and this George Edwards?" he drawled. "Because I have to tell you my intentions toward you aren't strictly honorable, ma'am."

She tipped back her head and laughed, a musical peal that brought an answering smile to Jackson's lips. "I'd have been very disappointed if they were."

"And you and Edwards?" In spite of the jolt of delight her answer gave him, he was well aware that she hadn't answered his question.

"Friends. Long-time, close friends."

He lifted his eyebrow. "Can't be that long a time. Seems to me you're a considerable bit younger than Mr. Edwards."

She nodded. "He's fifty-two, I'm twenty-four," she said without a trace of coyness.

Jackson was momentarily taken aback. He'd thought, by her sophisticated manner more than anything else, that she was older.

"And you're just friends?"

She raised an eyebrow and gave him a level look. "That's what I said, isn't it?"

He should have left it at that, because whatever

else there was between her and Edwards wasn't a damn bit of his business. But already an intensity crackled between them, incredible because Jackson hadn't even touched more than the palm of her hand.

Yet something primitive and male and possessive in him drove him to ask. "You sleepin' with him, Leona?" He was taking a big chance here. She could get huffy and kick his ass right out the door, exactly what he deserved.

Instead, a slow smile curved her lips and her long eyelashes dropped halfway down her eyes. She shook her head from side to side. "No, Mr. Nosey Zalco," she purred in that lazy, sexy voice. "I'm considering sleeping with you, though why I should I don't know, rude as you are."

His relief was so intense he didn't move for a long moment, but then he did and she was in his arms.

Chapter Thirteen

It was the fourth week of May. Tom had been in Frank exactly a month, and he had the sick and certain feeling that some vindictive, powerful god had taken an active dislike to him.

The construction job had ended abruptly, and he had tramped the entire town searching for work and had failed to find any. Penniless, he had no choice but to accept when word had come of an opening at the mine.

This morning, with his canvas lunch bag and tin water bottle over his shoulder, Tom joined the quiet, sleepy cluster of men beginning to assemble on the main street.

They were the early-morning shift at the coal mine, and it was still black dark, an hour before dawn. The air was cold and crisp; it would be hours yet before the sun cleared the top of the Turtle. Tom and his fellow workers wouldn't see it; by the time their shift ended, the sun would have slipped back behind the mountain.

Ironically, his few weeks of underground mining years before had qualified as experience, and today would mark the end of his first week as a pick and shovel laborer underground.

Tom had to draw deep on steely reserves to quell the disgust and horror that threatened to overcome him each time he faced the fact that at least for the foreseeable future, he was an underground coal miner again—with the certain knowledge that in less than a year, the mine would be buried beneath tons of rock, trapping men inside its depths.

When the crew were all accounted for, the foreman, Smiley Williams, led the way across the bridge that spanned the Crowsnest River and up the gentle slope to the mine entrance. Smiley was a sandy-haired veteran miner from Wales.

At the office near the entrance, Tom handed the small brass disc, called a check, to the lampman. It bore his payroll number and was hung on a large board with the others from his shift. The checks were an indication of how many men were underground, and their identities. If an accident occurred inside the mine, the checks were a way of knowing how many men were either safe, or trapped, or dead.

In exchange for the check, Tom was issued a kerosene lamp which he hung on the front of his belt. Some of the men, working in places where odorless methane gas was a danger, were also issued live canaries in cages. The canaries chirped and sang, but they were highly susceptible to the deadly gas.

If the bird suddenly fell over, the miners ran pell-mell for clean air, snatching the cage as they went.

Tom had learned that many of the softhearted miners, inordinately fond of their little birds, carried turkey basters of clean outside air in their back pockets and successfully resuscitated their canaries.

"You makin' out okay, Tom?" Smiley was beside him as they entered the mine shaft. In Tom's mind, the one slight consolation about this mine was that it was worked by the room and pillar system at near-ground level, so there was no need to drop hundreds of feet in a cage to reach the coal face.

"Fine, Smiley. And you?"

"Can't complain. When a man's got a good steady job, a strong back, and a stout roof over 'is head, 'ee's a lucky man." It was Smiley's standard answer. "I'm putting you on steady with Augusto Rossi and Joe Petsuko, lad. They're Eyeties, good men to work with. They don't talk the language so good, but who does, hereabouts? Young Percy Adams was their partner till yesterday, but he quit. Said they were working fools, and he couldn't keep up with 'em. Lazy, was our Percy. But you're not, you'll do fine."

His lamp lit, Tom walked rapidly along the uneven surface of the main tunnel to reach the chamber where Smiley had indicated he and his partners would be working. Within moments, sunlight and fresh air might never have existed.

The interior of the mine was both familiar and horrifying to Tom, like a recurring nightmare that had surfaced years after he'd believed it gone forever. The ceiling near the entrance was seven or eight feet, shored up at regular intervals by immense wooden beams, but the side tunnels were often so low a man had to walk bent double—and walking was something a miner did a lot of. These mine owners had never heard of traveling time. Tom was paid only for the number of cars he managed to fill each day. A miner walked in and out on his own time.

Water dripped onto Tom's head and shoulders from the roof and trickled incessantly down the walls. An endless stream ran alongside the tracks where pit ponies hauled coal cars along the rails to the surface, one sturdy little beast for every five loaded cars. Most of them were blind from having spent their lives in the underground darkness.

It was that darkness that Tom hated the most. Palpable and thick, it hovered at the edges of his feeble light and seemed to weigh him down with its density. Without the foul-smelling kerosene mine lamp, he, too, would be totally blind.

Outside, the air had been frosty, but there in the bowels of the mountain the temperature was always constant. The seasoned miners liked it—cool in summer, warmer in winter. Many worked yearround shirtless, sweat and greasy coal dust mingling on their brawny chests, never completely washed away. By the end of his shift, Tom's eyes, ears, nose, mouth, and fingernails would all be rimmed with the oily-tasting grit, and he'd reek of kerosene from his lantern.

"Ciao," a gruff voice greeted him when he finally reached his destination. "I am Augusto Rossi."

Tom's lamp revealed a burly man with a huge handlebar moustache, twinkling dark eyes, and a wide, white grin. "You are Tomas, huh? Smiley, he say you are coming." He stuck out a hand, hard as iron, and shook Tom's with great enthusiasm. Another man materialized out of the blackness, and Augusto clapped him on the shoulder. "This my good friend, Joe Petsuko. Torro, we call him. He is strong like a bull."

Again Tom's hand was shaken, and another set of white teeth flashed. Joe was short, but his muscles bulged like a wrestler's.

The three of them climbed up the wooden ladder to reach the workings at the coal face. Within a short distance of one another, they began hacking at the coal seam with picks, breaking away chunks and sending them down the chute into the waiting coal cars below.

The Italians were cheerful and noisy, breaking into song at frequent intervals, calling back and forth in their native language. The drudgery was interrupted only by Torro casually warning the others to move away because he was setting a small dynamite blast to loosen the seam of coal.

Long before the dust had settled, Tom's partners were back at work. He joined them, although visions of black lung danced in his head as the insidious dust entered his chest with every indrawn breath. He thought of Virgil; Zelda had confided to him what the doctor had told her about her father's lungs.

At noon, they took a short lunch break. Joe and Torro did their best to include him in their conversation, asking about his wife and family. Tom explained that he was single, boarding with the Ralstons. Both Joe and Torro knew Virgil, and they clucked their tongues and shook their heads at the news of his illness.

"The mine, she gets us all in the end, one way or the other," they agreed with fatalistic aplomb.

Soon, they lapsed into Italian, and Tom chewed and swallowed the egg sandwiches Zelda had packed, methodically discarding the small black portion his fingers touched, watching the rats claim it almost before it settled.

He still had four hours and thirty-five minutes to spend in Hades today.

"So how's school going, Eli?"

Mindful of his promise to Virgil that he'd do his best to talk to the boy, Tom was helping clean out the stables that Saturday evening.

Brilliant opener to a real conversation, Chapman, he chided himself, using the shovel to scrape away the last of the muck.

Eli shrugged. "All right, I guess." He sluiced a bucket of water over the boards. "Did you have to go to school when you were young, Tom? Dad didn't have to. He got to go to work when he was only nine. How old were you when you started working?"

"I was fifteen. I had no choice in the matter. My stepfather didn't believe much in education."

"Were you ever lucky." Eli hefted the wheelbarrow of dirty straw and wheeled it out to the compost. When he came back in, he remarked, "They take you in the mines when you're fifteen, and I'm nearly sixteen already." He shot Tom a conspiratorial look. "Don't let on to Zel, but I already been working up there some, mostly in the stables taking care of the pit ponies."

"Oh, yeah? I thought you were still delivering groceries after school," Tom said.

Eli shook his head. "I quit that dumb job a couple weeks ago. I can make more up at the mine. I got a chance to work every afternoon if I want on the picking table."

The picking table, Tom knew, was a shaking and constantly moving platform where the shale was hand-picked from the coal. The job was mind-deadening, standing over a conveyor belt hour after hour as the lumps passed by slowly.

He carefully masked the alarm he felt. "You want that job, Eli? It's pretty boring."

"Yeah, I want it." His response was fervent. "It's only a starter job. Pretty soon I'll get a chance to go underground same as you and earn big money."

Tom thought of the pitifully small paycheck he'd draw at the end of the week and wondered how in hell he could make the boy understand that the mine was the last place he should be considering.

"Why not stay in school awhile longer? You might get to like it better as you go along."

"I hate it." Eli's voice was vehement. "I hate every single minute."

Tom understood, because he felt exactly that way about the mine. But he was hopelessly out of his depth when it came to giving advice. "Maybe you oughta talk to your sister about it."

Eli snorted. "You ever try to tell her somethin' she don't want to hear?"

Tom remembered trying to tell her about where he was from, and he felt a swift pang of sympathy.

"I need to make money, Tom. See, I asked the doctor about my Dad," Eli said in a subdued tone. "Zel won't give me the straight facts. She thinks I'm still a little kid." There was frustration and anger in his voice now. "Doc Malcolmson says my dad shouldn't go back underground. He's not supposed to go back to work at all for at least a couple more weeks, till he gets over this bad spell with his chest. But Dad told me he's starting back next Monday, come hell or high water. I know it's because there's no money in the house." Eli shook his head. "We need what I could make real bad, but when I try to talk to Zel about it, she won't even listen."

He shot a sideways glance at Tom. "Maybe you could sort of just mention it to her, not about going underground or anything, just about me working after school on the picking tables?"

Alarm bells went off in Tom's head. He was getting involved in family affairs, and he didn't want to. "That's not such a hot idea, Eli. You oughta tell her yourself."

"Ah, it's hopeless even to try. All I said to her once was that Jackson never went to university and he made out just fine, and she went insane. But she likes you a whole lot more than she liked Jackson. She'd listen if you told her you didn't get any fancy university education, either. She'd see that you turned out all right without it, right, Tom?"

Wrong, wrong, wrong, Tom wanted to say.

Damn it all. Living with the Ralstons got more complicated by the day, bringing up issues that never seemed to have an easy solution. This one with Eli, for example. He understood all too well how the boy felt. Tom wished to God he could ease the financial strain on the family. And he knew how adamant Zelda was about the boy's education. She was right, too. Being a miner sure as hell wasn't what Eli should aim for, but it was the job Virgil had done all his life, and Eli worshiped his father.

Tom forked fresh hay into the stall. He hated messes like this. He'd spent most of his adult life avoiding them, but living with the Ralstons seemed to shove him into one right after the other.

"Please, please, will you have a word with Zel for me, Tom?" Eli was mixing a handful of oats into the horse's feed, and he looked up at Tom with abject pleading on his freckled young face.

Tom cursed under his breath and compromised. "If you do your best in school, no more skipping out, I'll try to get Zelda to agree to this job after school at the picking tables."

"Hooray. Thanks, Tom." Eli's grin revealed teeth still too big for his mouth.

"And I have your word about not dodging school?"

The boy grimaced, but he nodded. "If I get on the picking tables, I can work Saturdays. That'll help."

Eli went off to feed the chickens, and Tom climbed into the loft to fork down more hay. He looked over at the area where he and Jackson had slept weeks before, the place where now he and Zelda came to make love when the rest of the household was sleeping—the place where they'd be together just a few short hours from now.

The thought of her in his arms brought a deep, burning ache of pure desire. Zelda had taken to lovemaking with all the zest and enthusiasm of her exuberant nature. In his arms, she was passionate and free and inventive, a wild and totally natural lover, and Tom found it impossible to get her out of his mind when he was away from her.

But it wasn't only their lovemaking that he enjoyed.

Zelda was insatiably curious, and now that she had accepted the facts of his background, she had wanted to know everything he could tell her about the future. She had quizzed him until he was exhausted about politics, video cameras, birth control, education, social programs, women's rights. She had wanted to know about movies and the way they were made, books that had been written in his era, the kind of jobs women held. She had asked about family life and how it had changed between her time and his, highly annoyed with him when he had admitted, honest if slightly ashamed, that because of the lifestyle he'd led, there was little he could tell her about families.

Then she had got on women's fashions, and he had been at least able to invent what he wasn't all that certain about. He had enjoyed the combination of horror and fascination on her face when he had described bikini bathing suits and miniskirts and panty hose and thong workout gear.

Feeling wicked, he'd gone into detail over all the improvements in women's lingerie, which turned out to be a big mistake because it had brought on a lengthy inquisition about how he'd come to be on such familiar terms with such intimate items.

She exasperated and totally frustrated him at times because she had a decided opinion on everything, and just as Eli had said, there was no changing her mind once she made it up. She was both stubborn and single-minded.

She made him laugh, but she also made him think, which made her different from any other woman he'd known.

He'd almost forgotten that she also had one hell of a temper, but he was reminded when she unleashed it on him several hours after his conversation with Eli.

They'd made love in the loft, hot, greedy, violent. She'd discovered she liked being on top, and she'd ridden him with delicious abandon before collapsing boneless on his chest.

"Oh, that was wonderful. Do you think anyone heard us, Tom?"

He grinned into the darkness. He'd developed a habit of clamping either his hand or his mouth over her lips to muffle her cries. She asked the same question each time, and he gave the same answer.

"Not a soul. We hardly made a sound."

"I'd be mortified if Dad or Eli heard."

"They're both sound asleep." But the mention of Eli's name reminded Tom of his promise to the boy. Surely this was as good a time as any to make good on it.

"Eli mentioned he has a chance at a job on the picking tables at the mine," he began in a conversational tone.

Her whole body stiffened. "I hope you told him that any such thing is absolutely out of the question. I won't have him anywhere near that mine."

He wrapped his arms a bit tighter around her, stroking her back and trying hard to find the right words. "It's just after school, Zel. He can make a lot more than he ever did delivering groceries. He wants the job pretty bad. I told him I'd talk to you about it."

She rolled off him and was on her feet as quick as a scalded cat. "You should have known I'd never agree. You know how I feel about his education. He'd be too worn-out even to study after working up there."

Tom sat up. "He promised that if he got the job, he'd do his best at school."

She was shaking her head as she pulled on her clothing. "I hate the mine. Look what mining's done to my father. I want a better life for Eli, you know that."

Tom tried to reason with her. "He's not quitting school. All he wants to do is earn some money in his spare time and the mine's the only place a young man can do that around here. Cut him some slack, Zelda."

"He's not working on the picking tables, and that's final." She shoved her feet into her shoes and Tom could hear her fumbling with the laces. "I can't believe you'd encourage him. You've said often enough how much you hate the mines."

"I do." Tom kept his voice low, even. "But I'm not Eli; and neither are you, Zelda. Quit trying to live the kid's life for him."

He heard her draw in a breath and hold it for a long moment before she released it. "I hardly think you're well qualified to give me advice about *my* brother, Tom Chapman."

Her scornful words were like a blow to the solar plexus, immobilizing him. He heard her fumble her way to the ladder and climb down swiftly.

He heard the back door of the house open and softly close.

She was absolutely right, of course. He'd deserted his own brothers. What the hell made him think he had the right to make a single suggestion to Zelda about hers?

It seemed that Eli hadn't relied totally on Tom in this battle of wills with his sister, however. Directly after breakfast the following morning, Virgil took his cup of tea and his daughter into the front parlor and closed the door.

Tom and Eli washed the dishes in silence, both uncomfortably aware of the heated, husky sound of Zelda's voice and the quiet, low rumble of Virgil's. They were out in the yard, tossing the softball back and forth, when Zelda appeared.

Red flags burned on her cheeks, and her back was ramrod straight. She marched over to Eli. "Dad and I have agreed that you may accept the job, but if your schoolwork suffers, that will be the end of it, young man."

Eli whooped and threw his arms around her. Zelda hugged him back, and her eyes met Tom's over the boy's shoulder.

"I'm sorry." As usual, her apology wasn't easily made.

The night before her words had stung him deeply, but the hurt faded when he saw the tears shimmering in her brown eyes.

She'd been forced to compromise her ideals, and he knew all too well how that felt. She was doing it as gracefully as she could.

He smiled at her. "C'mon, Eli. Let's see if we can

teach your poor sister to throw a softball properly. Girls aren't born knowing how, like men are."

And, of course, that incendiary remark dried her tears on the spot, just as he'd planned it would.

June brought sunny, hot weather, and on the second Sunday of the month, Zelda bullied the entire household into working in the yard. Eli, pretending to complain but actually enjoying himself, slopped a fresh coat of whitewash on the fence and the outhouse.

Her father cleared away the undergrowth from the lilacs at the back of the yard, and Tom was on his hands and knees helping her weed the garden.

Never having gardened before, he expressed astonishment at the way the weeds grew far faster than the young plants.

"It's a conspiracy. We probably were meant to eat the damned weeds all along. Why else would nature do this to us?" he complained, and Zelda laughed at his nonsense, her hair tucked under the battered straw sunhat. She'd tucked her skirt up and was kneeling on an old sack, vigorously clearing weeds away from her cabbages when Jackson's cheerful voice sounded from the corner of the house.

"Hey, there, y'all look real industrious. Makes me feel downright lazy."

Zelda scrambled to her feet and tugged her skirts down, swiping at rebellious curls of hair that stuck to her forehead under the hat's brim before she realized just how filthy her hands were. She'd had gloves on, but she'd tossed them off, sensuously enjoying the feel of the rich, warm dirt on her skin.

Now she wished fervently that she'd kept them

on. Holding on to Jackson's arm was one of the prettiest, daintiest women Zelda had ever seen, and she felt a total frump in comparison.

Jackson introduced each of them, and Zelda forced a welcoming smile. "How do you do, Miss Day?" She tried to wipe some of the dirt from her hands and succeeded only in leaving ugly black streaks down the sturdy apron she'd tied on to protect her brown work skirt.

"Do call me Leona." She smiled a dazzling smile. She was wearing an impossibly chic little hat on her smooth golden hair. She had on a dainty white-sprigged dress with immense sleeves trimmed in fine lace. Zelda noted that the lace also edged her neckline, which was low enough to reveal a lush bosom. A delicate cameo on a fine gold chain clung to the base of her shapely throat. She had a soft blue shawl over her shoulders that Zelda identified as cashmere.

The dress, Zelda decided, was cut quite daringly low, taking full advantage of a spectacular bosom. The hand that held the shawl was as soft and white as a child's, without a single one of the chemical stains from developing fluid that constantly marred Zelda's hands. The nails were unbroken perfect ovals, without a trace of grime.

Zelda had the absurd urge to hide her hands behind her back, just the way little Eddy did when Isabella asked if he'd washed before dinner.

At that moment, Zelda happened to look at her father. He was standing almost shoulder to shoulder with Eli and Tom, and to a man, they were staring at Leona as if they were under some sort of spell.

They looked for all the world like dumbstruck sheep, and Zelda decided on the spot that she thoroughly detested Miss Leona Day. It was just like that rogue of a Jackson Zalco to admire a woman like this and bring her here.

"It's fine of you to come visit, Jackson." Virgil was beaming. He loved company. "How about we all go inside and have a cup of tea and a bite of lunch? It's getting around that time of day, ain't it, Zelda?"

Furious, she shot him a look. Now she was trapped. They'd stay all afternoon, and she and Tom would miss their walk up to the little cave. She'd have to make polite conversation with a woman she knew would have baked alaska instead of a brain.

Chapter Fourteen

It was impossible to look the way Leona Day did and be intelligent, Zelda concluded, pressing her lips together to stop herself from saying something unforgivably rude.

"I'll just go in and clean myself up a little and put the kettle on," she managed to say while looking daggers at Virgil.

Of course, he didn't even notice. He was too busy asking Jackson about his job at the hotel and shooting admiring glances at Miss Day.

"I'll come with you," Leona said with a fetching smile. "I can help with the tea."

That was the last thing Zelda wanted. "Oh, that won't be necessary, I can manage fine." All she needed, Zelda decided petulantly, was Leona around while she scrubbed dirt off her face and hands.

"But I'd like to help. Please allow me."

Zelda gritted her teeth and led the way into the house.

Of course the fire in the cookstove was almost out. So before anything else it had to be built up again, which involved kindling and blocks of coal and still more dirt on her hands and arms.

And the kitchen was an absolute mess. Zelda had forgotten that in her eagerness to get outside she'd told Eli just to soak the porridge pot instead of scrubbing it. The kitchen table wasn't cleaned off, either. There were still dirty cups and the sticky jam pot sitting there. Well, things couldn't get much worse, Zelda thought morosely.

"You go ahead and wash up. I'll tidy this away." Without a thought for her dainty dress, Leona tucked up her lace-trimmed sleeves and began scrubbing the sticky pot. "I've never been in one of these houses before. They're really comfortable, aren't they?"

Feeling like a commoner being patronized by a queen, Zelda didn't bother to answer. Instead, she whipped off her hat and sloshed water in the basin, using a cloth and soap to lather her face. She couldn't get all the dirt out from under her nails, and when she looked in the wavy mirror, her skin was flaming pink with sunburn. Her freckles had popped out like the weeds in the garden, and her impossible hair was every which way. Horribly conscious of Leona's perfect grooming as well as her scrutiny, Zelda used her brush with savage zeal and shoved pins in at random.

"I do so love your hair. I always wanted uncontrollable curls like those." Leona had conquered the pot, rinsed and dried it, and was now clearing off the table. "Even a curling iron won't make a dent in mine. It's straight as a poker."

Zelda glanced at the golden mass, smoothly coiled and perfect under the absurd little hat, and she wanted to snort. She didn't need this woman's pity, she concluded in a huff, refilling the kettle and setting it on to heat. She'd been about to excuse herself and change into her good blue dress. Now she decided stubbornly that what she had on would do just fine. Nothing she owned would stand up against Leona's costume anyway.

"Jackson told me you were a photographer, and of course I noticed your sign out front." There was something that might have been admiration in Leona's voice. "I wonder if you'd show me some of your work?"

It wasn't what Zelda had expected. She eyed Leona suspiciously. "Are you interested in studying photography, Miss Day?"

"Leona, please. And, no, I don't know the first thing about photography, but I am interested in having some pictures made for publicity purposes. I'm a singer, you see." Her voice took on a steely, determined tone. "I'm going to become the most sought after singer around, and photographs are the way to publicize oneself. I did talk to another photographer, a Mr. Beaseley, but the man absolutely set my teeth on edge." She shuddered. "He's a smarmy little weasel. I couldn't bear the thought of being in the same room with him long enough to have him take my photograph."

In spite of herself, Zelda had to giggle. Weasel was the perfect word for William Beaseley, all right.

"Do you sing opera?" Zelda knew very little about music, real music, anyway. She'd grown up listening to Virgil play the mouth organ, and before Jackson moved to the hotel, he'd entertained them several times with his unusual songs. He'd invited Zelda to join in on the chorus, but she'd realized years ago that she couldn't carry a tune to save her soul.

"Gracious no, never opera. That's much too highbrow for me. I never really had any training," Leona confessed without a trace of regret. "I'm the lowbrow dance-hall type, saloons and that sort of thing, lots of volume and innuendo." She winked.

Zelda was fascinated. "I'd love to hear you sing. Do you perform at concerts?"

Leona shook her head. "Not so far. I'm afraid I'm not considered very respectable, you see. I sing in the bar at the Imperial most Saturdays, and there's several dance halls in Lethbridge and Macleod that hire me three or four times each year."

She wrinkled her elegant nose and shrugged. "Not cultivated, but my audience is usually appreciative once I get their attention. And the work pays well." Her grin was wide and wicked. "Drunken men tend to be amazingly generous with tips."

Zelda swallowed. "Do you—I mean, isn't it—dangerous, being a woman, alone in such places?"

Leona nodded. "It likely would be without a gentleman friend on hand. Mine is known to be something of a sharpshooter, and we pretend that I'm his lady."

Zelda struggled not to look shocked, and again Leona grinned. "George is like a father to me, but the illusion works well. When I travel to other towns to sing, he either accompanies me or else sends one of his friends to protect me." She dimpled and blushed. "Now, of course, Jackson is there most of the time, and no one, no matter how inebriated, would dare challenge Jackson."

Zelda was captivated. Apart from handing out temperance pamphlets in front of drinking establishments, she'd never really set foot in a saloon. Secretly she'd always wanted to, just to see what it was like. A dozen questions popped into her mind, none of them polite enough to voice.

As if she'd read her mind, Leona volunteered answers to several without Zelda saying a word.

"Of course, I'm still sometimes mistaken for a saloon girl, which can be quite tiresome—"

Zelda silently substituted "prostitute" for the more polite terminology and stifled a gasp.

"—and actually, I get to know most of the working girls."

Zelda, not to be outdone, confided, "I've met several saloon women myself. They were not at all what I'd imagined."

Leona nodded. "Don't you find that people seldom are, once you get to know them? Several of the women from the Tenderloin have become my good friends, in fact." Leona looked straight into Zelda's eyes. "I suppose that offends you, Miss Ralston?"

There was a definite challenge in her voice, one that Zelda knew well; it was the same tone she herself used when, as Virgil described it, she climbed on her soapbox.

"Not in the slightest." She emptied the teapot and generously spooned in fresh from the tin of good English tea she saved for very special occasions. "I try my best not to be a moral bigot. As far as I can see, we women have enough to contend with in life without being critical and judging one another."

She was honest enough to feel embarrassed now at her own hasty judgment of Leona. "Back East, I participated in a campaign sponsored by the Women's League to save the Fallen Angels. That's what they were called there," Zelda explained. "The whole thing was a resounding failure."

"They didn't want to be saved, I suppose?" Leona looked amused.

"Absolutely not," Zelda confirmed. "One of them, a young woman about my age, explained exactly why, in graphic terms that I'll never forget. Her name was Rosie O'Dale, and she said—" On an impulse, Zelda tilted her head back, put her hand on her hip, and assumed Rosie's disdainful, nasal tones. " 'Now why would I wanna be like any of you respectable women? Everythin' belongs to your husbands. You ain't got a penny to call yer own, and you're called upon to give away fer free what I get paid good fer—nine chances outa ten, to that same man you cook and clean and kowtow to. At least I got a decent bank account to call my own.' "

Leona tipped her head back and laughed, clapping her hands in appreciation of Zelda's performance. "You've missed your calling. You belong on the stage, Miss Ralston."

Zelda flushed with pleasure. "Please, call me Zelda."

"If you call me Leona."

They grinned at each other.

"Rosie was absolutely right, you know," Leona

continued. "Wives often do have the worst of it. My friends have plenty of time to themselves. They can sit around and read, or tend a garden, or keep chickens if they want, or sew, or make fancy cookies. But they don't have to do any of those things, the way they would if they were married. And they can afford to dress in the finest of clothes. Still, according to them, a great many saloon girls choose to get married anyway. They want a husband and children, a family."

Zelda shook her head. "It gives one pause for thought, doesn't it? In our soul, we females are all the same. I suppose we're all just searching for love." She spread a fresh cloth on the table and sliced bread.

"I couldn't agree more. If you ask me, I think married women ought to be petitioning for some of the same rights prostitutes have, particularly bank accounts of their own and control of their money. Unfortunately, that's not a universal concept at the moment. Where do you keep the cutlery?" Leona was setting the table as if she'd done it many times before.

"You know, I was terribly nervous when Jackson suggested we come here today. As you can well imagine, I've had my difficulties with respectable women who don't approve of my choice of career or my ideas." She laid knives and forks and spoons carefully beside the plates and centered a dish of bread and butter pickles Zelda had set down.

"Jackson told me you were a woman well ahead of your time, Zelda, and that we'd get along, but you know how men are, they have no real idea of what we women really think. I suppose I was deliberately trying to shock you just now, to see how you'd react." She wrinkled her nose and dimpled. "I'm sorry."

Zelda met Leona's blue gaze and after a moment they giggled.

"It's exactly what I do myself," Zelda confessed. "In fact, I do it all the time, saying things to shock people. I think that for once, Jackson was absolutely right. We're going to get along fine." She tipped her head to one side and gave Leona a long, assessing look. "You know, I can't wait to take your photograph. I think it would be quite impossible to take a bad likeness of you. I have some new portrait techniques I've been dying to try, and you'd be a perfect subject."

"Oh, goodie." Like a child, Leona clapped her hands. "I can't wait. Could I come tomorrow at ten, or is that too soon? And I have several friends who desperately want their portraits done as well—my friends, the saloon girls. Are you interested, or shall I tell them you're fully booked?"

"Not at all. I'm sure I can fit them in." Zelda would happily photograph the women stark naked if they so desired—although she'd charge them extra, of course. She'd just make certain they came while Eli was at school, Virgil was asleep, and Tom was safely at work.

A shiver ran down her back. Lord, it actually sounded as if she might begin earning some money at her craft.

The June day suddenly seemed glorious as Zelda went to the door and called the men in for lunch.

* * *

In spite of her assurances to Leona, Zelda was distinctly ill at ease the following week when three exotic creatures of the night appeared at her studio door.

"Miss Ralston?" One of the three addressed her nervously. "My name's Billie Morton. Miss Day said you were expecting us this afternoon?"

At the gate, a closed carriage pulled away.

"Of course. Come right in." Zelda smiled a welcome, careful to hide any signs of her own apprehension.

She felt downright dowdy in her plain dark skirt and white shirtwaist, inexperienced with her single foray into the intimate rites between male and female, and terrified that she'd inadvertently insult these women. She desperately needed their business.

Their dresses were as demure as those she and her neighbors might wear to church. But the fabrics were obviously expensive, silk and satin whispering softly, feathers and ribbons on chic bonnets drifting in the breeze.

Zelda stood to one side so the fashionably clad trio could get past her, and the flower-garden scent of their expensive perfume filled her nostrils.

Once inside, the spokeswoman introduced the others. "This here's Ethel Parker, and this is May Howard."

"Call me Zelda, please." She shook hands, her photographer's eye assessing each, admiring Ethel's high cheekbones and exotic good looks. Billie was short and plump, wildly freckled, with a topknot of curly ginger hair peeping from under her elaborate bonnet. May was tiny, with birdlike features, darting black eyes and a fluttery manner. It dawned on Zelda that all three were just as nervous and ill at ease as she was.

"Please, sit down." She gestured at the ornate sofa she used as a prop. "Why don't I make a pot of tea? Then we can have a chat about the kind of photographs you want."

They perched together on the very edge of the sofa, for all the world like schoolgirls confronting the head mistress, and when she returned with the tea tray five minutes later, they hadn't moved an inch.

"Now." Zelda poured, added sugar, cream or lemon, and offered the scones Virgil had baked. "Leona wanted some studies that are rather exotic." Zelda showed them a few of the photos she'd already developed from her sessions with her new friend earlier that week. "And also some that are very casual."

Leona had been a natural at posing for the camera. She'd had no qualms when Zelda suggested they try a few of the unusual posing techniques Tom had described as being popular in his time, photographs that had none of the studied and formal composition that was popular in 1902, but were rather whimsical and relaxed.

"You're sure us coming here in broad daylight won't hurt your business none?" Billie frowned over her teacup. "Your reg'lar customers might not like it much, Miss Zelda. See, we don't want to spoil your trade, we told Leona—Miss Day—that we could come in off hours, in the early morning, say, or on Sunday. Nights ain't too good fer us, though."

These were businesswomen. On an impulse,

Zelda decided to be frank with them, more open than she'd been even with Leona.

"To tell the truth, my business is practically nonexistent," she admitted. "I'm a good photographer, but I have a habit of speaking my mind. I've even been arrested for it, which doesn't sit well with many of Frank's citizens. They prefer Mr. Beaseley." She looked up and met three pairs of sympathetic eyes. "I'm very grateful for your business. I could hardly sleep last night, worrying that I might offend you in some way." She gave a rueful grin. "My tongue can be my worst enemy. Dad says it flaps before my brain engages, and I never know what's going to come out my mouth next."

Instantly, the atmosphere in the room changed. Zelda could see shoulders relax, stiff backs slump a little, faces lose their polite masks, and honest smiles blossom.

Billie actually reached over and patted Zelda's arm. "Good grief, don't you worry none about us. We was the ones worryin', right, girls?"

There was a chorus of assent. "See, Miss Zelda, most decent folks wouldn't want us in their houses," May chirped. "So we was real nervous, comin' over here today."

"Imagine folks goin' to that worm of a Beaseley instead of having you take their photograph. Why, he traded some of us, promisin' us pictures, then went back on his word." Ethel's sloe eyes snapped with outrage, and the others nodded.

The mental image of skinny, bespectacled William Beaseley buck naked and engaged in the act of trading services with these ladies popped into Zelda's mind and wouldn't be dislodged. Did he leave his glasses on? Did his already protruding eyes bug out even more when. . . .

Zelda choked on her tea, sprayed it over her chin, fumbled for her handkerchief, and giggled helplessly.

"I—a mental vision—Beaseley—without his clothing—"

She couldn't continue, but they had imaginations every bit as vivid as hers and probably a lot more graphic. All of them chortled, whooping, each adding an indecent comment or two that set them all off again.

When they finally all regained their composure, the last barrier was gone.

After that, the session was a delight. It turned out that Ethel, May, and Billie were unanimous in wanting the most formal and prim of portraits made, their bonnets firmly in place, their gloves on, their faces regal and unsmiling, their knees pressed together under layers of petticoats.

Of course Zelda didn't ask who the portraits were meant for. Perhaps the women wanted them just for themselves, but by the time the session was over, she felt she'd made three more friends.

They paid in cash, and each of them added a generous tip, the first tips Zelda had ever earned at her craft.

Within the space of a few weeks, the photography business became not exactly busy, but certainly vastly improved over what it had been. For the first time since their move to Frank, Zelda earned a sizeable chunk of money to help pay the bills that had mounted steadily during Virgil's illness, and it was entirely attributable to Leona Day and the saloon girls.

"I'm so grateful to Jackson for introducing me to Leona, Tom. I've never had a close woman friend until now." She sighed blissfully. "I think I'd be entirely content for the first time in my entire life if only Dad would get feeling better."

They were on their way to what had become their favorite spot, the small cave on the lower side of Turtle Mountain. It was a hot, sultry evening in mid-July, and they walked along hand in hand, stopping now and again for a tantalizing kiss.

"He's still coughing half the night," Zelda added, "and he looks thinner than he was before, don't you think so?"

Now that the evenings were longer, they walked up the mountain whenever Tom's shifts permitted—which didn't seem half often to either of them. The mine was working three shifts, and on the afternoon or night portion of his rotation, their time alone together was limited.

He felt a surge of impatient desire for her. Instead of diminishing, his need for Zelda seemed to grow as the weeks passed, and his ties to the entire Ralston family deepened.

"Tom?" Her voice brought him out of his reverie. "What do you think about Dad? Do you think he's getting better, or not?"

Tom, too, was concerned about Virgil, but he didn't want to alarm Zelda any more than she was already.

"I'm sure this hot weather will help his chest," Tom reassured her. Privately, he thought the older man seemed to be slowly losing strength instead of gaining it. Eli had noticed, too, that his father couldn't manage the strenuous chores that he'd been accustomed to doing a short time before. Between them, Tom and Eli had quietly divided up the heavier work.

They'd reached the cave, and Zelda retrieved the old blanket she'd hidden inside and spread it out for them.

Unable to control the raging desire he felt for her, Tom drew her down to the ground, locking her in his arms, his lips taking hers.

She returned his kisses, giving him all of her response, showing him how much she wanted him.

Feverishly, he stripped off his own clothes, then began the task of undressing her. He was getting much more adept with the endless rows of tiny buttons, but Zelda, too, was impatient. She undid the final tedious row that held her pants, and laughed softly at his groan of relief when he was at last able to tug the garment down and off her legs.

"It seems such a long time," he whispered, trailing kisses down her neck, allowing his hands to wander intimately over her breasts and belly. In reality, it had been only four days, but even a single day without the delight of loving her now seemed an eternity to him.

"For me, too." She gasped and arched as his fingers slid down and touched the hard nub between her legs.

It was like setting a match to kindling. She writhed and opened for him, and his sanity fled as he entered her.

* * *

They calmed slowly, their bodies still trembling with the aftershocks of ecstasy. He rolled so she was resting on top of him, her hair spilling in wild glory across his chest.

"Tom, do you think Leona and Jackson ever . . ." Her voice trailed off.

"Ever what?" Tom teased her, pretending not to understand what she meant, trailing his hand across her narrow back and down over her buttocks, loving the feel of her satiny skin under his calloused hand.

"Don't be obtuse. It doesn't become you. Do you think they're—intimate, in this way?"

He laughed, amused at how primly she managed to phrase it. "I think there's a pretty fair chance, all right." In fact, he'd stake his life on it. He'd seen the hot glances that passed between those two, and he knew his partner's appetites.

"Did Jackson have a great many women before?"

Tom thought he had some idea where this was heading, and it might be wise to proceed with caution. "I wouldn't say a great many, no." It was a lie, but what the hell. The truth wouldn't serve any purpose, and it could get both him and Jackson into hot water.

"Was there ever anyone he thought of marrying?"

She'd never asked him that about himself. "Not that I know of."

"Why not, do you think?"

It was a tough question, because it wasn't just Jackson she was asking about. Although she hadn't said so, the issue had to do with him as well, and Tom knew it.

"Partly the way we lived, Zelda, the job we had.

We didn't stay in any one place very long, so it was hard to get to know anyone well enough."

He knew her well, though, and he knew she wouldn't settle for such a superficial answer, so he struggled to put the rest of it into words. "The way he grew up has a lot to do with it, too, I guess. Jackson came from Portland, Oregon, a big city on the West coast. His parents didn't take care of their kids, so he was put in one foster home after the other. He was a wild boy, and he got into lots of trouble. He always says if he hadn't joined the army, he probably would have ended up in jail. Settling down with a wife and kids just isn't in his nature, I guess."

Tom tensed. Of course the next question would have to be whether or not it was in his, either, but as usual, she surprised him.

She changed the subject.

Chapter Fifteen

"Is that where you met Jackson? In the army?"

Tom nodded. "We ended up in a branch of the forces called Army Intelligence. We worked well together, and we were sent on special assignments. We got to be close friends."

"I remember the first day we met in the police barracks," she went on. "Jackson said you'd had a head injury during some war. Was that true?"

"In a way." Since coming here, he hadn't even thought of the political intrigues that went on in his own time, and now it was hard even to remember why they'd seemed so important. "It wasn't a war, exactly. It was a mess that a bunch of stupid politicians got us into. Jackson and I were sent there to try to free a political prisoner, but it turned out he was already dead. We got caught in a place where we had no right to be, and the guards fired at us. Jackson got hit in the thigh, and a bullet grazed my skull. We managed to escape, but we both spent quite a while in the hospital, and that's when we decided it was time to leave the army."

She shuddered. "Many of the soldiers who fought in the War between the States have emigrated to Canada, and the tales they tell of war are horrifying. I do hope there won't be any more wars, Tom, at least for a long time. I don't know how I'd bear it if Eli went off to fight some ridiculous battle."

An icy shiver traveled through Tom as he thought of the world wars that would come in only a few short years. He'd avoided telling Zelda about such things, and he wouldn't tell her now. There were times when knowing what the future held was a terrific, terrible burden.

He wrapped his arms even tighter around her and closed his eyes. It felt so good just to hold her, to lose himself in loving her so that memory disappeared, and there was nothing except the urgency of the here and now. In another moment, he'd roll her beneath him and start all over again.

"Eli can quit this awful job he has at the mine now that I'm earning money with my photography," Zelda declared, and Tom abandoned his fantasies abruptly.

The subject of Eli was still a touchy one between them. He considered what she'd just said, and then sighed and shook his head. He just couldn't stay out of it, no matter how he tried.

"Have you talked to him about it, Zelda?"

"Not yet. I wanted to discuss it with you first." She moved away from him, rolling to the side and sitting up. "You will help me convince Eli that he should quit, won't you, Tom?" She frowned down at him. "In spite of what he promised, his grades are slipping. He's simply too tired to study the way he needs to. He has to have top marks if he's to qualify for a scholarship."

Eli had confided to Tom while they were chopping and stacking wood the previous day that he was going to ask to work extra hours at the picking tables, to buy himself a bike.

"I'm not getting in the middle of any more of these discussions between you and Eli," Tom declared now. "I understand what you want for him, but the fact is, he has to want it, too. You can't tell a boy his age what to do."

Zelda scowled at him and pulled on her pantaloons, then her chemise. "But you know better than anyone how dreadful it is to work underground. I'm so afraid he'll decide that's what he should do. If you just talked to him. . . ."

Tom, too, drew on his underwear and then his jeans. "I've told Eli how I feel about the mine, but he's not me, Zelda. He's soon going to be a man, with a man's choices to make. You might not agree with what he does in his life, but part of growing up is learning to make your own choices."

She pulled on her skirt and tugged her light cotton dress over her head. "Then you refuse to say anything to him about this?"

Tom looked at her, taking in the stubborn set of her chin, the rebellious expression in her brown eyes. "Yes, Zel, I do."

"I'd have thought for my sake you might have agreed." The snippy tone of her voice warned Tom that she was angry. "My goodness, Eli hangs on every word you say. You're his hero. I thought you'd understand how important it is to me that he doesn't ruin his entire life this way."

Something snapped in him. "For God's sake, Zelda, don't go putting the responsibility for your brother's life on my shoulders." The web that had drawn so subtly around him, the whole issue of the place he'd unwittingly assumed in the Ralston family unit, suddenly weighed like chain mail on Tom. He'd fallen into a role he'd never had any intentions of playing, with an unspoken projection of permanence that terrified him. The memory of his small stepbrothers and how irrevocably he'd failed them flashed into his mind.

"I've never once said I'm going to be around forever," he went on, his tone harsh. "If things go the way I plan, I'll be leaving next April. You know that, Zelda. It's wrong to begin relying on me to guide Eli, because when the opportunity presents itself, I'm going back to my own time." Even as he spoke the words, he knew that the entire conversation had somehow been leading up to this moment.

"And what if you can't get back there?" Her husky voice was polite and impersonal, as if she were asking a question of a stranger. "What if you find you're stuck here? What will you do then?"

He and Jackson had discussed that very thing the last time they'd seen each other. "Whatever happens, I'm not staying in Frank, Zelda." His words were deliberately harsh. "I'll probably get back into the business I was in before. Even in this day and age, there's treasure waiting to be found."

"With Jackson?"

"Yeah, with Jackson." Tom wondered why the

plan that had sounded so promising suddenly left him feeling bereft. "Of course with Jackson. He's my partner."

"Of course." She'd drawn on her stockings and fastened them, and now she finished tying the laces on her boots, her skirts still above her knees. She looked flushed and rumpled and sexy as hell. Regret filled him for moments of lovemaking lost in controversy.

"Well, we'd best be getting back. Dad will be wondering where I am and what I'm doing."

Tom doubted that. He suspected that Virgil knew exactly what they were doing when they disappeared like this.

Tom had wrestled with the morals of the situation, wondering if there was something he ought to say to Virgil. He'd never made love to the daughter of a friend before, and he had no guidelines for it. In the final analysis, he'd decided there was really nothing he could say.

Neither did there seem to be anything more to say to Zelda, and their trip back down the mountain was long and painfully silent.

Calling on every ounce of self-control she possessed, Zelda managed to get through the rest of the evening, until she could at last climb the stairs to her attic room.

Once there, she threw herself on her bed and buried her face in the feather pillow before she allowed the tearing sobs that she'd held at bay for what seemed an eternity finally to escape.

She wanted Tom. She wanted him physically with a need so great it stunned her, but she also wanted more. She wanted to spend more than these few stolen hours in his arms. She wanted to wake up beside him in the morning, to bear his children, to grow old alongside of him. God help her, she'd done exactly what she'd vowed not to do.

In spite of all her resolutions to the contrary, Zelda realized that she'd fallen in love with Tom Chapman. She was embarrassed and ashamed of herself for backing him into a corner the way she had, but she couldn't help herself. Some demon insisted that if she pushed hard enough, he'd admit that he loved her, too, that he wanted nothing more than to spend his life with her.

You are such a fool, Griselda Ralston. Just like he said, he's never misled you. You knew from the beginning that he was planning to leave. So why does it tear you apart now to hear him reaffirm it?

It was just before noon the following day when the mine whistles blew the special signal that meant there'd been an accident at the mine.

Zelda was in her cellar darkroom, enlarging the negatives from a set of photographs she'd taken the week before, and at the first ominous whistle, her heart seemed to stop beating.

Virgil, against the doctor's orders and Zelda's frantic protests, had returned to the mine, but he was on the night shift and still asleep upstairs.

Tom.

Tom was in the mine right now. She'd watched from the tiny window in her attic room as he had left for work in the early dawn, his canvas lunch bag over his shoulder. He'd sensed her eyes on him and had turned to give her a jaunty wave, their quarrel forgotten.

God, oh, please, God, no, not Tom. Terror held her immobile.

"Zelda? Zel, where are you, lass?" Virgil's urgent voice broke the spell. She dropped the negatives she still clutched and raced up the narrow stairs to the kitchen where Virgil, clothing tugged on any which way, was already shoving his feet into boots. "Trouble up at the mine," he said. Their eyes met, and in her father's blue gaze Zelda saw a reflection of her own fear.

"C'mon, lass, let's see what's going on."

Out on the street, it seemed as if the entire town was running, just as they were, for the mine entrance. White-faced women, their aprons still on, carried babies over their shoulders and dragged toddlers along by the arm. Men like Virgil who'd been sleeping after their night shift came staggering out of their houses, wild-eyed and rumpled. In everyone's faces Zelda read the same awful dread that made her heart hammer and her lungs feel as if she couldn't draw enough breath.

There was already a sizeable crowd gathered near the mine entrance, and it was impossible to sort out fact from fiction.

There'd been a cave-in, some said, or an explosion, no one knew for sure which. Miners were trapped. No one could say how many. Estimates ranged from four to two dozen. A rescue team had been sent in, but so far no one had come back out.

All that they could do was wait and pray.

* * *

Tom was working alone on a coal face inside a narrow, low-ceilinged tunnel. There was barely room to swing his pick, and for some time he'd been working on his knees, wearing kneepads he'd devised for the purpose. Sweat trickled down his forehead, and he stopped once to tie a bandanna around his head to keep it from running into his eyes.

His partners, Joe and Augusto—Torro—had proven to be fine men to work with. They were inordinately proud of their ability to mine more coal in one shift than most other miners could in two, and Tom had earned their respect by working just as hard as either of them.

Just now they were in a larger chamber some distance away. They'd set a dynamite blast a short while before. Tom could hear them joshing one another in their native Italian. At intervals, Torro would break into song, his rich tenor echoing eerily through the caverns of the mine. Often they'd laugh uproariously at a shared joke.

They were easy men to get along with, always good-natured. They'd labeled him Tomasso, generously offering delicacies their wives had baked, always politely speaking English when he was nearby. But Tom was well aware of the powerful and private bond that existed between the two of them, a bond not only of language, but of deep comradeship. He understood, because it was the same bond he had shared with Jackson.

There in the bowels of the mine, he missed Jackson badly. The dirty, mind-numbing labor would have somehow been easier if Jackson shared it, but, of course, he didn't wish his friend were there. He wouldn't wish this job on his worst enemy.

Tom raised the pick and took another vicious swing at the coal face, bringing a satisfying amount of black boulders raining down around him. Like the rest of the miners, he'd developed a sense for what were the natural sounds of the mine: the groaning of timbers; the routine series of whistles and warning sounds that accompanied the blasting that loosened the coal so it could be worked; the rumble of the coal cars along the tracks; the welcome echo of the voices of his fellow miners; and the continual, maddening trickle of water.

When the rumbling began, it came more as a sensation than a sound, a peculiar tingling in his hands and feet, and Tom stopped in mid-swing, alert and alarmed by the feeling. In another second, it escalated into a roar, and pieces of coal began to tumble down all around him. The floor shook and the walls of the cavern seemed to vibrate. Mercifully, his lamp stayed lit, and after an endless moment, the noise stopped abruptly.

Tom, his hands trembling and every cell in his body anticipating the entire low roof tumbling down on him any second, dropped his pick. He began to scrabble toward the main tunnel that would give him access to the chamber where his partners were.

"Joe? Torro?" Tom hollered as loud as he could. He listened, but there was no response.

In another minute, he reached the larger opening of the tunnel. Normally, he could have stood upright there, but the roof and floor had mysteriously become closer together. The timbers that supported the roof groaned and cracked ominously as he moved along, crablike, to the mouth of the larger chamber where his partners had been.

His feeble light barely penetrated the dimness, but it was immediately evident that a large portion of the roof had caved in.

Unspeakable horror filled him. Dust rose in a choking cloud, and even as he crouched there, another one of the timbers crumbled and toppled, releasing a small landslide of debris into the already-littered area.

"Joe? Where the hell are you?" His lamp wasn't bright enough to reveal the entire chamber, and at first, he couldn't find any sign of either of the men. Horror and slippery fear twisted in his gut, and his first instinct was towards survival.

Run! Run, toward the daylight, the fresh air. . . .

Instead, he crawled into the scant four feet of space that was all that was left between the collapsed roof and the jumble of coal and rock. "Joe? Torro?"

This time, a muffled groan came, and Tom scrabbled toward the sound. Joe lay trapped beneath a timber, half-buried in chunks of coal. He turned an agonized face toward Tom's light.

Tom put his shoulder to the timber, straining with every ounce of muscle in his body to move it, but it didn't budge an inch.

"Leave me, leave me. Go to Torro. He's buried under there—" Joe's eyes indicated a pile of rubble some yards away. "He can't breathe under there."

Tom crawled over frantically. Augusto's arm and one shoulder were above the rock, but the rest of him was buried. Tom had barely begun to free him when another tremor shook the rocks beneath him, and like an accordion, the distance between floor and roof lessened once again.

Joe began to pray in Italian, and Tom cursed in a steady stream, more frightened than he'd ever been. He fully expected the narrow passageway to close completely, trapping them all forever beneath tons of rock. But after an endless moment, the mountain seemed to stabilize once more.

On all fours with his back pressed against the roof, Tom dug as he'd never dug before. Throwing debris aside, he freed Augusto's head and shoulders, frantically trying to ascertain whether the other man was breathing.

He wasn't.

With a last, herculean effort, Tom managed to get him entirely out from under the rock. Cramped in the narrow space, he clumsily turned Augusto from his stomach onto his back, clearing his mouth, checking for a pulse.

None. No sign of life. His forearm was obviously broken, and beneath the coal dust, his face was already purple. As well as he could in the limited space, Tom began the Cardio Pulmonary Resuscitation techniques he'd been taught in the armed forces. Breathing into Augusto's mouth, pressing on his chest, he counted one, two, three, four. Augusto's mouth tasted of garlic and coal dust.

Breathe, damn you, breathe—five, six . . . you're strong like a bull, Torro, now breathe . . . You've got four little kids at home, you have to breathe—breathe. Press, three, four, five. Tom kept hitting his head on the roof, feeling the coal dust filter down his neck and back, into his eyes, his nostrils, and throat.

Dimly, he heard the welcome sound of other miners' voices, and he was aware that several men had crawled into the chamber and were frantically heaving at the timber that held Joe pinned. There was noise, a lot of it, wood cracking, men swearing and panting, "He's free, careful now, drag him out—"

"Gotta get out, she's gonna go again—"

Two men crawled over and said something to him, but Tom couldn't answer. He was blowing his very life into Augusto's inert body.

He could hear Joe frantically calling Augusto's name, and then the sound gradually faded, and the men beside him scuttled away.

Tom maintained the rhythm, breathing, counting out loud, "Three, four, five, six. . . ."

"Leave off, lad, he's dead. We've got to get out of here. The roof's going any second!" Close at his elbow, Tom heard the Welsh voice of Smiley Williams, filled with urgency, but he was so intent on what he was doing he couldn't answer.

"Tom, lad, he's a goner I say. Leave off now. We've got to get out of here quick. No telling when she'll go again—"

Smiley's hand was on his arm, trying to pull him away, but Tom shrugged him off, leaning over to cup Augusto's cheeks and breathe into his lungs.

All of a sudden, Augusto's limp body jerked spasmodically, and he drew in a ragged breath and then another, and moaned. Sweat was dripping off Tom, oozing from every pore. He was panting as if he'd run a marathon, and he knew he was grinning like a fool.

"Son of a gun, he's breathing, Smiley. Torro's

breathing. Let's get him out of here. His arm's broken. I'll try to steady it. See if you can get hold of his belt."

Hauling Augusto's inert body between them, they somehow wormed their way backwards to the opening where others were waiting, eager to help.

The small group of men had barely gotten Augusto's inert form out of the area when an ominous rumble sounded and the floor beneath their feet shook.

They cursed and scrambled along as fast as they could. When at last they felt relatively safe, Smiley gasped, "That'll be the rest of the roof comin' loose back there. We made it just in time. You don't half-cut things tight, do you, Tom, lad?"

Smiley's white teeth glimmered in a smile, and he shook his head. "Never saw the likes of that before. I've seen dead men, but I never saw one come back to life the way this one did."

When they reached the main tunnel, Tom used his own belt to stabilize Augusto's broken arm. He watched as the man was loaded on a stretcher and covered with a blanket, then placed on a coal car. The pit pony started off at a trot. A few hundred yards down the main tunnel Doctor Malcolmson was waiting with his medical bag ready.

"Doc, you tell that tough Eytie he's got Tom Chapman to thank when he comes around," Smiley declared in a loud voice. "Tom here put his mouth right over Augusto's and breathed into him, and damned if he didn't come back from the dead. Never saw the likes of it."

"What exactly happened?" The rotund doctor was

puffing to keep up with the mine car and the stretcher.

"He stopped breathing for a time. There was no pulse," Tom reported. "I performed CPR and he's breathing again, but I have no idea how long it was before respiration began. It seemed an eternity. He may well have brain damage."

"You a medical man, son?"

The doctor's light shone full into Tom's face and he shook his head. "No, I just have basic first-aid training."

"Whatever you did undoubtedly saved this man's life. Very commendable."

Together, the band of miners and the group of rescuers who'd come into the mine made their way quickly to the entrance. They faltered a moment when they caught sight of the crowd assembled behind a barricade the North West Mounted police had erected.

A huge cheer went up, and weeping women broke through the barricade and came running to embrace their black-faced men.

The sunlight blinded Tom. He turned his face up to it. He'd never realized before that sunlight had a taste, the delicious taste of freedom. He stopped and drew in a deep draught of fresh air and coughed up coal dust from deep in his lungs. He was shivering in the aftermath of the accident, relieved beyond belief to be out of the mountain.

He skirted the family groups, making his way to the lamphouse to turn in his light and collect his check.

"Tom. Oh, Tom, thank God you're all right." Zelda took him by surprise, catapulting into his arms with such force he staggered backwards several steps. Tom's filthy arms closed around her, and he could feel her thin body trembling.

Close behind her was Virgil, his craggy face split into a grin. "Had a bit of excitement under there, did ya?" He clapped a scarred hand on Tom's shoulder, his fingers digging in. "Glad you're out safe, son." There were tears in his blue eyes, and Zelda was weeping openly.

"Give me your lamp. I'll turn it in for you." Virgil reached over Zelda's shoulder and deftly unhooked the contraption, bearing it proudly toward the lampman's shack.

Zelda's arms were tight around his neck.

For the first time in his life, Tom knew what it felt to be part of a family, and the feeling brought a suspicious tightness to his chest. He had to swallow hard against the hot wash of tears that threatened. He cleared his throat and smiled down at Zelda, holding her a little away from him, aware all of a sudden how filthy he was.

"Hey, Zel, you're getting your pretty dress all dirty." Tom tipped her face up with his blackened fingers, leaving dirt marks on her chin. "C'mon now, what're you crying about? It was nothing at all, just a little bump."

Tears were streaming down her cheeks, and she sniffed and swiped at them with the back of her hand, giving him a ferocious look. "Don't you lie to me, Tom. I've been around mines all my life. I heard what the other miners on your shift said. You stayed behind to help Mr. Rossi, and the roof very nearly caved in on you. They're all saying you're a hero, but I think you're nothing but a—a damned pigheaded fool. You might have died in there."

He'd never heard her swear before.

She wrapped her arms around his waist, oblivious to the oily coal dirt that had already imbedded itself on her dress and her skin, oblivious as well to the smiling glances of neighbors who were watching.

She looked up at him, tears still pouring down her cheeks, her brown eyes locked on his. "I'm so glad you're safe, because I love you, Tom Chapman," she said in a fierce voice.

Chapter Sixteen

Tom and Zelda walked to the hospital that evening.

Tom was concerned about Augusto Rossi, plagued by visions of a coma or severe brain damage from the time the man had spent unconscious.

The hospital was small, and as they approached the men's ward, he could hear a number of voices, male and female, rising and falling in a jumble of excited Italian and English.

Hesitantly, not knowing what to expect, he entered the small ward with Zelda, who clutched the bouquet of roses she'd cut from Virgil's bushes.

Augusto and Joe were in adjoining beds, but it was impossible to catch more than a glimpse of either man. They were surrounded by visitors, and there were garden flowers, bottles of wine, and baskets of food strewn everywhere.

Joe had a gauze bandage covering one eye and a

sling on his arm. But he waved his free hand exuberantly when he spotted Tom and said something emphatic in quick Italian.

Everyone turned around and stared at him and Zelda. Then a plump and very pretty young woman, barely five feet tall and obviously very pregnant, leapt up from her seat beside Augusto and came bustling over.

"Tomasso!" She flung her arms around his waist, drawing his head down so that she could plant a smacking kiss on each of his cheeks. "I am Maria Rossi," she announced, holding his hands in each of hers and gazing up at him with dark, soulful eyes. "Never can I thank you enough for what you did for my Augusto." She turned to Zelda with a warm smile. "You are Mrs. Tomasso?"

Zelda blushed and shook her head. Mrs. Rossi looked from Zelda to him and drew her own conclusions. "Ahhhhh, soon, soon. What is your name?"

Zelda told her and Maria took one of Zelda's hands and one of his, drawing them over to the assembly.

"Come, come, meet everyone."

Instantly, they were surrounded. It seemed that half the miners in town were gathered around the two beds. They were introduced, and everyone soon sorted out who Zelda was. Many of them knew Virgil, and because Frank was a small town, they'd undoubtedly heard of Zelda's exploits, but, of course, no one mentioned them. Tom noticed, however, that she attracted a few long, curious looks.

To Tom's immense relief, Augusto was awake. He had a badly broken arm, cracked ribs, and bruises to every square inch of his body, but he seemed to have suffered no mental problems from the accident.

Pale beneath the coal dirt the nurses hadn't been able to remove completely, he was also groggy from the drugs the doctor had administered. He didn't remember anything except the first rumble and fall of rock, but Joe and the other miners had told him in great detail what had occurred. He reached out a shaky hand and shook Tom's, his strong face solemn.

"You breathe your life into me, Tomasso, now forever we are brothers," he said in a weak voice, and everyone around the bed nodded and made sounds of agreement and approval.

Tom was embarrassed. He was also touched by the solemn proclamation.

Joe had a bandage half-covering his head, and his eyes were swollen and blackened from a broken nose, but he, too, had survived without serious injury. He introduced his wife, a tall, stately woman with an engaging smile and light brown hair. She, too, was pregnant. Her name was Sofia.

Chairs were found for Tom and Zelda, and in spite of their protests, they were seated like royalty between the two beds.

Glasses appeared from the depths of a handbag and wine was poured for everyone, including Joe and Augusto. Some people left and others arrived, and the events of the day were told and retold with increasing emotion.

The nursing sister, a tiny bird of a woman named Mary Nettles, came in several times and sternly reprimanded everyone for the noise while pretending not to see the wine. She was offered delicate pastries from a basket lined in a white napkin.

In quick succession, Tom and Zelda were invited to a christening, a picnic, and a communal dinner to celebrate the arrival of someone's father and mother from Italy. It was impossible not to accept. The way the invitations were phrased, it would have seemed both rude and arrogant. They were urged to bring Virgil and Eli, and when someone remarked that Zelda had a photographic studio, great excitement ensued. She had to bring her camera with her to all the events and take pictures, everyone agreed.

The gathering had reached a noisy climax when at last Nurse Nettles came in again and, in a tone that brooked no argument, ordered everyone to leave.

Outside in the warm summer twilight, Tom and Zelda strolled home, still surrounded by a group of new found friends, some of whom also lived in the rows of miners' cottages on Alberta Avenue.

Cheerful voices called good night. Zelda was quiet as they rounded the corner and went up the back steps. Tom stopped her before she opened the door, gathering her into his arms, giving her the deep, lingering kiss he hungered for. He was exhausted, both emotionally and physically, but he wanted her with an urgency he couldn't contain.

Her lips parted for him, and she returned the kiss with all the intensity of her being.

"As soon as Eli's asleep, I'll meet you in the barn," she whispered. Virgil had gone to work that night, the way miners always did after an accident.

Tom spent the waiting time doing small chores—

pumping water at the well, filling the animals' troughs, chopping extra kindling for the fires, carrying in buckets of coal for the kitchen stove.

Next door, Isabella and Lars were sitting on the back steps, enjoying the evening's coolness after the heat of the day. Tom could hear the cadence of their voices as he worked.

Isabella giggled, and Tom smiled. It was a pleasure to hear her laugh in such a lighthearted fashion.

Silence fell and Tom glanced over at them, just in time to see their shapes silhouetted against the screen door of the lamplit kitchen. Isabella was locked in Lars's embrace. His head was bent, kissing her. After a long moment, they went inside, Lars's arm tight around Isabella's shoulders. The lamp went out.

After the initial shock of surprise, the knowledge that Lars and Isabella cared for each other made Tom feel good. But after a moment he frowned, thinking of Nestor Vandusen. Would the miserable little ass reappear or was he gone for good?

For everyone's sake, it would be best if Nestor was permanently AWOL. Isabella and the kids were happier than they'd ever been with him around, and if she and Lars could make a life together, so much the better.

Tom felt protective toward them. They were good friends.

He seemed to have a lot of good friends here in Frank, he mused. Isabella had come flying over to welcome him home when he got back from the mine today, relief and concern for him overcoming her usual shyness, and Lars had hurried over as well when he got home from work, pounding Tom's shoulder exuberantly, exclaiming how good it was he was safe.

Jackson had arrived at the same time, lightheartedly joshing Tom about being a hero. He'd gripped Tom's forearm hard when he was leaving. "Damned if you don't scare the living daylights out of me with capers like this one, old buddy," he'd drawled, and Tom had seen the barely masked fear in his eyes. "Don't do this to me again. I've gotten far too used to havin' you around, you ornery cuss."

Tom pumped one last bucket of water to fill the chickens' trough. He paused a moment, straightening and turning to look up at Turtle Mountain, its high peak silhouetted against the indigo night sky. The memory of those few moments when he'd been certain his life was over played again in his mind.

He shuddered. Was there some weird link between him and that damned, doomed mountain? He'd ended up living in its shadow, slaving with pick and shovel in its belly, making sweet, fierce love to Zelda in one of its caves. And, he reminded himself with grim honesty, he was also biding his time until the fateful night arrived when the mountain would slide down over half the town and—he hoped—send him and Jackson back where they came from.

It seemed barbaric to anticipate and to use such a tragedy to gain his own ends. He thought of the people who would die that night and shuddered. Back in his own time, reading about the Slide, he'd been philosophical and detached about those casualties. There were only about seventy, he'd marveled, a small miracle when one considered that five hundred others had survived, and after all, it had happened long ago.

Now, he agonized over those deaths. He knew the names and faces of the people living in these cottages, all of whom were fated to be buried in the Slide. Daily now, he wondered if there was any possible way to change history and prevent anyone from dying.

The back door of the house opened and quietly closed, and in another moment Zelda was beside him in the darkness. He reached out and took her hand, lifting it to his lips, pressing a kiss in her palm, sensing the delicious shiver that ran through her body.

She'd told him today that she loved him, and ever since, the words had been there, underlying everything else he'd done or thought or said. She'd touched a tender nerve in him, satisfied a deep need—and brought to the surface an agony of doubt.

Zelda was a woman of deep conviction, of fiery passion, of innate honesty. She'd spoken of her love freely, without asking for a similar response from him.

He had feelings for Zelda he'd never had for any other woman, that was certain. Physically, he wanted her with this passion bordering on madness, this insatiable hunger that never seemed to be filled. But to commit himself entirely to her meant staying in these early 1900s, marrying and giving up all hope that he would ever return to his own life, to the financial security he longed to regain.

He couldn't do it. He understood that complex,

imperfect world he'd been born into. He belonged there. He needed the financial security he'd amassed.

Did he love Zelda? He shied away from an answer, because he couldn't bring himself to make that commitment.

But what would happen to her when he left? Would she meet someone else, marry, bear children? Everything in Tom rebelled at that thought, even though he knew it was likely. She understood passion now; her body had awakened to its own potential.

Tom wrapped his arm around her and guided her toward the sweet-scented loft, his body already hard and throbbing. At the top of the ladder he turned and grasped her arms, lifting her up and into his embrace. He groaned as his lips closed on hers, his kiss nearly savage.

He needed her. God, how he needed her! Tonight there wasn't time or patience to peel away slowly her layers of clothing. He carried her down to the blanket he'd spread on a soft cushion of hay, shoving aside the barriers of skirts and petticoats. Her drawers maddened him, and he stripped them away, opening the buttons on his trousers, cursing at his clumsiness. At last, at last, he found her soft, wet folds and slid inside, groaning aloud as her body's silky heat enveloped him, her legs wrapping and holding him tight.

With his last ounce of control, he held back until he felt the tremors begin deep inside her. Then, at last, he exploded, her soaring cries echoing in his ears as he spilled and spilled, and the darkness and terror of the day's events slid away, purified by passion.

He'd cherish her for the time they had together, he vowed when reason returned. He'd take what each separate day had to offer, giving back everything he had to give, because, God help him, he couldn't promise her forever.

In the weeks that followed, the community reached out wide, welcoming arms and enfolded both Tom and the Ralstons to its bosom.

From the day of the accident, Tom found himself an adopted brother to the Italian miners. He and Zelda attended the christening they'd been invited to, a celebration that began early in the morning in church, then continued throughout the entire day at the cottage of the proud parents. There were unlimited amounts of homemade red wine, huge tubs of spaghetti and meatballs, dandelion salads, loaves of fresh bread, and enough homemade ice cream to satisfy a small army.

The men played *bocce* out in the yard, and the women exchanged recipes and home remedies and hair-raising tales of childbirth.

Zelda had brought her camera, and she spent the afternoon taking one photo after the other. It seemed that everyone wanted a photograph of their family to send back to relatives in Italy, and everyone either paid cash or bartered a service in exchange for her work.

By the end of the day, she'd earned more in one afternoon than she'd made during the entire past six months. She'd also traded three enlargements to Mrs. Petevello, who was an excellent seamstress, in exchange for two shirts for Eli and a new dress for herself.

August came, and a series of picnics began, held in the clearing on the outskirts of town. Eli and Virgil accompanied Tom and Zelda. Again, there was always wine, quantities of delicious food, as well as laughter and good-natured ribaldry and teasing.

There were spirited ball games at the picnics. Tom was an excellent pitcher, and Zelda, tutored by him and Eli, was soon in great demand because of her natural ability as a player. She could hit the ball far out into the field and run like the wind around the bases, her arms pumping as she held her skirts shockingly high, laughing uncontrollably as her hair tumbled out of its bun and curled in mad disarray around her shoulders.

One hot Sunday in late August, Tom watched her fly around the bases, and his heart seemed to twist in his chest at her beauty.

There was a subtle difference in her now, an awareness of her own sensuality. It telegraphed itself to every male in the vicinity and brought out a fierce jealousy that Tom had never suspected he was capable of feeling.

A tall, lean, and extraordinarily handsome cousin of Joe's named Aldo couldn't take his eyes off Zelda. Aldo was in his thirties, still single, always impeccably dressed. He had a head of shining golden hair, piercing green eyes, a classic aquiline nose and the type of aristocratic elegance and charm that had every woman from ten to eighty blushing and flustering in his presence.

He didn't work, but he always seemed to have

plenty of money. Joe had confided that Aldo came from the northern branch of the Petsukos, who were well-to-do in Italy. He was a businessman, in Frank to look into the possibility of building a luxury hotel and restaurant.

Everything about Aldo made Tom's hackles rise. As he watched him watching Zelda, Tom recalled the scene earlier in the day when Joe had introduced him.

"You are betrothed?" Aldo had asked her, even with Tom standing inches away telegraphing a cool-eyed, lethal warning.

But the other man's gaze remained fastened on Zelda's face.

"No, we are not," Zelda said coolly.

Aldo smiled. "Then perhaps you would take dinner with me one evening, Signora Ralston?" His English was almost perfect, with only the faintest trace of his native Italian lending a charming accent to his words. "The hotel dining room is not so very bad."

Tom had had enough. "The lady's with me," he said softly, a slow curl of anger unfolding in his gut.

"But of course." Aldo smiled. He shrugged, an elegant movement that displayed to advantage the muscles under the expensive hand-tailored shirt and vest. "But surely if you are not betrothed. . . ."

Tom's fists curled, and he met the other man's challenging gaze with a cold, hard stare. Aldo didn't flinch. From that moment on, the battle lines were drawn between them as far as Zelda was concerned.

Aldo made him angry, but what infuriated Tom was Zelda's attitude toward the situation. Instead of freezing Aldo out or blistering him with her tongue, she actually openly flirted all afternoon, and when Tom confronted her, she laughed up at him, her sun-kissed, freckled face mischievous.

"Oh, phooey, for a plain Jane like me to have two handsome gentlemen sparring for my affections is both flattering and funny," she stated, her brown eyes sparkling. "I'm certainly not going to spoil it all by insulting Aldo, Tom. He's really quite a dear," she purred, ignoring the way Tom's eyes turned stormy and dark.

"You're no plain Jane, Zelda. You're very beautiful, and you're mine." His voice held a warning, but again she ignored it.

"But I am not betrothed, am I, sir?" she said with impudent emphasis, her chin tilted high.

Tom lost his temper. "Get your shawl, we're leaving right now," he ordered. By now he should have known better than to order Zelda to do anything.

"I'm not ready to leave. I'm having a wonderful time. If you want to go, I'm sure Dad will accompany you. He's all done with his meal, and he's looking a bit weary."

Gritting his teeth, utterly furious with her, of course Tom stayed. It seemed that for the rest of the evening, Aldo was at his elbow, bringing Zelda a glass of lemonade, asking her questions about photography, brazenly ignoring Tom's lowering glances.

Finally, Tom couldn't bear any more. He leaned close to the other man, his nose a scant three inches from Aldo's aristocratic face. "I warned you once, pal," he said in a lethal tone. "The lady's taken, so buzz off or I'll plant my fist in the middle of your face."

People nearby became suddenly quiet, and a dozen pairs of eyes fastened on the scene. Tension filled the air.

"Tom, really," Zelda gasped in a shocked voice.

Tom ignored her, holding Aldo's eyes with his own.

This time the other man interpreted the message correctly.

"*Arrivederci, bella signora.*" He sighed. He gave Zelda a little half bow, made a mock salute in Tom's direction, and strolled off.

"How could you do a thing like that? I'm mortified," Zelda hissed. They left soon after, and she wouldn't speak to him all the way home.

That night was one of the times Tom cursed the fact that he boarded with the Ralstons. More than anything, he needed to haul Zelda off, probably kicking and screaming, to somewhere private where he could tear off her clothes and make passionate love to her until she couldn't so much as remember Aldo's name. He needed to fall asleep beside her and find her there, curled in his possessive embrace, when morning came.

Instead, he lay alone in his room, hot and prickly with desire, achingly conscious that she was only a few steps away—but so were Virgil and Eli.

That night, for the first time, he dreamed of marrying Zelda, of staying where he was, but reason returned when he awoke.

If he left, he would lose Zelda. If he stayed, there would be no financial security, not for a long time, perhaps never, only this grinding poverty that ate at his soul.

The fact was, Zelda had been born nearly a hundred years too soon.

Fall came late to the valley that year. The frost held off until the end of September. When it arrived, Virgil insisted on digging the last of his potatoes and carrots and parsnips himself, coughing and having to stop and lean on his shovel at intervals to recover his breath enough to continue.

Eddy and Pearl came into the yard and were helping him shake the dirt from the vegetables and put them into bushel baskets, ready to store in the root cellar under the house.

Zelda watched from the kitchen window, her own chest hurting each time he coughed. She ached to race out and snatch away the spade and dig the vegetables herself, but, of course, she couldn't. Virgil would be humiliated. This harvesting of his family's food was something he needed to do.

The summer had been good for him, Zelda told herself. She was sure he'd regained a little of his strength. In spite of Zelda's outright nagging, he stubbornly went on working underground, but he missed almost as many shifts as he worked, too worn-out from bouts of coughing to drag himself out of bed.

Damn the mines. They'd injured her father, they were luring her brother, they'd endangered her lover. . . .

The sound of her studio bell provided a welcome distraction.

Zelda hurried along the hallway to the front of the house, marveling at how often she was now summoned to take someone's portrait. Her business was at last becoming a success.

"Leona, come in, what a pleasure. How did your singing engagement go?" Zelda hugged her friend, then took the other woman's shawl and bonnet. It had been several weeks since they'd seen each other, and there never seemed time for a good long visit alone.

Leona was busy. She'd been hired by a hotel in Calgary to entertain a group of English visitors who were touring Canada.

She plopped down on the sofa now and rolled her eyes. "May God spare me from Englishmen. Their manners seem impeccable, but they are the most persistent pests when they want something." She giggled wickedly and rolled her eyes. "And what they wanted was me, of course. Several of them were both handsome and filthy rich, Zel, which made it much less of a bore having to fend them off tactfully. Wouldn't you know I'd meet that magical combination only after I'd fallen for Jackson?" She sighed. "Where on earth were they when I was still available?"

Zelda laughed. "So the trip was a success?"

"Very much so." Leona looked smug. "The proprietor has asked me to come back in the spring, and I believe Jackson was suitably devastated by my absence." Her eyes sparkled. "I didn't have to do more than hint to him about the Englishmen to make him absolutely green with jealousy."

Zelda remembered her own recent experience with a jealous lover. She couldn't wait to tell Leona about Aldo. There was something immensely satisfying in having two grown men act like idiots over one's favors.

Leona hardly took a breath. "And the portraits you made of me have resulted in still another job offer, this one in Fernie. You're a genius, Zel. I've decided to have you make still another set, with different poses. Look, I've come prepared." She opened the huge carpetbag she'd brought and dumped out a silky stack of dresses and a long ostrich feather boa. "I thought we'd do something sophisticated, but also just that slight bit naughty. This one's cut rather low in the bosom, and that one's sinfully tight across the back, and this one shows just a bit too much ankle . . ." She held up one gown after the other.

For the next hour, Zelda's camera clicked away as Leona changed from one fetching gown and provocative pose to the next.

When they were done, Zelda led the way to the kitchen for a cup of tea. She found that Virgil had already made a pot, and was sharing it with Pearl and Eddy. The children, both grubby and greedy, were wolfing down scones Zelda had made that morning.

Zelda introduced them to Leona, and in a moment she had them chattering away, telling her of their new kitten and the swing Lars had made for them in their backyard.

When the children were done with their milky tea, Virgil took them back outside with him, and Leona's face took on a meditative look. "They're sweet, even under all that soil. Do you want to have children someday, Zelda?" She sipped at her tea, her lovely face thoughtful.

"Yes, I do." The words didn't begin to convey the longing Zelda felt each time she imagined Tom's child growing inside of her. She'd even, God help her, given thought to abandoning the sponge she used so conscientiously, knowing that if she were to become pregnant, Tom would marry her.

And doing so would trap him, keep him there at her side against his will. How long would it be, then, before he began to resent her?

"I never imagined the time might come when I'd actually think of getting married and having children," Leona said quietly. "But nowadays, I think of little else." She paused, and then added in a rush, "The thing is, Jackson never speaks of marriage or a future together. It's maddening, because I'm accustomed to men proposing to me at the flick of an eyelash. One of the Englishmen, for instance, proposed no less than four times. I deliberately let Jackson know, to absolutely no avail. He laughed as if it were a huge joke." Her smooth forehead creased in a frown. "I even asked him once if perhaps he was already married, but he insisted he never has been. And I know he cares for me. It's something a woman senses." She shrugged and reached for a scone. "Well, I suppose it's just going to take longer than usual."

She met Zelda's eyes, and after a moment color rose in her cheeks. She broke the scone open and then crumbled a bit of it between her thumb and forefinger.

"The problem is, if he waits much longer, he'll be a father before he becomes a husband."

Zelda stared at her friend as the import of her

words registered. She gasped, then reached across and took Leona's hand. "Oh, my. Oh, my goodness. My dear Leona. You're expecting a child?"

Leona nodded, her face calm, but the way she clung to Zelda's hand indicated that she wasn't as relaxed as she pretended. "It's so silly to be in this situation," she said with a shaky little laugh. "I'm not a total fool, and I did take precautions. Heaven's to betsy, I had the best advice available. I asked the saloon girls what to use, and they showed me. But I suppose nothing's foolproof, and there were several times . . ." Her face turned scarlet.

"Well, I'm sure you know what I mean. At least, I hope that you do. I mean, I've suspected that you and Tom—" Her voice broke, her face crumbled, and she wailed, "Oh, Zelda, what am I going to do if he doesn't want to marry me? I'm afraid to tell him about the baby, in case he doesn't really love me after all."

Leona sounded so heartbroken Zelda wanted to weep with her.

"Of course he loves you, Leona. One look at his face when he's with you shows that he's besotted."

"Then why doesn't he say so? Why doesn't he ever once hint that he'd like us to be together? I know it bothers him that he doesn't earn much money, but I have an—an inheritance that would afford us a decent living. I've told him so." She attempted a smile, but it didn't quite materialize. "I'm almost rich, and I'm not ugly, and I'm certainly not old. So what is his problem, do you think, Zelda?"

For one of the few times in her life, Zelda couldn't think of a thing to say, because she knew exactly what the problem was. It was all too obvious that

Jackson hadn't said a word to Leona about it.

It was obvious he'd never told Leona about being from that future time, or planning to return to it, which of course accounted for his reluctance in planning a future here.

Zelda opened her mouth to spill out the whole incredible story, then closed it again with a snap. Even if she could manage to convince Leona the preposterous tale was true, her friend was going to be furious, or frightened, or deeply hurt at Jackson's deception—or more probably, all three, and she was already upset enough.

It was better to hold her tongue for the moment, Zelda decided. "You must tell him about the baby," Zelda urged. "I'm certain that when you do, he'll marry you immediately."

"And that's exactly why I won't tell him," Leona said in a vehement tone. "I couldn't bear having him marry me because he had to."

Zelda sighed. "I do understand." All too well. "I feel the same way about Tom."

And although it was painful to admit, Zelda also envied Leona with every fiber of her being. Fate had taken a hand in Leona's destiny. Married or not, she still would have a child, a living, breathing reminder of the man she loved.

When Tom went away, what would she have of him, Zelda thought bitterly? Memories were cold comfort to a heart that longed desperately for living, breathing flesh.

Leona dug a lace-trimmed handkerchief out of her sleeve and blew her nose. She squared her shoulders and got to her feet. "I must go. Tom will be back from work any moment, and it wouldn't do for him to find me here soaking the table with tears."

Zelda got up and impulsively wrapped her arms around Leona. "Whatever happens with Jackson, you know I'll be here for you. If we need to, we can raise the child between us. I'd adore having a baby around, and so would Dad."

"Think what that would do to your reputation," Leona said in a horrified voice, trying to lighten the atmosphere. She clung to Zelda for a moment, dangerously close to tears again. "You are a dear friend." She stepped away, smiling a shaky smile. "And, of course, we'd have all the saloon girls as godmothers. Wouldn't that just set this town on its ear?"

She walked to the door and opened it. "Heavens, I almost forgot. Jackson asked me to invite you and Tom to dinner with us at the hotel on Thursday evening, at six. It happens to be my twenty-fifth birthday. We're having a small celebration. You will come, won't you, Zel?"

Zelda promised they would.

"And, of course, you won't say a word about any of this to Tom?"

"My dear Leona, of course not. I wouldn't dream of betraying your confidence."

But when Leona left, Zelda wished with all her heart that she could talk the situation over with Tom. He was Jackson's best friend. He could insist that Jackson at least tell Leona the facts about who he was and how he'd come to be in Frank.

Jackson was a rogue. She'd thought so from the first moment she'd laid eyes on him, Zelda concluded. All she could do now was hope that he was an honorable rogue.

Chapter Seventeen

The dining room at the Imperial Hotel was grand, and Zelda tried not to stare around like an unsophisticated bumpkin.

Carpeted in thick red plush, it had an enormous chandelier in the middle of the ceiling. Framed paintings of most of the crowned heads of Europe as well as three very large and, she concluded, badly done studies of the late Queen Victoria hung one next to the other on the gold-papered walls.

The late queen could have used a good photographer.

A pianist—Tom whispered that he was the same little man who played honky-tonk in the saloon each evening—was playing something soft and, she assumed, classical.

Jackson had reserved a large, round table in a quiet corner, and as Tom escorted Zelda across the room, past the other diners, she silently blessed Rosa Petevello's inspired dressmaking.

In return for several portraits of her family, Rosa had made her a dress. Zelda had argued for a dark, utilitarian serge, but Rosa wouldn't hear of it. Instead, she'd concocted this lavish gown of emerald-green shot taffeta, its huge sleeves decorated with embroidered braid, the low bodice draped in such a way that it actually looked as though Zelda had an adequate bosom.

It was ridiculously opulent, and Zelda had fallen in love with it on sight. She had thought she'd never have occasion to wear it, but she had been unable to resist taking it home and hanging it in her wardrobe.

Yesterday she'd bought a pair of black patent-leather, high-heeled shoes, on sale of course. Today, she'd devoted herself to getting ready.

The afternoon had been spent cursing and struggling with her freshly washed hair until at last the curly mass rested in a high chignon on top of her head, with only a few rebellious curls escaping down her neck and over her forehead.

Bathed and perfumed and trembling with nerves, she slipped into the dress. But after a fruitless ten minutes of effort, she had to call Virgil up to help with the row of minuscule buttons and tiny hooks that held it closed down the back.

Virgil didn't have an easy time of it, either. When he finally managed and Zelda turned hesitantly to face him, worried all of a sudden that she might look ridiculous, his blue eyes filled with tears and he couldn't speak for a long moment. He held her hands in his and looked at her.

"You're the living image of your mama, when first I met her," he said at last, his voice trembling. "She was a beautiful woman, your mama."

"Oh, Dad, your eyes are getting bad," Zelda teased, but her voice, too, quavered. "I'm nothing like her. I take more after your spinster sisters. You know that."

But for the first time in her life, she felt almost pretty as she descended the stairs and went into the small parlor where Tom was waiting, playing a game of checkers with Eli.

The two of them looked up from the board, and their expressions confirmed Vigil's words; it was plain even before they spoke that they, too, thought her beautiful.

Eli whistled in a rude fashion, and she didn't even rebuke him.

Her heart caught in her throat when she looked at Tom and saw the admiration in his eyes. "Wow," he said softly.

He was heartstoppingly handsome in a dark navy suit and buttoned vest, with a white shirt and soft blue bow tie. The suit had been purchased from Murphy's Men's Wear, but it had been tailored, again by Rosa, to fit Tom's tall, broad-shouldered frame to perfection.

They attracted a good deal of attention now as they walked across the dining room. Zelda was aware of heads turning their way, of women assessing both her dress and her escort, of men giving her the kind of admiring, flirtatious looks she'd once believed would never be directed at her.

Her heart swelled, and she couldn't keep her foolish lips from smiling.

"Mr. Chapman, I presume? And this must be the lovely Zelda." Jackson grinned and bowed, debonair and impossibly handsome in his close-fitting black suit.

Beside him was Leona, resplendent in a deep garnet velvet dress. She smiled and called an excited greeting, and Zelda admired her poise. No one would have suspected there was a thing on Leona's mind except enjoyment of the evening.

A stranger sat beside her, an older man with a large white moustache and a shy half-smile. He got to his feet as they approached, and Jackson introduced him.

"Zelda Ralston, Tom Chapman, this is George Edwards, an old friend of Leona's."

Of course. Mr. Edwards was the protective friend Leona had told her about, Zelda recalled. She smiled, and he bowed in a courtly manner. He had very soulful eyes, Zelda decided.

She felt Tom's hand tighten spasmodically on her arm, and she winced and turned to frown at him.

His face registered profound shock, and he was staring in a discourteous fashion at the old man without even acknowledging the introduction.

"Tom," she whispered, prodding him with her elbow. "Tom, what is it? What's the matter?"

He recovered and held out his hand. "Pleased to meet you, Mr. Edwards," he managed, but his voice sounded strained.

They sat, Zelda with Tom on her left and Jackson on her right. She handed Leona the gaily wrapped birthday gift she and Tom had made, a photograph of Frank taken from up on the mountain, mounted in a handmade oak frame that Tom had fashioned.

Leona ripped off the wrappings, as excited as a child, and everyone exclaimed over the photograph.

It was one of the best she'd done, Zelda had to admit. She'd taken it on an early-spring morning when the sun had just come up and the mist, rising over the little town, had given it an eerie, fairy-tale aspect, cradled in the valley like a giant's toy.

A waiter hovered at her elbow, filling her stemmed wineglass, and Zelda stared at it, wrestling with her conscience and her convictions and her allegiance to the Women's Temperance League.

All three lost, and she raised the delicate glass to her mouth and took a long, delicious sip. Tonight she was a sophisticated woman of the world, and such women, she knew from her reading, enjoyed a glass of wine. She sipped again cautiously, feeling lightheaded and giddy and debonair.

But she soon began to have misgivings about Tom. If she didn't know better, she'd swear he'd been imbibing in spirits all afternoon, because he was certainly acting in a most peculiar fashion.

First he forgot to eat his soup, seemingly lost in a daydream. Then he knocked the entire bowl over on the tablecloth. There was a great fuss as waiters converged and mopped up the mess.

Almost immediately, he poured salad dressing on his potatoes instead of gravy, and the unfortunate waiter had to be summoned again to take the serving away and bring another plate of food.

Zelda began to worry that he was having some sort of seizure.

He kept losing the thread of what was being said,

making responses that had nothing whatsoever to do with the conversation.

Perhaps he'd been hit on the head at the mine and hadn't told her? She caught him innumerable times casting the most peculiar glances at George Edwards, and she couldn't for the life of her understand why. The older man was the soul of courtesy, very quiet spoken and good-natured, knowledgeable about a variety of topics, interested in everything the younger people had to say—altogether a charming gentleman with impeccable manners.

Zelda was actually losing patience with Tom by the time dessert was served. Jackson had ordered an elaborate cake with Leona's name on it, accompanied by bowls of rich custard and sliced fruit and a most delicious blackberry dessert wine. Tom didn't even taste his serving. He sat lost in some sort of daydream.

Zelda, however, enjoyed every morsel, but all the liquids began to make a visit to a bathroom an urgent requirement.

She was relieved when Leona winked at her, and announced, "Zelda and I are going up to my room to freshen up a little. We'll come down and join you gentlemen for coffee in a short while."

Zelda sprang to her feet and found herself just a trifle wobbly. She staggered, and Tom leaped up to steady her, knocking a half-filled glass of dark blackberry wine to the carpet, where it spread in an ugly stain.

Zelda, relieved that the wine hadn't hit her dress, felt mortified on his behalf. It was fortunate they couldn't afford this sort of entertainment on any regular basis, she concluded as she hurried off with Leona. He might look as though he'd been born to wear evening clothes, but elegant surroundings and polite conversation were definitely not Tom's element.

When the swish of the women's skirts faded and he was seated once again, Tom took a healthy gulp of the excellent brandy Jackson had ordered. He tried to get a firm grip on the feeling of disorientation and utter disbelief he'd been experiencing since the moment he'd met the man who called himself George Edwards.

Recognition had been instantaneous. But so was the shock of actually meeting someone he'd researched and read about in such detail, a notorious man long dead by the time Tom was born—now sitting not two feet away, very much alive.

George Edwards was the pseudonym used by the infamous train robber, Bill Miner, the man once labeled by the head of the Pinkerton Detective Agency "the master criminal of the American West." Over a period of years, Miner masterminded a number of robberies in both Canada and the United States, successfully escaping with substantial amounts of gold and money each time. He'd also been caught and sentenced to San Quentin twice. He'd managed to escape both times from the notorious prison.

Bill Miner was a legend. He was credited with originating the expression, "Hands up," and he'd often been described as a gentleman bandit because of his charm. The reason Tom had researched him so thoroughly was because he was the man who planned and executed the robbery of the Klondike gold bars, the lost gold that had brought Tom and Jackson to Frank in the first place.

According to Tom's research, Miner and his partner, Lewis Schraeger, would ambush the CPR train next April, the very night of the Slide, and escape with, then bury the fortune in gold bars near Frank.

Several times, Tom had watched *The Grey Fox,* a movie portrayal of Bill Miner's life. The story was a touching and sympathetic study of Miner that revealed the human side of the famous criminal. Tom realized now that the actor who had portrayed the man sitting only a few feet away had created an uncanny likeness.

Tom had recognized him instantly and had longed to throw caution aside and confront Miner. There were questions only the gentle old bandit himself could answer, such as how he'd ever managed to escape from San Quentin and how he'd survived the long months spent in solitary confinement inside that prison. But, of course, it would have been both rude and insulting to put Miner on the spot in front of everyone.

When the women had excused themselves, Tom's heart had leapt with excitement. Perhaps now was his chance. But Leona and Zelda were barely out of the room when Miner, too, got to his feet.

"If you gentlemen will excuse me, there's a matter I must attend to this evening. I do thank you for your hospitality, Jackson. Good to meet you, Tom. My regards to your lovely Zelda."

In a moment, he was gone, and Tom felt like howling with frustration. Furious, he turned on

Jackson. "Why the *hell* didn't you tell me you'd met Bill Miner?"

Jackson frowned and shook his head. "Bill Miner? What're you talking about?"

Tom gestured at the empty chair. "Leona's friend, George Edwards. He's Bill Miner. I recognized him right away."

Jackson still looked blank, and Tom grew even more impatient. "Miner, for God's sakes, the man who was the brains behind the robbery of the gold bars from the Klondike. The bars we originally came here to find, remember?"

Jackson looked stunned. "But I thought Lewis Schraeger was the guy who robbed the train and ended up in San Quentin."

Tom shook his head. "Schraeger was just Miner's partner. It was Bill who was the real brains behind the robbery." Swiftly, Tom filled in all the details, recalling everything he could remember about the wily old bandit. "I know for certain this is Bill Miner. Miner had a ballet dancer tattooed on his right forearm, and because of his coat I couldn't see that tonight. But he also had a tattoo mark at the base of his thumb, and that was there as plain as day on his left hand."

Jackson's mouth dropped open, and the stupefied expression on his friend's face made it obvious that until now he hadn't had a single clue as to Edwards's true identity.

"Tom, I always left that research stuff to you, you know that. Sure, I remember now you talking about Bill Miner, but I didn't connect it. Leona just told me Edwards was an old friend of her father's, that when her dad died, Edwards"—Jackson grimaced and corrected himself—"Miner, that is, promised him . . ." His voice faded, and the full implications of Miner's identity began to register on both of them.

"Of course she knows exactly who he is. She knows all about him. She has to, right?" Jackson's jaw hardened, his mouth twisting into a grim line. "No wonder she's been vague about so many things." His eyes narrowed and a muscle twitched near his mouth. "I'd like to know just exactly how involved Leona's been in Miner's career. All this talk about an inheritance from a great aunt. . . ."

In all their long years together, Tom could count on the fingers of one hand the number of times he'd seen his partner totally lose his temper. When he did, it was monumental. Right now, he was on the narrow edge.

"Cool down, Zalco. Give her a chance to explain before you jump to conclusions."

"Explain? How the hell do you explain something like this?" Jackson lifted the round globe of brandy and tossed it back in one swallow. His knuckles were white. "I'm gonna go find her and have it out right now."

Tom sighed, accepting the inevitable. "I'll come with you and get Zelda. Sounds as if you'll be wanting privacy for this particular conversation."

Jackson jerked his head in agreement.

On the second turn of the grand staircase, they met the women coming down.

"How sweet! You couldn't wait a moment longer." Leona smiled gaily and held her hand out to take Jackson's arm, but one look at his face made her draw back. "What is it? What's happened?"

"You and I need to talk, Leona. Right now." He seized her arm and began to hustle her back up the steps, but she jerked away from him, scowling.

"Jackson, for heaven's sake. Whatever it is has waited this long, surely it can wait until later. Zelda and I would like some coffee, and there's dancing in the ballroom. I intend to enjoy the rest of my birthday."

"This happens to be about you and your old friend, Bill Miner, Leona." Jackson's steely voice and narrowed gaze betrayed his anger.

Leona's face blanched and her eyes widened. She stared at him for a moment, and then turned to Zelda. "I'm afraid we'll have to have that coffee another time, Zel," her voice strained. She said, "Thank you for the photograph, and for coming to celebrate my birthday with me. I'll come see you soon and explain all this." She turned and marched up the stairs ahead of Jackson, her back ramrod straight.

Zelda stared after them, her eyes wide. "Who in heaven's name is Bill Miner, and what does he have to do with anything?" She sounded exasperated. "I would have said that Jackson had the explaining to do, not Leona. But I'm very relieved if you said something to him, Tom. He's really been most dishonest with her, and in her condition—" She caught a glimpse of his astounded face and pressed her hand over her mouth. "Oh, damn my tongue. All that wine—"

Tom stood as if paralyzed, poised between one step and the next. "Leona's pregnant. And Jackson doesn't have a clue." His words came out in a stunned whisper.

"I gave my word I wouldn't say anything," Zelda said miserably. "And I still don't understand who this Bill Miner person is, either."

He put his arm around her shoulders, drawing her close to him, unable even to imagine how tonight's events would affect their lives, knowing only that it would be profound.

She looked dejected, and suddenly it seemed important that he make her smile again. "C'mon, pretty lady. It's their problem. Let's you and I go down to the ballroom and see if I remember how to waltz."

He was becoming an expert at shoving the things he didn't want to think about into a giant trash can in his mind and slamming down the lid.

In Leona's room, Jackson stood, his hands balled into fists and planted on his hips, voice soft and lethal. "Well, Leona?" he asked, in a soft, lethal tone. "And don't bother telling me you didn't know who Bill Miner is, because I won't buy it."

She'd flung herself into an armchair and unbuckled her shoes, kicking them off and tucking her stockinged feet up under her skirts. Rich color stained her cheeks, and there was a dangerous light in her blue gaze when she looked up at him.

"For heaven's sake, Jackson, sit down. There's no need to loom over me this way. I'm not about to bolt."

He ignored her. "Bill Miner is a wanted man, Leona, by the Canadian police as well as the Pinkerton Detective Agency. He's robbed trains all over the damned place. He's done time in San Quentin and pulled off two jail breaks, and you tell me he's your good friend." His voice was deceptively mild. "You mind explaining just exactly how you come to be mixed up with him in the first place?"

She scowled up at him. "I told you. He was my father's best friend. He's been my—my guardian for years."

"Your guardian." Jackson shook his head, making his long ponytail switch from side to side. "What kind of father would appoint an ex-con, a known bank robber, as guardian to—" He stopped suddenly and looked at her, narrowing his eyes. "Maybe you'd better tell me a little more about your father, Leona."

With a furious movement, she uncurled her legs and sprang to her feet, mimicking his stance, her hands on her hips, leaning toward him.

"And maybe you'd better be a lot more honest with me than you have been, Jackson Zalco. You're with Pinkerton, aren't you?" There were angry tears shining in her eyes. "You've just used me to get close to Bill, isn't that right? No wonder you were so secretive about where you were from and why you came here to Frank. No wonder you never said a word about our future together."

Taken off guard, Jackson gaped at her. "Pinkerton? You think I'm a *detective?*"

She gave him a scathing look. "Stop acting, Jackson. Of course you're a detective. How else would you know so much about Bill?"

He stared at her, then sank down heavily on the sofa. "Son of a gun. I give you my word I'm no policeman, Leona. There's a lot I haven't told you about myself, but one thing's for damned certain, I'm not here to arrest Bill. I just want to know the truth about *you*. All of it, Leona." He leaned forward, scowling at her. "I'm in love with you. Don't you know that, you impossible female?"

If he thought that was going to make her melt into a puddle of sentiment at his feet, he was dead wrong. She tossed her head and looked even angrier than before. "How should I know? You certainly never said so till this minute, and you're only saying it now to divert me. Before I tell you one single word about myself, or Bill, or my father, you'd better do some explaining yourself, Jackson Zalco. If you're not some kind of lawman, then who exactly are you, and how do you know the things you do?"

She had him there, no contest. His anger dissolved and he sighed and patted the sofa beside him. "I've been puttin' this off because it's downright weird, and I didn't want you figgerin' I was some kind of nut case. Sit down here beside me, honey, this is going to take a while."

Leona shook her head. He might be over his temper fit, but she certainly wasn't. She gave him a frankly skeptical look and moved to the armchair again. "I can listen just fine from over here!" she snapped.

He leaned forward, resting his elbows on his knees. "Look, I know this is gonna sound as phony as hell, but it's the God's honest truth. My bein' here, in this place, is the damndest accident I ever had. Anybody ever had, for that matter." He sucked in a long breath and expelled it. Then, in halting fashion, he began to explain how he and Tom came to be in Frank in 1902.

He told of his own time, of his partnership with

Tom, of how they'd earned their living searching for lost treasure. He then spoke of Tom's research, the research that involved Bill Miner, and of their intention of finding the gold they'd felt was hidden somewhere near Frank. And he told her about the Slide.

Leona's eyes grew huge. "You're telling me that Turtle Mountain is going to fall down right on this town?"

"On some of it, for certain." Jackson sighed. "Next April. Same damned day we got here, April 29. Four in the morning."

For a moment she looked as if she believed him, but then she shook her head. "That's preposterous. Surely you don't expect me to believe such a tall tale." She cradled her hands over her flat belly. "I don't have any idea why, but you're lying to me, Jackson. You certainly have a vivid imagination, if nothing else."

He swore viciously and got to his feet. "You wait right here, lady. I'll prove to you I'm tellin' the truth." He limped to the door, slamming it.

Within ten minutes he was back with several items of clothing over his arm. He tossed the first into her lap.

"Those are my jeans, take a good look at the fly."

She looked at him haughtily, her eyebrows raised.

He grinned and pointed to the zipper. "Don't get modest on me, Leona. Just take a look. There isn't another pair of jeans around with one of these handy little devices, now is there? There are buttons on everything. I never even thought about zippers much before I landed here, but, believe me, I'd give a lot to have 'em installed on my pants again."

Next, he handed her the red sweatshirt he'd been wearing when he visited the Interpretive Center, with its "Life is a Beach" message blazoned across the front.

"Nobody's thought of writing on clothes like that yet, either, right? Not that I miss it so much. It tended to get tiresome, all those message shirts. But this soft old sweatshirt is the sort of thing I used to wear most of the time, and I sure as hell miss the comfort. Clothes now just aren't built for comfort the way they are where I come from. And here's another prime example." He dropped a scanty pair of men's black bikini briefs on her lap, grinning when she picked them up between her thumb and forefinger as if they were about to bite her.

"These are what men wear under their jeans in my day, and you know full well that the things I've got on right now under these pants don't bear much resemblance to those. More's the pity. Damned underwear these days just isn't comfortable or sexy, either."

Next, he fished in his pocket and drew out his wallet, exhibiting his charge cards and driver's license. From a hidden fold he took out the useless wad of money he'd drawn from a bank machine hours before the accident that had landed him in Frank.

Leona fingered the bills, staring at the date marked on them.

When she looked up at him again, Jackson felt elation and enormous relief flood through him. He could tell without having her say a word that she believed him.

Her full mouth was slightly open, and she was staring at him as if she'd never seen him before.

Chapter Eighteen

"Is there any way for you to get back there, to this—this place in the future, Jackson?"

He shrugged. "Can't say for sure. Tom and I've got a plan we hope will work. On the night of the Slide next April, we're gonna go to the exact spot where that Interpretive Center was and see if the actual event will reverse the time-travel process." He outlined it for her in detail. "We're gonna do our damndest to find a way back. We just don't belong here." He paused, looking at her. "And neither do you. I sorta thought you might come along if it works, Leona. You'd like it fine, where I come from."

Slowly her blue eyes kindled, "I might at that," she said. "First, though, I want to know all about this future place. Time. Whatever you call it."

Jackson nodded. "Later, I promise. But first,

we've got old business to settle here." He rested one booted foot on the other knee and smiled at her, a deceptive, easygoing smile that meant she wasn't going to get away with anything. "Right now I want to know everythin' there is to know about you and Bill Miner and your father, so start talkin', honey."

She scowled and he could tell she was debating whether to tell him the truth, even now. At last, she gave an exaggerated sigh and made an impatient little movement with her shoulders.

"Daddy was Bill's partner. They'd worked together for years." She glanced at Jackson and scowled. "Yes, of course, robbing trains, although my father retired for a while when he married my mama. She was a good friend of Bill's sister, Maizie. They lived next door to each other in Whatcom County, in Washington state. Bill used to come to see Maizie now and then, and once he brought my father with him, and when Dad laid eyes on Mama that was that."

Leona's smile was sentimental. "He stayed and got a job in the mill. I was born there, and we were happy." Her voice took on a different tone. "Then Mama got sick when I was four years old. She died, and Daddy left me with Aunt Maizie and went away with Bill again." She met Jackson's eyes, daring him to judge. "Daddy and Bill got caught holding up a stagecoach the following year, and sentenced to twenty-five years in San Quentin."

She swallowed hard, then continued, "Daddy died there, of pneumonia. Bill wrote and told me, and from then on, he wrote me often. Daddy had asked him to look out for me, and he did his best, even from jail. I found out later that Bill arranged somehow to have my tuition paid at a good boarding school until I graduated, and there was always money in an account in my name for spending and clothing. He escaped once during those years, but he got caught, and when he was sent back, they made it horrible on him." She shuddered. "He wasn't released until two years ago. When he finally got out of prison, he came to see me, and we've been together ever since." Her voice was filled with passion and affection. "Bill's like a second father to me. He's one of the kindest and best men I've ever known."

Jackson had been watching her face as she talked. He nodded, and it was a moment or two before he responded. "And have you ever gone along with him when he robs trains, Leona?" he asked, his tone quiet and matter-of-fact.

Her glance skittered away, and her lips set in a stubborn line. "How do you even know he's robbed any trains since he got released? He doesn't exactly want to go back to prison, you know."

"He has, though." Jackson might be hazy on details, but Tom had a steel trap for a memory, and he'd quoted dates and times.

Jackson repeated them now, and he could tell from the carefully concealed shock on her face that Tom was right. "Were you with him those times, Leona?"

She bristled, avoiding his eyes. "What I do is no concern of yours, Jackson Zalco. If you have your way, you won't be around here much longer. You'll go back to that place where they have those—those zippers on pants and that scandalous underwear for men."

He took her chin in his palm and forced her to look at him. "I thought you said you wanted to come along," he purred.

She twisted her head away. "Maybe I do, maybe I don't. I'd have to think about it."

Jackson leaned forward, his arms resting on the sides of her chair, effectively imprisoning her there. "I deserve to know whether or not you've been robbing trains, Leona. I'm not going to run to the cops if you have. Morally I don't give a damn one way or the other as long as you haven't taken to murdering innocent bystanders. But I do need to know whether some lawman—one of these Pinkerton gents you mentioned—could come along and arrest you some fine mornin' when I'm least expecting it. I need to know, Leona. Surely you understand that?"

She looked up at him, her eyes so intensely blue the color seemed to have bled into the whites. Her intoxicating, spicy perfume filled his nostrils, and it was all he could do not to lean a little further forward and cover her full lips with his own. He wanted her intensely at that moment. But first he had to know the whole truth about her.

"Leona?" he asked, keeping his voice lazy, but edged with a warning.

"Oh, for heaven's sake. You really are the most persistent man I've ever met, and not over the right things, either." She glowered up at him and finally heaved an exaggerated sigh. "Yes, if you must know, I've gone along with Bill, but only once."

Jackson didn't move, but the white-hot rage he felt nearly consumed him. "I'll kill him. I'll kill the bastard, I swear I will. You consider Bill Miner a second father? What was he thinking of, letting you go along on a train robbery? You could have been hurt or killed. Or ended up in jail." His knuckles were white on the chair arms. He cursed in a long, steady stream.

"Oh, phooey, be quiet. I just knew this was how you'd act. You're just as bad as Bill. If you must know, I *begged* him to let me go along on that robbery, but he wouldn't hear of it. He said all the same things you just did. So I helped him plan it, and then when he wouldn't let me go along, I just didn't think it was fair at all. So I tricked him. I knew where he and Schraeger were going, so I just dressed up like a man and rode there myself."

A mischievous, self-satisfied grin tilted her full mouth. "I joined them at the last minute. They'd already stopped the train, so there wasn't anything Bill could do about it. He was furious with me, but the robbery was a great success. We got a small fortune in gold dust and coins."

Her eyes sparkled with excitement. "I don't see why a woman should have to sit back and let you men have all the fun. I've considered going into the robbery business on my own. I could do just as well as Bill does, and a lot better than Schraeger." She sniffed. "Schraeger's an absolute idiot. He makes terrible mistakes, but Bill's loyal to him. They're partners, and Bill takes care of him." She shook her head. "Somebody has to. Schraeger's incompetent. I could do much better, working alone."

Jackson felt a pang of intense sympathy for the old robber. Miner was out of his depth with this impossible woman.

Hell, maybe they both were.

He slid his hands under her elbows and pulled her up, so that she was standing pressed against him, the back of her knees against the chair.

"You might not realize it quite yet, darlin', but your train robbin' career is over," he said in a voice that brooked no argument. "You're mine, Leona Day, and there's no way my woman's gonna be in danger like that ever again."

The problem, Jackson knew, was going to be finding something exciting enough to take its place, something that would consume her so that robbing trains wasn't quite so appealing.

She had too damned much energy, a quicksilver mind, a restless spirit, and, no thanks to Miner, too much money of her own. Singing to crowds of drunken men for a couple hours a day didn't even begin to challenge her.

Lovemaking exhausted her, of course, leaving her boneless and weak and sleepy, at least for a little while. His fingers adroitly loosened the fastenings on the back of her dress, and as they both impatiently stripped away the layers of clothing from her lush body, he grinned wryly.

As intriguing as the idea was, he knew that making love to Leona twenty-four hours a day wasn't any solution.

He'd just die the most pleasurable of deaths in a few short months, and she'd probably go right back to robbing trains.

He shrugged out of his own clothing and sat down on the sofa, with her straddling his lap, already half out of his mind with wanting her.

"Jackson?" Her voice was husky.

"Ummmmm." He was using his tongue and the

tip of his teeth on her nipple, his hands stroking down the satin of her back beneath the cascade of golden hair he'd loosed from its pins.

She sounded breathless. "There's something I need to tell you."

Urgency was building. "Can't it wait till later, honey?"

"No, it can't. Well, not much later. I'm going to have a baby, Jackson. Your baby. Our baby."

In the space of an instant, his life tilted and its axis changed, irrevocably, forever. His erection wilted.

"When?" He lifted her off his lap and sat her beside him while his mind grappled with this, trying to imagine his new role and failing totally.

One of the few things he'd ever been adamant about was that he'd never willingly choose to be anybody's daddy. He wasn't fit. He didn't have any idea how it was done. For some obscure reason, he'd relaxed his guard with Leona. Terror gripped him, and it was all he could do not to pull on his pants and run.

"I'm not certain exactly when. Sometime next June, I think." She was trying to sound casual and breezy, but he saw the anxiety in her eyes, felt the tension and the fine trembling in her naked body as he absently stroked her shoulder and arm.

She was scared, too, he realized all of a sudden. Not for the same reasons as him, though; Leona was scared of his reaction, scared that he'd run out on her.

He never would. He knew, between one heartbeat and the next, that although he hadn't counted on it happening, this was right for him. He wanted

Leona and his child. He'd learn somehow to be a father, a good father—the kind he'd never had. Virgil was a good father; he'd ask him for advice.

"Aren't you going to ask me how I let this happen?" Her voice was steady.

He smiled and shook his head. "From everythin' I've heard, it takes two of us to make it work, honey."

He gathered her close, her head on his chest, his face buried in her cascade of lemon-scented hair. "We'll get married," he said. "We'll get married right away." It was something he'd been contemplating anyway, working up to in his own good time. This just speeded things along a bit, that was all.

He sat back and smoothed her hair from her face, feeling good about the decision, smiling at her tenderly before he realized she was angry.

"So now you decide we'll get married, just like that!" she snapped. "Without asking me if that's what I want, or saying one single word about love. You never so much as mentioned marriage until you found out I was expecting, and now you think you'll do the proper thing and make a respectable woman of me?"

She sprang up, gloriously naked, her hands on her rounded hips, her hair swirling like a golden cape around her firm, uptilted breasts. "Well, you can go straight to hell, Jackson Zalco. I've had dozens of proposals in my life, and let me tell you, this one is by far the sorriest excuse for a proclamation I've ever heard. If you think I'd marry you just because of a baby, you'd better reconsider."

Now what? Jackson could only stare at her, dumbfounded by this new outburst. She was going to drive him insane before she was done, but if it was a formal proposal she wanted, then damn his hide, that's what he'd give her.

He stood up, naked as a jaybird himself, and took hold of her, forcibly sitting her down again on the sofa. She fought him, but he was much stronger, and after a moment she calmed. When it looked as if she might stay put for a minute, he dropped to one knee in front of her, still holding her down with one strong arm on her bare knees, hoping she wouldn't decide to use one of them on him, bare and vulnerable as he was.

"Miss Leona, I find myself overcome with your beauty, your charm, and your dainty ways," he began sarcastically, earning himself a clout on the side of the head.

"Ouch. Damn it all, woman, cut that out before I turn you over my knee. I'm tryin' to do this to your likin'."

"No, you're not. You're making a fool of me." She sounded absolutely furious, and he was appalled to see tears in her eyes, spilling out and down her cheeks. Remorse filled him.

"Ahhh, honey, I'm sorry." He reached out and thumbed the tears away. "Don't cry. I didn't mean to make you cry. I was teasin' but I'll stop and get serious now. Just give me a minute or two and I promise I'll get it right. See, I've never had any practice at this before."

He drew a deep breath and realized he was sweating with nervousness. With an agitated motion, he swiped at his forehead with his hand and wiped it on his own bare hip. The carpet was thin, and his sore knee was beginning to protest. He shifted to the other leg and took her hands in his. "Leona Day, will you marry me?"

His voice was actually trembling. He swallowed against the hot rush of sentiment that filled his throat.

What if he couldn't convince her? He'd never been all that good with words, not when he needed to be. "Not because of our baby, or because I figger I have to ask you." He looked straight into her blue eyes, trying to transmit all the things he didn't know how to say. "Just because I love you, and I need you for my wife." He'd suddenly had enough of being a supplicant.

"And that's the best I can damned do, so if you want anything more in the way of proposals, you're plumb outta luck, Leona." He got to his feet, leaning over to massage his knee. The pattern from the carpet was ingrained into his skin, probably for the rest of his life. He straightened and glanced at her, apprehensive as hell.

She was smiling at him, a tremulous smile, and although it was warm in the room, there were goose bumps on her naked skin. "Okay, Jackson."

She'd picked up some of his slang. It was his turn to scowl. "Okay what?"

"Okay, I'll marry you."

Incredible relief flooded through him. He pulled her up, crushing her against him so hard she gasped. He remembered the baby and tried to loosen his hold, but her arms were tight around his neck.

"When?"

"Whenever you say."

"I say, the sooner the better." An awful thought

struck him. "Tell me you don't want three thousand guests and a brass band."

She giggled. "I think that's only for virgins, and because of you, I don't qualify. No, I want it small and simple. I already have a dress that will do nicely, and if we can ever get the creases out of that suit over there on the floor, you can wear it."

"Thank God," he said fervently, cradling her against his naked body.

"Now, where were we when you started all this?" she purred, rubbing herself against him in a way she knew was destined to end in only one fashion.

"Don't worry, I marked the place." This time, at least there were no clothes to struggle with. He scooped her up in his arms and carried her to the bed. In the few moments before ecstasy drove all thought from his mind, it dawned on him that without intending to, he'd likely found the perfect solution to keeping Leona occupied.

Boarding with Isabella and her children had taught him that mothers didn't seem to have a whole hell of a lot of time left in a day to rob trains.

"I, Jackson, take thee, Leona Marie, to be my wedded wife. . . ."

Jackson and Leona were married Saturday, November 1st, 1902, and it snowed.

Zelda stood behind them, excruciatingly conscious of Tom close beside her in the crowded room, and she tried with all her heart not to envy Leona, but she failed miserably.

At her insistence, the wedding was taking place in the Ralstons' parlor, with the banquet to be served buffet style in the kitchen afterwards. Frank had no church as yet, and the hall where church services were normally held was large and drafty.

"In sickness and in health, for richer or for poorer. . . ."

Zelda was an emancipated woman who'd countless times rejoiced at her good fortune in being single. Yet at this moment she'd have given almost anything to be saying the words Leona was repeating.

". . . as long as we both shall live."

Her gaze slid to the side, and her eyes encountered Tom's. He was looking at her instead of the bridal pair, his blue eyes troubled and unreadable.

"By the power invested in me by the church, I now pronounce you man and wife."

The irony of the situation suddenly struck Zelda, and she smiled at him, a small, bitter smile.

There was Jackson, one of the most dedicated bachelors she'd ever laid eyes on, marrying Leona, a woman as fervently independent as Zelda was herself—and it wasn't just because of the baby.

Jackson's love for his bride seemed to pour from him like sunlight, with every glance, every touch. Zelda was close enough to hear him whisper, "I love you, Leona," as he slid the ring on her finger.

The words scalded Zelda's very soul, because Tom had never said them to her. She tried her best to smile through a haze of tears, and concentrate on the guests instead of herself.

Most of those present had a role in the proceedings.

Bill Miner, still masquerading as George Edwards, stood at Zelda's elbow. He'd given the bride away.

Zelda knew all about him now. Tom had given her the facts, and later, Leona had filled in the sentiment.

Her best friend's connection with a convicted bank robber bothered Zelda not at all. Her first impression of Miner had been that he was a fine gentleman, and if anything, his conduct had enhanced that impression. As for Leona's involvement in a robbery, Zelda was downright envious. She'd relish the opportunity to participate—as long as no one was injured, of course.

The ceremony ended, and Virgil played the wedding march on his harmonica. Zelda left Tom's side and hurried off to take photographs.

Eli ran a finger under his celluloid collar and wondered how much longer it would be until he could take the tortuous contraption off and get out in the snow.

During the past week, he'd been put in charge of all the jobs no one else wanted to do, which always happened when you were a kid. He'd had to keep the stoves and the buckets stoked with coal; polish everyone's best shoes; clear away the snow from the walkways. Today he had to bring in extra chairs for Isabella and Lars, and make sure Pearl and Eddy were quiet during the ceremony, as if anybody could manage that particular chore.

He shot a glance at his sister. She was bawling, and so were all the other women, including the bride, for Pete's sake.

He fervently hoped when this was all over, Zel would be in a better mood, but with the sobbing going on, maybe that was too much to hope for. At least he'd have his bedroom back, he consoled himself.

That had been the last straw, in his estimation, using his room as a dressing room before the ceremony. Zelda had declared that her tiny room in the eaves was too small and too cold to accommodate the bride.

"But I thought she was getting dressed over at the hotel," he'd groaned early that morning, when Zelda came to wake him with this latest mandate. "If she's already all dressed, what does she need to come up to my room for anyhow?" He yawned and buried his head in his pillow. It was barely six in the morning.

"Don't argue with me, Eli." Zelda looked around the room and made a disgusted sound in her throat. "This place is a sty. Get up and get to work. I'll be up to inspect before breakfast."

Eli was slumped on his bed trying to figure out where to hide his tin of tobacco when Tom stuck his head in the door. "I heard. Why don't you bring your clothes and things into my room? We can both hide out in there." He glanced at the tobacco tin. "Better put that under my bed right now, sport, before your sister sees it."

"Why is she so riled up over this wedding, Tom? She's actin' downright crazy." Zelda had ordered them all around and been increasingly short-tempered and unreasonable as the wedding day neared. She'd even snapped at Virgil, which was unusual. As for Tom, Eli'd heard her nearly take his head off late last night over something or other.

"I guess the excitement of it all is getting to her,

and she feels responsible for making the wedding a success," Tom said.

"Well, I hope I'm not around if Zel decides to get married herself," Eli declared, "if this is how she gets over somebody else's wedding."

Somebody else's wedding. Tom knew that was the crux of the problem, but there was more to it than that. Much more.

He figured Zelda would marry him if he asked, but he never had.

Zelda would bear his baby, if she was pregnant. But she wasn't, and Tom couldn't help the feeling of relief that knowledge gave him. He couldn't have accepted the idea of fatherhood with the equanimity Jackson was displaying.

Jackson had told Tom he wanted this marriage, that even if Leona weren't pregnant, he'd have gotten around to marrying her anyway, that nothing would change the plans he and Tom had made. Hell, they were still partners, he'd just take Leona along when they made their attempt to get back to the nineties, and if that attempt failed, they'd all take off together and find a way to make some money.

He'd been so complacent, so optimistic, that Tom had wanted to pop him one, because he knew it wasn't going to be that way at all.

He knew that Jackson's marriage meant the end of their old, easy partnership. Those times were gone forever. They'd started slipping away when Jackson had taken the job at the hotel, and Tom had gone into the mine.

He knew he could manage without Jackson, although he'd miss him.

The question burning in Tom's mind today was, could he manage without Zelda?

Chapter Nineteen

The realization that he loved her came to Tom with all the force of a hammer blow to his skull.

There was no way he could go and leave her behind. How had he even ever considered it? He was in love with Zelda. He'd gone out of his way to avoid recognizing it, but now, at this simple little wedding, surrounded by people he was close to, he at last acknowledged his feelings for what they were.

Somehow he had to convince her to go with him when the time came. He tried to imagine how it would be, up on that hillside in the early morning hours, on that fateful day next April.

Would the cataclysm of the rock falling do what Jackson and he were hoping—open a tunnel in time that they could pass through? Or, as Tom dreaded, would they simply have a bird's-eye view of the tragedy of Frank and be forced to resume their lives there, however disrupted, knowing that they were fated to live their years out in the first part of the century instead of the last? No one could say; they could only try.

And if by some miracle it worked for him and Jackson, would it work for the others, for Leona, say—or Zelda? If Zelda was there, Tom knew that Virgil and Eli would be as well. He'd never ask her to leave her family behind, and, of course, she'd never agree to do so. Was there a limit to the number of people who could pass through, assuming the route was there?

All they could do was try. And Tom had to convince Zelda to try along with him.

He asked her on a cold December morning, after they'd made greedy, impatient love once, and slower, gentler love once again.

Virgil was on the day shift, Tom on nights, which meant that as soon as Eli left for school, there was blessed privacy for lovemaking—a rare occurrence now that winter made trips to their cave impossible.

They were in Tom's bed, languorous and lazy from lovemaking. The room was icy, but they lay wrapped in each other's arms, snug under layers of quilts. The sun shone through the frost on the tiny window, and outside they could hear an occasional team and wagon go jingling past the house. It had snowed again in the night, and sounds were muted and faraway.

"We've got to get up, Tom." Her whisper tickled his ear. "The fires downstairs will be out if we don't stoke them soon, and I hate having to start them all over again. And you've got to go to the general store for me. We're out of sugar and flour, and I need to make bread. Tom?"

He wasn't listening. He was trying out words and phrases in his head, but none of them sounded just right. He tightened his arms around her and drew a breath. Why was it so hard to say?

"Zelda, I've been thinking. I want you to try and come with me when I go. Will you?" His voice was strained. "In April, the night of the Slide." He drew another deep, shaky breath and added in a rush, "I love you. I want you with me."

He felt her stiffen in his embrace. She was curled against his chest, and he couldn't see her face.

"I couldn't leave Dad and Eli." Her husky voice was thin, and she sounded breathless. "And you've never told them the whole story, Tom."

"I know that, I thought of that. I'll talk to them. I've already told your dad some of it. I'll explain the whole thing. I'll convince them to come along, too. If it works at all, I don't see why it won't work for all of us, as long as we're in the right place at the right time."

He wanted so much to believe that.

She squirmed away from him so she could see his face.

"Have you thought what it would mean, being back in your own time with all of us? Have you considered the responsibility, Tom? We'd be dependent on you, at least at first. Not just me, but Eli and Dad as well."

He'd thought about it. In his entire adult life, he'd never even had a pet relying on him, and now he'd have an entire family.

"I'll take good care of all of you, Zel," he promised

with quiet assurance. He'd figured it out in detail. "I have plenty of money. If you don't like any of the apartments or houses I own, we'll build one to suit you. In New Mexico if you like it there. If you don't, then somewhere else." His words tumbled out, spelling out the dreams he'd woven in the past weeks. "You can take classes in photography at any college. You'll be so amazed and excited at the new techniques, Zel, the modern cameras. We'll enroll Eli in a good school and get the best doctors in the country to treat Virgil. He'll be better in no time, what with the sunshine and the best of medical advice." He hoped that was true, although he wasn't certain.

"And what happens if it doesn't work the way you plan? What happens if we stand up there and watch the mountain slide and then have to go on here with the lives we already have?"

He was quiet for a moment. This was the part he didn't dare let himself contemplate. "Then we'll have to make the best of it, but I know it won't happen that way, Zelda. That one night, in that special place, up on the mountain where the Interpretive Center was, we'll get back. You wait and see." There was passion and excitement in his tone, and he scooped her close and kissed her hard. "You'll come with me then?"

She hesitated, and her nod was reluctant, but he chose not to notice. "Talk to Dad and Eli. If they agree, yes, I'll come. Because I love you, Tom."

Virgil shook his head. "No, lad, I can't do that." His blue eyes were troubled, his refusal definite and final sounding. "Thank you, son. But, no."

Tom looked at the older man, and his frustration made it difficult to hold his temper. "Why the hell not, Virgil? I don't get it. It's a chance for a better life for all of you, for Eli, for Zelda, for yourself."

"The young 'uns can go. I'm not stoppin' them, I never would. But me, I'm too old, too set in my ways." He grimaced and sucked on his pipe. "Can't teach an old dog new tricks, my own daddy used to say. This place you talk of sounds mighty strange to me, what with them cars and planes and talkin' pictures in a man's parlor, and all." He coughed, the deep, harsh sound that was beginning to punctuate every hour of his days. It seemed to go on and on, and when it subsided, his eyes were red and streaming and it was difficult for him to breathe. "Anyways," he wheezed, "seems it's a young person's world, this time you tell about. Old folks get stored away, so to speak, in those rest houses you told of, don't they?"

Tom cursed himself for ever mentioning them, but he couldn't deny that what Virgil said was true. When he thought of it, the nineties did seem centered more around the young, with the old often relegated to special areas where they weren't too visible.

Evelyn Lawrence was suddenly as clear to Tom as if she were present, and he felt a stab of shame. He remembered flipping the coin with Jackson, dreading the visit to the old people's residence, begrudging the few hours she asked of his time.

"Me, I wouldn't do too good in one of those places, Tom," Virgil was saying. "They likely wouldn't let me have my pipe or my tea when I wanted them. I'd as soon take my chances here, where things is familiar, when I get old."

"But you'd be with us, Virgil, with family. We'd never put you in a rest home." Tom knew he sounded desperate. Damn it all, he was desperate. "You know Zelda will never agree to come along without you." Tom hadn't planned to blackmail the older man, but he wanted this too much to give up easily.

Virgil nodded, and a sadness came over his usually cheerful features. "I figgered that. Tom, lad, I'm gettin' weaker every day. I won't be around much longer, and it's time fer some straight talk between us. Now, I've never interfered in what's between you and that girl of mine. I figger it ain't my place."

Tom felt color rise in his face, but he looked Virgil straight in the eye. "I love Zelda, and I'll take good care of her."

Virgil nodded and sighed. "No doubt you would, son. Yer a fine man. But Zelda's my girl, the best daughter a man could have. I'd like nothin' better than to see her settled before I go. She loves you, a blind man could see that, and when you look her way, I know the feelin's mutual. But it's come to me you just cain't give up on wantin' to go back to your own territory, no matter yer feelin's fer Zelda, no matter if she goes or stays. Am I right?"

Tom looked into Virgil's weary eyes and wished with all his heart he could answer differently. The words pained him.

"Yeah, you're right, Virgil." He held the older man's gaze steadily with his own. "I love Zelda," he said. "I want to spend my life with her, but I can't live here, as a miner, and be content. I want more. I have—I had—more, back there. I want to enjoy what I worked hard to get, if going back's possible. I want Zelda to enjoy it with me, and you and Eli, too."

"But whether we come or not, you'll still go up that hill next April's end?"

There it was. Virgil was far too wise to miss the flaw in Tom's proposal. "Yes, I will." The words nearly choked him, but there was no alternative to the brutal truth. "It's what I have to do."

Virgil nodded. "I ain't blamin' you, son. But there's the thing that rubs me, y'see. To my mind, you ain't puttin' my Zelda first. You ain't sayin' you care enough to choose ta live here in her world."

Tom didn't answer, because he saw clearly that Virgil was right.

He took his jacket off the hook and went out into the frigid December day. He made his way to the woodshed, found a huge sawn round and lifted the axe, bringing it down with such monumental force it took him moments to work the blade free.

He chopped steadily, until the stack of kindling and firewood was higher by far than the pile of uncut rounds. His shoulders and arms felt as if he'd fought a giant and lost.

It seemed to Zelda that the wedding was no sooner over than Christmas was upon her, and she was determined to make it a memorable one.

She'd resigned herself to the fact that it would be the only one she ever spent with Tom, and she told herself she wouldn't allow bitter thoughts or regrets to spoil it.

Virgil had told her of his decision and urged her to make her own, regardless of him. He wouldn't explain, even though she'd wept and argued and pleaded with him. He'd been unyielding.

So there was really no decision for her to make, because, of course, she'd never leave her father, sick as he was.

It felt as if she had a stone inside her chest as she threw herself feverishly into preparations for Christmas.

The Ralstons had spent the previous Christmas in Frank, and it had been lonely. They hadn't known many people, and money had been in short supply. They'd gone to a singsong at McIntyre Hall on Christmas Eve, but they'd spent Christmas Day alone, just the three of them, eating the chicken she'd roasted.

This year, everything was different.

The festivities had begun early in December with a sleigh ride organized by Smiley Williams for all the men on his crew and their families. That was followed in quick succession by parties and dances and community potluck suppers, as well as a snowy expedition one afternoon with Lars and Isabella and the children to cut and bring home Christmas trees.

Sundays all during December had been filled with friends dropping by or invitations to visit, and both Joe Petsuko and Augusto Rossi had been adamant that Tom and the Ralstons join their families for Christmas dinner. But Zelda had gracefully refused, explaining that she'd already promised Isabella they'd come next door and celebrate the holiday with her and Lars and the children.

The Zalcos were also invited, and Leona spent Christmas Eve day in the Ralstons' kitchen with

Zelda, cutting out and decorating gingerbread men for Eddy and Pearl, baking pumpkin pies and cooking a huge ham as their contribution to the meal the following day.

Eli and the men had been warned they were expected to help, but it turned out there were simply too many bodies in one small, overheated room.

Zelda sent Tom out for buckets of coal, and when Eli and Jackson had suffered their way through an enormous stack of dirty dishes, she relented and ordered them all out of the kitchen.

Within three minutes, Eli was out the door, going skating with his friends.

"Are you sure we can't help, ladies?" It was pitifully obvious that Jackson was praying Zelda wouldn't change her mind and decide she needed them after all.

"Go!" she snapped.

The three men let out relieved sighs and all but raced into the parlor with a bottle of Augusto's best red wine and a deck of cards, insisting they were going to teach Virgil to play poker. In a short while, male guffaws and pipe smoke were floating down the hallway.

"Thank goodness." Zelda sighed with relief. "Tom and Jackson are just too large to have underfoot, and it's impossible to have a conversation with you with those men around. Now, let's have a cup of tea before we do anything else, and you can tell me exactly what it's like, being in a delicate condition. Sit down here and put your feet up on this box. Do you have any idea when the baby is due?" She was proud of herself for maintaining a cheerful facade.

"May. I went to see Dr. Malcolmson, and he said

the second or third week in May." Their eyes met. Many times over the past weeks, they'd discussed the Slide that Tom and Jackson insisted was inevitable. Zelda had told Leona about Tom's invitation and Virgil's refusal.

"At least the baby will still be safely inside me for the trip," Leona said now.

Zelda managed a laugh. "You make it sound like you're planning nothing more than a buggy trip to Lethbridge."

Leona laughed, too. "That's because I truly don't believe there's much chance of this absurd scheme working, but if Jackson wants to try, I'm going where he goes. We're going," she corrected, patting the bulge under her apron. "I do wish you'd consider coming up there with us that night, Zel. Just in case it does work. Think of the adventure."

Zelda kept her eyes on her teacup. "I couldn't leave Dad. It might be different if he was feeling well, but his cough gets worse by the week. And there's Eli."

Leona made an exasperated sound. "I do wish Tom would come to his senses and just stay here with you then."

How often had she wished that herself?

"He can't," Zelda said, and changed the subject before the agony under her cheerful facade broke through. "Besides, I plan to do whatever I can to get as many people as possible out of town that night, out of the way of the Slide. Tom and I have already tried to warn people of what's going to happen, but they don't believe us. Tom patiently explained the whole thing to Joe and Augusto and the others, to absolutely no avail."

Leona grimaced. "I know. It seems no one will listen. Ever since Jackson told me about it, I've been trying to convince everyone I talk to, the miners, the saloon girls, that the mountain's going to topple over in April. They all laugh and say I've been listening to too many Indian stories, or else they look at me as though I'm some kind of witch." Leona shivered. "Let's not think of it just now. Let's think of Christmas instead."

Zelda agreed wholeheartedly. "You've still not told me what it feels like, having a child growing inside of you."

"It's the strangest thing. He moved for the first time just last week. Oh, Zelda, it was thrilling, like a tiny bird, fluttering around in there, and suddenly I realized there's a real and separate person, growing inside of me. I'm not ill in the morning any longer, which is a blessing, but my middle's expanding at a shocking rate. It's quite frightening, really. One can't help but think about the birth itself." She shuddered.

"Something the size of a fully grown baby is going to pinch coming out. Common sense tells one that, at least." She added, "I don't have anyone to ask questions. When I asked about labor, Dr. Malcolmson patted me on the head as if I was an idiot and mumbled about nature taking its course. Nature is all well and good, but I want *details.* I want to know exactly what to expect, even though I know full well it won't be pleasant."

"Why not ask Isabella? Her English is much improved, and she's been through it twice herself."

Leona considered the suggestion. "She seems very shy. She might be shocked into having the vapors if I ask the things I need answers to."

Zelda shook her head. "I don't think so. We've become close friends, and Isabella's actually very practical."

Zelda thought of a recent conversation she'd had with her neighbor concerning birth control. Isabella had hemmed and hawed, blushed crimson, and finally blurted out that she didn't want to become pregnant, and she knew that Zelda had handed out leaflets at women's meetings on the subject. Zelda had given the other woman the pamphlets and several of her own sponges, as well as an address where she could mail order more.

"Is there any news of her husband?" Leona knew that Isabella and Lars had been trying to locate Nestor Vandusen so Isabella could get a divorce and marry Lars.

Zelda shook her head. "Not a trace. I've helped her write queries for the eastern papers, and the North West Mounted are still trying to locate him, but there hasn't been a single response."

"That's such a shame, because she and Lars are obviously in love. He's wonderful with the children, but, of course, I suppose everyone's gossiping about them living in the same house alone together."

"Let them gossip," Zelda said vehemently. "No one bothered to say anything when Nestor was beating her senseless four times a week."

"Except you, my dear Zelda." Leona gave her a fond smile. "Jackson told me how he first met you, how you ended up in jail because you petitioned against Hugo Bateman for selling spirits to Vandusen." Leona looked at Zelda with open admiration in her eyes. "You're the most honest, compassionate woman I've ever met, and the bravest. I know Isabella thinks so, and all the saloon girls sing your praises to the skies."

"I'll be sure to use them as character referrals the next time Corporal Allan throws me in jail," Zelda said wryly, but she was deeply touched by Leona's words. They were balm, however slight, to the terrible hurt of knowing that Tom didn't love her enough to want her with him for a lifetime. If he did, he wouldn't want to leave.

This Christmas Day was the best Tom ever had.

Not that there was much to compare it with, he thought as everyone was squeezed at last around the laden table in Isabella's kitchen the following afternoon.

Until today, Christmas had never been a cause for much celebration in his life. But seated at this table, surrounded by his friends, he understood for the first time what the day ought to represent—friendship, laughter, celebration—the exchange of small, inexpensive gifts whose real value was in the love they illustrated.

The kitchen was unbelievably crowded.

Lars had built sturdy benches to extend the seating, and although there wasn't room for so much as an elbow between bodies, no one minded at all.

"Tom, you vill ask the blessing, please?" Isabella's unexpected request took him by surprise, and for a panicked moment, Tom couldn't think of anything to say.

He looked around the crowded table for inspiration. Virgil smiled encouragement, his thin face and faded blue eyes stamped with the now-familiar gray tautness that brought a twinge of anxiety to Tom. Virgil's cough had grown worse in the past weeks.

Next to Virgil was Eddy, his healthy little boy's face flushed, his eyes glowing with the excitement of the day. He clutched the replica of a flashy '90s sports car that Tom had whittled and painted a dashing red.

Leona was next, her golden hair piled high, her rounded belly lending an earthy note to her beauty. Jackson, seated beside his wife, winked at Tom, delighted at his discomfiture.

Eli's coppery hair was slicked down flat, and his bony wrists protruded from the cuffs of his shirt. He'd grown a good three inches in the past months. He was almost as tall as Tom, although his body hadn't filled out to match the new found height. He'd been unusually quiet all day, and Tom wondered what was troubling him. He'd have to have a talk with him soon.

Beside Eli was Zelda, and Tom's eyes lingered on her face. She was looking up at him expectantly, smiling her wide smile, her brown eyes soft, telegraphing her love.

His family. These people had become his family during the months he'd spent there, so far removed from the place and time he'd called home.

Tom had to clear his throat before he could manage the simple grace. "Thank you for good friends, good food, and a fine Christmas," he said, and everyone joined in the amen.

"And may the New Year bring peace and happiness to all," Virgil added, lifting his cup in a toast.

Jackson's eyes skittered to meet Tom's, and in the

look they exchanged was the awful knowledge of the coming Slide. This very house would be gone, along with the others along Alberta Avenue, during that April night now only four months away.

And if their plans succeeded, they'd be gone as well that night—Jackson, Leona, himself.

Desolation swept over Tom, and he turned his head to look at Zelda, spooning food into sleepy little Pearl's mouth, laughing at something Isabella had just said, her face radiating life and spirit and energy.

He couldn't leave her.

He couldn't stay with her.

Chapter Twenty

"Tom, you still gonna try and get back to that place you came from, when the end of April comes?"

It was a cold, sunny morning in mid-March, and Tom and Eli had gotten up at the crack of dawn to climb to a nearby lake, so high in the mountains that it was still frozen over. They cut holes in the mushy ice and did their best to catch enough fish for Sunday dinner the following day.

"Yeah, I am, Eli."

"Dad said you wanted us to try and come along, him and me and Zelda."

Tom's breath made a cloud of frost around him. "Yeah, I did. Still do, matter of fact. But your dad doesn't think it's a good idea."

"I want to come, Tom."

Tom checked the line that disappeared into the hole in the ice. One end was tied to his hand, and it didn't need checking; he'd know in an instant if a fish took the hook. Eli's words had taken him by surprise, and he needed a moment to think. "You'd be leaving your family behind, Eli. Your dad won't come, and Zelda won't, either, without Virgil. If the plan works, chances are good you'd never see them again."

"I want to go anyways." Eli's face was stubborn. "I want to see all the things you've told me about, the cars and planes and those video things, and rollerblades and ghetto blasters and rock groups. Besides, you told me you left home when you were fifteen, and you never saw your family again."

Obviously, Tom decided, he'd talked far too much. "The circumstances were different with me, Eli. I didn't come from a family like yours, one where people care about each other."

"Huh." Eli yanked up his line hand over hand, his mittens stiff with ice, his movements jerky. "If Zelda really cared about me, she wouldn't try and make me do what she wants all the time."

Tom noticed that Eli's voice, which only a few months before had tended to wander from bass to soprano in the space of one sentence, was now even and deep. He'd started shaving after Christmas, and his face was now that of a young man instead of a boy. The peevishness of boyhood was also gone, replaced by a quiet steadiness, but along with it there was anger.

"If she really cared, she'd listen when I tell her how much I hate school, and that I don't want to go to that sissy college she's got picked out back East. But I can't seem to make her hear me."

"You know she cares, Eli. She wants the best for

you, that's all it is." Tom knew his words were ineffectual at best. "If you don't want to go to college, then what do you want to do? D'you still want to work in the mines, or what? Have you thought about it?"

"I've been underground a few times. Smiley took me so I could see what it was like, and I guess it's not where I want to work." He hesitated, then said, "I think I'd like to be a Mounted Policeman." His voice was tentative. "I've thought about it, and I figger I'd like that a lot."

Tom was surprised, but when he considered it, he understood. The North West Mounted, in this early period, embodied adventure and romance. If he were Eli's age, he'd probably opt for a career as a mounted soldier, too.

"Have you told Zelda?"

Eli shrugged. "I tried. She won't hear of it, not unless I go to college first." His voice was scornful. "As if a fellow needs college to be one of the North West Mounted. I'll be seventeen next October. I've talked to Constable Liard, and he told me I can start right here in Frank if I want, taking care of the horses and running errands. Then I can be a trumpeter and stable boy at one of the forts, and when I'm eighteen I'd get to be a subconstable, and I could work up from there. Zel had a conniption fit when I mentioned it. I told her if I went away I'd send my wages home and everything, to help out, but she said if I tried it, she'd make them send me back. She could, too, until I'm eighteen. Constable Liard said I'd need a signature before they'd take me on, and I don't think Dad would agree unless

Zelda did. So the only thing left to do is go with you."

Tom knew he was standing on thin ice in more ways than one.

"Eli, you know that Zelda would never agree to letting you come with me, not in a million years."

Eli darted a quick look at Tom's face, and when he caught his eye, looked away again, concentrating on the fishing line. "I didn't actually plan on telling her."

Tom struggled to keep his tone mild, his voice even. "That would be a cruel thing to do, not just to Zelda, but to your father as well."

"Dad would understand." But the words were less certain. "I think he would, anyhow. Before he got sick, he used to stand up for me with Zel. He used to tell her to let me make up my own mind about things. But now, he seems too tired to argue with her. He's not strong anymore, not like he used to be."

A terrible sense of helplessness welled in Tom at the thought of Virgil. The older man was very sick again, confined to his bed, coughing endlessly in spite of the bottles of foul-smelling medicine the doctor dropped off regularly. He'd finally told the boss at the mine that he wouldn't be coming back.

"Is my dad going to die, Tom?" Eli's voice was quiet, but there was a tremor in it. "He never gets over that cough, and he seems to just get weaker and weaker all the time. It's all he can do to get out of bed to go to the outhouse some days."

Tom's heart sank. He'd been expecting and dreading the question, and none of the answers he'd mentally prepared seemed right now that Eli had asked it.

"We all die at some point, Eli. Nobody knows for sure when. Your dad's got a strong body, and he's a fighter."

But no one could fight long when their lungs were destroyed.

"If we could get him to the future, could the doctors there maybe help him?" There was stark appeal in Eli's voice, and again, it was a question Tom had asked himself countless times. The answer was never conclusive.

"They might be able to. They can do lots of things that they can't do now, even lung transplants. But people still die, Eli, then or now. I just couldn't say for sure."

There was silence for a long time. The afternoon was swiftly fading into early twilight. A pale blue mist settled over the lake, and dark snow clouds began to gather over the top of Turtle Mountain.

Tom squinted up at them and pulled his line free of the water. "It's time we packed it in and went home, kid. Looks like it might be going to storm, and we got four fish. Not bad for a day's work."

They were halfway home when Eli spoke again. "I wanna tell you something, Tom, but I gotta be sure you won't tell Zelda."

Being Eli's confidant wasn't easy. Tom sighed and promised.

"I quit school, Tom. I haven't gone more 'n a couple days a week since Christmas, and for two weeks now not at all."

Tom tried not to show how concerned he was at

that revelation. "Where've you been spending your time?"

Eli shrugged. "Around. With some guys I know. We built this cabin in the bush over by the river. And I've been working extra at the picking tables whenever I can."

Tom knew hours of idle time for a teenager could spell big trouble. "How come Zelda hasn't found out you're not in school?"

"Our teacher for the advanced class, Mr. Beebe, left at Christmas and didn't come back. His dad was ailing or something. The new teacher doesn't care who's in class and who's not." Eli sneered. "He's corned half the time. He doesn't even take attendance. That's why I need to come along with you and Jackson, Tom. There's nothin' for me to do in this place." He drew a ragged breath. "Please say I can come."

"You'd have to have permission before Jackson or I would let you even try, Eli."

"Shit!" The expletive was explosive. "No matter what I want to do, there's some reason why I can't do it. I feel just like a prisoner, like I'm in jail or somethin'."

"Your family cares about you." Tom's voice was sharp. "You should be glad they take an interest in what you do with your life."

"Yeah, well, Zelda doesn't seem to realize it *is* my life."

Tom didn't reply. There didn't seem to be anything he could say to Eli that would ease his frustration, and he'd given the boy his word that he wouldn't tell Zelda.

Talking to Zelda about her brother didn't solve a

damned thing anyway. Each time the subject arose, it seemed to precipitate a quarrel between them, and the last thing he wanted was to quarrel with her. He was all too aware that the time they had left to spend together was growing shorter with each passing day.

Maybe he'd have a talk with Jackson about Eli. Jackson cared about the kid. Maybe together they could figure out a way to keep him out of trouble.

"Tom, old buddy, long time no see."

A week after the fishing trip, Jackson was waiting when Tom came out of the washhouse. He'd just worked the night shift at the mine, and he blinked like an owl in the brilliant sunlight.

"You wanna grab some breakfast over at the hotel? I need to talk."

"Sounds good. I've got some things I want to hash over with you, too."

The table Jackson chose was in a private corner, reserved for hotel staff. Tom cradled the steaming mug of coffee between his palms, squinting at his friend. The bone-deep tiredness that came after working a ten-hour shift underground was creeping over him.

He'd listen to what Jackson had to say first, he decided. That would give him a chance to eat and maybe wake up a little. Then he'd bring up the subject of Eli.

"So what's shakin', partner? Leona's okay?"

Jackson grinned and gave him a mock salute with his cup. "Damn, it's good to hear you use new-fashioned slang. If we ever get back home, I'm gonna have to take a crash course. Leona's in the best of health, gettin' a nice round belly on her. She sends her regards." He waited until their heaping plates were in front of them and the waiter had moved away.

Tom turned his attention to the flapjacks and bacon and eggs on his plate, pouring syrup over everything and attacking it with honest hunger.

"I want you to refresh my memory on that gold shipment, Tom."

"Gold shipment?" Tom frowned, his tired brain unable to make the connection.

"The damned gold shipment that landed us here in the first place.

The Klondike gold that was stolen and buried somewhere here." Jackson sounded impatient. "Fill me in on all the details again, okay?"

Tom chewed a mouthful and swallowed, washing it down with coffee. "It was the last of the large gold shipments out of the Klondike," he recalled. "It arrived in Vancouver in mid-April, 1903." He shook his head and gave Jackson a wry grin. "Two weeks from now," he amended. "It'll be fired into gold bars, and secretly shipped via Canadian Pacific Railway across the country to be deposited in the Eastern banks." It was strange to think that the events hadn't happened yet.

"The research I did showed that three men ambush the train in a narrow canyon just west of here." Tom took another hefty swig from his cup. It was confusing, trying to tell the story in the present tense. He decided to tell it the way he remembered it best, as if it had already happened.

"One of the guards recognized the leader of the gang, identifying him as our friend, Bill Miner. The other man was Lewis Schraeger, and the third remained unidentified. As you know, Bill, better known as the Grey Fox, because of his ability to slip away from the law, was wanted on both sides of the border for similar robberies. The police discovered later that Miner had lived quietly right here in Frank for some time, using the alias of George Edwards, working as a land surveyor."

"He actually does work as a surveyor, y'know. He's good at it, too," Jackson commented. "Says some dude in San Quentin taught him the trade. Sorry, didn't mean to interrupt."

"No problem." Tom took up the story again. "The night they took the gold, Turtle Mountain did its thing, and the authorities concluded that Miner and the unidentified third man must have died in the avalanche, because they were never seen or heard from again. Lewis Schraeger was eventually arrested in Montana for cattle rustling and charged with the murder of a rancher. He was sentenced to twenty years in San Quentin, questioned numerous times about the train robbery, and offered a lesser sentence if he told what he knew. But although he admitted knowing Bill Miner, he refused to talk about the robbery or the location of the hidden gold. He had TB, Dr. Lawrence attended him, and the minute Schraeger was cold, Lawrence left the prison service and came here to Frank."

"But Lawrence never located the stuff?"

Tom shook his head. "I'd hoped those diaries Evelyn Lawrence had would shed some light on the whole thing, but . . ." He glanced around and shrugged. "You know the rest. We ended up here, doing field research instead."

Jackson rested his elbows on the table, his face animated. "I've figgered out why Lawrence never found the damned gold, Tom."

"Lay it on me then." Tom yawned and signaled the waiter for another coffee refill. "But you better make it quick. I'm going home to bed in another five minutes. I'm beat." He nodded his thanks to the waiter and sipped the strong brew.

Jackson waited impatiently until they were alone again. "Lawrence couldn't find it because the gold was gone." He paused, his voice filled with excitement. "Don't you get it? We knew where it was, and we either dug it up the minute we got back to our own time, or we took it with us here and used it as a grubstake to finance a new business for ourselves. But my money's on us gettin' back to the future and diggin' it up."

Tom shook his head. "You've lost me. How could we do either?"

"Easy. It makes perfect sense. It came to me when I was havin' a game of cards with Miner last night after the saloon closed. Leona asked me if she could tell him about us, about the robbery and the Slide and all, and I couldn't see any harm in it. I was there when she did, but the peculiar thing was that Bill didn't seem to know diddly about that Klondike shipment. Never heard of it until Leona told him, insisted he doesn't have any contacts anymore on the railway. He's been fixin' to retire, plannin' on takin' a boat to Europe next summer. Leona was gonna go with him till I came along. He even talked Schraeger into takin' a job on some ranch out in the valley. That's why we haven't seen him around. Leona says Schraeger's dumb as a stump.

Bill has all he can do to keep him out of trouble."

"So what?" Tom was weary. All he could think of was getting back to the house and collapsing into bed for a few hours. "Bill probably heard about the shipment at the last minute and changed his mind about retiring. Who knows how it happened? It did, which is all that matters."

"I know. Just calm yourself a minute and I'll explain. Like I said, we got talkin' about it last night, him and me. I get along real good with old Bill. He's a true gentleman. Anyhow, he asked all sorts of things about this robbery he was supposed to have pulled off, the exact time and place, the way he stopped the train. You know any of the exact details, Tom?"

"Quite a few, I guess. I found copies of the reports the guards made of the robbery, and there were references to it in other material I had."

"You'd be able to write them out, maybe, if Bill needed them?"

"I expect so."

"Because he's gonna do it, Tom. He's one of the few guys around who absolutely believes me when I tell him about the Slide and all, and how we got here. He's horrified at the idea of the mountain burying half the town, but like he says, apart from trying to warn folks, there's not a whole hell of a lot we can do to prevent it. So we might as well take advantage of it and do the robbery. Nobody got killed or anything during that heist, did they?"

Tom shook his head. "Not that I read about, but you've got to remember, a lot of the details were pretty sketchy. There wasn't exactly video coverage of the whole thing." He frowned as the import of

Jackson's words sank in. "What do you mean, we might as well take advantage?"

Jackson met Tom's eyes, his gaze deceptively mild. "That's what I've been tryin' to tell you, Tom. I'm goin' along with him. Bill Miner, me, and Schraeger. We're gonna rob the damned train and split the take. When I bury my share, we'll know exactly where to look, you and I, either back in our own time, or if worse comes to worst and we're stuck here . . . Well, hell, in the confusion after the Slide, we can just leave town, all of us, you and Zelda, me and Leona. We'll use our share to break free from this damned place, Tommy."

All of a sudden Tom was wide awake. "God Almighty! Have you lost your mind? Train robberies are a criminal offense. You could end up in San Quentin right along with Schraeger. Or get yourself shot. That shipment is under armed guard."

"Wake up and smell the gold, partner." Jackson gave him a withering look. "You know that didn't happen. You just told me the exact way the whole robbery went down. Smooth as cream, nobody hurt, good guys get away with the loot, bad guys get to talk to the Feds, the whole shipment insured, everybody's satisfied. It's not as if you and I haven't operated outside the law before, Tommy, m'boy. Remember those undercover jobs for the good old U.S. of A.? They weren't exactly what I'd call Boy Scouting. We knew damned well if we got caught, we'd probably do jail time in some stinkin' foreign prison, and our own government wouldn't lift a finger to defend us, because what we were doing was highly illegal. If you ask me, this is one whole hell of a lot cleaner than that stuff was."

Tom couldn't disagree, but neither could he approve of what Jackson was planning. "Does Leona know about this, that you're planning on going along on a robbery?"

"Not yet." Jackson's smile was grim. "But, believe me, there's not a whole lot she's gonna be able to say about it." He rested his forearms on the table and leaned forward. "Tom, don't get all moral on me here. This is our one big chance to break free, whatever goes down the night of the Slide. If we get to travel back, then hot dog, we know where the gold is. If we stay on this ass end of the century, we clear out of this burg, travel the world again, watching out for opportunity, just the way we did before."

Jackson slumped back in his chair. "I'm sick to death of slingin' booze, and you can't tell me you really want to spend your life workin' your guts out with a pick and shovel in a coal mine, either." He raised his hands, palms up. "Far as I can figger, this is our one chance at somethin' better. You're the man who always said money's what really matters when the chips are down. Don't you remember your theme song, 'I've been rich, and I've been poor, and rich is better'?"

He grinned, the exuberant, wicked grin that made him look both charming and dangerous. "You write down every single detail you can remember about the robbery and the gold shipment, and after we study it, I'll go play cops and robbers with Bill the Gentleman Bandit." He winked. "Technically, how the devil could I rob a train in 1903 when I wasn't even born till 1954? Way I figger it, if we get back the way we plan, we're gonna make a mint on movie rights for this whole caper."

"You can't even ride a horse." Tom knew it was a ridiculous objection, but none of the rational ones had worked on Jackson.

"I'm about to learn. Bill's got a couple extra saddle horses. He's gonna teach me. And he's got a nice little side arm I can borrow as well. I may not be able to ride, but I'm one hell of a good shot, you got to admit."

"You've lost your mind. This is the screwiest idea I've ever heard."

"You got a better one that'll get us some dough?"

Tom didn't. Ever since they'd arrived, both he and Jackson had racked their brains to find a grubstake. But the old adage was as true now as it had been in his time. It took money to make money. All the same, this idea was insane.

"Finding lost treasure is one thing. Deliberately stealing it is another. Forget it, Jackson. If we get back, we've got enough assets without the damned gold."

"And if we don't—which you've got to admit is pretty likely—then what, Einstein? We'll have missed our only shot at living the rest of our natural lives in any sort of comfort." Jackson's jaw was set, and the usual easy humor in his voice was missing. "I'm set on this, Tom, so stop tryin' to change my mind for me."

Tom lost his temper. "No chance of that! You're so damned stubborn you'd never listen to reason, anyhow." He got to his feet and slapped money down to cover his breakfast. "I'm going home to bed." He walked out of the hotel, acutely aware that for the first time in all their years together, he and Jackson had just had a serious quarrel.

And he'd never even gotten around to mentioning the problem of Eli, either.

Zelda's whole body was trembling, her hands most of all. Tears of fury and impotent frustration trickled down her cheeks as she lifted the mug of cold tea, spilling some on the tablecloth before she got it as far as her mouth.

The table was littered with the congealed remains of the breakfast she'd cooked. No one had eaten the eggs or oatmeal or bacon; Tom still hadn't come home after his night shift and she and her brother had fought bitterly while the food grew cold.

The kitchen was empty now, but it still seemed to echo with the angry words she and Eli had just hurled at one another. There was no sound from her father's room upstairs. He'd come down during the worst of the quarrel, and when Eli had slammed out of the house, he'd made his way back up to his bedroom, coughing all the way.

"Morning, Zel." The kitchen door opened and Tom came in, hanging his coat on a peg and setting his lunch pail on the counter. "Sorry about breakfast. I had some with Jackson at the hotel."

She set her cup down and folded her hands in her lap to stop their trembling.

Be calm, she warned herself. Don't accuse—Be reasonable. Ask. It might just be Eli, making it sound as if Tom had betrayed her trust.

"I suppose the two of you are making plans, now that April's almost here." Despite her good intentions, it came out sounding accusatory.

"Yeah, something like that." Tom found a mug

and poured tea into it, adding cream and sugar and slumping into a chair across the table from her as he stirred it. "Time's getting on, all right."

"Did Eli happen to mention that he's planning on going with you?" She cleared her throat. "The night of the Slide?" She did her best to control her voice, but it trembled. "He wants to try and go along with you, he says."

"Yeah, as a matter of fact, he did tell me that." Tom lifted the mug and drank. "I'd have said something to you about it, but he asked me not to."

So he had known, just as Eli said. Hurt and anger knotted into an ugly ball in her middle, and she pressed her hands against her abdomen. "Were you and Jackson planning to leave me a note perhaps?" Pain made her sarcasm vicious. "Thanks for everything, Zelda, and oh, yes, before I forget, I've taken your brother with me?"

"You know I wouldn't do that." He sounded exasperated.

"I don't know anything of the kind." She glared across at him, choosing to ignore the weariness on his face, the dejected slump of his shoulders. "I do know that from the very beginning, you and Jackson have filled my brother's head with—with these preposterous stories about this wonderful place you come from. All along, you've lured him into wanting to visit this—this utopia." Her anger was getting the better of her, and her voice was rising. "How could any boy Eli's age resist the temptation to go along with you when you spin such tales and encourage him to be irresponsible about his schooling?"

Tom set his cup down with a bang. "Let's get one

thing straight here, Zelda. Neither Jackson nor I have ever tried to talk Eli into coming with us. And I told him he'd have to have permission from you and your father before I'd even consider such a thing."

"And I suppose you've never encouraged him either in this foolishness about running off to become a bugler at some forsaken Mounted Police post?"

"He mentioned that to me, too. Actually, I didn't think it was such a bad idea."

"Not a bad idea?" Zelda felt impotent rage building inside her at his callous attitude. "Eli's a sixteen-year-old *child,* Tom. He has the opportunity to make something of himself if he'd only buckle down and finish his education. You knew that he'd quit school, too, didn't you?"

He met her eyes, and he didn't have to say a word. She read the answer in his expression.

"How could you not tell me?" Her voice was steady, but it felt as if something were breaking apart in her chest. "How could you know such a thing and not do something about it?"

Tom shook his head, rubbing his hand through his hair. "He told me in confidence, Zel. I've been racking my brain to figure out what to do about it."

"Well, you needn't trouble yourself any longer. He won't be pestering you to join your little party at the end of April, either. Dad signed the consent form this morning so Eli could go and work at the Mounted Police barracks as a stable boy."

She set the cup she was still holding down with such force that it broke. Tea spilled across the cloth and dripped to the floor, and she ignored it, clutching her hands to steady their trembling.

"So after all the dreams I had for him, my brother's going to end up an ignorant, uneducated, bumptious *law*man."

He gave her a long, steady look. "There are worse things for a young man, Zel. The North West Mounted will become one of the most respected law enforcement agencies in the world during the next decade. If Eli wants to join them, he'll end up having an exciting career."

"I've had about enough of you telling me what's going to happen in the future." Her words came out in a hiss. "In case you hadn't noticed, we lesser mortals live in the here and now, and try to cope with things as they are instead of the way they will be."

She began to gather up the dishes, viciously scraping the remains of the food into the chicken bucket.

Tom, too, got to his feet, leaning his hands on the back of the chair. "And in case *you* hadn't noticed, Eli isn't a little kid anymore who's going to do what you tell him." His voice was cold with anger. "I've been trying to get that through to you for months now. Maybe what you want for him isn't what he wants for himself, you ever once think of that? For God's sake, Zelda, live your own life and let Eli live his." He gave the chair an angry shove and walked off down the hall. "I'm going to bed."

Furious tears rolled down her face as she poured boiling water from the kettle over the dishes in the basin. So his advice to her was to live her own life, was it?

What kind of life did he think that was going to be after he left? Because in spite of his declarations of love, Tom was still doing his level best to leave her behind forever. The fact that he wanted to do so hurt her even more than this business with Eli. Reason told her it was hopelessly romantic to think that he loved her enough to choose to stay in an age in which he didn't belong, but she wished it all the same. God, how she wished it.

And if the effort failed and he had to remain here? With the dishtowel she swiped angrily at the tears on her face. She'd spent a lot of time thinking it over. Would she be waiting for Tom the morning after the Slide, ready to resume their relationship where it had left off, if, by some miracle, he was still around?

She sniffed and straightened her shoulders. "Pride, Zelda Ralston," she muttered. "Your pride in yourself as an independent, self-sufficient woman must get you through this."

And one thing was certain, she decided as she slammed dishes from one basin to the other, sending soapsuds cascading down the front of her apron and onto the floor.

She was not going to be any man's humble consolation prize, no matter how much she loved him.

The dishes weren't finished, but she ignored them. She dried her hands on her apron, and on legs that felt like blocks of wood she turned and went down the hall, into her studio.

There, amidst her work, she felt stronger. Here was evidence that she was independent, a career woman, more than just a pathetic old maid who'd fallen in love with the wrong man.

She closed the door behind her and leaned against it, her breath coming in short, hard gasps.

She felt so betrayed by Eli, by her father, but most of all, by Tom.

He, more than anyone, knew of the hopes and dreams she'd had for her brother. She'd confided in Tom, allowed him to see how much it meant to her to have Eli make something of his life. Now he'd conspired against her, encouraged her brother in this course of action that he knew would hurt her irreparably.

Her eyes went to the calendar on the wall. April 29 was circled in red crayon, a scant five weeks away. She'd been scoring off the days, not because of the coming Slide and the need to evacuate the house—she'd long ago come to terms with that—but because it would mark the end of her time with Tom. She walked over and ripped the calendar from the wall, tearing it into small bits and letting them fall to the floor.

At least that part of the waiting was over.

Chapter Twenty-one

She didn't remember going up the stairs, although she must have climbed them.

Tom's bedroom door was open, and she was relieved to see that he wasn't yet in bed. He was sitting on the chair by the dresser, his dark, curly head bent, seemingly lost in thought. He looked up at her, and she steeled herself against the naked appeal in his blue gaze.

"I want you to pack your things and leave, immediately," she said, keeping her voice flat, devoid of any feeling. "I'll return the remainder of this month's rent, of course."

Her tone of voice and her impersonal words brought him slowly to his feet. "So you figure this whole thing is my fault, is that it?"

She turned away from him and wouldn't answer, but with one quick step he moved up behind her.

He took her shoulders and forcibly turned her, so she had to look at him.

"You're making a big mistake here, Zelda."

"I made a mistake, yes, but this isn't it. Now take your hands off me. Whatever there was between us has ended, and I think it best you leave as soon as possible." She reached up and tried to remove his fingers from her shoulders, but they were like iron clamps. She'd have bruises, some detached part of her reasoned.

"Zelda." Her father stood in his bedroom doorway just across the hall, concern evident in his face. He'd obviously heard what had been said. "You mebbe want to think this over, lass. It's not Tom's fault Eli's quit school, now is it? No sense doin' somethin' you'll be sorry for later."

"I know exactly what I'm doing, Dad. I want Tom out of here, now." She turned on her heel and marched back down the stairs and along the hallway. She snatched her old brown coat from the peg by the back door and walked out blindly into the mocking sunshine of a splendid spring morning.

Tom made a move to follow her, but Virgil put a restraining hand on his arm. "Best let her go, son. Sorry this had to happen. I tried to talk to her before you got home, but I didn't get no further than you did. When women get an idea in their noggin, there's no changing it sometimes." His shoulders sagged. "Poor old Zel. She's real broken up over Eli quittin' school, and she's vexed with me fer signin' the paper so's the lad can join the Mounted." He looked into Tom's eyes. "And you'll be leavin' her, too, most likely. That's what this is all about, I reckon."

Tom knew it was the truth.

Half an hour later Tom shoved the last of his belongings in a box and tucked it under his arm. One thing about it, he hadn't amassed a whole pile of stuff, so moving didn't involve much packing.

"I'm off now, Virgil." Tom stood in the older man's doorway, awkward, wondering what in hell to say that would convey even some of his feelings.

Virgil was lying down, the patchwork quilt pulled over him. He struggled to a sitting position, punching the pillows into a backrest behind him. "Well, son, I'm right sorry to see you go. Where you thinkin' on stayin'?"

"The Miner's Hotel, probably. I've heard they have pretty decent rooms, meals included. Won't be anywhere's as good as here. As soon as you're on your feet, come on over for a game of poker." The muscles in his throat felt tight, and he forced a smile.

"I'll surely do that."

"Good." Tom set the box down on the bed and scrubbed his face with his hand, weary to the very bone. "I love her, Virgil. I'd take her with me if she'd come, but she won't."

Virgil shook his head. "She can't leave, you can't stay. That's the sum of it. It's a damned shame, but nothin' to be done. I'll miss you, son."

Tom knew Virgil wasn't talking only about now. Suspicious moisture gathered in the older man's eyes.

"I'll miss you, too. These have been some of the

best months in my life, living here with you and your family. I can't thank you enough—"

"Get away with ya. It's been a two-way street. You've worked like a navvy around here, and paid us hard cash into the bargain. Made me ashamed sometimes, lollygaggin' around in this bed the way I do these days. But won't be long now till I'm better, what with spring comin' on."

Tom was certain that they both knew it wasn't going to happen.

Day by day, Virgil was growing weaker. He still managed to get dressed and come downstairs, but the effort was greater every day. The struggle to make it back up the steps to his bedroom was more and more painful to witness.

"Take this, lad." Virgil was holding out a crumpled dollar bill, probably the last one he had. "You'll need a mite extra, what with payin' rent an' all."

Tom's heart swelled up in his chest, and he wanted to weep. "Thanks, Virgil, but I've got enough."

"Long as you're sure. Don't be scared to ask, if ya come up short."

Tom took the calloused miner's hand with its broken nails and myriad scars tight in his own, trying wordlessly to convey all that he felt in that simple clasping, afraid that he was failing dismally.

"Thanks so much for everything, Virgil." The words were inadequate, but in the end they were all he could find. "I'll be back to move you out before the end of the month. You need anything, send Eli for me."

"Right you are." Virgil sank back on the pillows as the interminable coughing started, waving Tom out of the room when he hesitated at the door.

Tom made his way down the stairs, pausing in the kitchen to stoke the stove with coal so the fire wouldn't go out. Zelda was nowhere around, but he hadn't expected her to be. There was nothing friendly about this parting, and nothing he could say would make it easier.

He stared down into the flames in the firebox. Deep inside, he'd always known he was incapable of sustaining a loving relationship with a woman. He'd never planned to hurt her, but he'd succeeded anyway. He replaced the stove lid with an impotent bang and shoved his arms through the worn sleeves of his coat.

At the door he turned and looked around the kitchen.

He'd spent such happy hours in this room, in this house. It was the first house he'd ever lived in that felt like home, but that was due to the people who lived here with him. He loved them, all of them, each in different ways.

Virgil was the father he'd never had.

Eli had somehow eased the guilt over the brothers he'd lost long ago.

And Zelda . . . Oh, God, when he thought of Zelda, the sense of desolation in his gut was so vicious and powerful he wanted to double over and retch.

Instead, he made his way to the Miner's Hotel and paid for five weeks' room and board—the five weeks he had to get through somehow before he left Frank forever.

* * *

Two weeks passed, then three. Lars Olsen sought Tom out to say good-bye. He'd been hired by the owner of a construction company in Fernie, a town sixty miles west of Frank, to build a hotel and a number of houses. He was taking Isabella and the children with him, and he was elated.

"Now I vill have steady vork, and near Fernie I have found a farm. The house is not good, but I vill build a new one for Isabella and me. You vill come and wisit, Tom, our honored guest."

Tom had never been able to convince Lars that the town of Frank was doomed. He was immeasurably relieved now that his friend wouldn't be around to witness the Slide when it happened. Tom had spent hours trying to plot a way of making certain that Lars and Isabella and the children would be safe when the time came, and it seemed that fate had taken over for him.

The two men grasped each other's hand. "Except for our friends, Isabella and I are glad to be leaving this place," Lars confessed. "Still there is no vord of this svine Isabella is married to, so from now, in this new place, ve vill use my name and forget all about him. She is my vife now, common law, yah?"

Tom nodded approval. "That's the best way to go, Lars. Vandusen will likely never show up. He's probably gotten himself shot or something. Unless the law's changed from what I know, you can have him declared legally dead after a certain amount of time goes by. I wish you a lifetime of happiness, my friend."

"And you, Tom." A shadow passed over Lars's cheerful face. "I am sorry about you and Zelda. I had hoped to dance at your vedding, yah? Can you not take her some daisies, say you are sorry for vatever it is between you? Vomen, they need petted, now and again, Tom. She is a fine voman, Zelda. I vould marry her myself, if I did not love my Isabella."

Tom's smile was stiff. "Thanks for the advice, buddy. Tell Isabella good-bye from me, and hug those kids, okay?"

"And you vill come and wisit, yah?"

"If I can, I will."

Tom watched Lars stride off. He'd become a good friend, and Tom would miss him.

Tom went to the Ralstons' house three times during those weeks, desperate to see Zelda, talk with her, and if possible, mend the breach between them. Each time, she met him at the door with a cool hello, her manner polite and formal.

Twice, Virgil was sitting at the kitchen table, pitifully glad to see Tom and gossip with him for an hour, and Zelda immediately put on her coat and left, saying she had errands to run.

The third time, Tom deliberately arrived late in the evening.

"I'm afraid Dad's in bed already," she said, standing in the doorway, barring his way. The lamplight behind her turned her hair to flame, and he couldn't see her features clearly, but just the sound of her voice fulfilled an aching need in him.

"I figured he would be. It's you I want to talk to, Zelda. Can I come in?"

"No. I'm sorry, Tom. No. Nothing's changed between us. As far as I'm concerned, we have nothing more to say to one another."

"You may not have, but I do." It was all he could do to stop from reaching out and dragging her into his arms. As if she sensed it, she took a careful step back so that she was out of his reach.

"Whatever it is, I don't want to hear it." The steely note in her husky voice was suddenly gone, and she sounded close to tears. "Please, Tom," she begged in a ragged whisper that broke his heart. "Please, please don't come here anymore. I can't bear it."

She closed the door softly, and for a moment he contemplated smashing it down. His fists clenched and it took moments before he had control again. Then he turned and almost ran down the steps.

She was right. Nothing had changed. Nothing could change.

He didn't go to the house again, relying on his frequent visits with Eli to keep abreast of what was happening with Zelda and with Virgil. They met whenever Tom's shifts and Eli's work at the police barracks allowed, usually once or twice a week.

Eli had became equally obsessed with law and order and the forthcoming Slide. He questioned Tom about every detail, particularly the story of the miners trapped inside the mine.

"I've tried to tell Corporal Allan what's going to happen, but he remembers you from when you first got here and he thinks it's all a story you made up. He believes you're not right in your head, Tom, no matter how I try to tell him different."

There had been times during the past weeks when Tom himself had wondered about his sanity, but he didn't say so to Eli.

They were sitting in the Frank Cafe. Tom ordered them glasses of milk and slabs of apple pie.

"How're things with you and Zelda?" He needed to hear about her, to know that she was safe and well. He knew that she'd finally rented a house on several acres on the outskirts of Frank, in a location he was certain was far from the Slide.

He'd been appalled that she was staying in the vicinity at all. He'd advised her to move to Blairmore, when they were still talking, but as usual, she was doing things her own way. Unfortunately, the house she'd rented wouldn't be vacant until the twenty-seventh, just two days before the Slide.

"She still mad at you for quitting school?"

Eli shrugged. "She's still mad, all right. But not like she used to be, when she'd holler and yell, then get over it. She just doesn't act like she used to. She's real quiet, she never laughs like before. And she seems kind of far away all the time."

He frowned. "I keep tryin' to get her to start packing up to move, but all she says is that Dad's too sick, that if she waits maybe he'll get feeling a little better. But I think it's her more 'n Dad. Her eyes are red a lot, like she's been crying. I can't get her interested in nothing at all." He forked up a huge mouthful of pastry, chewed slowly, and swallowed, his Adam's apple bobbing. "I wish you and Zel could get back together, Tom," he said in a plaintive tone. "She was real happy when you were there."

Tom had given up any pretense of eating. It felt as if a lump had lodged in his throat. "Yeah, well, sometimes these things just don't work out. Is your dad worse, d'you think?"

Eli's young face became somber, and he laid his fork down as if the pie had suddenly lost its appeal for him as well. "He's not very good, that's for sure.

He mostly spends the days in bed or just sitting in the parlor by the stove. He's always cold, and his cough is worse. He can't get his breath too good."

Tom took several folded bills from his pocket and shoved them across the table to the boy. Eli had objected to the money when Tom had offered during their first meeting, but Tom had made him understand how much he needed to feel that he could help, in some small way.

But this time Eli shook his head. "Zel asked where I got the money last time, and she kept on and on at me till I had to tell her. And she says to tell you we're managing fine, and she won't accept no more money from you."

Impotent rage almost choked Tom. Why in God's name did she have to be so stubborn? "I'll be over early on the twenty-seventh to help you move."

Eli frowned. "Zel isn't gonna like that, either. She walks outta the room if I so much as mention your name, for Pete's sake."

"She doesn't have a lot of choice in the matter this time. You and she can't do it alone, and I want her and your dad settled and safe."

Before I go. The words were unspoken, but they were there all the same. There was silence between them. Tom signaled the waiter for coffee, and after it arrived, Eli said, "Can you draw me a map, Tom?"

"Of what?"

"You told me the miners tunneled out the night of the Slide. I need to know the exact route they used. You said seventeen out of twenty men on the night shift tunneled thirty-six feet up, to where a seam of coal outcropped. I want to know where."

"I'm not certain I can pinpoint it exactly. What

I'll do is try and locate it underground. What'd you plan to do with the map, Eli?"

"Give it to Smiley, or one of the other foremen. Even if they don't believe me, maybe just looking at it will help when the time comes."

Tom sighed in frustration. "I've told Smiley and everyone else I could get to listen to me exactly what's going to happen, but they just figure I'm a well-meaning crackpot. Maybe you'll have more luck." Tom smiled at the earnest young man. Being at the police barracks had brought out the best in Eli, proof that the choice he'd made was the right one for him. "I'll draw what I can and try and find the place inside. I'll give it to you the next time I see you."

Drawing the map for Eli reminded Tom that he'd also told Jackson he would write down all the details he could remember of the train robbery. He'd deliberately held off doing so, hoping that Jackson would come to his senses in the meantime.

Now he wrote out everything he could remember. That evening he shoved the closely written sheets in his jacket pocket and walked to the Imperial where Jackson was working behind the bar.

Tom hadn't seen his friend since the morning they'd quarreled. He sat on one of the bar stools, sadly aware that behind the wide, welcoming grin, Jackson was wary of him.

"Hey, Tom, how's it goin', good buddy?" He tapped Tom's shoulder with his fist and plopped a brimming mug of draft down.

"Have one on me."

The bar was quiet. Jackson polished an already spotless glass with a white towel, his every movement reflected in the long mirror behind him. "Heard you've moved from the Ralstons'. Leona was talkin' to Zelda."

"You probably know what went down then."

Jackson nodded. "Yeah. Sorry to hear about you and Zelda. Hear you're bunkin' over at the Miner's. You coulda come here, y'know. I'd' a got you a room. My old one's empty now that Leona and I are sharing a suite."

It was obvious that Jackson was ill at ease. For the first time in their long friendship, Tom, too, felt awkward.

"Thanks, but I'm fine where I am. It's not for very long, anyhow." Tom waited while Jackson served whisky to two rough-looking men at the other end of the bar. "You remember that matter we talked about last time I saw you," he said in a low tone when Jackson came back. "You still going along with it?"

Jackson's easy smile didn't waver, but the glance he shot Tom was cautious. "Same plans as before," he said softly. "Same time, same place."

"I wish you'd change your mind."

Jackson moved his head slowly from side to side. "Sorry, partner. Not a chance."

Tom stuck his hand in his pocket and withdrew the pages he'd written out, handing them to Jackson. "Maybe this'll help then."

Leaving the beer untouched, he walked out of the bar.

* * *

"Good afternoon, Miss Ralston." Corporal Allan stood just outside the studio door, and as soon as Zelda opened it, he stepped inside.

His massive bulk made the room suddenly too small. His eyes made a swift survey behind Zelda, lingering on one photograph and then another. She'd been planning to pack everything into boxes this afternoon, in preparation for the move, but she hadn't started yet.

Her heart slammed against her chest, and fear blossomed. "Oh, my goodness. It's Eli, isn't it? He's been hurt—"

Allan gave her a startled look and shook his head. "No, no, the lad's fine. He's running an errand for me at the moment. No, Miss Ralston, I'm here on police business."

Instantly, the thought of Leona and Bill Miner and train robberies ran through her head, and her stomach roiled. She fought to keep her expression from revealing any of her thoughts, and the animosity she felt toward Allan now took precedence over fear.

This was the man who'd had her arrested and flung into a filthy cell like a common criminal, she reminded herself. Well, he'd get nothing out of her.

"May I?" Without waiting for an answer, he stepped neatly around her. He moved directly to an enlargement she'd made of a provocative photograph of Leona, reclining on a chaise longue with rather a lot of bosom and leg exposed and a feather boa draped across her arms.

Zelda's heart sank as Allan studied it in silence. She would say absolutely nothing, of course, no matter what atrocities he threatened her with. But what would become of Leona? Surely they couldn't imprison a woman big with child. She'd have to contact other members of the Women's Temperance Union immediately, and see if they would assist her in coming to Leona's aid.

"Hmmmm." His already florid face was crimson when he at last turned to another photo, giving it the same intense scrutiny. "Eli tells me your father is not well. I hope his condition is improving?"

If only it were. "I'm hoping the warm weather will help," she said evenly.

"Extend my regards." He went from one photograph to the next, studying them as if they were police exhibits. "Yes. Well. Your brother told me you were an exceptional photographer, Miss Ralston, and I see he didn't exaggerate. Well, now." He clasped his hands behind his back and rocked on his heels.

Zelda felt like screaming with frustration. Why didn't he just come out with whatever it was he wanted?

"I haven't had occasion to speak with you in quite some time, Miss Ralston. Am I to understand that you've given up your attempts at closing down the local drinking establishments?"

Zelda lifted her chin high and looked at him defiantly. "Without the support of the law, there wasn't much chance of success, was there, Corporal? And as I'm sure you know, my neighbor's husband fortunately left town before he succeeded in murdering her, so the motivation hasn't been as urgent in recent months." She didn't add that her convictions weren't as clear-cut as they once had been.

"I see." Zelda could have sworn there was a gleam

of humor in his eyes. "Well, since you've become a law-abiding citizen, I wonder if you'd consider doing photography for the North West Mounted?"

Taken aback and totally confused, she repeated stupidly, "Photography? Me? For the Mounted?"

"Yes. I'm afraid some of it isn't at all suitable for a lady, but your brother assured me you were a professional, not given to hysterics or the vapors. You see, we need photographs taken occasionally, portraits of our members, of criminals we've arrested, of crime scenes, and unfortunately, sometimes of the victims of violent crimes as well, bodies and so forth. We've contracted until now with Mr. Beaseley, but unfortunately, he's developed something of a, ummmm, a drinking problem, and is no longer reliable."

His gray eyes met hers in an assessing stare. "Are you interested in taking on the contract, Miss Ralston? The Mounted will pay whatever reasonable rate is mutually acceptable."

"Yes. Yes, of course, I'm interested." She'd have to be a fool to refuse. It was exactly the sort of work she'd dreamed of getting, both steady and lucrative. It would help immeasurably with the doctor's bills, steadily increasing as Virgil's illness worsened. "I'm—we're—moving soon, to a house on the other side of town."

"Eli mentioned that. It's actually much closer to the detachment, so that will be an advantage, should we need you in a hurry. That's good then. Settled." He nodded, turned to the door, and hesitated. He whipped around to face her. "Your young brother is a fine young man, Miss Ralston," he said in a formal tone. "We're very fond of him at the barracks. He'll make a good policeman when the time comes. He's both honest and intelligent, and hardworking to boot. I understand you helped raise him, madam. You are to be commended." He shot her a keen look. "He's indicated you are less than pleased at his being associated with the North West Mounted."

Knowing she might be about to lose the opportunity that had just presented itself, she still had to tell the truth. "Lawmen are generally not well educated, Corporal. They're generally a rough lot, in my opinion." It was still painful to acknowledge her failure. "I wanted more for Eli, I wanted him to have an education, so that if he chose, he could become a lawyer, or a doctor, or whatever profession appealed to him. I was—I am—" she swallowed the tears that seemed to lurk just behind her eyelids these days—"bitterly disappointed that Eli quit school and chose to work for you." She turned away, forcing her voice to remain even. "I am despondent about it, Corporal. You see, until this past year, Eli was a good student, with a promising future."

"And what happened to change that, madam?"

She told Allan about the abrupt departure of Mr. Beebe, and, not bothering to mince her words, described the drunken sot who'd succeeded him and brought about Eli's final refusal to go to school. She didn't add that in her heart she also laid a large share of the blame on Jackson and Tom and their stories of adventure, although that conviction gnawed at her still.

Corporal Allan nodded thoughtfully. "And, of course, Eli is at a time in his life when he wants to begin testing himself, making his own decisions. The transition to manhood isn't always an easy one."

Zelda bristled. She'd heard quite enough on that score from her father and Tom. "Quitting school doesn't seem very sensible to me or very mature. I would think that even a policeman could appreciate that, Corporal."

"I am an advocate myself of education, Miss Ralston," he replied politely, apparently not offended. "Not to sound pretentious, but I am rather well versed in such areas as mathematics, Latin, and history. In fact, I was a teacher in a rather elite school for young gentlemen before I left England in search of adventure with the Mounted."

He thought for a moment and seemed to come to a decision. "How would it be if I suggested to young Ralston that he spend his idle evenings exploring some of my textbooks with me? I have rather a good collection, if I do say so myself."

It took a moment to register. "You're—you're offering to tutor my brother?"

He raised his bushy eyebrow. "One can only lead a horse to water, madam. Whether he chooses to drink is quite another matter."

"Yes. Of course. I understand." She didn't at all. She had no idea how this had all come about, but it seemed a miracle. "Oh, I'd—I'd be most grateful if you would try, Corporal. I'll have a word with Eli—"

The ferocious look he gave her silenced her.

"Indeed you will not. Worst thing you could do. Let Eli make his own choice, Miss Ralston, or I guarantee he will refuse to open a single book. I've had a great deal of experience in this regard, and, believe me, pushing a young man of Eli's age and temperament into doing something you think best for him will always result in his running as fast and as hard as he can in the opposite direction."

Zelda could only stare at him. It came to her suddenly that she'd been hearing the same advice over and over, in different ways, from her father, from Tom, from Eli himself, and ignoring it. For some reason, hearing it from Allan forced her to recognize it as truth.

"I'll do as you suggest," she said quietly. "I still have a sum set aside for his education, so whatever your fee—"

Allan looked horrified. "There will be no talk of fees, Miss Ralston. I thought I'd made myself clear. The matter is not your affair. It will be entirely between Eli and myself. We will work out a suitable arrangement between ourselves. He would be furious to learn that his sister was involved in any way."

Slowly, she nodded, aware for the very first time that Eli was no longer the little boy she'd protected and cared for all these years. Her role as mentor in his life was over, had been over for some time, although she'd been far too stubborn to recognize it.

The realization left her feeling empty and immeasurably sad, but it also was a kind of freedom, one that would take time to get accustomed to. Her relationship with her brother had changed. She must try to establish a friendship with him, instead of a stewardship.

Tears welled and spilled over. She reached out her hand, taking Corporal Allan by surprise. It took him a second to respond, but at last he clasped her hand in his huge warm paw.

"Thank you, Corporal." *For far more than you realize.*

"Perhaps a glass of water, Miss Ralston?" He was so obviously horrified and ill at ease with a weeping female that her tears gave way to amusement. She wished she'd known long ago that female tears had this effect on him; she might have avoided several nasty confrontations just by dabbing her eyes with a lace handkerchief.

The moment Allan detected the faint trace of a smile on her features he looked vastly relieved and dropped her hand like a hot scone. He stepped back several paces and adjusted his Stetson so it was again at a precise angle to his square jaw. "Well, that takes care of everything then, Miss Ralston. You'll be notified whenever we need your services."

He turned to the door, then paused. "There is one other annoying little matter." He cleared his throat several times. "Your brother has repeated to me—and, unfortunately, to half the populace of the town—a disturbing rumor about Turtle Mountain. He's been most vocal about it. Embarrassingly so. I have had to warn him about the dangers of hearsay. Now, I know where the tale originated, of course, as you do. I believe you were present when it was told the first time."

He fixed her with that intense stare. "I understand Mr. Chapman boarded here for some time. Is he still in residence? I would like to have a word with him."

Would she ever hear Tom's name without this sinking feeling in her stomach, this desolate emptiness that threatened to destroy her?

"Tom doesn't live here anymore."

"Where can I find him?"

"I have no idea," she lied. "Probably at the mine, doing his job like any other honest man." She wasn't about to tell him where Tom was or to allow him to criticize him in any way. "I think you should know that in my opinion every single word Tom Chapman said that day was the truth. My family, and as many of our neighbors as we've been able to convince, are going to evacuate our homes on or before April twenty-eighth, Corporal." She drew a deep breath and looked him straight in the eye. "I believe, and so do they, that there will be a devastating Slide early on the morning of the twenty-ninth, and that much of this village will be destroyed and lives lost." She gave him a pleading look.

"Corporal, you could help so much. You could order all the houses along these rows evacuated. You could warn people about the Slide. They'd pay attention if the alarm came from you."

Zelda's heart sank, because already he was shaking his head in vehement denial. "Rubbish. Poppycock, Miss Ralston. It was my opinion a year ago, and it remains my opinion today, that Mr. Chapman suffers delusions, and that unfortunately, he's good at making them sound convincing. He's obviously heard the tales the Indians have spun for years about the Turtle, and his demented mind has enlarged on that fantasy. Why, I'd be laughed out of town if I took stock of such insanity."

"Tom is not crazy." Her hands were on her hips and she glared at him. Once again they were adversaries. "I'm ashamed of you, Corporal Allan. I thought it was your duty to protect the citizens of this town, but obviously all you're concerned about is your own reputation. You're going to be a sorry man afterwards, knowing you had the opportunity to save lives, and didn't do it."

"I intend to protect the town and its inhabitants, Miss Ralston. I have already told Eli he is not to go about mouthing this nonsense, and I shall pay Mr. Chapman a visit and warn him to cease and desist with his foolishness, or I shall be forced to take further action."

"You'd better be quick about it then. April twenty-ninth is next Wednesday. You have four days left to prove yourself an utter fool, Corporal."

Chapter Twenty-two

"Morning, Zelda."

"Good morning, Tom."

Zelda rubbed her damp palms down her apron and tried for a composed smile. "Would you like some coffee? Breakfast? I've left out a few supplies."

"No, thanks. I've eaten." His words were easy, but his look made her breath catch in her throat.

How could she have forgotten how tall and broad he was, how muscular? His black, shining hair was longer than she remembered, curling down his neck and over his ears, and his lean, rawboned face was thinner, his deep blue eyes shadowed.

Her palms ached to reach out and touch him, to feel his warmth and solidity surround her. She turned to the stove, lifting the lid and adding an unnecessary block of wood to the flames.

Eli had told her Tom was coming to help this morning. She'd insisted hotly that she didn't want or need him, but with new found dignity Eli had simply said, "He's coming anyway."

Half of her had dreaded this encounter, and the other half had longed for it. Now that he'd actually appeared, she felt exhausted before the day had even begun.

She'd been awake half the night, listening to Virgil cough, getting up to boil the kettle and to bring him a cup of hot tea or a dose of useless cough medicine. She'd also worried about the move and wondered how on earth she'd manage to be around Tom all day without breaking down.

She turned and caught him staring at her. His eyes lingered on her mouth. With a feeling of utter desolation, she remembered exactly how his kisses felt, the gentleness of his lips on hers before passion built, the scratchy feel of his beard on her cheeks, her neck, her breasts.

"It's good to see you again, Zel." The words came out on a sigh.

She nodded, not trusting herself to speak.

"I've hired an extra wagon, that way Eli and I can make the move in half the time. And a couple of young men from the hotel should be here any minute."

She didn't have the energy to object, although she hated the thought that he was spending money on her. She had to be self-sufficient, learn to exist without him or his help.

At least when today was over, she told herself, she wouldn't need to see him again. One more day, if his plans worked, and he'd be gone forever. Once that was a certainty, it might get easier for her to bear.

"Dad's poorly this morning. The sooner we get him moved and settled again, the better." She'd get through this, she told herself, if they just stuck to this mundane, everyday sort of conversation. "He's still asleep. He was up most of the night coughing."

"Let him sleep as long as possible then. We'll move your kitchen things and the furniture from the main floor first, and you can come along and get the stoves going and a room organized for Virgil."

With the help of the two young men and the extra wagon, her household things were loaded quickly into the wagons. Eli took hot tea and porridge up to Virgil when he awakened, promising to keep his father from exerting himself in any way. Virgil was determined to help with the move, despite the fact that it took all his energy just to make it down the stairs to the kitchen.

Soon the first load was ready to go. Tom was driving, and Zelda was conscious of his broad, strong hands on her waist, boosting her up to the high seat.

He climbed up beside her and clucked to the team, and they started off. She racked her brain, trying to think of a neutral subject they could discuss. This was a dangerous time. Once they arrived at the other house, they'd both be too busy for idle conversation.

"I had a visit from Corporal Allan a few days ago," Zelda began. "He asked where you were. Did he speak with you?" At least the narrow-minded corporal seemed a safe topic, and one they could agree upon.

"Yeah, we had a little heart to heart." Tom's mouth curved in a sardonic grin. "He still figures I'm mentally deranged, and he warned me that I'm not to mention the word 'Slide' to a living soul, or he'll toss me in the lockup."

She shot him a worried glance, and he shook his head, a rueful look on his face. "I've pretty much given up trying to warn people, Zel. They either laugh at me or make the sign to ward off evil spirits."

"Yes, I do know what you mean."

They rode along in silence, and the tension between them seemed to grow with every bounce of the wagon. Zelda groped frantically for another safe subject.

"This house I've rented was occupied by a group of young men. I'm afraid it might need a bit of cleaning." She'd felt totally indifferent about the move. She'd rented the first house available with rent she could afford in an area safe from the Slide. Beyond that, she hadn't been able to summon up any interest whatsoever. A house was a house.

"I looked it over, but now I barely remember what it was like," she prattled. "I do remember there was a ground-floor bedroom for Dad. The stairs have been hard for him to manage lately. There was a large front room I thought would do for a studio, although I wonder if anyone will want portraits, after the Slide." She couldn't imagine what it was going to be like, afterwards. She only knew she'd be alone, and if she dwelled on that, her fragile control would shatter. It was better not to discuss the coming catastrophe.

Perhaps Tom felt the same way, because he switched the conversation. "You heard from Isabella?"

Relief flooded her. "Yes, I had a letter from her last week. She's learning to write English very well. They've bought a farm, and Lars is fixing up the house. The children have a goat, some chickens, and a pony. There's a school not far away, and Eddy will start next term."

Isabella had also confided joyfully that she was now pregnant with Lars's child, and Zelda had burst into tears when she read the awkwardly phrased message. First Leona, now Isabella. Zelda wished with all her heart that the little sponges hadn't worked so well for her, that she, too, could look forward to a baby—Tom's baby. A boy or girl with his blood in its veins, his hair, his eyes . . . Something, anything, of him, some living reminder of the love they'd shared. But her monthly courses told her it wasn't meant to be.

"Leona's coming to the new house this afternoon to help us get settled." Leona was blooming, her body lush and heavily rounded with the coming child. "Of course she mustn't lift anything heavy."

"If Augusto and Joe and their wives were around, they'd help, too," Tom said. "But I'm glad they aren't."

The Italians, professing not to believe a word of Tom's warnings, still had taken the week off work, packed up their families, and gone to a wedding in Lethbridge.

"They'll come back to find their homes under tons of limestone rock, but at least they'll be safe," Tom said. "They both left me keys. If there's time today, I'm going to load up some of their belongings and bring them to your place, if that's all right with you?"

"Of course, by all means." Zelda could feel hysterical laughter building inside of her.

This was so ridiculous, this whole conversation. The two of them were chatting like polite strangers, when for months they'd been as close as two humans could be, sharing not only their bodies, but their most intimate thoughts and feelings.

She was so aware of him, close beside her on the narrow seat of the wagon. She could feel his muscles tense as he guided the horses, smell the good clean smell of him. She was even aware of his breathing, deep and even.

She knew so much about him. She thought of the small triangular patch of hair just above his tail bone, of the scar below his right shoulder blade, of the ache in her heart when he'd told her of the terrified little boy he'd been, hiding from his vicious stepfather. All that secret knowledge brought a strange comfort. He might be leaving her, but at least those images were hers to keep forever.

Tom steered the team along the faint track through the poplars that led to the rather isolated house she'd rented.

"I wish you'd moved to Blairmore, Zelda," Tom burst out abruptly as the two-story house set among the trees came into view. "Sure, you're safe here from the rock, but nothing will be the same in Frank after the Slide. Most people will pack up and leave, terrified of the mountain. This'll be a ghost town in a couple years. You'd be way better off getting established in the town of Blairmore now, before the Slide."

She bristled at his words. "I'll move where it suits me. It's absolutely no concern of yours."

"Damn it all, you're a stubborn woman." They were in front of the house. He pulled the team to a halt with an abrupt motion that startled them. "You won't take my advice, and it's perfectly obvious you hate having to accept my help today." His voice was irate. "You wouldn't even let Eli take the money I wanted to give you a couple of weeks ago. Why won't you let me do what little I can for you, Zelda?"

This was exactly what she'd been trying to avoid. Recklessly, she slid off the seat before he could get down and help her, almost losing her balance as she hit the ground. She steadied herself on the wheel of the wagon and glared up at him.

"Because I don't want you easing your conscience by paying me off, Tom Chapman." Her voice trembled, not with tears, but with outrage. "I don't want your charity. Money's not what I need from you, you stupid man. It's not what I ever needed. I don't have the same reverence for riches that you do." Her tone oozed sarcasm. "I'd certainly never trade investments and bank accounts for love." It was vicious. It was intended to wound, it was exactly what she'd wanted to say to him all along.

Rage sizzled in the look he gave her, but he didn't say anything.

She tossed her head and stalked to the back of the wagon, aimlessly grabbing an armload of smaller boxes. She struggled with them up the steps and across the wide porch, marching into the house with her back ramrod straight and her head high.

She slammed the door behind her and then wilted, close to tears. She would not, could not, let him see how devastated she felt.

"Pride, Zelda. Keep busy," she said aloud. Dumping her load just inside the kitchen door, she forced her attention away from Tom and onto her new home, and her heart sank into her worn boots.

The kitchen was filthy, the plain wooden floors inches deep in dirt and littered with useless bits of trash the former residents had abandoned. The wallpaper was stained, the kitchen stove rusted, and when she drew aside the filthy curtain, she found the cupboards crawling with tiny ants.

Dreading what she'd see next, she moved in a horrified trance from one room to the next. The men who'd lived here must have partied for days before they left. There were empty liquor bottles everywhere and indescribable filth.

Tom found her in the doorway of the ground-floor bedroom, the room she'd planned for Virgil. A straw mattress had burst, and the room stank of moldy hay and mildew. The windowpanes were so dirty light hardly penetrated, and the room reeked of urine.

"These people were worse than animals," she fumed. "How could anyone live like this?" Her shoulders slumped, and she added in a whisper, "And how am I ever going to get it clean enough for us to move in today?"

He reached out to touch her, to comfort her, but she moved back, signaling a warning with her eyes.

His jaw tightened and he stuck his hands in his back pants pockets. "I've checked the outbuildings. They're almost as bad as the house. But the well is fine. I've got a fire started in the stove, and the chimney seems to draw okay. I've put two buckets of water on to heat."

Her spirits lifted an infinitesimal inch. Tom would help her clean. It wouldn't be so bad after all.

"Eli and the men are waiting for me to come back. I've unloaded all the stuff from the wagon—it's out on the porch."

And just like that he was gone, leaving her to deal with this monumental disaster on her own. She stood and gaped at the empty doorway, unable to believe Tom would desert her this way. But she heard the horses and the wagon rumbling off.

Well, she *had* insisted she wanted to manage her own life her own way. Wouldn't you know he'd take her at her word just when she needed him most?

She rolled up her sleeves and began to sweep the worst of the rubble out, but it was a mammoth task. Panic took over, and she dropped the broom and scurried from one room to the next in a tizzy, unable to organize any single task, overwhelmed by a sense of impending disaster.

She hadn't accomplished a single thing by the time she heard the wagon returning. She clasped her hands together and for the first time in her life seriously considered having both hysterics and the vapors as she went out the door.

For a moment, she couldn't believe her eyes.

Instead of furniture, the wagon was loaded with women. Leona waved gaily. Billie Morton and Ethel Parker called cheerful greetings. Tiny May Howard looked like a child between the taller women, but she was the first to hop down.

The saloon girls had come to Zelda's rescue.

They were equipped with buckets and mops as well as tins of calcimine and brushes and baskets of food.

"Tom said you needed us right away," Leona explained cheerfully. "The girls were mostly sleeping, but we got them up. We'd better put on gallons of coffee, though, and I had the cook at the hotel make us a picnic lunch. I can't go more than an hour these days without eating, so I told him to make a generous amount."

There were three women Zelda hadn't met before, and Leona introduced Beatrice, Julie, and Susannah. Smothering yawns behind their palms, they trooped through the house, exclaiming in delighted horror at the mess.

"It's a fuckin' pigsty," Zelda overheard one of them say.

She repeated the words under her breath, feeling deep satisfaction at their expressiveness. She couldn't have put it better herself.

Sleepy or not, they were an efficient crew. Within a half-hour, they'd organized what needed done and assigned duties. They set to work, chattering like magpies, telling risque stories—most of which Zelda didn't begin to understand. They drank quantities of the coffee she brewed, giggled as they scrubbed floors, scoured windows, tore off dirty wallpaper, and brushed fresh white calcimine over bare walls.

By the time the wagons arrived with the furniture, the entire house was clean and sweet smelling, and the ladies were lounging on the freshly scrubbed porch, enjoying sandwiches and cakes and still more coffee.

Ethel Parker, exotically beautiful even in a plain gingham dress and a soiled apron, sat beside Zelda.

"I don't know how to begin to thank you," Zelda said.

"No thanks needed," Ethel responded. She watched as Tom nodded at Zelda, jumped down from one of the wagons, and went around the back to lift Virgil down and help him across the yard and into the house.

Zelda got to her feet. "That's my dad now. We'll need to set his bed up right away in his bedroom."

"Let us handle that. We're good with beds." Ethel gave a wicked giggle. "Isn't that Tom the fellow who's been going around saying the Turtle's gonna slide over the town tomorrow night?"

"Tom Chapman, yes." Zelda kept her voice and face free of expression, but Ethel shot her a calculating, sidelong glance anyway.

"You believe him?"

Zelda nodded. "I'm totally convinced he's right. That's the reason I moved out here. He says the rock isn't going to come this far, but it's going to bury that whole row of cottages where we were living."

Ethel nodded slowly. "How about the Union Bank? He say whether that gets buried? I got all my savings in the Union."

"The bank won't be buried, Tom says. Or the Imperial Hotel."

"What about the Tenderloin?"

Zelda shook her head. The area where the girls lived and worked was well out of the Slide's range.

"Well, that's sure a relief." Ethel gestured at Tom.

"This fellow of yours, he some kind of prophet or something?"

"He's not my fellow." Zelda deliberately ignored the rest of the question.

Ethel gave her a skeptical look. "Horse twaddle. One thing girls like us get to know real well is when somebody's head over heels," she remarked. "Men get that way and it's as if other women don't exist anymore. Ain't so hot for our business, I can tell you. Your Tom's like that. Doesn't so much as glance at any of us, and, believe me, men *always* look at us. It's plain as the nose on your face how he feels about you, Miss Zelda."

"You're wrong, Ethel. He's leaving tomorrow for good, and I'm staying here." She was proud of her matter-of-fact tone.

Ethel snorted through her elegant nose. "Don't you believe it for a minute. Even if he goes, he'll be back."

"I greatly doubt that. Not where he's going." Zelda's ironic smile was cheerless.

Tom slid his arm around Virgil's back, shocked and horrified at his fragility and the harshness of the coughing that racked him.

He could hardly walk, and Tom supported him into the house, into the fresh-smelling little room where several women had set up his bed and swiftly made it.

Tom did his best to hide his dismay. Virgil had aged years in the short weeks since Tom had last seen him. His flesh seemed to have fallen away. His russet hair had turned white, his once-strong body was skeletal, and the lively blue of his eyes had dimmed to a frightening weariness. His shoulders had rounded, his chest sunken, and each breath was an audible effort.

It was obvious this man who'd been the nearest thing Tom had ever had to a father was fast coming to the end of his life. Tom knelt, unfastening Virgil's shoes and pulling off his stockings. The fact that Virgil didn't protest was mute evidence of his weakness.

Loosening the rest of his clothing, Tom eased him down on the stack of pillows and tucked the blankets snugly around his shoulders. Virgil's eyes were closed before Tom left the room.

Mechanically, Tom climbed back on the wagon and clucked to the team, his brain a maelstrom of bittersweet memories.

Virgil, bailing him and Jackson out of jail, offering them a place to stay. Cooking his special mush for them at dawn, shaking Tom's hand at the mine entrance after the accident. Playing his harmonica at Jackson's wedding, offering his last crumpled dollar bill in case Tom needed it.

Like an automaton, Tom packed the possessions that meant the most to his Italian friends and loaded them into the wagon, their wine-making equipment, the new carpet Sophia was so proud of, the spinet Joe had ordered from New York, Rosa Petevello's prized sewing machine.

At the empty, lonely house on Alberta Avenue, it was a welcome release to chase and curse and finally catch all of Zelda's chickens and stuff them into the crate he'd fashioned to transport them.

Tom was loading the noisy birds and the last of Virgil's tools on the wagon when he spied a man in what had been Isabella's backyard. No one had moved into the house next door, much to Tom's relief. Along with all the others in this area, it would be buried deep under the Slide less than forty-eight hours from now.

"Hey, Mister, can I help you?" Surely no one was about to move in now.

The man whipped around, and with a sense of shock Tom recognized the stocky figure and flushed, bloated features of Nestor Vandusen.

He stood, bull-like, staring at Tom, and then he shouted, "Where is Isabella? Where is my Eddy, my Pearl? Where have they gone?"

Tom walked to the fence. "And just where the hell have you been all this time, Nestor? You walked out on them. You expect them to just sit around waiting for you to come back?"

Nestor's nose was even redder than before, his clothing dirty and tattered. He was careful not to come near the fence, but he glowered at Tom from halfway across the yard, his stocky shoulders hunched, his hands balled into fists.

"Isabella, she is my wife," he blustered. "Where did she go?"

"I haven't a clue, Nestor." Tom was about to turn away when the other man sidled closer, and Tom was amazed to see tears trickling down his veined cheeks and honest desperation in his crusted, red-rimmed eyes.

"I love her, my Isabella," he sniveled. "I need her."

Tom felt both pity and disgust for the man. "Yeah, well, you had one hell of a strange way of showing it, Nestor, and now you're way too late. The best thing you can do is clear out of here, because tomorrow night that mountain"—Tom tilted a thumb up at the lowering Turtle, dark now against the evening sky—"is going to come tumbling down over this town and bury these houses. Clear out of here while you can."

The words didn't register. Mumbling, Nestor turned away, making his way to the back stairs of the empty house. He fumbled a key out of his pants pocket, unlocked the back door, and disappeared inside.

What the hell! Tom shrugged. Nestor would probably rattle around in the empty house for a while feeling sorry for himself, then stagger off to find a bottle to climb into.

He'd send Lars a telegram in the morning, telling him that Nestor had turned up. Lars would take care of it from there.

Tom finished loading the wagon.

He was half a mile down the road, idly wondering what the hell made a man like Nestor Vandusen tick, when words suddenly popped into his mind along with the vivid memory of a huge, sad, old woman.

"Loving has to be learned, just like any other skill," Evelyn Lawrence had said to him in what seemed another lifetime. "I never learned."

Well, neither had Nestor, Tom mused. Then, like a powerful fist straight in his gut, it came to him.

He hadn't learned, either. He jerked on the reins and the patient team pulled to a stop. Sweat broke out on his forehead and he sat, dumbfounded by what seemed a revelation.

For an entire year, he'd seen and experienced

love in all its various forms, and yet it seemed he hadn't learned a thing.

Nestor had abandoned Isabella, and now, much too late, decided he loved her. Wasn't Tom about to make the same mistake?

He loved Zelda, and yet he was choosing to leave her. It suddenly seemed both stupid and wrong, the actions of an idiot and a coward. When it came down to it, there wasn't much difference between him and Nestor Vandusen.

The rest of what Evelyn had told him was there in his mind, clear as a bell. "I got to thinking money was the important thing," she'd said.

And so had he. He'd been ready to abandon everything of real worth, because he thought the same cockeyed thing.

Urgency rose in him. He hollered and brought the reins down on the backs of the astonished team with a resounding slap, and they broke into a trot.

Evelyn Lawrence had learned too late. Nestor Vandusen had learned too late.

Slow learner though he was, maybe there was still time for Tom Chapman.

Chapter Twenty-three

Virgil was sleeping, peacefully for once, in his spanking clean, white-walled bedroom.

Zelda sat in the kitchen, tired to the bone, sipping a cup of tea. For the first time all day, the house was empty. Soon, she'd light the lamp, but for now, there was still just enough natural light coming in the clean windowpanes.

A short time ago, all the women had gone back to town, calling good-byes, making ribald comments to her and one another as they climbed in the back of the rented wagon.

Zelda's heart swelled when she thought of all they'd done for her that day. The house and even the outbuildings were clean and tidy, all the Ralstons' meager possessions in place. Even the chicken coop had been limed and strewn with fresh straw, in preparation for her chickens.

Tom was bringing them. He should be there soon. Her stomach clenched, and she realized she was listening for the sound of the wagon.

The sounds in this isolated spot were different than she was used to in town. Night birds called in the trees outside, and she could hear the creek not far away, gurgling over the stones.

There were no miners' voices, calling greetings to one another, no boisterous youngsters playing kick the can or catch, no mothers ordering children into the house. Missing as well was the constant sound of the trains, bringing boxcars to the mine and taking them away filled with coal, and the sharp whistles that marked the endless progression of shifts.

Here, there was only silence—at least for this one, last night. Zelda shuddered, thinking of the following night and the Slide.

What would it sound like? What would it feel like, being close to such a catastrophe? The ones who survived would have to be strong. There'd be a need for food. She'd already put a huge pot of beans to soak, and in spite of her weariness, she decided to set bread before she went to bed. She'd bring as many of the homeless home as she could. Her father would want that.

From the bedroom just down the hall, she heard Virgil cough, and she tensed. But for once the coughing didn't continue, and after a moment she sat back in her chair again.

"Your father belongs in the hospital," Dr. Malcolmson had told her two days ago.

"Is there some new treatment then, that will help him?" she'd asked, praying it might be so.

But the kindly doctor had sighed and shaken his

head. "I'm afraid that's not likely, but it might be easier on you, Miss Ralston."

Her temper had flared. "My father took care of me for years," she'd snapped. "I can manage quite well caring for him."

But could she? Virgil was all but bedridden, needing attention round the clock. Eli came by whenever his job allowed, but the brunt of the nursing was up to her. Especially at night, she felt terribly alone and very frightened.

The crunching of gravel told her the wagon was coming down the rutted path in front of the house, and every nerve in her body tensed. She leaped to her feet and lit the lantern, turning the wick as high as she dared. She didn't want to meet Tom in the dark.

The horses were trotting, as if Tom was in a great hurry to get this day over with.

She smoothed her hand over her hair and unfastened her soiled apron, tossing it over the back of a chair as she went to the door.

She'd help him unload and stable the horses. It would go faster that way. He could leave sooner.

He reined the horses in, and almost before the wagon stopped rolling, he jumped to the ground.

"Zelda." The single word echoed in the evening stillness, and the urgent, passionate way he said it made her heart lurch and then hammer. She stood where she was, one hand on her throat.

"Zelda," he said again, and this time the word had all the impact of a caress. He crossed the yard with determined strides and took the porch steps two at a time.

"What—" she began, but the query ended in a

gasp as he caught her roughly in his arms. She could smell sweat, and chickens, and the good smell of his body. Automatically, her arms went round him.

"I think I'm supposed to get down on my knees or something," he said, his voice thick with emotion. He moved her back, just far enough so that he could look down into her face. "Zelda, I love you. Will you marry me?"

She gaped up at him. "You've—you've taken leave of your senses." If he hadn't been holding her, she was certain her knees would have given way. Her mind was blank with shock.

"No, damn it all, I've just come to my senses." She could hear the smile in his words. "Zelda, marry me. I've been a total ass, but that's over now. Say that you'll forgive me, that you'll marry me." He gave her a small, impatient shake. "Tonight, if we can find someone to do it. Right away, right now."

She was beginning to recover. She shook her head and tried to step away from him, but he held tight.

Her brain was starting to work again. "What would be the purpose, Tom? You'll likely be gone tomorrow night, and you know I can't—"

"No. I'll be here. I won't be leaving."

She frowned. "Nonsense. You'll change your mind." She thought she understood. "It's because you don't think your plan will work, is that it? You think you'll end up staying here whether you want to or not." He was simply hedging his bets. That's what this was about.

"You're wrong, Zelda. I'm not even going to try. I'm staying."

"That's ridiculous. If you don't try, you'll always regret not making the attempt to return to—to where you came from." She moved back, out of his arms, trying to distance herself from the terrible temptation he was offering. She prayed for strength, for clearheaded vision.

"I won't be the reason for that regret, Tom. If you stay, you've said yourself you're liable to have to work hard, just to earn a living. All those comforts, those—those investments, those—" She struggled to remember the things he'd described so lovingly, the things she'd come to resent. "Those—motorcycle things, and your—what about your real estate? Your bank accounts?"

He shook his head impatiently. "They just don't matter anymore, none of them. You matter, Zel. You're all that matters to me now. I'm staying here."

She folded her arms around herself, her fingers digging into her shoulders. He'd taken her by complete surprise, but now she was beginning to feel again. The weeks of misery, the months of waiting in vain for him to say exactly this, were suddenly vivid in her mind. She began to tremble.

Instead of relief or happiness, all she was aware of feeling for him at this moment was anger, red and blinding.

She'd had nothing but her pride for so long. She wasn't about to relinquish it now, just because of some whim that had come over him. She summoned up outrage and insult. She deliberately recalled the awful pain of the past weeks, and suddenly she wanted to strike him, to lash out with her fists and her feet at the unfairness of it all. He was finally offering her everything she'd ever dreamed of, and now she was too proud and too terribly frightened to take it.

"So you've changed your mind, and now you think all you have to do is ask, and I'll simper and fall weeping at your feet, grateful for the honor of being your wife, Tom Chapman?" Her voice vibrated with the scorn she'd summoned up to protect herself.

"You believe that because you're a man, you can make all the choices, go or stay, give love or withhold it, marry or not." She ran out of breath and gulped. "Well, I have choices, too, and I—I choose not to marry you, not tonight, not ever. Get back on that wagon and leave, Tom. When the Slide comes tomorrow night, go back where you came from, where you—where you be—belong." Her voice broke shamefully on the last word, and she whirled around, but his hand caught her arm in a fierce grip.

She fought him with all her strength, kicking and lashing out with her fists and knees, but he cursed and grabbed her other arm and held on until she quieted. He turned her to face him, holding her immobile, his fingers clamped around her upper arms, his chest heaving with emotion and the effort of restraining her.

"Damn you, listen to me, Zelda. You have every right to be good and mad at me. I've been a fool, and I'm sorry for that. But I'm telling you that I'll spend the rest of my life making it up to you if you give me the chance."

She shook her head furiously from side to side and tried to fight her way out of his grasp all over again, but again he held on.

"Stop this and listen. I knew this woman once," he said with savage intensity. "Her name was Evelyn. She was old and fat and rich, and she was dying, and she was all alone. She told me that money's cold comfort at a time like that, and if I'd had any sense, I'd have listened a lot harder than I did. But it all came back to me tonight, what she'd been trying to get through my thick skull about money and love. And what she said goes for pride, too, Zel, you hear me?" He shook her, desperate to make her understand. "Is that what you want, to get old and die all alone like Evelyn Lawrence, with just your damned pride to comfort you?"

She looked up into his face. It had grown darker, and she couldn't see his features clearly, but the timbre of his voice seemed to penetrate her every pore.

"For the first time in my life, I know exactly what I want." He sounded confident and very sure. "I want you for my wife. I want to make a home for us, for Virgil, for Eli, for the kids you and I'll have together." His voice became softer, thoughtful.

"I want to know when it comes time to die that I've loved and been loved by my family, the way Virgil has, that I'm leaving behind more than just a damned bank account, or real estate, or rolling stock. Love is what you leave, Zel, and it's probably what you take with you, too. I had to come back here to find that out, and now that I have, I won't let you and your stiff-necked pride and your bad temper spoil it for both of us."

Inside the house, Virgil coughed and quieted again, and she had a vision of what the future would be like alone. Her father would die soon; for the first time, she acknowledged it honestly, and the pain was almost unbearable.

She was terrified of the agony Virgil's death would bring.

She was so afraid of being totally alone. But if she lowered the only defenses she'd ever had—her pride, her fierce temper, her matter-of-fact acceptance of herself as a spinster—what would take their place? She'd be defenseless.

Tom had lifted his head at Virgil's cough, his body tensing. "Believe me when I say I love you, Zel," he murmured again when the coughing subsided. "I love him, too. I'll be here for both of you, I promise." The whispered words were heartfelt, with an unspoken acceptance of all that was to come.

It was so hard to trust. She struggled against it. "I can manage on my own. I always have."

"Of course you can." His voice was sad. "Both of us can manage, we're strong people. But it would be so much better to share. Tell me, Zel, do you still love me?"

There it was, the one thing she couldn't deny. She trembled and her throat worked. "Yes." The answer was instinctive, as automatic as the blood coursing through her veins. "Yes, I love you. I will always love you." The assertion brought its own strength, and with it, at last, came peace.

She stopped struggling, both physically and emotionally. She felt rather than heard the shuddering sigh that came from him, and its echo vibrated through her as well.

"Then for God's sake stop fighting and say that you'll marry me."

She groped for courage, and it was there. "Yes. I will marry you, Tom."

His arms came around her, and she thought her ribs would crack. He pressed his face against her hair and groaned. "You're such a stubborn woman, Zelda Ralston."

She nestled against him, and it felt as if she were home. She made a disparaging sound in her throat. "I don't hold a candle to you in that regard. Heaven knows what our children will be like. They'll probably drive us both to distraction."

Children. Her heart soared. She'd have his children.

He bent his head and kissed her, first with jubilation, then more gently, and finally with growing hunger. Then sudden angry squawking came from the chickens crammed uncomfortably into the wooden crates.

They laughed, reminded of what still had to be done.

"I'd better get this stuff unloaded in the shed and them in the coop, unharness these poor horses and give them a rubdown and some grain. They've had a hard day." He released her with reluctance.

"Will you—would you stay here with me tonight?" Her question was shy.

He planted a quick, hard kiss on her lips. "Nothing could drive me away."

Tom awakened to the sound of Virgil's harsh coughing coming from downstairs. The bedroom was still black dark. Zelda lay nestled in his arms, her long slender body deliciously warm and naked under the quilt. She didn't stir, exhausted from their lovemaking and the work of the previous day.

Cautiously, Tom untwined his body from hers and slid from the bed, fumbling for his pants and shirt and socks, shivering in the chill. He fumbled for a match and lit the candle on the dresser, shielding the faint light with his hand so Zelda wouldn't be disturbed. His watch said it was twenty minutes to three. He strapped it on and made his way along the hallway and down the steep stairs.

Virgil was propped nearly upright on a mound of pillows, the only way he could rest these days. He turned his head toward the candlelight, and although there was recognition in his eyes at the sight of Tom, there was also agony as the paroxysms shook his frail body and he struggled to draw air into his damaged lungs. His contorted face was purple, and small blood vessels had broken on his cheeks and nose. The fingernails on each gnarled hand were a deep cyanotic blue.

Feeling helpless, Tom sat down on the edge of the bed and began to rub Virgil's back. He'd seen Zelda do this in an effort to ease the attacks. Through the flannel nightshirt, he could feel the frantic beating of the older man's heart, and his own chest ached with the awful knowledge that Virgil's lungs could no longer draw in enough oxygen to sustain his body.

Under Tom's palm Virgil's back was skin and bone, each rib and vertebrae standing out in harsh relief through the flesh. Muscles that had once been strong from hours of digging coal with pick and shovel were now atrophied.

The coughing finally ran its course, and Virgil was able to take one shaky, desperate breath and then another. He groped for a handkerchief and blotted away the tears that the coughing created and slumped back on the pillows. Then, indomitable as ever, he gave Tom a shaky grin.

"Thanks, lad," he wheezed. "Good to see you." Speech was an effort, and it took moments before he could manage the rest. "So you've come home, have you? I knew you and that lass would come to your senses afore it was too late."

"We're getting married, Virgil. As soon as we possibly can. I'm staying here, with all of you, if you think you can put up with me."

Virgil's gnarled hand curled around Tom's forearm and squeezed, and the tears that glistened in the candlelight weren't from coughing this time. "I'd like that right fine, lad." His smile was tremulous. "I always knew here was where you belonged."

"I'm going in the kitchen to light the stove, make us both a cup of tea," Tom said, struggling against the hot rush of emotion that Virgil's words brought. He drew the quilt up over the older man's shoulders and clumsily tucked it in. "Be right back."

But by the time the stove was lit and the tea steeped, Virgil had fallen heavily asleep again. Marveling at how fond he'd become of tea, Tom poured himself a mug of the strong, hot brew and pulled on a jacket and a pair of boots.

Outside, the first faint traces of dawn were beginning to lighten the eastern sky, and a chorus of birdsong filled the cool mountain air. Tom shivered, not just from the chill. It was the morning of

April 28, the last morning Frank would exist in its present form.

He and Jackson had been in the village exactly one year today, and sometime this morning, Jackson would ride off with Bill Miner and Lewis Schraeger. Late in the afternoon they'd stop the eastbound train, hoping to make off with over a million dollars in gold.

Tom's mind skittered over the things that could go wrong with their plans, and apprehension twisted his gut. He'd tried time and again to reason with Jackson, but his former friend had become a stranger, caught up in the excitement and romance of taking part in a train robbery. Nothing Tom said affected him.

If they succeeded, as history indicated they would, they were all to meet shortly after midnight tonight, on the mountain where the Interpretive Center was located. Tom had promised Jackson he'd bring Leona with him, and, of course, he'd stick to that plan despite the fact that he wasn't going to try to return to the future himself.

But he needed to say good-bye to Jackson. He'd decided to give his friend his bank cards and the information needed to access all of his accounts and investments. Jackson might as well benefit from everything; Tom had no use for any of it there.

The day would be a busy one. He planned to make one final effort at getting the people in the miners' cottages to leave their homes and go somewhere safe for the night.

He looked up at the mountain, massive and inky dark against a lighter sky, its rolls of limestone jutting forbiddingly out over the valley.

He squinted at his watch.

It was eight minutes after four. As he watched, the hands moved inexorably forward. One minute, then two.

4:10. An icy tremor passed through Tom's body and his eyes lifted again to the mountain. Its limestone peak would break away exactly twenty-four hours from this exact moment. Ninety million tons of rock would come tumbling down, breaking into fragments that ranged from tiny chips to chunks the size of a house. It would last less than a hundred seconds, and it would bury everything in its path.

For Tom, the very worst thing was knowing that he couldn't stop it from happening, and neither had he been able to convince most people that it would even occur.

He remembered all too well the embarrassment and pity he'd felt for the wild individuals in parks and on street corners in the nineties, loudly predicting the end of the world or an invasion by little men from outer space. The loonies, he'd called them.

Talking to people about the Slide made Tom sympathize with those unfortunates, because now the embarrassment and pity on people's faces were directed at him.

He sighed and dumped the remains of his tea on the grass. No matter how humiliating, he had to try again today, going from door to door at the cottages on the eastern flats—the cottages directly in the path of the Slide.

Behind the house the disgruntled rooster in his

strange new chicken house crowed, and gradually light seeped over the valley like golden dust.

Morning had come to Frank, the last morning before the Slide.

Chapter Twenty-four

April 28, 1903.

It was unseasonably warm all that day and well into the evening in Frank. Crocuses bloomed everywhere, and mothers finally allowed their children to discard heavy winter underwear and put on summer clothing. As dusk fell, the ball game at the recreation field broke up and, amidst shouts and laughter, players and spectators slowly made their way home.

The hotels geared up for their nightly sessions of drinking and gambling, and in the cottages wives cooked dinner for the miners getting off day shift, or shushed noisy children so the night shift workers might steal another hour of sleep.

A heavy mist formed over the top of the Turtle as the sun went down.

At the North West Mounted Police barracks, Corporal Allan unlocked the barred door of the cell and handed a supper tray in to his prisoner. Tom took it, watching for a single small mistake on the corporal's part that would allow him to overpower his captor and escape. But the corporal was a cautious man and a good policeman. He shut the cell door with a bang and locked it, delivering the same lecture he'd given Tom two hours before when he'd arrested him.

"You were duly warned, Chapman, about this ridiculous talk of the mountain falling. I distinctly remember telling you that if you persisted, I would be forced to take action," he said, turning the huge key. "And yet there you were, going from door to door, frightening innocent women and children with your fabrications. A night behind bars will hopefully convince you of your folly."

Tom stared at the plateful of stringy pot roast and congealing gravy, sick to his very soul. During the hours since his arrest, he'd tried to reason with the corporal, promising absolute silence on his part if only he were released that evening, but Allan was resolute.

"First thing in the morning, you can go. You seem a reasonable enough chap, apart from these delusions of yours. Have you seen a doctor about them?"

Tom gave up on reason. "Could I at least speak to Eli Ralston? I have to get a message to his sister, Zelda. She's expecting me for supper and she'll be worried."

"The boy is off with Constable Liard. They're helping one of the ranchers round up cattle that were driven off by wild dogs last night. They should be back by dark."

How long would it be before Zelda became alarmed? She knew he'd planned to pick up Leona just before midnight and head up to the site of the Interpretive Center, to wait for Jackson. He'd told her that morning what Jackson was up to, and she'd been horrified.

"Are you sure no one was killed during that robbery, Tom?"

"Fairly sure."

"But if it doesn't work tonight, if Jackson can't return to the future, he's going to be a wanted man. He and Leona will have to live like fugitives. And there's the baby—"

Tom had nodded. "It's going to have to work, Zel. It *will* work, I'm sure of it."

"And you, Tom?" Her voice had been a husky whisper, and he had seen the uncertainty in her eyes. "You haven't changed your mind?"

He'd drawn her into his arms and had stopped the words with his lips on hers. "I'm already home, Zel."

But at this moment he wasn't home at all. He was in jail. Unless he found some way out, he'd spend the night of the Slide ignominiously behind bars, unable to say good-bye to Jackson or to witness the event that had haunted him, day and night, for a full year. Panic threatened and he forced it down.

"Could I have a pen and paper, Corporal?"

Allan handed in a nib pen and a small inkwell.

"I, Tom Chapman, hereby appoint Jackson Zalco to be my power of attorney for all purposes. This appointment shall endure beyond any mental or physical impairment I may suffer from, and is effective from April 28, 1995. . . ."

It was already dusk by the time Constable Liard and Eli finally got back to the barracks and a half-hour after that when an outraged Zelda burst through the door.

"This is ridiculous, Corporal Allan." Her rich, deep voice reverberated through the room, and from his seat behind the battered table he used for a desk, Allan rolled his eyes heavenward.

"This man is my betrothed," Zelda declared. "I demand that you release him this instant."

Allan drew himself to his full height and scowled at her. "Betrothed or not, Mr. Chapman is here for his own protection, Miss Ralston," he pronounced. "He will be released first thing in the morning."

"You are an *idiot!*" Zelda began hotly. "By tomorrow morning this entire town—" She stopped abruptly, because Tom was finally able to catch her eye and shake his head from side to side, warning her against a statement that might land her in the cell next to his own.

"Corporal, could I have a word in private with Miss Ralston?" Tom tried to sound as humble and contrite as possible, even though it galled him.

Allan looked from Zelda to him. Before he could answer, the telegraph in the corner of the room began chattering, and with a muffled oath, he walked over to see to it.

Zelda at once moved close to his cell. Swiftly, he explained what she had to do, slipping her the closely written sheets of paper with the bank and credit cards folded inside. Allan had checked him for weapons but hadn't taken his wallet. Zelda tucked them into her handbag.

Constable Liard came in from outside, and Corporal Allan called him over. Snatches of their conversation reached Tom and Zelda, and they exchanged a horrified look.

"Train robbery . . . gold shipment . . . three armed men . . . Pinkerton detectives. . . ."

"You take over here, Constable. I'll ride out and meet the detectives." Without another glance at either of them, Corporal Allan hurried out.

Zelda reached her hand through the bars and convulsively grasped Tom's. Then she turned to Liard, and suddenly became distraught and fragile and totally feminine. Her husky voice quivered and tears trickled down her cheeks.

"Constable, you know that my father, Virgil Ralston, is very ill. Mr. Chapman has been helping me with him . . ." Her hands fluttered helplessly. "With Tom behind bars, I *desperately* need Eli at home tonight. I'd be most grateful if you'd allow him to escort me back to our home now and stay with me tonight? He'll be here first thing in the morning to tend to his duties, I assure you."

Tom understood. She couldn't leave Virgil alone all the hours it would take to accomplish what she had to do tonight. And she wanted to be certain as well that Eli was in a place she knew to be safe from the Slide.

Liard frowned. "We're busy, I'm afraid it's not—"

Zelda dissolved into pitiful sobs, her face hidden in her hands.

Liard hastily agreed.

* * *

In the darkness, it took much longer for the horse and buggy to reach the top of the hill than Zelda had anticipated, but at last she and Leona arrived at the precise spot Tom had indicated on the map he'd drawn.

Nearby, the horse moved restlessly and whinnied, and far down in the valley where the village lay, dogs howled in a constant, mournful chorus. They sat side by side on a fallen log, and Leona huddled deeper into her warm cape.

"It's absolutely freezing up here, Zel. Thank goodness we finally got this fire started." Leona shivered again, and Zelda tucked the blanket she'd brought closer around their knees. "What time do you think it is by now?"

Zelda squinted in the firelight at the watch she'd pinned to the lapel of her coat. "One-fifteen."

"Where the hell are they? Jackson said midnight at the latest." Leona sounded on the verge of tears, near hysteria, and Zelda could feel her own determined optimism slipping away and utter abject terror taking its place. She made an herculean effort to calm herself and decided to distract her friend with chatter.

"Do you think the animals know what's going to happen tonight, Leona? I've never heard the dogs howling this badly, and if it hadn't been for Eli, I'd never have gotten the horse harnessed to the wagon. He was almost uncontrollable." If only she herself could control the nerves that made her fingers tremble and her stomach contract. Unable to sit still, she got up and put another small branch on the fire.

Her thoughts, as they had done all evening, went to Tom, and she wished with all her heart that he was beside her right now. No matter what happened, his presence would have made everything easier.

"Do you think the police might have caught them?" Leona sounded as forlorn and terrified as Zelda felt.

Zelda reached down and grasped Leona's icy fingers in hers, and against her arm she felt the baby inside Leona's distended middle move restlessly. "Absolutely not. Tom was certain about that. He said that they got clean away—"

"Hush." Leona squeezed Zelda's arm, her nails digging in. "Listen."

Far off, they heard the sound of horses' hooves making their careful way up the narrow mountain trail, and then the muted jingle of harness.

"It's them. It has to be!"

With Zelda's help, Leona struggled to her feet. They held hands, peering into the darkness at the edge of the small clearing.

"Jackson?" Leona's call was anxious. "Is that you, Jackson?"

"Yeah, honey. Me and Bill." He sounded infinitely weary.

There were only two horses. The riders pulled their mounts to a halt and all but tumbled from their backs.

"Oh, my God, what happened?" Leona shrieked.

Jackson was supporting Bill. A makeshift sling had been fashioned from the older man's shirt, and it was stained with blood. He seemed only semiconscious.

Jackson half-carried him near the fire and lowered him to the grass, propping him against a stump. Appalled, Zelda and Leona did their best to make him comfortable, wrapping their blanket around him, adding more twigs to the fire. He was shuddering, but in spite of his obvious discomfort, Bill tried to smile up at them.

"Just a scratch," he declared in a thin voice. "Nothin' to worry about. Survived plenty worse than this little bee bite in my time."

Zelda knelt by the injured man, and Leona crouched awkwardly, unsure as to how best to help Bill. They had no water or bandages, nothing with which to cleanse the wound. The worst of the bleeding seemed to have stopped, so it was probably best to leave it exactly as it was and just keep him warm, they both decided.

"But where's the gold? I thought you were bringing a wagon with the gold." Leona heaved herself to her feet and moved close to Jackson, her arms clasped protectively over her abdomen.

Jackson reached out and drew her close, making a disgusted sound in his throat.

"What happened, Jackson?" Leona demanded. "And where's Schraeger?"

Jackson snorted. "That miserable slimeball. Heading for the U.S. border, most likely, and good riddance. He's the one who shot Bill. He was aimin' for me, but Bill got between us."

Leona gave a muffled shriek and put her hand over her mouth.

"The whole damned operation was a catastrophe," Jackson said in a weary tone. He looked around and suddenly became alert.

"Where the hell is Tom?"

"In jail." Zelda got to her feet.

"Jail? Sheeit." There was a definite edge of panic to Jackson's cursing. "What the *hell* is he doing in jail? Can we get him out in time? How long've we got, anyway?"

Zelda shook her head. "There's no need. They'll let him out in the morning. He'd already decided not to try and go with you, although he wanted to be here to say good-bye."

"He's staying here with Zelda," Leona supplied. "They're going to get married."

"Can't say I blame him for that," Jackson said after a moment, but there was a world of sadness in his voice. "How'd he get himself thrown in the can?" He laughed harshly. "Wish I could josh him about that. He nagged me somethin' awful, warnin' that I'd end up in jail if I went along with Bill, and now he's the one behind bars."

Zelda quickly explained how Tom had been arrested, adding, "Please, tell us what happened to all of you."

"Well, looked as though everything was going good at first," Jackson began with a sigh. "We stopped the train just like we planned, smooth as clockwork, tied up the guards, not a shot fired and nobody hurt. Loaded those blamed boxes into the wagon."

"Heavy as sin they were, too." Bill's voice came thin and reedy from where he lay, but he chuckled as if the whole thing had been a fine joke.

Jackson took up the story again. "We had bandannas over our faces, but one of the guards snatched Bill's off and recognized him. You're just too damned well known to Pinkerton's men, Bill."

"Price of fame, I reckon," Miner replied with an attempt at a smile. "They've been after me a long time."

"We knew," Jackson continued, "that as soon as the guards got loose they'd telegraph ahead and warn the cops, so we rode hard, hauled that damnable wagon clear to the outskirts of Frank."

Absently, he rubbed his lame leg. "Stopped by the creek down on the flats. It was gettin' dark already. We figgered on dividin' up the gold there. The Slide would bury the wagon and Pinkerton's men, and the Mounted would think we got buried along with it. Bill and Schraeger were gonna take their share and head to the border. I was gonna bring Tom's and mine up here and bury it so's we'd know where to look if this door we're plannin' on goin' through tonight actually opens and lets us travel."

"Trouble was," Bill said quietly, "the gold was already gone."

"Gone?" Leona's voice was horrified.

"Somebody else had stolen it. Probably somebody back in Vancouver, but they'd been damned clever." Jackson took off his hat and rubbed his hand wearily over his forehead. "They'd substituted bricks for the gold bars and nailed the boxes shut again." He gave an ironic chuckle. "We risked our asses for a couple boxes filled with bricks." His voice dropped, husky and filled with regret. "Too bad Chapman isn't here. He'd get a real kick out of that. He kept telling me this was a rotten idea, and he was right. Anyhow, when Schraeger saw those bricks, he flew into a black rage and blamed me. Pulled his gun and was about to kill me, but Bill saved my life."

"Oh, say, I doubt that, Jackson." Bill still sounded amused. "Schraeger was always a lousy shot. He likely just missed and hit me by accident."

Zelda was trying to fit this into what Tom had told her. "So the whole story of gold buried under the Slide was nothing more than a myth?"

"Appears so." Jackson sighed. "According to the research Tom did, Schraeger's gonna end up in San Quentin for rustlin' cattle and murderin' a rancher." He gave a grim chuckle. "Serves the bastard right. He was questioned about this robbery, but he wouldn't say a word. He let the authorities believe that his partners and the gold got buried by the Slide."

Again, Bill Miner chuckled. "Too humiliatin', I'd say, even for Schraeger, to have to admit we went to all this trouble just to steal a box of bricks."

"He got tuberculosis in jail. He may be dumb, but he still realized he could barter some favors from old Doc Lawrence if he spun a tall tale about the gold bein' buried here."

Bill's voice was somber. "San Quentin's a hellhole. A man would trade his soul for decent food and warm blankets in there. I know, I spent nineteen years, five months and twenty-seven days inside." He shuddered. "I ain't fond of the idea of goin' back, I can tell ya."

"You're not." Jackson's tone was hard-edged. "You're comin' along with Leona and me, as long as this bright idea of Tom's works, and I hope like hell it does. Otherwise, way things are goin' tonight, we'll maybe both end up in San Quentin."

They were all silent for a moment, aware that

what Jackson said was nothing less than the truth. The doorway to the future had become the only certain freedom for Jackson and Bill Miner.

Jackson was the one who broke the tense silence. "Thing was, Tom's research was dead accurate. The facts all fit Schraeger's story. The gold bars missing, the train robbed, the Slide burying everything." Jackson sighed. "Damn, I wish I could see Tom's face when he hears the real story. He always said you couldn't trust what history books said was fact. Tonight sure proves him right." His voice became choked with emotion. "Tell him I wish you both all the happiness in the world, Zel."

She suddenly remembered what Tom had asked her to do. She hurried and retrieved her handbag from the wagon, extracting the packet Tom had entrusted to her. "He wanted me to give you this, Jackson. He said he has no need for any of it, and he wants you and Leona to use whatever you can. He said it's a belated wedding gift, and he wants you to take good care of his motorcycles."

Jackson struck a match and quickly perused the power of attorney and the letter Tom had written. He stared at the bank and credit cards, the money, and the keys and then shoved them into his pocket. He cleared his throat, but still his voice was thick when he spoke. "I'm gonna miss him real bad, you tell him that, Zelda. And tell him thanks. Tell him—" He had to swallow before he could go on. "Tell him we'll have a burger and fries on him when we get back."

He dug out his own wallet, extracting all the cash he had. "This won't be any good to us. It's little enough but you might as well use it." He handed the bills to Zelda.

Bill had been paying close attention. "I take it money's changed somewhat, where we're goin'?"

Jackson explained briefly what had happened to him and Tom when they tried to use their money the first day in Frank, and he showed Bill the credit cards Tom had given him. "These will give us access to all Tom's accounts. He's given us a lot of money."

"Give me a hand, here, young feller." Jackson knelt beside Bill and helped him unstrap a money belt Bill had concealed under his clothing. The old bandit held it out to Zelda.

"Take it," he insisted. "It's a grubstake fer you and that young man of yours." His sardonic grin came and went under his moustache. "I never did trust banks none, so I always carry cash and bury gold. It's gonna be fun, seein' if the gold I hid here and there'll still be underground." He thought about it. "Mind you, if this plan don't work no better than the robbery did, I'm gonna need that all back again."

Zelda thanked him and took the heavy canvas belt. After a moment's hesitation, she strapped it on her own waist, under her coat.

"It's late. What time is it getting to be?" Leona's voice was anxious.

Once again, Zelda checked her watch, and her heart gave a great jerk and began to hammer when she read the hour. "It's three fifty-five. The slide will come at four-ten. There's only fifteen minutes left."

"Time to move." Jackson stamped the fire out and looked around the clearing. "We need to be right over there. That's where Tom and I ended up the last time. Zelda, you come with me. We'll take the wagon and the horse and get you good and safe way over there. The Slide came real close to the Center and we're not takin' any chances."

Leona threw her arms around Zelda, tears coursing down her cheeks. "Good-bye, my dearest friend. If this baby's a girl, I'm naming it for you," she said brokenly.

Zelda planted a wet kiss on both Leona's cheek and Bill Miner's.

Jackson tied the saddle horses to the back of the wagon. "Hurry up, Zelda."

She ran after him. At the last moment, she remembered the snapshot Tom had asked her to find. She dug it out of her coat pocket and handed it to Jackson. "Tom asked if you'd give this to a woman named Evelyn Lawrence, if she's still alive when you get there."

It was the picture Zelda had taken in the summer, using a timing device Tom had made for her. The two of them were standing in front of the little cave, high on Turtle Mountain. Their clothes were rumpled. They were looking, not into the camera's lens, but at one another, and their expressions made it plain they were in love.

Jackson took the photo. "Was there a message along with it?"

"Tom said just tell her good-bye and thanks, and that he found the real gold."

Jackson tried to speak and couldn't. He hugged Zelda hard, and she could feel hot tears on his whiskery cheek before he limped back to where the others were waiting. The moon was bright, and Zelda could see them all clearly.

The horses moved this way and that, stamping their hooves and rolling their eyes, and somewhere below her the dogs were still howling in an endless chorus.

She turned and glanced across the valley. Turtle Mountain was a dark and silent mass against an indigo sky.

Chapter Twenty-five

When Constable Liard came in from patrolling the town at 2:30, Tom made one last urgent plea to the weary young policeman.

"The corporal said I could go in the morning. Technically, it's morning already. Let me out now, please."

Liard shook his head. "Sorry, can't do that. When the corporal says morning, he means more like seven or eight. Why don't you try to get some sleep now?" He poured a cup of cold coffee and grimaced as he drank it. When Tom didn't move from the cell bars, Liard sighed and said, "Y'know, I remember the day I arrested you and your friend, must be a year ago now."

"Exactly a year ago, April twenty-eighth." Tom confirmed.

Liard nodded. "I often think of that money you had. Still can't understand how that could be, you having money that looked like it was printed in 1986."

"There's one simple explanation, Constable. I was telling the truth then, and I'm telling the truth now. That Slide I talked about?" Tom knew his voice rang with the truth. "It's going to happen tonight. Soon, in fact. What time is it now?"

Liard pulled out a pocket watch. "Two-thirty."

"There's one hour and forty-five minutes left. Please, Constable, let me out of here." Tom racked his brain for something—anything—that might work on Liard. "You ever been in love, Constable?"

Liard didn't answer, but his neck and face flushed pink, and he didn't meet Tom's eyes.

"You know how that feels then, wanting to be with someone you love, needing to take care of them," Tom said softly. "I'm in love with Zelda Ralston," he stated. "I'm going to marry her. I need to be with her and her family, now, tonight, when this happens. Please, Constable Liard, please, let me out of here. Even if I'm the raving lunatic Allan thinks I am, what the hell can I do at this hour?"

Liard thought it over for another endless five minutes, then got up, and unlocked the cell door.

Yellow lantern light streamed from the kitchen window. Tom ran up the steps and threw the door open.

Virgil sat hunched in an armchair. He had an old afghan wrapped around his shoulders, but he was shivering in spite of it. He stared at Tom, relief spilling across his ravaged features.

"Zelda?" Tom was out of breath. He'd run all the way from the barracks, stumbling often on the dark path, cursing the absence of flashlights. "She's up on the hill?"

Virgil nodded. "Left long before midnight with the horse and buggy. She was taking Miss Leona with her." His breath was short, his reedy voice anxious. "She'll be safe up there, lad, you're certain of that?"

Tom wasn't certain of anything, but he nodded anyway. "She'll be fine, Virgil." How long would it take him to get there? He looked at the clock on the mantle, and his heart sank.

3:20. No time. . . .

"Where's Eli?" Virgil looked worn out and cold. He ought to be in bed.

Virgil's forehead creased in a frown and he shook his head. "Boy should'a been back long ago." He started to cough, pressing a wrinkled handkerchief to his mouth. Long moments passed before he could continue. "Went to the mine with a map you'd given him," he managed to gasp. "He wanted the boss on the night shift to have it, so's he'd know where to dig to get out." He coughed again, and Tom stared at him, aghast. The coughing went on for what seemed an eternity.

"First," Virgil wheezed when he could speak, "I said no to Eli, wanted him to stay here by me, safe." Virgil's face grew crimson with the effort to suppress another bout of coughing. "But I got thinking how it is underground, lad. . . ." Virgil couldn't finish. The paroxysm took over and he coughed, bending double with the effort.

Tom didn't need an explanation. He'd lived through too many bad dreams himself of being buried alive, deep in the bowels of the earth. It was every underground miner's worst nightmare.

"He must'a gone in with the crew," Virgil gasped, voicing what Tom had already surmised.

Tom scooped Virgil up and carried him along the passage to his bedroom. He felt as light as a child in Tom's arms.

Laying the older man gently on the bed, Tom piled up the pillows behind him and drew the quilts around his shoulders.

"You stay here and remember, when the Slide comes down it won't come anywhere near here. I'll go see what's keeping Eli."

All Virgil could do was nod, but his eyes telegraphed his relief, his gratitude, and his love.

With every hurried step that led him closer to the mine, Tom's horror grew. If Eli hadn't come back, there was only one explanation. As Virgil said, the young man had gone into the mine, intent on helping the miners when the Slide came down and trapped them.

Tom knew that twenty miners were on the night shift, and that only seventeen of them survived the slide. Three had perished. Was one of the three Eli? He had no way of knowing, but he had to do whatever he could to prevent it, and that meant going into the mine.

As he raced across the mine bridge that spanned the Crowsnest River, running as fast as he could up the gentle slope to the lampman's shack, Tom was dimly aware that dogs were howling in the darkness of the valley.

It was ten minutes before four.

Tom knew the lampman, an old miner named Jimmy Grant.

"Eli Ralston," Tom gasped. "Is he inside?"

Jimmy nodded, his kind, wrinkled countenance filled with concern. "Ayup. The lad had a message for one of the night shift. I gave him a lamp." He knew, of course, of Tom's association with the Ralstons. "Is poor Virgil took bad?"

Tom nodded. It was no more than the truth. "I have to get to the boy, right away."

Jimmy handed over a lamp.

"Jimmy," Tom said urgently. "Get the hell away from here. Tell the men on the mine tipple the mountain's going to go in just a few minutes. Run, Jimmy. Run for your life, all of you."

The old miner stared at Tom as if he'd taken leave of his senses.

At a dead run, Tom made for the entrance.

He was already racing down the manway, heading deep into the bowels of the mine when, in the mist-shrouded darkness outside, high above the town, a single boulder broke free and tumbled down the face of Turtle Mountain.

Across the valley, on the hill above the town, Zelda squinted in the moonlight, trying and failing to make out the individual shapes of the three figures standing in the clearing, their arms wrapped tightly around one another.

Her heart hammered like a wild thing in her chest, and the silence was thick and heavy.

The earth might have stopped on its axis. Even the dogs were no longer barking. It was difficult to breathe.

The moment stretched on and on, and for an instant, she was certain it was all a dream.

Nothing at all was going to happen. It was a huge joke on all of them. She opened her mouth to call to Leona, but before a sound could escape her lips, a solid, icy wall of air struck her and she was thrown violently to the earth.

An horrendous sound, like a gigantic clap of thunder, reverberated through the valley. The horses neighed in terror, rearing and pawing the air with their hooves.

Zelda's scream was drowned in the cacophony of monstrous noise as ninety million tons of rock broke away from the face of Turtle Mountain. They careened down and down, into the valley and halfway up the side of the hill where she cowered, her face and body pressed into the earth.

It seemed to last an eternity, but it was only a short hundred seconds before echoing silence and a gray mass of dust hung like a shroud over the valley.

Trembling, coughing, barely able to breathe, Zelda struggled to her feet.

Below her, where the town of Frank had slumbered only moments before, there was now a sea of jagged rock.

She cried out and whirled around, searching for her friends, needing the reassurance that others besides herself were alive in this holocaust. She felt the hairs at her nape stand on end.

A building shimmered in the dust-filled air, a strange, cantilevered construction surrounded by concrete walkways, with glass walls that seemed to glow in the light of some invisible sun. The glass reflected a peaceful vista—a valley covered in tumbled gray stones, and high above, the scarred and ancient face of Turtle Mountain, placid and worn.

A sign hung on chains from a board, blowing gently in a slight breeze. "Frank Slide Interpretive Center," Zelda read. "Built 1986."

Three figures made their way slowly up the walk, toward a doorway, two men and one very pregnant woman.

"Leona." Zelda's scream rang out in the silence. "Jackson, wait—"

They paused and turned. Zelda began to run toward them, but she tripped on a root and fell flat, her breath whooshing from her body. For a moment, she lay sobbing, struggling to breathe. When at last she clambered to her knees, she watched in disbelief as the building, solid, real, began to shimmer in the eerie light. Before she could get to her feet, it disappeared like smoke.

There was only the dark, dusty clearing.

Except for Zelda and the horses, it was empty.

Tom raced down the mine tunnel, stumbling and half falling, his lamp bobbing, shooting rays of dim light at crazy angles into the blackness. He'd been running for some time before he saw the dim glow of another lamp as a miner came toward him down the track, leading a pit pony hauling cars of coal.

"Have you seen—" Before Tom could finish the sentence, the earth shuddered around them. The other man cried out in alarm, and the tunnel heaved and twisted.

Tom grabbed a beam and put his hands over his head as a shower of rock and coal tumbled down.

"Explosion!" the other man screamed. "Run for the entry!" His foot caught in the tracks, throwing him violently to the ground.

Then, like the breath of a demon from hell, a blast of hot, putrid air came blowing down the narrow passageway, flinging Tom against the side of the mine shaft.

Other panicked voices sounded now as men came running from the depths of the mine, racing for the mine entrance, fearful of the dreaded afterdamp, the deadly gaseous mixture resulting from an explosion. They stumbled and many fell headlong as the tracks heaved and twisted and buckled beneath their feet.

"Eli!" Tom's shout echoed eerily through the dust-filled tunnels. "Eli!" he roared again.

A tall, lean man with glasses stopped long enough to say, "I saw the lad near the cabin not ten minutes ago. Be careful, the water's rising back there."

The cabin was the small room inside the mine set aside for officials, several hundred feet down a side tunnel. Tom, running in the opposite direction to the others, dodged frantic bodies as he hurried down the manway and turned into the down-sloping tunnel where the cabin was. The ever-present trickle of water underfoot became deeper, and Tom was soon slogging through an ever-increasing murky stream.

He almost tripped over Eli's limp form. The boy lay half-submerged in water in a crumpled heap just outside the cabin, and at first Tom thought he was dead. His entire face and his shoulders as well were covered with blood, and awful fear overcame Tom as he threw himself down beside him. Icy water splashed over them both, and Tom reached an arm under Eli, raising him out of the wet, trying to ascertain where he was injured.

After a frantic moment, he realized that the blood all came from one deep gash on the back of Eli's skull. He fished a handkerchief from his pocket and pressed it to the wound, and Eli flinched and groaned. His eyes fluttered open, blank and confused. After a second, recognition dawned and he struggled to sit up, but the exertion made him retch. He vomited on them both and slumped back, his eyes rolling.

"It's okay, kid. I'm gonna lift you up over my shoulder, and we'll head back to where the other men are."

They'd have to make it quick. Tom remembered that the Slide had altered the course of the river that ran through the valley, and that parts of the mine—the areas where the men might have otherwise escaped—had become rapidly flooded with water.

Drowning in there didn't appeal to him any more than being buried alive. The earth shuddered once again beneath him, and Tom gritted his teeth.

"The Slide—" Eli's voice was weak and panicked.

"It's over. The worst is over. All we need to do now is get out of here." Tom got to his feet, grunting as he lifted the boy over his shoulder in a fireman's carry. They were both soaked, and the water was icy and rising fast.

Tom shivered and started rapidly back up the incline toward the entry. He panted and staggered under Eli's weight, aware of the sound of water rushing along the tunnel behind him.

It was already up to his thighs. Eli seemed to grow heavier with every step.

"I can walk now, Tom, put me down."

Tom did, keeping a tight grip on the boy's arm. Together, they stumbled and threshed their way to the main tunnel. There, the mine was deathly quiet. The floor had ceased its shuddering, but Tom was horrifyingly aware of being trapped in the belly of the mountain beneath tons of rock.

The other miners had rushed to the main exit, which Tom knew was blocked. As he and Eli joined them, the breathless men were trying to ascertain whether they could dig their way out. One of them, a burly man with an English accent, had worked the mine since its opening day and knew every inch of the timbering and tracks.

"We're a good three hundred feet from the outside, laddies. We'll run out of air before we ever dig through that lot," he pronounced, and a murmur of consternation rippled through the men.

They already knew that the lower level was rapidly filling with water, making escape from the exits there impossible.

Several had climbed three hundred feet up ladders to the old workings of the mine, searching for an alternate way out. They returned now with the awful news that gas was collecting rapidly up there, and that the air shafts had been completely sealed off.

Some men were already working at the entrance, making little progress against the snarled mass of timber and rocks. Every man was aware that if the air shafts had been damaged, their supply of fresh air would rapidly disappear.

Panic began to spread.

"There's a way out of here, up through an outcropping of coal some distance back along the tunnel." Tom's voice was quietly assured.

The men nearest him repeated what he'd said to others, and after a moment the entire group of miners were silent, listening, as he repeated what he knew to be true, detailing exactly where the outcropping was. "It'll take us a while, for we have to dig up through the seam to the surface. We'll take it in shifts. It's a small seam and cramped quarters."

"How'd'ya know you're right, man?" The voice in the darkness was accusatory. "How'd'ya know it's not just a wild-goose chase you're suggestin'?"

"I know, believe me," Tom replied. "Who's with me?"

A chorus of voices answered. They made their way along the tortuous tunnels to the area Tom indicated, and within a short while, shifts were assigned and men had begun doggedly hacking away at the narrow seam of coal.

The passage was narrow, and only two or three men could work at a time. At first, the others kept their spirits up by singing, and the strains of "Clementine" and "Oh Susannah" rang through the inky darkness. They pooled their lunches, and when the men digging were forced by exhaustion to relinquish their places to a new shift, their reward was a tiny bite of sandwich and a single sip of cold tea.

Hours passed, and it began to be apparent to everyone that the supply of oxygen was diminishing. The laboring men grew weary after only a short time, and the ones who took their places were morose and silent.

Tom had settled Eli nearby, making him as comfortable as he possibly could, and after each of his own stints in the claustrophobic passageway, he returned to Eli's side. The boy slipped in and out of consciousness. Once he whispered, "Are you sure we got it right, Tom?"

"I'm sure." Tom's voice rang with certainty, and Eli relaxed and slept again. But cold sweat trickled down Tom's forehead and off his nose, and the terrible dread that had been building in him during the past futile hours threatened to overwhelm him now.

The truth was, he wasn't sure at all. The memory of a diagram in a book he hadn't laid eyes on in a year was all he'd had to go on. The corridors and tunnels underground were convoluted, and any sense of direction became easily distorted.

What if he had the men digging in the wrong place?

What if historical facts could be altered after all, and he and Eli and all these brave men were fated to die in the belly of this cursed mountain?

The latest trio came scrambling wearily back into the main tunnel, and Tom got to his feet. "I'll take this shift," he said, aware that no one argued for a turn now the way they had a short time before. It was three in the afternoon. They'd been digging since six that morning.

Two hours later, only Tom and two other men still persevered.

The others, oxygen-starved and losing all hope of escape, slumped dejectedly against the mine wall, their heads bent and resting on their knees. Some prayed audibly while others sat silent.

Tom's head swam with dizziness. Every muscle hurt, and he could barely lift the pick to swing it. His partners, a man named McKenzie and another called Farrell, were also struggling. Tom was aware of their labored breathing.

Then, with no warning, McKenzie's pick broke through a layer of hardpan, and like a benediction, a stream of brilliant sunlight blinded the three men crushed shoulder to shoulder in the narrow shaft.

Fresh air streamed in, and they could see blue sky high above.

"We've made it!" McKenzie hollered. "We're out!"

They'd tunneled through thirty-six feet of coal and clay, and they were free. Tom closed his eyes and said a fervent prayer of thanksgiving.

Elation turned to horrified disbelief when the exhausted miners looked down at the valley and saw the devastation and destruction the Slide had wrought. Far below, tiny figures clambered over rocks, frantically searching for survivors.

Nothing was left of the rows of cottages where some of the men had left wives and children only the night before.

Fifty yards below, in an effort to free their fellow workers, frantic miners dug ceaselessly where the mine entrance had been. There was nothing now to mark it except a sea of stone.

McKenzie called down to them, and a glad shout went up. The men digging sent their caps flying into the air and began scrambling up the rocky slope, elated that in the midst of tragedy, there had been a miracle. Their fellow miners were safe.

Tom, with Eli beside him, looked down at the

stricken valley, emotions too powerful for words coursing through him.

The vista was both horrendous and familiar. It looked, now, the way it had when he'd first seen it, one year ago and decades from now. His gaze went to the hillside across the valley, and for a second his mind played tricks on him.

He thought he saw the Interpretive Center there, white-roofed and shining in the sunlight, but, of course, it was a mirage.

Where were Jackson and Leona right now? Were they somewhere below, in the ruins of the town, or had the pathway been there for them, when the Slide came down?

And most important of all, where was Zelda?

Apprehension roiled in his gut. With an arm around Eli's waist, supporting the groggy youngster every step of the way, Tom began to climb down the treacherous slope.

Chapter Twenty-six

It was long past dawn by the time Zelda arrived home.

The events of the night had left her dazed and shocked, and all she could think of was making certain the ones she loved were safe. Surely Tom would be free by now, waiting for her return.

Her exhausted horse, the two riderless ponies in tow, picked its way around the massive rock fall and started wearily up her rutted driveway.

Relief washed over her when she saw that the house, unharmed, looked just the way she'd left it. Could it only have been the night before?

She felt as if centuries must have passed, that when she looked in a mirror, her hair would be white, her face lined and old.

She slithered down from the buggy, aware of the weight of Bill's money belt around her waist. She hurried up the steps, concerned that there was no smoke coming from the chimney.

The kitchen was empty, the stove out, the air frigid. She could hear Virgil coughing. Her heart hammering, she raced down the hallway.

"Thank God you're safe, lass." Virgil's voice was little more than a whisper.

A terrible premonition made her throat go dry. When at last she could speak, she whispered, "Tom? Eli?"

Her father met her gaze, consternation in his red-rimmed eyes. "The mine, lass. Eli went to warn the miners, and Tom went after him. It was just before the Slide, and neither of them came back. I'm worried. Go, now, and see what you can find out in the town."

Zelda found Dominion Avenue choked with horses and buggies and purposeful men and women hurrying here and there. A citizens' meeting had been held at dawn in the lobby of the Imperial Hotel, organizing search parties to look for survivors, soup kitchens to feed the hungry, and volunteers to organize temporary shelter for the homeless. Everyone was doing what they could to help.

Among the first to prepare food, organize shelter, and gather clothing were the women from the Tenderloin, and it was Ethel Parker who told Zelda there'd been no word so far as to the fate of the underground miners.

Frantic, Zelda asked one man after another if anyone knew whether Tom or Eli had actually gone into the mine. The answer was always a shake of the head.

The lampman, who'd know for certain, and the men working on the tipple who might have seen them the night before, were all presumed dead, buried beneath the rocks.

Zelda fought against hysteria. It was unthinkable, to have come through all that she had, only to lose the ones she loved. She wanted to run, fast and far, until the masses of limestone and the terrible mountain itself were far behind her. She wanted to go home and crawl into bed, pull the blankets up over her, allow her mind to go blank and empty.

But there was work to do. "Send anyone who needs a meal and a makeshift bed to our house," she told Ethel, and she hurried home.

It was when she took her coat off that she again became aware of the money belt, heavy on her waist. Unhooking it, she looked inside.

Her mouth dropped open. Inside were neat bundles of hundred dollar bills. She drew them out, one after the other, her lips moving as she counted. Forty—perhaps fifty thousand dollars in all. It was a fortune.

It was freedom, from the mines, from the poverty that Tom hated.

Had it come too late?

She couldn't—wouldn't—let herself stop hoping.

She stuffed the money back in the belt and shoved it under her mattress. Then she lit the stove, cared for Virgil, and began to cook, forcing herself to think only of flour, yeast, molasses, salt.

She put her alarm clock on the kitchen table.

Tom had said the miners would dig their way out

by five in the afternoon. When that time came, Zelda would be there, waiting.

In the town, a few bodies were recovered, but most would remain forever beneath the Slide. Some occurrences were unexplainable. A baby girl was found alive on a bale of hay which had been inexplicably flung from a livery stable a half-mile to the east. Another child, Fernie May Watkins, had been tossed from her bed and was found, cold, dirty, and crying, on the rocks not far from where her family's cabin now lay buried.

Shortly after five in the afternoon, word flashed joyfully from one survivor to the next. By some miracle, the miners had dug their way out. They were safe, they were making their way down the mountain. Cheers went up and everyone rushed to greet them.

The bridge across the river was a useless mass of twisted metal. A rope had been strung from bank to bank, and a makeshift raft shuttled the miners across. Wagons waited to transport any who were injured to Dr. Malcolmson's hospital, and friends and relatives waved and cheered and wept as the ferry brought the first load of men across the frigid water.

Shouts and glad cries of welcome greeted them as they climbed off the raft. Many faces, inky dark with coal dirt, were streaked white with tears.

Photographers were on hand to record the event for posterity.

Zelda hadn't given a single thought to a camera.

Frantically, her eyes went from one man to the next, but Tom and Eli weren't there.

The ferry returned for a second load, and she prayed and cursed and strained to see across the water. But the remaining men stood huddled in an undistinguishable mass on the far side of the river.

The raft was halfway across again when she saw them. Tom's arm was tight around Eli and both their black faces split in identical wide, white grins when they spotted her.

She ran forward to the water's edge, waving her arms and calling to them. Alarm filled her when she saw the dried blood on Eli's face, but the moment the raft landed, she was reassured. Eli was upright, and he was smiling. He couldn't be too badly injured.

"Zelda." She heard Tom's voice, and the tears she'd been holding back for hours began to rain down her face. A welter of thoughts and feelings filled her heart and mind as she threw her arms around both of them.

Eli hugged her and Tom kissed her, and she tasted coal dust and thought of love, of the mysteries of time and place that had brought them all there at this particular moment.

For those few minutes up on the hillside in the early, awful dawn, with the sound of the Slide still reverberating in her ears, she'd looked into the future. This grim cascade of limestone that lay now like an ugly scar across her valley was still there, but it was no longer the overwhelming tragedy it seemed here and now.

Instead, in that future time, the Slide was peaceful, strangely beautiful. Time had changed it from tragic to awe-inspiring.

"We're safe, Zel, all of us. That's really all that

matters." Tom's lips tickled her ear, and she smiled up at him through her tears.

As soon as possible—today, tomorrow—they'd wed, with Virgil and Eli on hand to celebrate with them. She thought of the money belt, and the freedom it represented.

"Jackson and Leona?" His voice was anxious.

"Gone," she managed to say, relief and sadness mingling inside of her. Dear friends, lost forever to the future.

But they'd talk of them often, she and Tom. They'd remember.

She thought of the glowing white building and shivered.

She had so much to tell Tom, but there was plenty of time.

They'd grow old, sharing their memories, loving one another with a steadfast intensity that had no age.

Like the limestone rocks, they'd weather as years passed. The tragedy of the Slide would become only a memory to relate to their grandchildren, a distant echo, a reminder of the beginnings and endings that make up eternity.

With a thriving business and a stalled personal life, Shelby Manning never figures her life is any worse—or better—than the norm. Then a late-night stroll through a Civil War battlefield park leads her to a most intriguing stranger. Bloody, confused, and dressed in Union blue, he insists he has just come from the Battle of Fredericksburg—more than one hundred years in the past.

Maybe Shelby should dismiss Carter Lindsey as crazy—just another history reenactor taking his game a little too seriously. But there is something compelling in the pull of his eyes, something special in his tender touch. And before she knows it, Shelby finds herself swept into a passion like none she's ever known—and willing to defy time itself to keep Carter at her side.

_52074-5 $4.99 US/$6.99 CAN

Dorchester Publishing Co., Inc.
65 Commerce Road
Stamford, CT 06902

Please add $1.75 for shipping and handling for the first book and $.50 for each book thereafter. NY, NYC, PA and CT residents, please add appropriate sales tax. No cash, stamps, or C.O.D.s. All orders shipped within 6 weeks via postal service book rate. Canadian orders require $2.00 extra postage and must be paid in U.S. dollars through a U.S. banking facility.

Name____
Address____
City ______________________________ State______ Zip______
I have enclosed $______in payment for the checked book(s).
Payment must accompany all orders.☐ Please send a free catalog.

TIMESWEPT